In Forgery Divided

In Forgery Divided

David A. Tatum

Fennec Fox Press

In Forgery Divided

This is a work of fiction. All the characters and events portrayed in this book are fictional, and any resemblance to real people or incidents is purely coincidental.

Printed in the United States of America
First Trade Edition, 2016

ISBN-13 978-0-9912844-9-8

Fennec Fox Press
Ashburn, Va 20147
http://www.FennecFoxPress.com

Cover art by Alex Kolesar
http://nn4b.com/

Dedication and Acknowledgments

To Alex Kolesar, for providing some wonderful cover art.

To my brother, Jonathan Ken Tatum, who helped tighten my prose and solved the problem I had with the end of the book.

To my mother, Betty Jo Tatum, without whose financial and logistic support I wouldn't have had the time to write.

And finally to my late father, librarian extraordinaire and book expert George Marvin Tatum, who instilled a great love for writing throughout our whole family before he passed away.
I miss you, dad.

Chapter I

Maelgyn groaned, straining against the force of magic holding him down, but he was too weak to break free, or even to shift his position to something more comfortable. Grimacing, he relaxed his muscles and stared at the stone walls, resigning himself to await his captor's return.

Maelgyn was one of the Sword Princes of Svieda, the third most powerful nation in the known world. He was Duke of the Duchy of Sopan, the wealthiest province in the entire Kingdom. He was the man who defeated the only true High Mage in all of recorded history, and was well on his way to becoming a High Mage himself. He was responsible for the end of the Borden Isles Rebellion, a civil war which had lasted for eight decades. He could be considered pretty high up on the list of the world's one hundred most powerful and important people.

And, at the moment, he was too weak to get out of bed.

Moments later, the heavy oak door of the room swung open with a slight creaking noise as its black iron strap hinges strained at the weight. A slim woman with a brown ponytail and bangs that hung down in front of her eyes walked in and sat down on the bed next to him, rubbing his cheek softly with her fingers.

At least, he was with his wife, Euleilla, even if she was holding him down with her magic like prisoner.

"I told you," she fussed. "Until Dr. Wodtke says it's okay, I am not going to let you out of that bed."

"You do remember that I am the Sword Prince of Svieda, Duke of Sopan Province?"

"Of course, love. You do remember I'm your wife?"

"Of course," Maelgyn sighed. "But since you are using your magic to insist that I 'not get out of this bed' from anywhere in this building, could you at least let me talk with some of the people who we both know I need to talk to?"

Euleilla frowned. "Am I boring you?"

Maelgyn snickered. "Love, if you happen to be fishing for compliments, you can be assured that you are a very... *interesting*... woman. But I can't shirk my responsibilities as Sword Prince, injured or not, especially not while we are still at war with Sho'Curlas."

Euleilla smirked at him. "Now am I the sort of person who would fish for compliments?"

"You're the sort of person who would let me marry you without realizing it," Maelgyn snorted. She looked briefly hurt, but the teasing way he had said it reassured her enough so that she could wait for him to finish the thought. "Don't get me wrong, love, I'm glad you did – I'd never find a better woman to marry if I searched the entire world – but you must admit that shows a bit of a penchant for deviousness."

"I thought you knew what you were doing!" she protested playfully. Despite the war, Maelgyn's recovery from the severe injuries he sustained dueling the deranged High Mage Paljor had given them ample opportunity to talk out a few issues from their sudden marriage. It may have begun because of a technicality, but lately they had taken to teasing each other about it. So far, the teasing had done them both a world of good.

"Somehow, I think you know I don't believe that for a minute," Maelgyn snickered. "Now, maybe it was my fault we got married – I'll grant that – but you knew I might not be aware of the law by which we were married. That makes you a very, very devious woman." His expression turned serious. "Which is probably a good thing, because I'm probably going to need the help of a devious woman at my side, considering where my life seems to be leading me."

Euleilla cocked her head, which pulled the hair away from her eyes briefly – long enough for him to see the scars that had once been her eyes. Euleilla usually hid those scars behind her hair even from him, but recently she had been less cautious about it in his presence. Few people knew of her condition, however, because she was able to hide it not just with her hair but also with her magic. Her exceptional skill with magic allowed her to 'see' her surroundings, to some extent. That 'sight' became even sharper with the still-nameless *schlipf* now growing under the skin of her wrist. The couple had made a bargain with the living Elven weapons, and both of them could warn them of any dangers that might be approaching them.

"Well, put that way, I suppose I'll admit to being just a tiny bit devious. But that is unofficial, off the record, and not something you'll ever hear me admit again."

"Just get out of here, vixen, and get me the people I need to talk to!" Maelgyn growled.

"Certainly, husband," she said. "Now that Wodtke agrees you can handle the stress of it, anyway. Tur'Ba is about to arrive to take on his duties as your personal servant, so I can leave assured that you will be taken care of. Who should I track down first?"

Maelgyn groaned at the news that Tur'Ba was going to be looking after him. He liked the Dwarf, who was well on his way to resurrecting the skills of the legendary Dwarven Axemen by himself. In that way, and as a friend, Maelgyn valued the Dwarven boy. However, as his 'servant,' Tur'Ba was much more... enthusiastic... than Maelgyn would have liked. Especially since Maelgyn had only designated the man his 'servant' as a favor, and not because of any skill in service the young dwarf possessed.

Tur'Ba's enthusiasm for the position led to him conspiring with Euleilla to keep Maelgyn on his back and in bed at all times until Dr. Wodtke had cleared him. However, Tur'Ba's company wasn't as pleasant as his wife's, and he was even more restrictive of Maelgyn's movement.

"Promise me you'll return as soon as they're all assembled?" he begged.

"'Kay," Euleilla laughed, smiling at him teasingly.

Maelgyn rolled his eyes. "And don't start that one-word-answer-to-every-question thing right now. I love you, Euleilla, but sometimes you drive me crazy with that."

"Of course I do," she reassured him, leaving him with a quick kiss before heading to the door. "It's my job as your wife to drive you crazy, now and then."

Walking to the outer gates of the castle with her foster father, Admiral Ruznak, Euleilla sensed several of the people she was supposed to assemble already inside the gates. So Euleilla was unsurprised to find Sir Leno and Admiral Rudel, the highest ranking military officers in Maelgyn's command, talking with Wangdu the Elf, Onayari the Nekoji, El'Athras the Dwarf, and Dr. Wodtke. Euleilla knew that Maelgyn was especially anxious to see Wodtke – he was getting increasingly restless in his sick bed. Sir Leno hadn't been expected to attend, but it was just as well that he did, since his attendance would effectively put the entire interim government for the Borden Isles in one room.

"The funeral was quite an extended affair, it was," Wangdu said with his rather peculiar Elven dialect. "It isn't often a traitor is honored more than a king, it isn't."

El'Athras snorted. "Uwelain was no traitor. If anyone was a traitor, it was that damned Paljor and his entire line."

"Regardless, both events took much of our time," Onayari agreed. "Thankfully, we were only requested to be present for the burial, and not the ceremonies afterwards. The people understand that His Highness needs our care."

Euleilla nodded. "My husband can now meet with you all, and requests your attendance. Dr. Wodtke, I think you'll have to save him from Tur'Ba before he gets so frustrated he murders the boy."

The doctor laughed. "I'll go check on him before your meeting. What is today's order of business, may I ask?"

"I'm not entirely sure," Euleilla said. "But he especially wants to see the Admiral."

"Me?" Rudel said. "There is no need for my ships to do anything until we are ready to return to the mainland. The island is secure, and I would know before him if there was some threat coming from the sea."

Euleilla hid a smirk. She had an inkling as to what was going on, but there was a possibility she was wrong. Besides, she never gave away *any* information of *any* kind if she could avoid it. Well, okay, nowadays she also let Maelgyn know most of what she knew, but they were married – that didn't count. "Ask him," she said. "So, shall we go?"

"Of course, Your Highness," El'Athras replied.

As they made their way through the stone hallways of the Borden Island Castle, Euleilla tried to pry more information she would 'keep to herself' out of the secretive Dwarf's claws. He had become the spymaster for Maelgyn's team, while still a Count of Svieda and ruler of his own Sviedan Province in his own right. However, he was sometimes a bit too tight-lipped with his information without realizing it, and kept secrets when he didn't need to... or even when it was dangerous to.

"So how are the Seats reacting to the new laws we are making?" she asked, hoping he would not deflect her questions, this time.

"Well," El'Athras began somewhat reluctantly, "I won't say they're happy about everything. They still want us to appoint a new Sword Prince for the Borden Isles, but we've pointed out that the issue of who is next in line to become a Sword is a little clouded at the moment. Even if we knew, there would be some difficulty bringing any of the possible candidates here until we're sure the sea lanes are secure, so they've mellowed a bit on that. They'll accept us designating an official regent, but we know nothing of the candidates they have presented to us." He sighed. "Plus, there's the need to replace Baron Uwelain, and they haven't yet worked out a proper system for naming a Baron when their Sword is not around to appoint one. What we really need is someone with enough natural authority that they can respect his decisions... like, say, your husband, My Lady. I may, technically, outrank the current Barons, but they don't trust me since I'm just a Dwarf and a stranger to the Sviedan system."

"And no-one trusts an Elf, they don't," Wangdu mused. "Though I would not blame them for that, I wouldn't."

El'Athras snorted in disgust. "Which, as you've probably figured out, means that Maelgyn's probably the only one who can get us out of this mess."

"Maelgyn *wants* something to do," Euleilla sighed, shaking her head. She had seen, all too clearly, just how frustrated her husband was getting with his enforced bed-rest. "He'll be happy with the task. But with his injuries... well, he hasn't been able to, so far."

"Trust me, milady," Dr. Wodtke snorted, glaring at the Dwarf she had taken as a lover while still addressing the younger woman. "I've made absolutely certain that Athy understands just how impossible it is for your husband to do... well, just about anything, right now."

"Maelgyn's just as bad on his end," Euleilla chuckled. "I'm still having problems keeping him from overdoing things. He hasn't lost his temper with me, yet, but with others—"

They were just outside of Maelgyn's room when they heard the aforementioned Sword Prince's fierce voice roaring out. "I'm fine! Just leave me alone!"

"As I was saying," Euleilla sighed, shaking her head ruefully. "We'd better go in there and save Tur'Ba before Maelgyn kills him."

The small group of people entered the room to see Tur'Ba carrying a rather smelly concoction that several of them recognized as a Dwarven medicine. It appeared he was trying to feed it to a protesting Maelgyn while they all watched on, amused.

"Stop that," Dr. Wodtke snapped. "I already told you that won't work for him."

"But it's always been good for my family when they were injured!" Tur'Ba exclaimed.

"That's because you have a family of Dwarves," Wodtke said slowly, gritting her teeth to keep from shouting. "And Humans don't react to that medicine the same way. It'll just make him sick."

Well, Euleilla thought, remembering the one time Tur'Ba had managed to convince Maelgyn to try it. *Yeah, I guess he was rather 'sick' by the next morning... if you can call it that. He rather enjoyed the 'being drunk' part of it beforehand. He's a rather amusing drunk, but he's not exactly a very pleasant person to be around when he's recovering from a hangover...*

"Doctor," Maelgyn sighed thankfully. "Please tell me that I can get out of this bed today!"

Wodtke shook her head in resignation. "I was reluctant to let you deal with the stress of this meeting. Well, let me check you out, first, and we'll see how things go. But don't be so impatient – you're lucky to still be alive."

After a short exam, however, she reluctantly found herself giving him the news he was hoping for. "I suppose you can start walking around, again, but you are not allowed to wear armor or carry a sword, and you must take things slowly and rest frequently. It might do to make sure someone is with you to lean on, since you'll probably find it hard to walk around unsupported. And don't use your magic to help you move! Magic was all that was keeping your body from falling apart after that duel, I know, but now that your muscles are knitting themselves back together you need to use them without the crutch of magic to get strong again."

"But at least I can move, now," Maelgyn replied. Euleilla had to smile when he started laughing. "It's about time."

Rudel, seeing that the Doctor was done, stepped up and bowed to him. "You called for me, Your Highness?"

Maelgyn, having forgotten the others were in the room, nearly jumped in surprise. He took a moment to ensure he hadn't re-injured himself before giving his answer. "Yes, yes, of course. I may be able to walk again, but I am still unable to handle all of the day-to-day necessities surrounding the establishment of an interim government. In my condition, I need to delegate much of that to other people. With that in mind, I will be asking you to take on a certain job for me."

"If you wish, your highness," Rudel said.

"There are several things that must be done before our return to the mainland, and time is of the essence," Maelgyn began, starting to tick off items on his agenda with his fingers. "First, Paljor's records say he made three sets of armor out of the hide of that Golden Dragon he killed. We have the one he was wearing, but we have yet to find the others. He must have a storeroom somewhere that he kept them in. We must find it before our next meeting with the Dragons – they will want their kinsman's remains returned to them. But that isn't the only issue – I must appoint a new regent, who will rule this province until we can determine which of my family members is in line to be the next Sword Prince, before I may rejoin our mainland armies in the war against the Sho'Curlas."

"We think we have already found the armor, we do," Wangdu said reluctantly. He had insisted that the return of the armor was unimportant. Paljor's damaged armor, alone, would be proof enough that they had avenged the murder of one of the Golden Dragon's elders. Maelgyn overruled him, however, so the Elf volunteered to lead the search. "As well as more evidence of the mad elf Hrabak's mischief, we did. We've found papers, we have, of his involvement both this rebellion and the Abindol rebellion. We also know Hrabak once had a villa or laboratory of some kind on this island, we do, and that he may have experimented on enhancing the magical potency of the Borden Isle royal line, he might."

"Was Paljor the result of one of these experiments?" Maelgyn asked, alarmed. If there was a way for an Elf to turn a human into a High Mage, and that Elf was both an enemy and a madman, there was definite cause for alarm.

"Perhaps to some degree," El'Athras said. "Wangdu translated the notes which discussed this lab, and they make it seem as if most of the experiments were a complete failure. Paljor comes from a line of powerful mages, as do you. He may have been a natural High Mage, but—"

"But we can't be sure he was a natural High Mage, so that doesn't necessarily rule anything out," Maelgyn mused. "What could Hrabak possibly gain with this new interest of his?"

"When we get back to the mainland, I'll see if my spies can dig up any information on Hrabak's experiments," El'Athras said. "The 'Mad Elf' is secretive, but my people can still get some information on him."

Maelgyn cocked his head at the Dwarf, curious. "And just how do they do that? You seem to know an awful lot about the internal workings of other nations."

"Dwarven spies are the best in the world, and that's all you need to know," El'Athras replied. "You have other things to worry about at the moment. Just be thankful that my spies are now on your side."

Maelgyn wanted to press for more information, but realized he would get none from the Dwarf for the time being. With that in mind, he moved on to another topic he'd been trying to discuss before getting sidetracked. "In that case," he said, "We should return to our efforts at setting up the government here. I've been thinking about this long and hard, and I believe I have an idea for someone who could become the new Duke Regent of Borden Isle, if he'll take the job."

"That should help," El'Athras snorted. "At least one problem would be solved, if we had someone to deal with the local government."

"When I put together this expedition," Maelgyn began, "My initial thoughts were to make Baron Uwelain the regent, with my first alternative being Admiral Ruznak. But the Baron was killed and the locals are... still somewhat hostile to Ruznak."

"I wouldn't have made a good choice, anyway," Ruznak muttered. "I'm old and I don't have any kids of my own – my line would be a very short one."

"I still think it should be an older member of our party, however," Maelgyn sighed. "An unknown young man is less likely to command much respect, regardless of how competent they are. And I think it should be someone with experience leading a number of men... which leads me to only one conclusion."

"Rudel," Euleilla finished for him, smiling.

Maelgyn looked miffed that she had figured it out before he could say it, but then nodded. "Indeed. Hand me a sword, love. Admiral, if you would kneel?"

Rudel hadn't taken it in at first. He had no noble blood in him. To be elevated to a knighthood, or even to a low-ranked lordship such as a baronet, might be expected had he led them to a major victory, but to go from civilian to Duke Regent was inconceivable. He almost stumbled to his knees with the realization Maelgyn meant him, but then he quickly regained his composure, but caught himself and turned it into a proper kneel as Maelgyn slowly stood up off his sick bed.

Euleilla presented Maelgyn her own sword – one formerly belonging to Paljor. It was not one of the ten Swords of Svieda, but rather the well-made katana that had been used in the duel with Maelgyn. She claimed it for her husband as a prize following the battle, but she had enjoyed the weight and balance of the weapon so much that he let her keep it.

If they hadn't known any better, one might have assumed that it, too, was one of the Swords. It was not as fancy, and lacked many of the adornments that the royal emblems wore, but it was a brutally functional blade intended as a weapon of war. Wangdu had examined it, himself, and strongly suggested she hang onto the blade, as "it might come in handy, it might."

Regardless of whatever other qualities it might have, the sword would work for the impromptu ceremony Maelgyn was initiating. "Admiral Rudel," he intoned, beginning a formal dialogue which had been used by Svieda for centuries. "Do you understand the honors due a title of nobility, and the rights and responsibilities that go with such?"

Rudel steeled himself before answering with the sort of crispness one might expect of an officer of his years, though there was still a hint of disbelief in his voice. "Yes, Your Highness. I understand them."

The flat of the blade was rested against his right shoulder. "And will you swear, upon your life and honor, to wield these powers granted to you for the good of Svieda, and to accept those responsibilities such a title will require of you?"

"Of course!" Rudel exclaimed before catching himself. "I mean, I will, Your Highness."

Maelgyn's lips twitched upward at the sudden outburst. He tapped the flat of his blade to the left shoulder of the sailor. "Then rise, Duke Rudel, Regent of the Borden Isles, and accept the duties and powers that I entrust to you."

Maelgyn sat down to think and rest, suddenly beginning to feel the strain of moving around so much. Appointing Rudel would help satisfy the demands of the Borden Island Council, and give him someone to hammer out the details of restoring the province to the kingdom.

Rudel would miss the sea, but Maelgyn was sure he would find excuses for travel by ship from time to time. Rudel's family would have to be summoned from Sopan, and there would be other problems to deal with, as well – but those matters could be handled by someone else, and at a later date..

"I think that's enough for today," Dr. Wodtke said.

"I agree," Maelgyn acknowledged, a little surprised at how tired just that brief ceremony made him. "But there will be more to take care of in the morning."

Ten figures huddled around a huge beechwood table in a study near Maelgyn's chambers several days later. It used to be a banquet table during the reign of Paljor's predecessor, but had been retired in favor of a stone table shortly after his coronation. The pitting and scoring on it were several years old, but it still smelled slightly of stale food. It was the only mobile table of sufficient size they could get their hands on, however, and so they took it into the study to make a war room.

Maps and other papers were strewn on every flat surface of the room, but the only chair was the one at the head of the table brought in for Maelgyn to rest at. Not that he was resting in it – he'd been pushing to spend more and more time on his feet, arguing with Wodtke repeatedly about his treatment. Quite frankly, he was restless, so instead of using the seat his doctor insisted upon he was up and (slowly) pacing about the room. That seat had been offered to the young sailor now giving this report.

"The rumors coming from the mainland are hazy. Rumors say the bulk of the fighting is somewhere between Happaso and the Royal Province, but that we're holding them under the joint leadership of Sword Princes Brode and Arnach. That said, our position is very tenuous – the entire province of Rubick is in ruins and undefended. It wouldn't take much for Sho'Curlas to take it. They've already shown themselves willing to violate the sovereignty of Squire's Knot, which would give them an opening on that border."

"Have you heard any word of dragons, Altan?" El'Athras peered at the young deckhand who was giving them account of the war.

"Dragons? Not recently," the youth said, frowning. "The last Dragon I heard about on the mainland was a small flock of Golden Dragons heading for these isles, but that was a couple years ago. Before that... well, there was that Red Dragon that the Swords helped hunt down about six years ago. Let's hope there aren't any more of those – the war is bad enough!"

"My thanks, lad," said Maelgyn, flinching slightly at the mention of a certain youthful indiscretion of his. "Safe voyage to you on your return." Tur'Ba took the merchant sailor aside and paid him for his time. With a clumsy bow, Altan took his leave and scurried out of the room.

"He's probably right about the front line," said El'Athras. "My spies tell me that Sho'Curlas has positioned its Black Dragon troops here, here, and here." He gestured to several locations on a map showing the pre-war border between Svieda and Sho'Curlas. "Yet its main encampment is currently occupying Sycanth, and they have yet to push all the way through the Royal Province. I don't know why Sho'Curlas hasn't brought them into battle yet – a mystery that will continue to weigh on me until they are."

"They'll be brought in eventually. I need to get back to the fighting, and soon."

"There's no help for it, your highness," Rudel said. "You won't be in the fighting any time soon. Wodtke says you are pushing the limits of your recovery already, and to be honest there's still work for you here in the Borden Isle's. I may be serving as Regent, but the Golden Dragons won't know that. They'll be waiting word of your fight with Paljor, and they aren't likely to accept that word from anyone but you."

"And without the Golden Dragons, we'll have done all of this for nothing. Well, maybe not nothing, but it'll be a while before the Borden Isles are stable enough to provide us much support in the war effort." Maelgyn took one last glance at the map before sighing and shaking his head. He grabbed his Sword and belted it around his waist. "I'd better get to my exercises, and the rest of you need to get to work. When I return, I will want a list of everything else I'm still needed for here on the Borden Isles. It's high time I start taking care of those things."

Maelgyn stood in the courtyard a short time later, practicing a set of maneuvers with a sword and a long dagger in slow motion, almost as if he were performing some complicated but graceful dance with weapons in hand. Under the close supervision of both Ruznak and Wangdu (for technique) and Wodtke (to keep him from overworking himself), Maelgyn had restarted his training, albeit very slowly and very lightly. Wangdu, reflecting on the fight against Paljor, suggested Maelgyn try and add a second blade to his repertoire, and Maelgyn was making great strides despite his injuries. He still felt as if he was wasting his time.

"And yet I'm still stuck here!" Maelgyn snarled aloud, kicking a training dummy in frustration. It was a mistake – not only did the sudden exclamation startle those watching him perform his daily routine, waves of pain were sent shooting up his somewhat atrophied leg muscles. His knee gave out on him, and he very nearly went tumbling to the ground – saved only by his wife catching him magically.

"Are you alright?" she called, concerned.

"Thanks. I thought you weren't going to watch, today?"

"I was coming down to see if you would join me for lunch."

"He will be okay," Doctor Wodtke assured them, having sprinted over immediately to check out the injury. Ruznak also rushed to his side. "He did nothing to further injure himself, although some of my stitches appear to have been pulled slightly on his knee. The others have held, fortunately, so he won't bleed to death. He just needs to learn his limits while recovering."

"I don't have the time to go slowly. War does not often allow for 'limits,'" Maelgyn groused.

"You'll have less time if you ignore those limits," Wodtke mused absently, prodding his knee in a clinical fashion. "That's enough exercise for today. Go rest up."

"When will I be able to meet with the Golden Dragon elders, Doctor?" Maelgyn asked, not moving. "I need to get out of here, and soon."

"'Soon,' eh?" the Doctor laughed bitterly. "I'm sorry, Your Highness, but it'll be weeks before you're up to the journey."

"Or it would be on foot or horseback," Euleilla said. "Doctor, what about my suggestion?"

Maelgyn perked up. "Suggestion?"

Wodtke shrugged. "He could do it, but Athy says it would be undignified, and probably not the right way to go to a diplomatic meeting. I'd take his advice if I were you."

"And I agree with him," Ruznak said, glaring at his foster daughter even though he knew she wouldn't see him. They had argued about her idea the night before – and rather extensively, as well. He had thought he'd convinced her not to mention it.

"What suggestion?" Maelgyn demanded.

Wodtke hesitated, then nodded to the younger woman to explain. "A cart," was all Euleilla would say, however.

"A cart?" he repeated slowly, not liking the idea right away. Still, Euleilla was his wife, and he would give her a chance to explain.

"If you were willing to rest in a cart the entire trip, you could make it without tiring yourself or straining your injuries," Euleilla replied. "At least, that's what I asked the doctor if you could manage."

"You could, that is, if you spent the whole trip riding in the cart, and let Euleilla and I tend to you the whole way," Wodtke continued. "You lost a lot of blood during your fight with Paljor, and you have yet to recover from that. I've only been letting you train very slowly, for very brief periods, and under my strict supervision, but you've also had to return to your bed after each session. Believe it or not, sitting in a bumpy cart for several hours straight will wear on you more than that."

"You're right – I don't believe it," Maelgyn remarked snidely.

"You're being held together by stitches and bandages, and anything too strenuous would likely open them up. You will still have to walk up the path to reach the gates into the Golden Dragons' Lair, which is harsh terrain. I think you're just barely capable of it at this point, and only if you get there well rested. You might even need to be carried back down the mountain, even if you can get up there. But... well, I doubt you would harm yourself any farther. I could – reluctantly – go along with the idea, but only if you swore to follow my instructions for the entire journey."

"We would have to take a cart with us, anyway, whether you rode in it or not," Euleilla pointed out. "If you intend to go along with your plan to hand over the dragonhide armor Paljor made, we'll need something to carry them to the mountains. We certainly couldn't take them up any other way, unless we were going to wear them... which would be less diplomatic then an 'undignified' arrival on a cart."

"But—" Ruznak began.

"It isn't like the dragons would even see him on the cart, gramps! The horses can't be made to approach their lair, so we would have to hike up the mountain pass for the last leg of the journey. No-one would see him until he reached that point." Euleilla argued.

"And if he must be carried back down the mountain afterwords," Ruznak intoned, finally managing to get a word in. "Will the dragons still respect him, or will they think of him as weak?"

"They will see to what extent my husband put his life on the line in their service," Euleilla said fiercely. "If they choose to see him as weak, after he brings back and delivers proof that he killed someone they could not, then I won't want them as allies."

"Her Highness is right, she is," Wangdu said, approaching them.

All four people spun to see the elf approaching, startled. He had a funny smile on his face – one none of them could quite understand the meaning of. "If there is one thing which will turn the Dragons into true allies, it will, it would be to show them that you went to great pains to help them, it is."

"And how would you know, Elf?" Ruznak snapped. He wasn't being rude, exactly, but he wasn't accustomed to being ganged up on. It was hard enough to keep himself civil when his foster daughter was contradicting him – let alone when a complete stranger did. "The Dragons have hated your kind for millennia."

If anything, that peculiar smile just grew. "Ah, but I have hated my kind for millennia as well, I have. Nevertheless, I know of Dragons far better than anyone else in the world, I do – even better than the Dragons know themselves...."

Maelgyn started to turn to Wangdu to ask what he meant, but stopped in pain as the movement strained his leg again. It could wait. At the moment, Maelgyn just needed to get off of his feet.

Chapter II

The cart had to move very slowly on the rough road to the Golden Dragons' lair, managing a walking pace, at best. What would normally be a one day journey on horseback took three, and by general agreement the party decided to camp at the bottom of the mountain before attempting the climb to meet with the dragons. With the guards on patrol, Euleilla, Wangdu, Dr. Wodtke, and El'Athras were the only people in camp, leading to a more relaxed atmosphere than they would have managed had his entire entourage from the previous meeting with the Golden Dragons and their guards been present.

Maelgyn, who was feeling rather stiff again after being cooped up in a cart for three days straight, insisted on some sword training after the camp was set up. Nothing strenuous, he agreed, but just something to stretch his muscles. Euleilla 'sparred' with him, using her iron-tipped staff to gently poke at some holes in his defensive form. Unfortunately, she prodded him just a tiny bit too hard, hitting one of his injured rips, and he collapsed nearly right away. He instinctively reached out with his training sword to steady himself, but the steel lodged in the dirt and wrenched itself sideways as he fell.

"Oh," she cried, realizing what she did and collapsing to his side,

Wodtke and Wangdu rushing to join them from their spots around the campfire. "Are you okay?"

"I'm fine," Maelgyn groaned, gingerly sitting up while the Elf and the doctor examined him. "But I'm afraid I broke your sword again."

Euleilla used her magic to check and see what he meant, and found that the steel broadsword she had forged for him using her magic many months ago – and reforged following its destruction during the duel with Paljor – was bent and unusable. She could easily repair it, she knew, but she knew it could never compare to his royal Sword. The ten heirloom katana forged for the royal family of Svieda were often regarded – with cause – as the greatest swords ever made, and the best her unaided magic could achieve wouldn't even be close to their quality. She did, however, have another option handy.

"I will fix it, of course," she replied, waving her hand with a flourish over the broadsword and bending it back into its proper shape. The gesture was unnecessary, of course, but was often ingrained into any mage from an early age as a training technique. Euleilla usually ignored such trivialities, but this time she was doing something the rarely attempted: Studying the actual structure of the metal itself, so as to ensure that her earlier repairs hadn't left it defective. "It is a workable sword, I suppose, but my abilities are rather limited. I would rather you use a better sword in a real fight."

"I'm training in a two-sword style," Maelgyn pointed out. "And the other sword is much better. We're mages, so surely you should know how important it can be to have a weapon you can afford to break in a battle – one of our more commonplace techniques involves voluntarily shattering our own swords and using the fragments as projectiles."

"True," Euleilla admitted. "But that technique is more often used with your opponent's sword rather than your own. And I'm not saying to get rid of it entirely, but I think you would want to use a better sword in most fights." She paused. "I have a better sword already, husband. A prize I am unlikely to use, myself, and one which truly you deserve."

Wangdu, listening curiously while examining Maelgyn's injuries, suddenly glanced up. He knew exactly what she was referring to, and he had a comment of his own. "Milady, that would perhaps be a more generous gift than you know, it would."

"I don't care," Euleilla admitted. "My preferred weapon is the staff, and he is my husband. I struggle to 'see' where the blade ends, so it would be best in someone else's hands."

"What are you talking about?" Maelgyn asked, confused.

"I still hold the sword Paljor dueled you with," Euleilla explained, unstrapping the sheathed blade from her belt and offering it to him. He hesitantly reached out and took it, drawing the blade slightly to inspect the steel. "You let me keep it after the battle, though I am not sure if you were in your right mind when you agreed to give it to me. I think you should keep the prize, after all. It is a fine katana, by all accounts, and is almost as well-made as your royal blade."

"It is more than that, it is," Wangdu snorted. "Would you tell me, would you, if you have the same problem 'seeing' the end of Maelgyn's sword, you do?"

Euleilla paused, stretching out her senses. "Yes, I suppose I do. We've always practiced together with the blade I made for him, so I never noticed before...."

"Both blades were forged the same way, they were," Wangdu noted. "A mage who knew the skill of blacksmithing, he did, made Paljor's dueling blade. Such swords are a rarity, they are, but these blades are both even more special than that, they are – their blades were tempered in Dragon blood, they were, and their hilts were wrapped in Dragon skin. Likely the same Golden Dragon's blood and hide that you were sent after Paljor for killing, you were, and so they may be even more magically resistant than the Sviedan Swords themselves, they might. There is a reason the Royal Swords of Svieda are so prized, they are. Human hands have never forged better weapons, they haven't."

Maelgyn paused, using his magic to examine the weapon as closely as he could. He found that, like Euleilla, his magical senses seemed to barely be able to touch the blade. He knew that sensation from the ten Swords of Svieda, though it was significantly more pronounced in this katana. "How odd. What properties does this blade actually have, though? I suppose it's largely immune to Human magic, but what else does tempering it in Dragon's blood do?"

"Not much," Wangdu admitted. "It's nearly impossible to break, it is, and may be mildly poisonous to Elves, it might... although for that poison to be really effective you would need to deliver what would be a fatal wound on a Human with it, you would. It might even survive piercing a Dragon's skin, it might, while most other blades would be melted, they would."

Maelgyn glanced at the sword Euleilla had given him with new respect. "A blade to even the odds against those races traditionally considered stronger than Humans," he mused.

"I believe that was the idea, I do," Wangdu replied doubtfully. "But that sword alone does not bridge the difference as much as you might think, it doesn't."

"And now I wield two such blades," Maelgyn continued, amazed. "And hold the magic of a High Mage at my fingertips, now that I've proven myself against Paljor."

Euleilla smacked him gently on the back of his head. "Don't get a swelled head."

"That is wise advice, it is," Wangdu agreed. "There is always someone stronger than you are, there is. You did not truly compare to Paljor, you didn't, but you were able to use a distraction against him, you were. Paljor did not truly compare to me, he didn't, though with the element of surprise he was able to pin me to a wall. Elves such as I do not truly compare to our Ancient Enemy, we do not, but our warriors won many battles against them, they did. The Ancient Enemy had no equals, they didn't, but were wiped out by the Dragons, they were."

Maelgyn grinned ruefully, rubbing the spot where Euleilla had struck him. "I guess I was being a bit arrogant there, wasn't I? My apologies. I was merely thinking of our chances in the Sho'Curlas war. These weapons could prove... quite valuable." He paused, looking thoughtful. "I have to wonder, though... who were your Ancient Enemy? I have heard many references to them, but never what they were. If they were more powerful than the Ancient Elves, than—"

"They are not to be spoken of, they aren't," Wangdu snapped briskly. "If you truly wish to know, you do, then you may ask the Dragons, you might. But I will not speak of them, I won't – they are gone, they are, and so cannot be a part of any plan you might make."

"But what were they? Elves, Humans, Nekoji—"

"They were themselves, they were," Wangdu insisted desperately.

"But there have only been five major races," Maelgyn pointed out.

"Wouldn't they have to be one of them?"

"You must ask the Dragons, you must. I will speak no more of this, I won't."

With that, the Elf walked away, refusing to acknowledge anyone. Maelgyn turned to El'Athras curiously.

"I've never been able to tell what they were, either," the old Dwarf said, shrugging. "I've tried to find out, but only the Elves and the Dragons know. The Elves won't discuss it, and the Dragons... well, they're pretty hard to talk to, as you know. Rumors are pervasive – some say they were shapeshifters, related to the Merfolk, while others claim they were Elves who corrupted themselves with forbidden knowledge. A few people even think they were Humans who achieved powers greater than any now possess today. I just don't know."

"A discussion for another time," Wodtke broke in, completing her examination of Maelgyn's recovering wounds. "If we wish to make the trip up the mountain tomorrow, we should all go to bed and rest. Coming, Athy?"

"Of course," the Dwarf replied, jumping to follow her to their shared tent. A look sent Maelgyn scurrying after Euleilla, as well, as she prepared to redress his wounds.

I suppose this means I've got more questions for the Dragons, now, Maelgyn mused as he entered their tent. *At least these might get answered tomorrow. The one whether an alliance between Svieda and the Golden Dragons could ever be made, however... well, now, I wonder if that one will ever be answered.*

All of the questions Maelgyn was hoping for an answer to were out of his mind by the time he reached the entrance to the Golden Dragons' lair. He was wheezing hard, his head spinning and his legs about to fail him from the physical exertion needed to get him that far. He hadn't believed Wodtke about just how much this short walk would stress him. Fortunately, he had a moment to catch his breath before they were greeted.

"I see you have returned," a Golden Dragon the size of a small horse intoned, stepping out of the shadowy crags of the cave entrance. Maelgyn couldn't be sure, but he thought it looked like the same one he had met with before – Khumbaya, if his memory was right. "I trust this means you have news for us?"

"Paljor is dead," Euleilla answered, acting as Maelgyn's spokesman. "My husband killed him."

The Dragon turned his eyes towards the young Human woman. "I do not know you. Who is your husband?"

"I am," Maelgyn replied, straightening his posture slightly. He was now certain of the Dragon's identity, recognizing the voice if nothing else. "As I'm sure you know. Don't annoy my wife by asking her questions you already know the answer to."

"My apologies, it was merely a formality," Khumbaya replied. "And I find it quite courageous of you to stand up to a Golden Dragon when you can barely stand up on your own. What proof do you have that Paljor is dead?"

"Many proofs," Euleilla replied. "My husband's condition came from fighting your enemy, and I believe you should honor his word for having done so."

Khumbaya chuckled in a very Draconic way. "Your mate is as much of a spitfire as you, Sword Prince Maelgyn. The pair of you should know better than to risk angering a force neither of you would stand a chance against."

"But if you want evidence," Euleilla continued as if he hadn't spoken. "We have the swords Paljor used, the armor he built out of your Elder's hide, his blood on one of those armors, and witnesses such as Wangdu the Elf and El'Athras the Dwarf to speak to his demise. If that is not sufficient, we may be able to convince the people of the Borden Isles to exhume his dead and rotting corpse for your perusal."

Khumbaya seemed to lick his lips slightly, but shook his head. "Unnecessary. We felt the battle take place even up here, and your husband's word is enough for us to believe him. That you were willing to bring evidence is proof enough of your victory – we require nothing more."

"Nonetheless, we will gladly present you with the armor," Maelgyn said, having recovered his breath enough to speak for himself. "So that you may honor your dead Elder as your kind decides."

Khumbaya looked puzzled, and Wangdu mildly embarrassed. "Why would we want her hide? We have our own."

Wangdu cleared his throat to get their attention. "Humans usually bury their dead in tombs, they do, so that their families will have a place to come and mourn," he said to the Dragon, then turned to address Maelgyn. "I tried to tell you this sooner, I did, but Dragons do not bury their dead, they don't."

"Then what do they do with them?" Maelgyn asked.

"Dragons are... carrion eaters, they are," Wangdu explained carefully.

Maelgyn paled, feeling queasy as he realized what was being said. "I see. Well, in that case, I suppose we can find a use for three dragonhide armors, ourselves, even if one of them is slightly damaged." He turned back to Khumbaya. "But this is our proof that we have done as you asked, and so I now request to meet with your Elders to discuss the matter of our treaty, as we had agreed before."

"One of my brothers left to summon them before I even greeted you," Khumbaya explained. "I am merely here to... 'entertain' you until they are ready for the meeting."

Maelgyn nodded. "In that case, perhaps you know the answer to a question our Elven companion refuses to answer." Wangdu stiffened, but didn't show any more reaction than that as the expected question came. "Who were the Elves' so-called 'Ancient Enemy,' and why are the Elves so reluctant to discuss them?"

Steam blew out of Khumbaya's nose. "An interesting question that few could answer. No Elf would be comfortable talking about them. Even we Dragons have no good memories of their kind."

"But what *were* they?" Maelgyn asked. "Another type of Elf? Humans who—"

"They were like nothing you have seen before," Khumbaya interrupted. "In ancient times they were called 'Tengu.' While their torsos and heads resembled large-nosed Humans or Elves, they had wings similar to a Griffin's but with golden feathers. Their arms were covered in what looked like Golden Dragonhide, but their hands had bird-like talons rather than human fingers or the claws my own people wield. Like the Merfolk, they were shapeshifters; they could change their form to resemble that of Humans or Elves. More complex changes eluded them, however, and they could never reduce the size of their noses – that was a distinctive trait, and allowed them to be discovered on multiple occasions.

"They wielded many powers. Their arms could shield them from intense heat of the sort only Nekoji or Dragons can bear.

With training, they could perform Human magic as well as any human. Their greatest strength, however, was also the same form of magic that the Elves wield – they could manipulate creation itself, producing the Kappa, the Minotaurs, the Orcs, the Hydra, and many less intelligent creatures and plants. They were also better than the Elves at enslaving their creations – Griffins, Dragons, Satyrs, and even some tribes of Centaurs betrayed the Elves. None of the Tengu creations, loathsome as they were, would ever be described as 'traitors.'

"They had other natural talents, as well. They could send poison through the winds with the help of a fan-like weapon known as a *hauchiwa*. These poisons came out of their talons, and could be delivered in stronger doses by a strike of their hands. We Dragons were immune to this poison, but few other creatures were. Even without the poison, however, their wings and *hauchiwa* could create furious gusts of wind that could knock a Griffin or even a smaller Dragon out of the sky.

"But while those were powerful weapons, they had a stronger power which made them... difficult to kill. Their strength would grow in the daylight, and the sun could restore them to perfect health from even the most lethal of injuries in a matter of hours."

Wangdu, who had been quietly listening, shook his head sadly. "They came to us, they did, presenting themselves as gods. We worshipped them, we did, and gave them our tribute and our service. They made us slaves in return, they did. They experimented on us, they did, killed us for sport, raped our women, stole everything from us. Finally the Elves rebelled, they did, realizing that the Tengu were not what they had represented themselves to be...."

"Indeed," Khumbaya growled. "And in the process of rebelling against the Tengu, you became as cruel and evil as them. You, too, experimented on other races – our forefathers the Green Dragons. You, too, enslaved other races – the Dwarves, in particular, for their skill in navigating in the dark, as well as Griffins and the Ancient Dragons you created. The only thing that separated you from the Tengu, in our eyes, was that you were not the type to kill or torture others for sport. You did what you did in defense of your people, not for selfish reasons. It was your leaders who wronged the Dragons, my ancestors felt, and for that reason, only your leaders were destroyed when we rebelled. The Tengu, however, we destroyed utterly."

"No-one has admitted seeing a Tengu for centuries, they haven't," Wangdu agreed. "But my kind has not lived up to your forbearance, we haven't, I fear."

Steam heralded the entrance of another dragon who quickly showed he had been listening in. "There are a few Elves that we Dragons respect, still. One is our friend the Lady Phalra of the Bandi Republic, who once worked as a healer for our kind. You, Wangdu, are another. Perhaps a few others, less visible, who it would be tiresome to name. But there are many Elves throughout the world who we would gladly kill if the opportunity presented itself."

The steam cleared, allowing Maelgyn's people to see this new dragon for the first time. It was older, and somewhat larger – Khumbaya looked to be the size of a small horse, but this Dragon looked as if he were about the size of a large warhorse. His golden scales were more dull, and the teeth he displayed were pitted with cavities from millennia of use. *This*, Maelgyn realized, *must be one of the Elders*.

"Sir," Maelgyn said. Despite Wodtke's earlier admonitions, he used his magic to help him stand to full attention. "We have fulfilled the quest you presented us with, and avenged your lost comrade. Furthermore, we have reunited Svieda and the Borden Isles, fulfilling the condition set decades ago for your return to our treaty of old. We have been told an enemy of ours intends to employ Black Dragons against us. Will we have your support, should we require it?"

The Elder Dragon stared at him, cocking his head slightly. "I think you should rest, your Highness. Your injuries will not heal properly if you continue to use magic to compensate for them."

Wodtke glared in the direction of the young Sword Prince. Maelgyn flushed in embarrassment. "I felt it important to present myself to you properly. A few minutes of magical enhancement, here or there, should not make a significant difference in my recovery."

"Commendable," the Elder replied, though his tone implied he was more amused and impatient than impressed. "But unnecessary. We Dragons prefer our allies to be practical rather than diplomatic."

Maelgyn didn't release his magic, however. "I was not aware we had concluded an alliance, just yet."

The Elder snorted. "Of course, of course. Well, we will respect our treaty of old, that much is certain, so you may relax. We do not go back on our word, and we swore to keep the old treaty if you and the Borden Islanders were ever reunited. But we are considering whether to offer you more – in addition to providing protection from other Dragons anywhere inside your territory, as our original treaty remains in force, we are willing to help guard six Human cities of your choice on the mainland for the next one hundred years. In exchange, you will defend our lair and our nesting sites as much as can reasonably be expected from both foreign invaders and poachers. If both of us are satisfied after that time, we may agree to extend the alliance even further."

Maelgyn hesitated. "'Nesting sites?' What 'nesting sites' are you talking about? I'm not sure we can commit to defend those, given I have no idea what a Dragon's nest is, exactly, nor where you will put them. And my understanding is that Dragons need to 'nest' for about a thousand years – the chances that we will be able to keep to any for that length of time, regardless of how fair it is or how sensible it would be to keep it, is... nearly zero. I cannot know the minds of the unborn grandchildren of my unborn grandchildren."

Steam once more snorted out of the Elder's nose. "Of course we would not ask you to defend the indefensible, nor to swear an oath on behalf of your descendants for the next thousand years. And we have heard of dragon nests being in... inconvenient places, in the past, which lead to many of the conflicts between Golden Dragons and Humans. You have nothing to fear in that regard from us, however; the volcanoes of the Borden Isles present us with a special opportunity. A rare opportunity to incubate our eggs and hatch them faster – our next generation, if we can nest in these volcanoes, will be born in decades rather than centuries. The nests will be inside the volcanoes where they will trouble no Humans. We will only need a single century or so of your protection, and the truth is that all you must do is protect your own borders and prevent poachers from approaching us in order to protect our nests. That much commitment should be within your grasp."

Maelgyn hesitated. "It should be, yes. But something I don't understand – why are you even bothering with the alliance? We will be 'defending our own borders' anyway, after all. Forgive me, and I can't believe I'm arguing this point, but I don't see what is in this alliance for you, and that makes me suspicious."

If Maelgyn didn't know any better, he would say this latest blow of steam was laughter. Dragons weren't exactly known for their laughter, though, so it couldn't be that, could it? "Our reasons are simple: We know we can trust you to keep your word. If your people were to fall, we would be dealing with an unknown power... and for the next century, during the nesting period, we cannot afford that uncertainty. And we can always use additional help protecting our younglings from poachers."

That was something Maelgyn could certainly understand. His recent experiences dealing with the Nekoji – a race nearly hunted to extinction by poachers – showed that the Dragons' fear of poaching was not unfounded. He didn't believe that was their true reason for strengthening their alliance with Svieda, but it wasn't healthy to question the honesty of a Dragon. Their listed reasons were enough of an excuse for the time being.

"Very well. I would gladly accept the aid of such a noble people," Maelgyn finally answered.

"We will be able to join your order of battle when you require us," the Elder said. "But with the nesting, we ask for a short delay to organize ourselves. We will send with you an observer with you, to survey your war and report back to us when we are needed."

Again, Maelgyn knew that he wasn't being told the whole story, but he accepted the explanation he was given without comment. Dragons never told lies, though they were rarely said to tell the whole truth. Maelgyn accepted that they were honestly interested in entering into an alliance with Svieda, and so he would gladly take that help.

"Very well. And who shall be accompanying me back to the mainland?"

"Me," Khumbaya grumbled unhappily. "I will join you. Though I do not look forward to the journey with you – your ships move so slow."

Maelgyn turned his attention back to the younger Dragon, who seemed somewhat disgruntled. "I intend to leave in a matter of days. How long will you need to prepare?"

"We are Dragons, your Highness," the Elder reminded him. "We need no armor, no weapons, no provisions of any sort. We are our own armor, our own weapons, and we eat what we like, when we like, and have few concerns for anything else. Khumbaya can leave immediately, assuming your ship is ready to sail. The rest of us merely wish time with our families."

"Very well," Maelgyn sighed, trying to think whether the shipboard stocks were sufficient to provision a dragon for the trip. "Then meet us in the castle's harbor in three days. We should be ready, then."

Chapter III

"I don't think suggesting to the Dragons that you plan to leave in three days was wise," Wodtke said. Maelgyn had made it most of the way down the mountain by himself, but only thanks to the illicit use of his magic – he was now being forced to lie down in their cart, and the doctor was unhappy with the effect on his injuries. "You'll be lucky if you can *walk* again in three days after the way you strained your injuries on that mountaintop. An ocean voyage probably won't be possible for you when that Dragon arrives."

"Even if I'm bedridden the entire trip home, I will be leaving for the mainland in three days time," Maelgyn declared, eyes flashing. "I have dallied here long enough. I need to be in position to take command of my armies when they arrive, even if I'm not in perfect health when I do. As it is, I may already be late."

Wodtke opened her mouth to protest, but then closed it and shook her head. Instead, she turned to address Wangdu. "Well, it's pretty obvious I'm not going to be able to talk him out of that. He still needs to heal, however, before he gets back into this war, so is there anything you can do to speed his recovery? I understand that Elven magic includes amazing healing powers...."

Wangdu shook his head slowly. "There are things I can do,

there are, but I will not do them now, I won't. It would have lasting consequences, it would. If you keep his injuries clean, you do, then he should have ample time to recover on the ride to the mainland, he should. It is much better for all of us, it is, if his injuries heal more naturally, they do. Just like it is better for him, it is, if he does not use his magic to compensate for his injuries, he doesn't. Still, if he really wanted my help, he did, I might be willing to try something, I might."

"I am right here, you know," Maelgyn pointed out wryly. "You could ask me if I'd be *willing* to undergo Elven healing techniques. The answer, by the way, is that no; I have it on good authority that it is, ahem, dangerous to allow an Elf to heal you." With that, he tapped the wrist circled by the vines of his *schlipf*.

Wangdu nodded. "That is wise advise, it is. At the very least the process is very painful, it is, and at the worst an Elf can... change you, he can. For good or ill, being changed by an Elf is never a pleasant experience, it isn't."

"If we needed Elven healing magic to keep from antagonizing a dragon, it might be worth it," Euleilla said. "But I would also rather my husband not undertake this 'change.' Perhaps if he took at least one more day before starting the journey back home, we could manage it. I've been looking over Rudel's reports, and it will be a hard thing just to get the ship fully supplied in that time."

Maelgyn hadn't even considered that when he set his personal deadline. He was just thinking about getting himself home as soon as possible, and hadn't considered the fact that the rest of his people wouldn't have had time to prepare. However, he wasn't sure what he could do to fix that mistake. "I'm afraid it's too late. Unless you can think of some way to delay Khumbaya after he arrives at the castle, we'll have to leave pretty much right away."

"I can think of one way," El'Athras grumbled from his perch at the front of the wagon. He'd been too busy driving the cart to pay much attention, for the most part, but he heard enough to know this was the perfect opportunity to bring up a difficult topic. Part of it was that he was naturally suspicious of everything (especially Dragons who weren't giving out the whole truth), but he had quite a few questions that he wanted answered. "We are still investigating several of the artifacts we recovered from Paljor's offices. Many of them look like they are not of Human origin, and Wangdu believed at least a couple of them looked rather Draconian when he examined them. Perhaps our new 'friend' will be able to explain what they are, and how they wound up in Paljor's possession in the first place. And perhaps he could explain what the notes in Paljor's papers about certain secret conversations between him and the Dragons mean."

"It would not be wise to antagonize the Dragons, it wouldn't," Wangdu warned. "They are some of the most powerful creatures in existence, they are, and they do not take kindly to having their innate honesty questioned, they don't."

Maelgyn nodded slowly, considering it. He didn't want to risk alienating a new ally. On the other hand, a short delay might be advisable, and if they really did have artifacts of Draconian origin, it would be wise to get them identified. "Ask your questions, but do it politely. In fact, avoid their conversations with Paljor entirely – he's dead, after all, and was no friend of theirs in the end. Finding out what those artifacts are might be important, and could give us the time we need. But whatever you do, don't get the damned Dragon mad!"

"I'll be careful," El'Athras grumbled.

"I thought we would be leaving, today, so that I could get an eye on your main cities," Khumbaya grumbled, standing in the courtyard. "It's clear weather, with good headwinds for flying toward the mainland. And I thought Sword Prince Maelgyn would be here to greet me upon my arrival."

"His Highness is preparing for the journey," El'Athras explained, having been the one to greet the dragon upon his arrival. "Had you not joined us, we would be leaving some time tonight, but your presence requires some added equipment and provisions – we don't expect you to fly alongside the ship the whole way, so we are preparing a place on the boat for you to rest. We should be ready to set out tomorrow, but we've run into a puzzle that you might be able to help us with while we wait. In searching Paljor's estate, we found some unusual items. Wangdu suggested your kind might know what they are."

Khumbaya snorted out a breath of steam as he followed the Dwarf. "Unlikely. We dragons are quite self-sufficient, and rarely create artifacts of our own. Elder Veila was carrying none of those artifacts when she was assassinated by Paljor, and I haven't heard of any thefts from our hoards, recently."

"That may be," El'Athras admitted, opening up the door to a warehouse in which they had been storing some of Paljor's effects. "But these artifacts may not have been lost recently. Many of them seem... rather old."

He pointed to an ancient scrap of metal with roughly etched decorations on the surface and the tattered remains of several leather straps that were now too rotted to properly reconstruct. The one-time piece of armor was too large for a Human, and really was even too large for a Golden Dragon, but was obvious in what it was: A breastplate for some huge beast of burden.

"This once belonged to the Ancient Dragons," Khumbaya explained soberly once he completed his examination, gently tracing the scratches with a single claw. "Not many examples of its like survive. This one looks to have been made after the defeat of the Ancient Enemy, when we finally broke free from our Elven slave-masters. We would fill these grooves with a poisonous paste, and their entangling plants would be unable to properly grasp us. Our skins protect us from being pierced or cut by most Elven weapons, far better than any armor that could be made of metal, but we had to worry about nets or similar devices leaving us immobile and thus vulnerable to those few weapons that could hurt us. We Golden Dragons are smaller than our Ancient Ancestors, however, so we would have no use for this piece any more. The design, however, could be fitted for any of our modern kin, with some effort." He paused. "You say it was Sho'Curlas that was training Black Dragons?"

El'Athras nodded. "And we have proof that Paljor and Sho'Curlas were conspiring together. We hope that no armor was made and that Paljor was merely preparing to sell this design to them... but that brings up the question: Where did Paljor get it, and what were the Sho'Curlans planning to do with it? There are no more great armies of Elves to entangle the Black Dragons. As far as I know, Wangdu is the only Elf now operating in Svieda, and even *he* wasn't there as of two months ago. Only Oregal has Elves in enough numbers to threaten a dragon, and even they are so scattered as to be no significant danger to them."

"There are a few other nations which could manage to field a sizable company of Elves," Khumbaya argued. "We Dragons keep track of them, after all, to make sure they never become a threat to us."

El'Athras cocked his head. "I have spies in every nation, and I'm not aware of any large concentrations of Elves anywhere."

"There are a number of Elves in Squire's Knot," Khumbaya explained. "Or there were. Most of them left days before an army from Sho'Curlas invaded, and we have no idea where they went. Also, thousands of Elves still live in Oregal, scattered as you say. And in Poros...."

El'Athras waited, but it seemed the Dragon wasn't going to continue. "Poros?" he prompted.

"We have suspicions," Khumbaya growled lowly. "But I will not voice them, as we know nothing with certainty. Dragons refuse to slander others."

El'Athras frowned. His spies had been getting increasing inconsistent information out of Poros, but this was the first time he'd heard of Elves living in that home of the original Human civilization. No, wait – the second. "Before we left for Borden, four Elves we know to be from Poros attempted to assassinate Prince Maelgyn. They left when Maelgyn managed to acquire one of their *schlipf* and Wangdu intervened, but I never trusted the explanation they gave for why they left. They could easily have killed both Maelgyn and Wangdu, but I think they didn't want to leave any proof of their presence that could be shown to others. To kill the both of them, I'm pretty sure they would have had no choice but to use weapons and techniques that would leave certain evidence of their presence."

Khumbaya nodded slowly. "Again, we only have suspicions, not proof."

"Well, perhaps there is something to that," El'Athras nodded, keeping his eyes on the breastplate. He didn't even glance at the Dragon as he asked his next question. "Do the Dragons know where someone here on the Borden Isles, which are largely isolated from the mainland, might have found this piece of Draconic armor?"

El'Athras knew he was pushing it after Maelgyn's orders, but this was vital information. Fortunately, the youthful Golden Dragon missed the implication in that statement completely. "The Borden Isles were home to an Ancient Dragon stronghold during the wars with the Tengu, and again after the rebellion against the Elves. Our lair now encircles much of that stronghold, but relics of the Ancients are strewn across other parts of the island. We take the ones we can find, but we know there are some we have missed."

"Is that the only reason you can think of?" El'Athras asked suspiciously.

"Yes," Khumbaya growled, steam blowing out his nose. "But you obviously have another idea. What is it, Dwarf?"

El'Athras realized he had trapped himself. He had no choice, now – he had to confront the Dragon with his suspicions. Hopefully, he would survive the response.

"I speak of my own suspicions, not those of Maelgyn nor anyone else, but my first thought upon finding these was that, perhaps, the Golden Dragons had sold these things to Paljor."

There was a very long pause before Khumbaya responded. "We Dragons have no need of Human money. There were rumors that some of our Dragon Clans were paying a tribute to the lands they stayed in before coming to Borden Isle, but we have never had any fears from the fortified walls of our volcanic lair that Paljor could demand tribute for."

"Then where did this armor come from?" El'Athras demanded. "You can't expect me to believe he just found it! Someone must have at least told him where to look."

Khumbaya advanced on the Dwarf menacingly, but then reconsidered. "Well... there may be something to that. I don't believe the Ancient Dragons would have just lost something this valuable – if they no longer needed it, they would have hidden it to keep it out of Elven hands. We don't know where all of their hiding spots were, but we do know it is unlikely someone would just stumble on it. Paljor would have had to know where to look... and there are few creatures left in the world who would be able to tell him."

"Anyone you know?" El'Athras asked.

"If any of our Ancient Enemy survived, they might know where an old battlefield was that such things could be found," Khumbaya said. "But they are all dead. There may still be living Elves old enough to have lived in that time, but these things were kept secret from them. No younger Dragon would be able to tell anyone, even if one desired to. This is indeed a mystery. I swear to you that it would not have been any of the Elders I know of, however – some are old enough to possibly be aware of existing treasuries of the Ancients, but their hatred of Paljor was so great it could not have been feigned."

"Then perhaps a Dragon not from the Borden Isles?" El'Athras suggested, intrigued. He knew that no Dragon would have sworn that oath if they weren't telling the truth, but he couldn't imagine that anyone other than a Dragon would know the armor's location.

"Perhaps it is possible that there is a traitor to the Dragons somewhere," Khumbaya half-heartedly agreed. "Though it could not be a Red or Black Dragon; they cannot talk to humans. Nor an Ancient or Green Dragon, for they are both extinct. And there are very few Golden Dragons aside from those on Borden. So the question then becomes, who are they, and where are they?"

"I have people combing through Paljor's records," El'Athras noted. "Hopefully, they will find something soon."

"Hopefully." Suddenly, Khumbaya leaped, striking the Dwarf and pinning him to the ground underneath his fore-talons. He lowered his mouth to El'Athras' ear, bearing his teeth menacingly. "By the way, Dwarf. I understand your kind feel they must ask these questions, but keep in mind it isn't wise to anger a Dragon. We are not exactly... patient... when it comes to insults."

El'Athras swallowed. "Right. I'll keep that in mind."

"Now... when do we really leave?" Khumbaya released him and backed away.

"In the morning, as I said," El'Athras replied as stoically as he could muster, standing up and dusting himself off. "His Highness is still recovering from his injuries, but has become most insistent. He gave you the date he wanted to leave, but the rest of us knew that his health would suffer if we allowed him to leave that quickly. It took everything we had to convince him that he should take even one more day of rest, and he only granted that because there were a number of legitimate concerns for our provisioning."

"I see. Well, we Dragons can be patient," Khumbaya huffed. "Were there any other questions you had of me?"

"A few other pieces of the same set of armor, I believe. Nothing else Draconian in origin, according to Wangdu, although even he couldn't tell me the origin of a few of these artifacts. Perhaps you can help me...."

*

The voyage back to the Sviedan mainland was not pleasant. In addition to transporting Maelgyn and his entourage, the crew of the *Greyholden* also had to find cargo space for a number of items recovered from the treasuries of Borden Island: Dragonhide armor, artifacts El'Athras believed to have originated with the Sea Dwarves that needed further study, a selection of scrolls from Paljor's archives recording his dealings with Hrabak, and even spare weapons and sets of armor to help equip soldiers on the mainland. All taken with the agreement of the Seats of the Borden Isle, as a portion of their contribution to the war against Sho'Curlas.

But finding space for that was child's play compared to the issues the ship's cook had with trying to feed both the entire crew and its passengers... or rather, one particular passenger.

"Look, I'm not happy with it, either," the cook snapped. "Do you think I like cooking split pea soup seventeen days in a row? I hate it – absolutely *hate* it. But it's all we have, and so you either eat it or starve. Got that?"

"I am a Dragon, you simpleton!" Khumbaya roared, flames from his nostrils very nearly igniting the ship's rigging accidentally in his carelessness. "I cannot eat this... this 'split pea soup.' I eat meat, and nothing else!"

"Well, you've cleaned us out of salted beef and salted pork," the cook growled back, making a passable imitation of an angry Dragon himself in the process. "Though how you managed to down that rancid junk is beyond me...."

"I was *very* hungry," Khumbaya admitted sheepishly. "And truth be told, it didn't sit well at all..."

"Well, I warned you about that. But did you listen? No. Now, you have no choice *but* to listen. We have nothing to cook with on this ship except for seawater, split peas, and flour. You have three choices. You can eat ships biscuits – but you've already said they make you ill. You can eat split pea soup – but you're refusing that now. Your final option is to catch something for yourself. If you manage that, fine, but otherwise... don't bother me when I'm trying to feed everybody *else* on this horrid little warship, got it?" The cook walked away from the cowed Dragon, shaking his head in disgust. "All I wanted was for them to properly stock the ship while we were in port. We could have stocked pickles, properly preserved meats, properly wrapped cheeses, spices, wines, good fruits and vegetables, and all sorts of things that would keep this crew healthy. Did we do that? No. All we get is more flour, more split peas, and more rancid meat before we're rushed out to sea with only half our provisions on board. I don't know why I even try...."

Maelgyn watched the middle-aged man who had just argued a Dragon into submission disappear below deck, and chuckled in amusement. "I think I like that man. What's his name, again?"

Ruznak, standing next to the hammock that the Sword Prince was resting in, pursed his lips. He had taken command of the ship for the journey back to Borden with Rudel left behind as regent, and had made it a point to learn everyone's names. The ship's rather flamboyant cook was a pretty easy man to remember, however. "I believe his name is Kiszaten, your Highness. He is a good cook, and brilliant at making do with whatever is given him, but I fear he isn't exactly a good seaman. He could do well as a professional chef with his own establishment, but I don't think he's exactly suited for the limitations that most navy cooks must make."

Maelgyn frowned in thought. "What about as an army cook?"

"I fear the same limitations apply," Ruznak explained.

"How about as the personal camp chef to royalty?" Euleilla, sitting in her own hammock at Maelgyn's side, suggested. "Tur'Ba makes an excellent servant and bodyguard, but I fear that Dwarven cuisine doesn't exactly fit my tastes well."

Ruznak laughed. "I'm sure he would be honored. I fear, however, that your inner circle is getting a bit large, your Highness – you seem to be picking people up right and left."

"What do you mean?" Maelgyn asked, a little insulted. He glanced over at Euleilla. "I'd say I've done a good job of encircling myself with highly skilled people from all over Svieda."

"Well, I have my reservations about some of them," Ruznak huffed, but then grinned. "Though I certainly think you did a fine job picking a wife. I don't mean that all of your decisions have been bad."

"I'm so glad you think your foster daughter makes a good Princess," Maelgyn replied dryly. "But obviously you don't like some of my other companions."

"Again, not all of them," Ruznak dithered. "I find El'Athras to be an excellent spymaster. Rudel was a wise choice as regent over the Borden Isles. Lady Onayari is an excellent representative of the Nekoji people, and I feel will make a brilliant advisor as she gets more involved in court functions. However, there are a few people I'm not so sure about...."

"Such as?" Maelgyn asked impatiently. Even Euleilla looked somewhat upset at her foster father, more for the people he had left out than the ones he had included.

"Well, Sir Leno seems like a nice enough fellow, but he doesn't really seem to have a place in your camp. He's no military expert, he holds little or no influence over any of your soldiers, he is not a specialist in any field you have need of... just why is he one of your advisors?"

It was Euleilla, not Maelgyn, who answered that question. "Sir Leno, my husband and I have all gone through very unique paths on our way to becoming mages, and all of us have what you might call... well, for lack of a better term, an incomplete set of skills. I know many ways to use magic that are unknown to a traditionally educated mage, but some of the rather simple and basic methods never even occurred to me. Maelgyn is very adept in countermagic, but had to improvise for many of his other magical skills. Sir Leno struggled to find an instructor after he'd learned the basics, and turned to books... but most dealt more with magical theory and alchemy, rather than magical combat. This is the reason he is with us, gramps – not to be an advisor in the political sense, but in the magical one."

Ruznak was impressed. He had rarely heard Euleilla speak so much in one sitting, much less in one breath. Furthermore, the only person he had heard her speak more vehemently in the defense of was Maelgyn, back when she first asked permission to accompany him in his journey to Sopan – and she wound up marrying him only a short time later. Maelgyn had been quite oblivious to the discussion at the time, but Ruznak knew the girl was smitten from the very first moment she talked about him. Clearly, she had no romantic intentions with Sir Leno, but her respect was clear.

"I suppose that makes some sense. But he's not the only one – what about Wangdu? I know El'Athras seems to like him, but I don't exactly trust any Elf."

"I don't either," Maelgyn agreed. "And I'm pretty sure he'd lose his faith in me if I did – one of the things he's often told me is that I should never trust an Elf, not even him. However, it seems as if our enemies have an Elf behind their throne, so we should have one to counter him."

Again, Ruznak could see the logic in that, and Wangdu wasn't exactly one of the people he felt shouldn't be in the inner circle. He had just hoped to make his point before bringing up the people he liked, but feared were in over their heads.

"What of Tur'Ba? I know you were obliged to take him with you, but despite how enthusiastic he is I don't think he makes a very good servant," Ruznak explained.

"Nor do I," Maelgyn chuckled. "But that's okay – while on the road I don't really need a servant, and when at home I have hundreds."

"Fair enough – since it seems you're stuck with him as a matter of honor. But you should reconsider your decision to officially make him one of your bodyguards," Ruznak explained. "He's a Dwarf, and while they're stout, hearty fellows they don't exactly make good fighters."

Euleilla cocked her head, remembering a wall of dead bodies formed from the ambush on Borden Isle. *And that was only with a couple weeks of training with an axe. He's had more than a month, now, and will have more time in the future – how much better can he become?*

"Wrong," was all she said, however.

Ruznak blinked. That was the foster-daughter he remembered – enigmatic, one word (and usually a one syllable word, at that) answers to complex questions, with no explanation and rarely with much clarity as to just what she actually meant. However, she was just as vehement as she had been with Sir Leno.

"If... if you say so," he said finally. It had been a while since he'd been on the receiving end of one of those, and he was no longer quite so used to it. He had one more name to throw out there, however – if the royal couple somehow managed to find an excuse for this one, he'd give up. "Then what about Rykeifer?"

Maelgyn sighed. This was becoming tedious. He put up with the questions for Euleilla's sake, but it sounded as if even she was tiring of them. "What of him?"

"Making a militia captain one of the lead generals of your armies?" Ruznak replied, shaking his head. "I'm sure he's a good man, but he really lacks the proper experience, don't you think?"

Maelgyn frowned. Ruznak had a point on this one. Rykeifer's inclusion had not been a planned one, but rather an afterthought following the small-scale battle he had fought against a band of raiders. However, he had been rather impressed with the young man during their first meeting – he presented himself as overqualified to be a simple militia captain, and Maelgyn didn't want to waste that raw talent. Still, Rykeifer had yet to prove himself in any other role.

"I suppose I may have been overzealous with his promotion," Maelgyn agreed. "But, consider this: The armies of Svieda are supposedly opened for anyone of any social class to enter and become either officer or footsoldier. So tell me, why are almost all of the officer positions taken by noblemen?"

"Well, under the feudal system, a Lord leads his own soldiers, your Highness," Ruznak replied, knowing he was stating the obvious but hoping there was a point.

"In theory, yes," Maelgyn explained. "But Svieda's system of soldiering isn't a true feudal system – the Law of Swords, while written to prevent infighting amongst the Royal family, changed out government when it instituted the checks and balances needed to deal with the, ahem, overly ambitious of the Swords. Poros had a true feudal system and it turned into one of the most violently divided nations in the entire world. Svieda tried to correct those problems: We took the Republican system from Oregal to ensure the rights of the peasants and protect the nation from poor leaders, the Feudal system from Poros to ensure that we had sufficient numbers of mages to defend the land, and we added a modified form of the ring-giver system from the days that Humans were little more than wandering tribes to satisfy our inheritance laws. Our government may be a bit confusing, but I think most of us have found it a fair system for royals, nobles, and peasants alike."

"It usually is," Ruznak admitted. "But we had laws to ensure that our nobility would be ideally suited to act as great warriors and mages. It is understandable that most of our officers would be nobles."

"True," Maelgyn agreed. "But I fear that belief has allowed many promising soldiers who do not have such a lineage to go ignored. Rykeifer may be one such man, a promising soldier who has been ignored because he lacks the pedigree of most officers."

"Still," Ruznak insisted. "He has never commanded anything more than a few hundred militiamen. Are you sure you want him over all the other proven, experienced soldiers under your command?"

Maelgyn shrugged. "I'm not as certain of his abilities as I am of the others in my court. Keep in mind, however, that I am even more inexperienced than he is. Rykeifer has earned a chance by his deeds. Until he proves otherwise, I will consider his advice... just as I do any of my other counselors. Whether they came to me by proving their skill, through an honor debt, or because I had the good sense to marry their foster daughter."

Ruznak sighed, then bowed slightly. "As you say, your Highness. But please... try not to add to your retinue too much in the near future. A chef is okay. An artisan or a scribe might also be an okay addition. But no more, okay?"

It was sound advice, but Maelgyn felt as if the mood was getting too serious. He needed to do something to add a spark of humor back into what was supposed to be a friendly discussion, not an argument. The idea for just what to say came to him in a flash, and he smirked. "Anything you say... Gramps!"

Sekhar started shouting warnings of danger right away, and Maelgyn rolled out of his hammock to run away. It was a fun scene, as Euleilla 'watched' her foster-father chase her husband up the ship's mast. Maelgyn was moving slower than usual because of his injuries, and Ruznak was letting him escape of course. A smile came to her face.

Well, I'm glad they're still getting along...

Chapter IV

Maelgyn stood on deck, surveying the port as the *Greyholden* was coaxed the final few yards into the dock by the yard hands' lead ropes. Sailors jumped into action, securing fenders so the ship's sides would not scrape against the pier itself, and fastening the mooring lines that would secure the ship in place.

Maelgyn frowned. As the capital city of its namesake province, the port city of Happaso was normally a bustling hub of trade, with dockworkers constantly loading and unloading vessels at all piers. Today, though, *Greyholden* was one of only a few ships surrounded by activity. A port like Happaso should have still been teeming with trade, in a desperate attempt to feed the supply lines for the front. The question became whether the lack of activity was because the supply lines were being fed from a different direction, or whether the supply lines weren't being fed at all.

It was a question to answer another day, as the gangplank was lowered before he could ask those questions. Euleilla came up to his side as they made their way down the ramp to the small delegation standing at the pier to greet them.

"Welcome, your Highness. I am Senator Ontai, mayor of Happaso and the head of our parliament. I believe we have met before, but I don't know if you recall..."

Maelgyn gave him a diplomatic smile, but felt something was off. The man would be the highest ranking man in town absent the Sword or his Regent, but the lack of an honor guard of any sort was one more oddity to puzzle through.

"We had heard you might be coming, but not when. I'm afraid we haven't had time to prepare a proper reception...."

"Given the circumstances, I think a lack of certain formalities is perfectly understandable," Maelgyn said, motioning to where a group of town councilors were lined up ceremonially in place of the usual soldiers. "We've been largely out-of-touch with the front lines for a while, now. What is the word?"

"A lot has happened," The mayor said. "Come to the Citadel, and we'll explain it all."

Maelgyn frowned impatiently, waving for the rest of his entourage – including the newly recruited Kiszaten the chef, who was quite happy to be away from shipboard supplies – to join him. The gathering crowd seemed quite startled at some of his companions – many had never seen a Nekoji before, much less an Elf or a Dragon. Dwarves were more commonplace, but usually stuck to their own kind – to see two traveling in the company of one of Svieda's royals was enough to turn the whole city into rampant gossips. And then there was the young woman hanging on his arm – word of his marriage might not have trickled through to the locals, yet, but any woman on his arm would have drawn attention. "You can save the details until we're in the Citadel, Senator, but considering the necessities of war, I'd like you to give me the highlights while we make our way there."

Ontai hesitated for only a fraction of a second before nodding. In the few times Maelgyn had met him before, the man had always fretted too much about the wrong things, but he was very efficient. "Very well, your Highness. There is much to tell."

"I have many questions, and this reception is only adding to them," Maelgyn said. "We've heard that Rubick is gone, but not why. We've also heard that there's been fighting throughout the Royal Province, and maybe even in Happaso. Are the Sho'Curlan's really that close? Where is the front line?"

"There isn't one." Ontai paused, considering how to phrase what he was about to say. "Sho'Curlas is encamped in what once was

Sycanth Province, dispersed throughout most of the old cities and townships. They also have holdings throughout much of the old Royal Province, which we are trying to push back into, but their units are so scattered there isn't anything as simple as a line. I think this has something to do with Sho'Curlas' attempts to secure the conquered territory in Sycanth and improve their supply lines before making a concerted effort to match our armies, but I'm not privy to whatever strategy they are employing myself."

"Of course not," Maelgyn agreed.

"Our defensive forces are based throughout Happaso and Glorest, for the most part, mostly comprised of the survivors of Sycanth and the Royal Province combined with local provincial armies. A tent city with the bulk of the soldiers gathering from elsewhere is forming just outside of town, and it is hoped they will be able to join the war effort soon. That includes a portion of your own armies, I believe."

"I will have to visit them soon, then," Maelgyn said.

"Of course, your Highness." Ontai took a deep breath before relaying the next bit of news. "Rubick is in flames – literally. A series of raids set fires that grew to wild and unmanageable proportions in the farmland and the forests. Cities and towns have been abandoned for fear of the flames, and the people are scattered – the province cannot hold if anyone comes to claim it, so we are doing our best to see to it that Sho'Curlas doesn't send any significant forces across that border."

"Damn," El'Athras whistled, shaking his head. "Even if the war ended today, that sort of devastation will take years to rebuild from. Maybe even decades."

Ontai nodded. "As we are unable to protect that region from invasion, most of the plains between Happaso and Largo are defenseless. Raiding parties – such as the one which briefly held Squire's Knot a few months ago and which set Rubick ablaze – will continue to be a problem for the foreseeable future, but our generals don't believe they will bring in a full-scale invasion force; that might provoke a war with nearby South Poros, and we doubt they want a war on two fronts."

"Any word on Black Dragons being used in the war? I have received intelligence that Sho'Curlas is training Dragons...."

Ontai's eyes widened. "No! Nothing like that. Well, we've heard rumors that Dragons had taken residence in Sycanth alongside the old border with Sho'Curlas, but nothing more than that. If they're anything more than rumor, they haven't involved themselves in the war yet."

"That is fortunate... for them," Khumbaya growled, trailing the group. His size made travel through the narrower streets difficult, but roads built for horse traffic were large enough for him to walk comfortably... and he had been so quiet since coming ashore that Ontai and the other senators had almost been able to ignore his presence.

"I heard from a Dwarven Emissary that you were on a mission to restore our treaty with the Golden Dragons," Ontai said, glancing at Khumbaya nervously. "I take it you were successful."

El'Athras frowned. "What dunderhead informed you of our mission? That man needs to be disciplined for his loose lips."

"I'm afraid I don't know his name," Ontai explained. "But I will gladly point him out if I see him again."

Maelgyn was as concerned as El'Athras, but those worries could wait until he had settled in. "That is something we will have to deal with later – secret missions should not gossiped about, whether the gossip is an emissary, a king, or a simple footsoldier – but I am more immediately concerned with other news. You say our armies are still here and in Glorest, and the enemy forces are settled into Sycanth. I figured they would be closer to the front line, which would mean in the Royal Province itself. Surely, if we held any cities or towns, our armies would be there. How much of the Royal Province do we really hold, then?"

"I'm afraid the Royal Province is little more than one huge battleground," Ontai explained. "Cities and townships are constantly changing hands, and no-one is able to hold any territory in that area for long." He paused. "Though the Royal Castle, last I heard, was back in our hands."

Maelgyn froze for just a split second. He had never held out any real hope that he would be the one to lead the successful re-capture of the capital of Svieda, so he never believed he could be king. However, in the back of his mind, there was what might have been charitably called a fantasy that he could be King, with Euleilla as his Queen, and he could bring about a golden age in Sviedan history. A childish dream, he knew, which was why he forbade that dream from ever entering his conscious thought... but now, it was essentially over.

"Who is King?" Maelgyn asked. Most of those present had understood what Ontai's reference to the Royal Castle meant, but Euleilla and Khumbaya both were startled as they figured out the meaning as well.

"His Majesty, the Sword King Brode IX now rules from the Royal Castle... for as long as the Royal Castle holds, anyway," the mayor sighed. "It's been sacked twice already, and I doubt the castle's depleted defenses will hold for long should a new army approach, since there's no time to repair the fortifications. Sword Prince Arnach, my liege lord, was with him, step for step, up until the final assault on the Castle. He fell in that battle, though not fatally, and has been recovering from his injuries ever since. You'll find him in the camp outside of town, when you visit."

"Just one more reason for me to visit."

"Indeed. Only a few Swords are still alive to command the gathered army, I fear. Sword Arnach is in the ranking Sword in camp, though his injuries preclude any active service for now. Sword Princess Idril is... missing, though we still have hope that she is alive and somewhere in Sviedan territory. She and her immediate entourage got separated from their army as they marched here, and she's very late in catching up to them, but we have yet to hear of her death or capture. Sword Wybert is in the camp, accompanying the cavalry you sent here, but his own injuries will make leading our armies somewhat difficult. Sword King Brode is in the Royal castle, and you are here. Your father was captured alive, but we have heard nothing since, and Sword King Gilbereth and his sister were both killed in the initial fighting. Sword Prince Ambrosius went into battle alongside Arnach and Brode early on, but he's gone missing and is believed dead."

Maelgyn closed his eyes. The other Swords were his closest family, and now he had lost three of them in less than a year. Another – his own father – was imprisoned in a foreign land, and still others were missing or wounded. Euleilla's hand quickly closed over his, giving him a sympathetic squeeze, but there was little else she could do to comfort him.

The silence stretched on for a moment, almost becoming

uncomfortable.

"Your highness?" Ontai inquired tentatively.

Maelgyn looked up. "I see," he replied hoarsely.

"Were their Swords captured, were they?" Wangdu asked, gesturing to show he meant the blades which leant their title to the Sviedan royals, rather than the people.

"The Sword of Rubick was captured briefly, but Brode recovered that one with the castle of Svieda. Sycanth's Sword was captured, too, of course. The Sword of Leyland was found on the battlefield, which is partly why we suspect Ambrosius is dead. Assuming Idril is still alive, we believe she still holds the Sword of Stanget. The Royal Sword was taken before the Royal Castle fell," Ontai replied. "But I'm sure you knew of that one, already."

"Yes," Maelgyn said, remembering Hussack's betrayal clearly.

"I have heard nothing from Largo regarding your regular infantry," Ontai continued, deciding to change the subject as quickly as possible. "But, as I mentioned before, Sword Wybert is in town. He arrived alongside a sizable contingent of cavalry forces and Nekoji infantry only a few days after the Royal Castle was retaken. Sword King Brode's first act of any significant was to confirm the treaty you had negotiated with them." There was a long pause. "Many of his decisions since, however, have been... questionable."

"Questionable?" Maelgyn repeated, frowning.

"Never mind," Ontai said quickly, knowing he had spoken out of turn. "Sword Arnach will explain everything when you see him. Now, we must hurry – the Citadel's chefs will have prepared a meal upon hearing of your arrival, and it is never wise to annoy the chefs...."

"Maelgyn!" Arnach cried happily, hopping over to the tent's edge on one leg to embrace his cousin fiercely. This was Maelgyn's first trip into the tent city of soldiers growing outside of Happaso, and he had directed his guide to take him straight to Arnach's tent. Euleilla and the others were somewhere outside, setting themselves up inside the Sopan-controlled district. "I have to say, there have been many moments these past few months when I feared we would never see each other again."

"You weren't the only one," Maelgyn said, helping support his cousin as they made their way over to the seating. "This has been a pretty wild few months."

"I heard about your expedition to the Borden Isles from Wybert. Well, I actually heard about it from a bunch of the rumor-mongers throughout our camp before Wybert arrived and confirmed your plans for me. I take it, from the Golden Dragon sitting outside devouring our supply of rotten salt beef, that your trip was a success?"

Maelgyn grimaced. Apparently, the ability of his people to keep a secret wasn't nearly as strong as he would have liked. "Well, we reclaimed the Borden Isles and restored the old treaty with the Dragons with the hope of improving upon it. Then again, it was supposed to be a secret expedition, and it seems as if that part of it wasn't handled too well."

Arnach laughed dismissively. "Yes, well, any undertaking that great cannot be kept secret forever. So, explain to me just how you managed something the rest of Svieda's been trying to do for eighty years in just eight weeks?"

"It was more like two weeks, actually – the rest of the time was spent in me healing and travel back and forth from the Islands...." Maelgyn said. He went on to describe his entire journey, from the time he left Arnach and Brode following the assassination of their late King to his recent meeting with the Dragon Elder.

"Interesting," Arnach said when Maelgyn was done. "Any clue as to what the Dragons really want?"

Maelgyn shrugged. "Your guess is as good as mine. I've considered a number of possible motives, but none of them seem all that likely."

"Well, we'll worry about that another time," Arnach said. "Now... about this young woman you married...."

Maelgyn groaned. "Please tell me you aren't going to object. I've had to put up with enough of that nonsense back in Sopan, already...."

Arnach grinned. "Well, it wasn't exactly your typical courtship story for a Sviedan Royal, much less for one of the Swords. You have to expect some questions to be raised, at least."

"I wasn't exactly 'expecting' anything," Maelgyn pointed out. "As far as I knew, I was simply escorting a young woman across the mountains while concealing my identity. It seems as if I really need to pay better attention to our local laws."

"Turned out well enough for you this time, it seems."

"Well, I am quite glad to be married to her, if that's what you mean," Maelgyn agreed. "But I was unprepared for it. I love Euleilla, and nothing short of our deaths will break our marriage... but there sure are a lot of things I have to get used to."

"Well, you do have my support," Arnach said. "I'd like to meet this young woman of yours, of course, and I might have some questions of the both of you, but it sounds as if she's got you properly smitten. I won't have any objection to anyone you care that much for." He hesitated for a moment. "Brode, on the other hand...."

Maelgyn frowned. "You're not telling me that *Brode*, of all people, would have a problem with a Royal being involved with a commoner? The same Brode who, after being caught in a rather compromising position with an innkeeper's daughter, swore he would defy tradition and marry her? And when *that* girl refused to marry him, he moved on to a flower seller! Why would he object?"

"Brode has been acting... well, very strangely since taking the throne," Arnach sighed. "I don't think he would have objected a few weeks ago, but now...."

"Happaso's mayor said as much," Maelgyn replied. "But he didn't give any examples. What, exactly, is he doing? Could he just be... well, trying too hard to be a proper King, or is this something that couldn't be explained by that?"

Arnach rubbed the week-old beard on his chin in thought. "Well, I suppose some of it could be that. See, he seems to have gone... well, overly traditional in his views, and in ways detrimental to our well-being. You noticed the lack of shipping in the harbor? He's been trying to ban neutral powers from trading in our ports. That power is beyond him at the moment – he needs council approval for that kind of thing – but he can do it for ports which are 'close to the front.' He's been espousing some old Porosian beliefs that Svieda hasn't bothered with since its founding. 'In this time of crisis, we should look to our roots' has been the theme of many of his recent speeches. And in his personal life, he's been very distant. Oddly, he also seems rather obsessed with cleanliness all of a sudden – he seems to take baths an unusual number of times."

"Oh?" Maelgyn said, suddenly alert. "Hmm. By itself, peculiar, but with everything else? And I've taken a recent disliking to our Porosian 'roots' after an assassination attempt by some Elves out of Poros. It's a bit much of a coincidence. Before I voice any of my suspicions, though, I need to talk with him. I have to see just how odd he has become."

"That may be hard to do," Arnach sighed. "He doesn't take private meetings with anyone, and while I wouldn't call his public face 'inaccessible,' he doesn't like being out of his private suite more than is absolutely necessary as Sword King. Not to mention his throne is currently in the dead center of the largest battlefield in all of history...."

At that, Maelgyn smiled cockily. "Well, I'd expect him to summon me into that battlefield, soon. I've learned a few tricks that he should find useful for the war effort since we last parted."

Arnach rolled his eyes. "Tell me about it! You, a High Mage slayer. Someone at the next Mage's Council should suggest a rank higher than High Mage, just for you. Your ego must be threatening to take over by now."

Maelgyn laughed bitterly. "Not exactly had a chance to let it try, lately. I... wasn't exactly in good shape when the battle ended."

"As bad as me?" Arnach asked, lifting his injured leg for emphasis. Ontai had, during their dinner in Happaso's Citadel, described the leg as having been 'broken.' A splint and numerous bindings hid it from view, but with the insight his magic allowed he could see that 'broken' was an understatement. One of the bones in his leg had snapped in two... and the two pieces which that bone had once been were showing a spiderweb of cracks throughout. Thanks to the advances that magically-applied medicine had discovered, there was a slim chance the bone might heal... but Arnach would go through the rest of his life with a pronounced limp, if not worse.

"How did that happen?" Maelgyn asked, awed by the damage.

"Oddly enough, I don't know," Arnach said, letting the leg gently fall back to its resting position. "I think my horse fell on me, but I don't really remember. So, are you going to answer my question or what?"

"Huh? Oh! My injuries," Maelgyn replied. " I was closer to death than you, but I'll recover fully in time. I don't think our injuries are truly comparable – I was a step away from death by blood loss, but most of my bones and internal organs went unscathed. I suppose I could mention some cracked ribs, but that's nothing compared to your leg. I've been stitched up more than that old rag-doll you used to play with when we were younger, but I'm already healthy enough to do most anything. Doctor Wodtke doesn't think I should try anything too strenuous like fighting or horse-riding any time soon, but I should be back to where I was before that fight once I'm done recovering. You..."

"Eh, I'll live." Arnach shrugged. "Being one of the Swords is a dangerous thing in time of war. This is mild compared to Wybert's difficulties – I'd hate to have to go around with two pegs in place of my legs."

"I doubt you're fit to take me on a tour of the camp, however," Maelgyn pointed out. Truth be told, he was rather reluctant to take a walk through the tent city, anyway.

When he had stepped outside of Happaso's city gates and beheld the army camp, Maelgyn was quite impressed. It was one of the largest military camps in history, and it looked it. There were towers all along the outside, joined together with an improvised wall of wood that stretched for miles. Closer inspection, however, revealed that the towers were actually retired siege weapons, now long past any usefulness for their original purposes with and covered in rust along the armored section. The exposed sections were covered in various fungii and rotting away. The walls were not put together well enough to provide any reasonable defense, and there were gaps that hadn't been quite so visible from Happaso City's walls.

Inside those walls, conditions were frightening. There were many semi-permanent structures that had the same rotten-wood construction as the outer walls. The whole camp city smelled of human body odor, mold, decomposing garbage, and the like. Many of the inhabitants weren't much better, their clothes ratty, their bodies unwashed, and their equipment in a scandalous state of disrepair.

The older warriors of Maelgyn's party – Wangdu, El'Athras, and Ruznak – seemed unphased, but most of his friends – even the younger veteran warriors like Sir Leno – were astounded at the state of the encampment. Even Euleilla, who Maelgyn remembered calmly walking through the visceral material of hundreds of dead after their battle at Elm Knoll, looked rather perturbed at the conditions.

There was, however, a bright spot. A newer portion of the camp was being kept clean, well maintained, properly organized, and free of the squalor that populated much of the rest of the tent city. This was the part of the camp that Maelgyn's assembled cavalry, led by Wybert and Gyato, had taken as their own. When Maelgyn first stepped into their part of the camp, he was impressed to see the Dwarven Wolf-riders were busying themselves making repairs, converting old tent-spaces into semi-permanent structures, fixing up the old siege towers, and so forth. While most of the encampment made the soldiers look like refugees from some great disaster, Maelgyn's cavalry had turned their little section into the start of what might become a real extension of Happaso's fortifications when the war ended.

Arnach was basing himself in the heart of the tent city, which placed him at the heart of the squalor but also at the center of his troops. It was partly why Euleilla and most of the others refused to accompany Maelgyn as he visited his cousin. Only Tur'Ba, who was standing guard outside of the tent, and Khumbaya, who seemed oddly curious about Arnach, had walked with him.

"Perhaps I'm not able to take you on a tour," Arnach admitted. "But I would like to meet your friends... especially your wife. I doubt they'll come here, will they?"

Maelgyn shook his head. "Even Euleilla refused. Which is very odd of her, I must say – she once demanded that I allow her to accompany me into anything, no matter how dangerous."

"Give her points for good taste," Arnach sighed. "She knows you'll be in no danger, here, so why should she have to put up with this cesspit? She's better off staying in your people's district. She's probably aware that someone needs to prepare your lodgings your stay here, if she's anything like I've heard."

"That sounds like her," Maelgyn agreed with a wistful smile. "And I bet she would have come if I'd asked her... or if I were planning to stay here for very long. This camp is horrendous!"

"That's what happens when you've just about run out of money in a war," Arnach explained. "Tents go unmended, sanitation is left up to the individual, and construction ceases on all but the most urgent projects. We can't even provide the mayor of the city with a well-equipped honor guard! I think we're all very pleased that your men brought their own supplies with them, and that those supplies were more than adequate to hold them for several months, but it is the infusion of cash coming in from Sopan and the Borden Isles that will do more to keep us in this war."

"Truth be told, I wasn't expecting to find my people here in the reserve section," Maelgyn pointed out. "They might not always be so, but it's quite plain that they're the fittest warriors on our side, especially after the hardships yours have been through. I would have thought we'd have called them to the front lines, by now."

Arnach shifted uncomfortably. "Remember when I said Brode had gone 'overly traditional?' Well, he seems to think that Svieda is a nation of Humans, and so only Humans should be allowed to fight at our side."

Maelgyn frowned. "That makes... absolutely no sense at all. Next thing you'll tell me is he's forbidding mages from involving themselves in a fight."

Arnach swallowed. "Well, no... but only because the legislature blocked that move. Like I said, Brode's been acting... strange."

More than strange, Maelgyn thought to himself, his earlier suspicions coming back. *If this is what I think it is....*

"Anyway," Arnach continued, breaking Maelgyn's train of thought. "My doctors have said it's okay if I want to move to a new part of town, as long as someone pushes me around in this cart and I don't try to walk on my leg. Any chance I could get a push?"

"I'm not exactly medically cleared for strenuous work, myself," Maelgyn pointed out.

Arnach laughed. "Maelgyn, sometimes I'm very impressed with you. At your age, you've already managed to do things we Sviedans have been trying to accomplish for ages. You've reclaimed the Borden Isles. You've battled the most powerful mage to ever live, and beat him. You managed to expand Svieda's borders by two whole provinces, both very significant. But sometimes...."

Maelgyn blinked. "What? What am I missing?"

"You have a strong young Dwarf waiting outside the door. You have a bloody Golden Dragon at your call. Now, tell me again... any chance I can get a push?"

"Um... I'll go ask."

"Good," Arnach said. "Because I'm really interested in meeting your wife. It'll be interesting to see if she's another thing to add to the list of 'impressive accomplishments' you've made for yourself these past few months."

Chapter V

"So, you are the young woman who stole my cousin's heart," Arnach said, grabbing Euleilla's hand and kissing it in the courtly fashion expected when dealing with a Prince's bride. "I'm quite pleased to see you."

Maelgyn saw her grin, and knew what her response would be before she said it.

"Hi," she answered simply.

Arnach blinked, startled at the overly casual greeting. She was standing in a way that told him that she was entirely comfortable meeting with him, and he detected a definite hint of humor in that smile, but he didn't quite get the joke.

"Um, so, how did you and Maelgyn meet?"

Euleilla cocked her head. "Fighting," was her carefully considered answer.

Arnach shook his head, nonplussed. "Um, care to explain that answer?"

Euleilla put a finger up to her lips daintily. "Nope."

A long, deep intake of breath signaled Maelgyn that it was time to step in. Arnach was clearly trying to rein in his temper, and someone needed to explain things before he exploded.

"She did this to me all the time when we first met," Maelgyn explained. "Answered any question with all the uninformative one-word answers you could imagine. I thinks she was trying to drive me insane."

"Yeah," Euleilla agreed, smiling teasingly.

Arnach was still perturbed, but he had to grin at that one. "So... when does she stop this little game and start actually talking to you?"

"Stop?" Euleilla repeated, sounding as if the thought had never occurred to her.

Maelgyn laughed, pecking her on the cheek. He put his hands on her shoulders, pulling her into him. "I don't think she'll ever stop entirely, but she does eventually get to where she'll give you more than one word answers sometimes."

It was then that Arnach noticed the glittering of magic powder lightly dusting the air around her. "So... what's with the powder?"

"Secret," Euleilla replied before anyone else could.

Maelgyn sighed reluctantly. "He is family, love. He should know...."

"Later," she decided after a moment's consideration.

Arnach cocked his head, eyes narrowing. "A secret? Involving a magically controlled cloud of dust?"

"As Euleilla said, we'll tell you later." Maelgyn looked around – they were in a tent and out of the public eye, but it was only semi-private. El'Athras was in one corner, quietly discussing something with a couple Dwarves that Maelgyn didn't recognize, while Wodtke stood as close to him as he would allow while he was 'working' with his spies; Gyato was discussing something with Onayari; and Sir Leno was chatting up a young serving girl he'd met in Happaso city. "Somewhere with fewer ears – some of the people in this room know it already, but not everyone."

"Dare I ask what kind of a secret?"

"Private," Euleilla shot back.

Arnach sighed. "Well, I guess that's all of an answer I'll get for the moment, huh?"

"Yep," Euleilla agreed.

"Well, then... I don't suppose you'll tell me much of anything about yourself, will you?" Arnach asked.

"Later," Euleilla answered. Then shook her head. "Actually, I'll be glad to tell you pretty much anything... but how about we wait until dinner? I usually find such conversations much more pleasant over a meal...."

"So she *can* actually speak more than one word at a time," Arnach laughed. "Yes, it would be a much better dinner conversation."

Euleilla shook her head. "It *has* been a while since I've had the opportunity to practice my, uh, normal method of getting to know someone. My husband has often spoken of your sense of humor, so I felt you'd appreciate the joke. Or at least not hold it against me. As my husband said, I spent weeks treating him much the same way. I figured you could handle a few minutes of it."

Arnach looked at Maelgyn, standing over her shoulder. "You lasted through that for weeks? You definitely have my respect."

Maelgyn glanced briefly at the girl in his arms. "Well... I suppose it was worth it."

"I think you might be right," Arnach agreed. Once more, he reached for Euleilla's hand... but this time gave it a squeeze. "Welcome to the family, milady. I can't speak for all of us, but I think my cousin made a good choice."

The dinner that evening proved to be a pleasant affair, with a number of amusing anecdotes from Maelgyn and Euleilla's unexpected courtship keeping the mood light as more serious matters dealing with the state of the war and the country were discussed. Afterwords, when most of the dinner guests – Wangdu, a Dwarven contingent led by El'Athras and Wodtke, Leno and his serving girl, Gyato, Onayari, and a few others from Arnach's own inner circle – had departed, the secret of Euleilla's blind eyes was revealed to the older Sword. Arnach took it better than most, expressing even more appreciation for her – and for Maelgyn's decision to stick with her – after recovering from his initial revulsion over what had been done to her.

What Maelgyn hadn't been aware of until later was that Ruznak had departed that night. He had sailed off well before they met for dinner, intent on returning to his life in Rocky Run now that his services were no longer needed.

Seeing how upset Euleilla had been when getting the news the next morning – though only from subtle cues he wasn't sure anyone else picked up on, such as the way her magic fluctuated or slight tensing of muscles along her jawline – Maelgyn felt that she deserved what might be considered a 'day off.' With that in mind, he offered to take her for a relaxing stroll.

"A 'stroll?' Through *this* camp?" Euleilla asked. "I will go with you, if you wish, but I doubt any 'stroll' would be so relaxing."

"Well, I wasn't planning on going into the parts that smelled like a swamp," Maelgyn said, smiling gently. "Just a... well, you might call it an 'inspection of the troops,' if you will. We'd stick to those areas that the Dwarves have developed. There may not be much to speak of, for now, but El'Athras' people are cleaning more and more of the camp up as we speak. I just wanted to see what kind of work they were doing."

Euleilla sighed. It might help her keep her mind off of her foster father's departure... and off of the things to come. "I suppose that wouldn't be too bad. We really should go and visit Sword Wybert while we're at it – we haven't seen him since coming into camp, and I really should visit my former liege lord out of courtesy."

"Of course," Maelgyn replied. When he arrived at the camp, and even before visiting Prince Arnach, he immediately set out to find the people he had tasked to lead the cavalry expedition. The only one he had found was Gyato, who gave a very detailed report. The report was so detailed that it was unnecessary to find the others... but Euleilla was right – as a courtesy, if for no other reason, it would be wise to track down the rest.

"Then let us depart," Euleilla said, magically prodding him into offering his arm. "I fear we will have a lot to do before long, and it would be wise to start enjoying whatever 'relaxation' this stroll can offer as soon as possible."

They toured the Sopan and Dwarven-run parts of camp, arm in arm. Along the way, they encountered a number of industrious Dwarves trying to make the whole situation better. There was one team smoothing out a section of road leading into the 'underdeveloped' part of camp with what looked like a large stone wheel that they were pushing along. Some were cleaning or repairing old tents. A few were sharpening swords and repairing armor and other tools needed for the encampment.

They found a grizzled veteran Dwarven warrior telling stories to a gathering of much younger and less experienced Dwarves, Nekoji, and Humans. They found a Dwarven Wolf Rider, tending to his steed as it gave birth to a litter of pups – both Dwarf and Wolf would likely be out of action for weeks, if not months, as they cared for the young animals. They even found a batch of children being taught letters by one of Maelgyn's Human troops.

They encountered familiar faces, as well. Tur'Ba, who Maelgyn had given time off to 'train as a Dwarven Axeman' while they were in the camp (really, just an excuse to get the well-meaning Dwarf out from underfoot), was apparently passing on some of what he learned to others.

"...many disadvantages to being an Axeman," the young Dwarf was saying as the royal couple approached. "We are defenders, first and foremost – when we go on the attack, we limit ourselves. We work best in tight quarters. We have to work hard, to compensate for our small stature and relatively slow speed by learning how to use the axe exactly right. Being a Wolf Rider means being the true elite of our kind, as the Wolf Riders are the greatest light cavalry in the world. But a cavalry alone cannot hold the caves, and so we need to re-develop the only other effective unit we Dwarves have ever fielded: A defensive infantry force known as the Dwarven Axemen. We Dwarves don't work well when we try and become generalists in the art of warfare – we must be specialists. No one Dwarf should try to use both techniques at once."

Several of the people seated around him – most of them Wolf Riders – merely hoped to add a new skill to their current abilities. Of the others, most were members of a caravan of Dwarves who had joined up with the march on the road between Largo and Happaso. Maelgyn recognized two of the few who were in neither group, however, as individuals El'Athras had identified as trustworthy former members of his 'spy network' now forced to seek other jobs. They could no longer act as spies, and lacked the finances to become merchants, but it would take years to train them as archers, engineers, or Wolf Riders. El'Athras had asked Maelgyn for suggestions about what to do with them... and while he had no answers, it looked as if they were trying to take care of themselves.

Their names, he had been told, were Tur'Ka and Tur'Tei – which, if Maelgyn's interpretation of the Dwarvish (a language he only knew a very few 'important' words of, he had to admit) was correct, had to be pseudonyms. Tur'Ka literally meant 'The Youngest Male of the Interrogator Clan,' while Tur'Tei was 'The Youngest Male of the Spy Clan.' Unless there really were clans in Mar'Tok which chose the name 'Interrogator' and 'Spy,' it seemed likely that they had been given these names to protect the names of their real families.

Dwarven names gave Maelgyn headaches. El'Ba, back in Mar'Tok, had once told Maelgyn that he had six sons and two daughters. All of his sons and daughters were named 'Ba,' each with different prefixes that denoted their 'age' in the clan... which wasn't always their real age. No'Ba, for example, the 'Only Daughter of the Ba clan,' was actually the oldest girl in the Clan, and had been for many years. However, she had a younger sister, 'Ka'Ba,' or 'The Youngest Daughter of the Ba Clan.' If El'Ba ever had any other daughters, they would be called 'Neka'Ba,' or the 'Second Youngest Daughter of the Ba Clan,' even though Ka'Ba was actually older than she was. But on one certain occasion, the name would change: When the Dwarf Maelgyn knew as El'Ba died, Do'Ba (the 'Only Son of the Ba Clan') would have his name changed to El'Ba. The current El'Ba was once Sennetur'Ba, or the 'Twelfth Youngest Son of the Ba Clan.'

And it only got more confusing for Maelgyn when he learned that Sentur'Ba, or the 'Tenth Youngest Son of the Ba Clan,' who was El'Ba before the current El'Ba, had several children of his own... including ones named Do'Ba, Tur'Ba, and No'Ba who were not the Do'Ba, Tur'Ba, or No'Ba that the current El'Ba was related to.

Fortunately, Maelgyn hoped, he would never have to tell apart Tur'Ba son of the current El'Ba from Tur'Ba son of the next El'Ba.

"How goes the training?" he asked, hoping to clear his mind before thoughts on the Dwarven naming system gave him a headache.

"I am told that the best way for me to advance my skills at this point is to teach," Tur'Ba said, smiling up at the prince. "So allow me to introduce my pupils."

Euleilla stepped forward, bowing formally to the class. She may have become royalty by marrying Maelgyn, but even royals were asked to respect the traditions of the fighting academies in Svieda by bowing to the students before addressing them. By bowing to his class she was honoring Tur'Ba greatly.

"Students, I strongly suggest you learn all you can from this young Dwarf," she said. "Tur'Ba is well on his way to restoring a skill long lost to your people, and the proof of its effectiveness is standing before you, today. Without his talents as a Dwarven Axeman, even as a simple student of the skill, I would have been killed during our recent expedition to the Borden Isles. When I was incapacitated, he built a wall of my enemies bodies while protecting me, and I am sure that he has only gotten better since then."

The students looked at Tur'Ba with a newfound respect as Euleilla withdrew. Maelgyn lead her aside, whispering in her ear, "That was a nice thing to do. I'm sure they'll listen to him, now – I wasn't so sure, before."

"All I told them was the truth," Euleilla pointed out. "He has learned much in very little time. If he can teach more of his people to fight as well as he does, the Dwarven Axemen may return as a force and we could experience a Dwarven Renaissance."

"All the better," Maelgyn said. "I know it seems like 'taking advantage' to look at the politics of this, but I almost feel I have to: If we can use this 'Dwarven Renaissance' you're talking about as proof that Mar'Tok is only gaining by joining Svieda, we could make things a whole lot easier for El'Athras. And if things are easier for him, they become easier for us, too."

Euleilla shrugged. "I wasn't thinking of that... only that Tur'Ba deserved recognition for his deed. I fear I haven't thanked him enough, and this was one way of... what is going on, here?"

Maelgyn blinked, unable to see anything out of the ordinary, but then the magical senses Euleilla had taught him to use allowed him to figure out what she was talking about. A powerful source of magic – likely from a Nekoji, given the extent of the power – was flaring as if someone was trying to wield it. It didn't seem to be a threat, and Sekhar certainly wasn't feeling any dangers out of the ordinary nearby, but it was certainly strange. Maelgyn felt that it certainly bore investigating, but wasn't quite sure how to proceed.

"What do you think we should do?" he asked.

"I've sensed this, before," Euleilla explained. "Once, in Mar'Tok. A few other times since... all from Onayari."

"Your 'Nekoji mage?'" At her nod of confirmation, he continued, "Well, that's interesting. It doesn't seem as if Onayari – or whoever it is – is doing a good job of controlling that power."

"Why don't we go over and try to find out what she's attempting to do?" Euleilla suggested. "Maybe we can help."

They walked around the tents and cabins to find Onayari practicing with her spear in the courtyard. It was one of the most elegant examples of spear-work Maelgyn had ever seen. Even Euleilla, who practiced as competently as a master with many types of polearms such as spears, found herself astonished at the complexity and skill in the demonstration. The other Nekoji were watching her, but not as admirers – rather, as gawkers, as if they were watching some great disaster in the making. It was... remarkably disconcerting, seeing how the onlookers were reacting to such an astonishing display of talent.

Euleilla was certain that Onayari was the source of the magical flare-up they had been feeling, but by the time they had arrived all trace of that magic was gone. But the current exhibition – even though she could only perceive it with her own magic – was quite enough to hold her interest.

Other observers were just as impressed, it seemed, but there was some palpable sense of sadness from the Nekoji as they watched her – or maybe something akin to disappointment. A few even looked ashamed of her.

When it was over, and she completed her practiced drill, Maelgyn started clapping. Euleilla did, as well, and quite enthusiastically – never had she seen the like. The other Nekoji looked at them, embarrassed, but did not look offended. They slowly and silently dispersed, few looking back.

Onayari, herself, allowed a flicker of some unidentifiable emotion to consume her face for just a moment. Few Humans were familiar enough with Nekoji to recognize their facial expressions, but Maelgyn had tried to read her – perhaps it was fear, perhaps it was shame, but it was something unpleasant. Then she relaxed, allowing a calm mask to slip over her face before approaching the royal couple.

"Your Highnesses." She bowed in greeting. "I am quite pleased you liked my... demonstration."

"It was a remarkable feat," Euleilla answered. "I could be considered a master with many a polearm in addition to my usual staff, according to my foster father, and know well many ways to use a spear. However, I could not duplicate several of the moves I saw you make, or at least not with the precision you made them. You have my respect."

"And mine, as well," Maelgyn agreed. He glanced around, noticing that there were still a lot of sensitive ears close to them. "We would like to discuss something with you in private. Would you mind terribly if we went somewhere that we could talk?"

"Not at all," Onayari replied. "My exercises are done for the morning. We Nekoji usually either snack all day or eat one one large meal when we wake up and another when we are about to sleep, but I'm afraid I've gotten into the habit of eating like a Human or a Dwarf. I would enjoy a 'lunch' about now."

Food was served out of a new building the Dwarves constructed to be an inn for civilian travelers and guests in the future. The meal was delicious, and a lot heartier than standard fare. Unlike the common mess, where most soldiers ate for free, the inn charged for its food, and Maelgyn was quite willing to pay. The establishment was quiet, private, and was probably the best food anyone could get without leaving the camp city, which made it the perfect place to have a conversation.

"So," Onayari asked, dicing her stuffed trout. She was using traditional Nekoji silverware, a set of sharp metal coverings that could be slipped over her fingertips to allow her to eat cleanly with her hands, much as her ancestors had done with their natural claws. These 'claws' had not been used during their journey to the Borden Isles, and looked to be in pristine shape. She seemed to be having trouble with them, however, having to adjust them all the time. "Just what did you two want to discuss with me?"

Maelgyn forced down the amused smile threatening to find its way onto his lips as he watched the metal claws slip off her fingers, flipping over so that the hole for the thumb stuck itself into her meal. "Um, well, Euleilla has been noticing something unusual recently, and we were hoping that you might know something about it."

Onayari narrowed her eyes, fishing the uncooperative utensil out of her lunch and cleaning it out with her natural claws. "What sort of 'something unusual?' Are you seeing some sort of conspiracy forming, are you worried about the state of the camp, or is it something else?"

"I believe it is 'something else,'" Euleilla replied. "Although I must admit, I am also worried about the state of this camp."

"It was a serious mess when we got here, wasn't it?" Onayari agreed. "But the Dwarves seem to be taking the job of getting it back into shape very seriously."

"They'll need more funds if they want to do the job right," Maelgyn sighed. "'Sword King' Brode is refusing to supply enough money for more than even half-rations across the campsite. I'm opening Sopan's coffers to help pay for the obvious needs, but I've gotten no direction about where that money is most critically needed. I'm half-tempted to ride on out to the Royal Castle and confront my cousin about it in person. Maybe I can knock some sense into him."

"You aren't fit to travel long distances on horseback," Onayari said, still fussing over her utensils. "And the journey would be even worse on foot."

"That's why I'm only *half*-tempted," Maelgyn muttered, stirring his soup. "Wodtke wants me to let myself heal for several more weeks before I even get on a horse, so there's no way I'm seeing Brode unless he comes here. But it wasn't the state of the camp, my cousin, or my health that we wanted to talk with you about."

"Then talk," Onayari snorted. "I may not have anything pressing to take care of at the moment, but my time is not infinite."

Euleilla nudged Maelgyn when it didn't seem as if either of them wanted to go first. He glared at her briefly – not that she could see it – before addressing the Nekoji woman.

"My wife has a few unusual talents when it comes to magic," Maelgyn said. "One of those talents is the ability to see the magical potential a person has, and exactly how much of that potential has not yet been realized."

Onayari stiffened, letting her recently recovered utensils slip off her fingertips again. This time she didn't even seem to notice when they landed in her food. Maelgyn saw that her 'fur was rising' as her people often said. "I... see," she hissed.

Nekoji body language was still a mystery to Maelgyn, and Euleilla couldn't see any reaction at all, but it was obvious she knew what they were talking about... possibly better than they did.

"Most Nekoji have great magical potential," Euleilla continued. "But Maelgyn had been told that there hadn't been a successfully trained Nekoji mage in hundreds of years... which made it quite curious when I felt a Nekoji who was controlling some of their magic.

It took our ocean trip to pin you down as that Nekoji mage."

Onayari took a deep breath, and then sighed. "Well, your husband is correct, your Highness. There hasn't been a successfully trained Nekoji mage in hundreds of years."

"But—"

"However, there have been several failed attempts," Onayari continued, ignoring the interruption. "Most of them learned nothing of magecraft. A few, however, merely lack the consistent control over their magic to qualify as a mage."

Maelgyn waited for her to continue. When she didn't, he said, "And you are one of these 'failed Nekoji mages?'"

Onayari nodded. "My training was... not pleasant. It left me near death on many occasions, and others trained in the same way as I did not survive."

"So why do your people send their children to train as mages, knowing that they'll have to undergo such training?" Euleilla asked. "It doesn't sound as if it's worth it."

"It isn't," Onayari agreed. "And Nekoji parents don't send their children to train this way." Her magical powers flared briefly, pulling the Nekoji eating utensils onto her hand... but in the process warping it into uselessness. "I am somewhat different from what you humans call a 'failed mage.' I understand most 'failed mages' have good control over magic, but no power to back up that control. It is reversed for the Nekoji – I can manipulate powerful magic with no effort, but I have almost no control over it. So, attempting the very basic act of 'pick up a metal object' will cause me to, at best, destroy that object while picking it up." She tapped the mangled metal claws to emphasize her point.

Maelgyn paused. He remembered hearing of such mages in a history lesson. In the early days after the founding of Poros, the only way to learn magic was to enter a temple. These temples were dedicated to certain gods or goddesses that no-one believed in any more – gods and goddesses that he now realized were actually Tengu and Elves playing the part. Supposedly, the 'god' would come down and teach a select group of humans in the temple a method of employing magic, in return for their service. The training, however, was harsh and brutal, and many people failed to live through the experience. Many survivors displayed symptoms very similar to what

Onayari was describing. Only a very few were successful. Those early mages were almost worshiped, themselves, as their talent showed them to be "gifted by the gods."

Humans eventually figured out that the 'gods' in question were training them with flawed methods – perhaps intentionally so. New techniques for teaching and learning magic were developed that weren't so steeped in mysticism and religion. Leaders of those older religions would initially look upon magic learned in this manner with distrust, and spread fear – no longer teaching magic, themselves, as they came to consider it 'evil' if not under their control. Once the war between the Ancient Elves and the Tengu ended, however, the old 'gods' were recognized as the frauds that they were. Some of the newer religious orders even developed methods of curing those who had been so poorly trained, allowing them to use magic properly.

"This might be fixable," Maelgyn said finally. "It will take a great deal of effort, and I will need to research it, but I think it's possible to train someone out of this kind of problem."

"How?" Onayari demanded, desperate.

"This was once a more common problem than it is, today," Maelgyn replied. "There were treatments, but I haven't heard of a case among Humans in centuries. It will take some research. Perhaps if the library at the Royal Castle is still intact...."

"I will come with you when you leave for the castle," Onayari insisted. "This has been a serious issue in my life for some time. Most other Nekoji do not quite trust me, as my magic has occasionally had... unpredictable results. I've even been known to use magic unconsciously, in my sleep, so I worry they may have cause to fear me."

"In a few weeks, then," Maelgyn agreed. "When I am healthy enough, we go to the castle."

Chapter VI

Maelgyn read the letter a third time, just to make sure he wasn't imagining things. He checked, and double-checked, and triple-checked, and still wasn't sure that what he was seeing was correct.

"Tell me that this is a hoax," he said.

Wybert sighed, and Arnach shook his head. They, too, weren't able to believe their eyes at first. Arnach had even taken it to El'Athras to make sure there were no signs of forgery.

"The handwriting is correct, and the lettering wasn't traced," El'Athras noted. "And even a skilled forger would find that seal nearly impossible to duplicate. The messenger even vouched for its authenticity, claiming that he received it from Brode's hand directly."

"It doesn't look like Brode's handwriting to me," Maelgyn objected, desperately hoping for some reason to reject the missive.

"Not as you remember it," Arnach said. "It doesn't. But Brode injured his writing hand in one of our earlier battles. He's been trying to write with his off hand since becoming Sword King, and this matches his earlier missives."

"If it weren't for what the message says, I don't think we would be questioning it," Wybert admitted. "And it is consistent with Brode's other, more recent orders."

"What does the message say?" Euleilla asked. She was the only person in the room who was neither a Sword Prince nor a Ruling Count. Neither she nor Gyato had read the letter, and so neither of them knew quite how to react to the three Swords' dismay.

Maelgyn cleared his throat, trying to control himself. "I guess I can read it to you:

"From Sword King Brode IX, Duke of the Royal Province of Svieda, Acting-Duke of the Province of Glorest, Commander in Chief of the United Sviedan Armies, etc., etc.

"To Commander, United Sviedan Reserve Camp no. 3, Happaso City, Happaso Province:

"Greetings. We have received your request for additional funds to improve conditions at your camp. We have also received the requests for certain units in your camp to be called to the front lines, as they wish to provide proper representation from their provinces in the coming battle.

"In response to the first request, We are sorry to say that it is not possible at this time. As you already know, our national treasure acquired much of its wealth from the gold mines of Sycanth. Sycanth, as you are well aware, is in enemy hands and therefore is not able to provide funding at this time. The taxes of other localities – specifically, Rubick, Largo, Sopan, Borden, Leyland, and Stanget – have not been received. Glorest, Happaso, and the Royal Province of Svieda do not collectively have enough of a tax base to fully fund your camp at this time. We suggest you employ a strategy of living off the land, and possibly look toward those delinquent provinces for additional funds."

Euleilla cocked her head, and interrupted Maelgyn's recitation. "That would be... problematic. According to the last reports we got from El'Athras' intelligence network, the local governments in Rubick, Leyland, and Stanget are in utter shambles, and are not capable of collecting taxes at this time."

"Not to mention Borden, which is in just as bad a shape," Maelgyn agreed.

"What about Largo?" Arnach asked, looking towards the two other Swords. "Or even Caseificio and Mar'Tok, which he failed to acknowledge in his letter?"

"Much of what would have gone to the national taxes this year I spent the day I heard the castle fell," Wybert noted. "The proceeds going largely to the supplies my men took with them when they marched here to join your armies. Those supplies have already been exhausted, it seems, or were taken with Brode into the Royal Castle to help rebuild it."

"And it's not like the esteemed El'Athras or I would have had any opportunity to raise such a tax since signing our treaties," Gyato reminded Arnach. "I will say, however, that what money we could provide immediately has already gone to the repair and refurbishment of this camp. Mar'Tok's Dwarves are even working without pay to get things habitable here, which should tell you something."

Maelgyn scratched his head reluctantly. "And I'm already spending what I can, though many of my funds are already committed."

"What did you spend them on?" Arnach asked, not accusatory but curious.

"Initially, we were unsure of how things would settle on the front lines," Maelgyn explained. "In a War Council, we decided that it was too dangerous to 'put all our eggs in one basket,' as it were. There is wisdom in concentrating your forces as much as possible, but it is a good idea to protect your rear as well... so, while I spent some of the money in order to supply the cavalry on its journey here to the front, I committed funds to establish a second defensive line."

"Where?"

"Largo," Wybert answered. "Along the river. The Northern point is a small feeder-river called Rocky Run that starts from the Mar'Tok mountains, southern border is the Naslat Ocean and Largo City."

"My home town was on Rocky Run," Euleilla added. "In fact, it was named after the river. Small town, but it was the perfect site on which to build a bridge and fortification to protect the Northern part of the new line. And bridges and fortifications cost money."

"Sounds like you've done quite a lot with it," Arnach said, shaking his head. "This is getting us nowhere. Continue reading the letter – I think your wife should hear the rest."

Maelgyn nodded. "Where was I? Oh, yes:

"Regarding the second request, We have heard it and considered it. However, it is Our understanding that most of those forces requesting front-line duties are cavalry forces. At the current time, as We re-

establish the defenses needed to protect the Royal Castle, We have no need of cavalry. Furthermore, matters politic demand that all non-Human and non-Sviedan forces be kept in reserve. We must go back to our roots to win this war, and Svieda's roots are Human in nature.

"We suggest that you disband the non-Human forces currently encamped in your facility. It will be easier to stretch those funds if you remove those unnecessary elements from your budget."

Maelgyn paused, then shook his head. "He just signs and seals it after that."

Gyato snarled. "Is he referring to my people as 'cavalry?' My people have no cavalry, and need no cavalry. It is a great insult to say we are one. It puts us on the level of horses and wolves..."

"I am less concerned about the insult than I am some of the other things in that letter," El'Athras sighed. "No need of cavalry means no offensive plans. Brode intends to fight a defensive war, and it is not possible to win a purely defensive war."

Arnach hesitated. "While it's not an order, a King's 'suggestion' should not be completely ignored. The only way around it is to take the 'suggestion' and expand upon it. He doesn't want Nekoji or Dwarves in this camp... so maybe we should give them something to do outside of it?"

Wybert frowned. "Like what? We can't exactly launch an offensive on our own, and what else would we do with them?"

Gyato ruffled his mane at Wybert's question. "Well, 'they' could do any number of things. Since it seems as if one of the greatest concerns is money, perhaps my people should go to the cities of Rubick, Stanget, and Leyland, and offer their services to whichever Regent or Sword is in charge as tax collectors."

"My Dwarves would make better tax collectors than your Nekoji," El'Athras grumbled. "We understand money better. Though I see your point – if we aren't allowed to be soldiers, we should at least be able to do something in this war effort."

Maelgyn drew a deep breath. "Decide nothing for the moment. I would like to speak to Brode about this in person and see if I can make him see reason – I know my cousin well enough that I might be able to get through to him. Doctor Wodtke says the last of my stitches can be removed in three days, which will allow me to travel on horseback. This is pushing it as fast as she's willing to let me, mind – she originally wanted me to wait several more weeks – but I don't see much choice. If I cannot convince Brode to change his mind, our new alliance will amount to nothing and Svieda will fall."

"Speaking of the alliance," El'Athras began. "Does anyone know where Wangdu went? I wanted his view of this letter to see if he could think of something I didn't, but he's nowhere to be found. Your aide, Tur'Ba, was the last one to talk with him. He said he was going on a 'journey,' and I was hoping one of us knew where that journey went to."

Maelgyn sighed. "If he were officially part of this army, I could insist he tell us of his plans. He is not. I think he's officially a citizen of Squire's Knot, but it's hard ot say with Elves. He is working entirely for himself. But while I have no control over his comings and goings, I believe he can be trusted with some of our secrets."

"The last time I saw him, we were talking about how Brode had changed since ascending the throne," Arnach noted. "Your Elf friend seemed unusually interested in that for someone who had never met Brode."

Maelgyn had a suspicion what Wangdu was going to check – it was something he feared, himself – but now wasn't the time to bring that up. There were too many people listening in to this meeting for that suspicion to be voiced. He decided to offer an alternate explanation, turning to address Gyato. "I discussed a certain confidential matter relating to one of your people, Count Gyato. He might be looking into it, himself, though where he would go for that information I am unsure."

"Regardless, he's not here now, and so any plans we make must be made without him," El'Athras sighed. "I've been hearing from my spies that Sho'Curlas is planning a new offensive of some sort, but we have few specifics. We do know that they are continuing to target the Royal Province, though if they manage to claim it they will immediately move on to their next target, which will be, well, here. Rumors are that the Dragon Riders are involved in this latest ploy. Perhaps we should send Khumbaya back to Borden, to bring the other Dragons back to help us."

"Not without clear evidence that the Black Dragons are being used," Maelgyn said. "I don't want to annoy them when there's a possibility that this is a false alarm."

"I don't think it's a false alarm," came a shaky voice by the tent's doorway. The council of war turned to see a pale Sir Leno standing at the door. He turned to address El'Athras immediately. "Your Lordship, we have a message from your people."

"What is it?" El'Athras asked.

"The Royal Castle is again under siege... and the Black Dragons are part of that assault."

The war council expanded considerably as the news came in. Khumbaya left immediately to call his people to action, but it would be several days at the earliest before they could arrive. Everyone who might have any ideas had been asked to come to the emergency meeting. There were generals like Onayari all the way down to personal cooks like Kiszaten attending. Arnach had the groomer of his personal horse present, and El'Athras had brought Dr. Wodtke despite the later having no knowledge of military tactics. While this was a strategy session, it had also become a last meeting of friends and family before they were asked to leave the relative comfort of the campsite and journey to battle.

That led a lot of confusion, which led to noise, which led to even more confusion. Someone would need to take charge of the meeting, and everyone who could was reluctant to do so.

Maelgyn sighed, and caught Arnach's eye. "You or me?" he mouthed.

Arnach shrugged, then took out an old coin and flipped it. Glancing down at the coin, he pointed to himself without looking too happy about it.

He slowly stood up, mindful of his injured leg, and brought out his sword. He banged it, hilt-first, into the table, loud enough to draw everyone's attention.

"Excuse me, people, but we do have to take care of some rather important matters, so can you all quiet down enough for us to get started?" Arnach called out, his voice dripping with exasperation. Most of the assembled crowd had the good graces to appear somewhat embarrassed, and everyone stopped talking. "Good. Now, Lord El'Athras. You have discussed this with your spi— er, messengers. Could you please tell us what you have learned?"

El'Athras stood up and stepped into the center of the crowd where he could be seen by everyone. "Of course, your Highness. I have had teams of Dwarves observing several Sho'Curlas encampments, watching for any signs of movement. Well, two days ago one of the largest of these camps moved all right – they broke down their camp and moved straight to the Royal Castle. They were unable to take the castle immediately, and are now beginning siege operations.

"My people are surveying the situation from both sides. So far, on our side, we've determined that repairs on the castle had been completed sufficient to hold off an assault as long as no heavy siege weapons were brought to bear. Sho'Curlas brought more than mere siege weapons – five Black Dragons struck fast and hard, then left. We assume their departure is only temporary, to rest and resupply, before a final assault is made. Some of the castle defenses remain standing, but the damage done will limit their effectiveness.

"The attacking force is the largest single organized unit we have yet to see brought against us in this war, and it is under the command of Prince Hussack. More soldiers may be on their way – there are sixty thousand enemy soldiers in various encampments throughout Sycanth, and Sho'Curlas could easily pull as many as three hundred thousand more soldiers from the rest of their army without even touching the defensive garrisons in their fortresses and cities. As far as what Brode might have available to him inside the Royal City's walls, well, we haven't even been able to get a diplomatic courier inside since the last Sword King was assassinated, so we can only guess."

Maelgyn and Arnach both stiffened, remembering that day in the throne room when the last Sword King of Svieda was assassinated. "Is there any hope of the castle holding?" Arnach asked at last.

"Not for very long," El'Athras sighed. "With luck, it might hold out a few days – a week, at best, and only if the Dragons aren't brought out again. That may be long enough for the Golden Dragons to arrive, but it may not. And whether they arrive or not, it seems unlikely to matter."

"Then someone must act, to save the Royal Castle," Wybert cried. "I know that most of us in this room have had recent... difficulties, accepting some of Brode's declarations, but he is still our king, and we still must do what we can to rescue him."

"What do we have that can reach the siege in time?" Maelgyn asked, trying to do the math in his head. The army at Happaso castle wasn't ready to march at a moments notice – largely due to the poor funding and poor conditions – so it would take some time to get it ready to move. Between that necessity and the time needed to march to the Royal Castle on foot, it would be almost impossible for Human infantry from their encampment to arrive in time. He wasn't sure if there were any other garrisons closer by who could help, but the numbers of infantry needed to lift the siege probably weren't there. It would have to come down to the cavalry.

"Not much," Arnach sighed, knowing the distribution of their forces better than anyone else. "Between what was brought from Sopan and what we had in camp, there are maybe six thousand Human cavalry ready to go. Wait another day and we could probably assemble as many as twenty thousand, but considering the state of the roads between here and there the castle would fall before you could get them there. You can add the Wolf Riders, if you want, and the Nekoji infantry – I have no idea of their current numbers or how long it will take them to get ready, but they're probably more ready to move out than our regular cavalry is. That's about it."

"My people can leave tomorrow," Gyato snapped, affronted. "All of them."

"As can mine," El'Athras sighed. "Although I can't lead them – not at the speed they'll need to travel."

"Yes, who to put in charge of this expedition?" Arnach mused. "Neither Wybert nor myself can do it, thanks to our leg problems. It would need to be someone important, though..."

Maelgyn sighed, standing up stiffly. "I guess that leaves me. I'll take the lead."

Dr. Wodtke was the first to respond, before Arnach could even acknowledge him. "Your Highness, you are not healthy enough for that kind of travel, much less battle."

Maelgyn snorted, though relaxed when Euleilla put a hand on his shoulder. He knew that the Doctor meant well, but this was the Royal Castle. If it fell this soon after its recapture, morale would crumble, and they would likely have to concede the Royal Province altogether. That would open the door for Sho'Curlas to strike into Rubick, and with Rubick gone Stanget and Leyland would be quick to follow. Half the country gone, their armies scattered, morale low, and without a king... no, a loss, here, would be decisive. And if none of the Swords went along with the reinforcements, would anyone believe they weren't marching to their deaths?

"A few remaining stitches that can be removed on the journey there and I'm out of action? I realize, Doctor Wodtke, I should ideally wait for a few weeks before riding off to battle, but I don't think we can wait for ideals. Thank you for your concern, but I'm afraid that the needs of Svieda outweigh my own in this matter."

Wodtke shook her head. "There are others who could do this – Gyato, or even a lower ranked officer such as Sir Leno. It does not have to be one of the Swords."

She was wrong and she knew it. Maelgyn just had to look at her before she turned away in surrender. "Sir Leno and Count Gyato will both be accompanying me, as will my wife, but I will lead our soldiers into battle. My health aside, our talents as mages will be invaluable to this expedition. Perhaps our only chance at victory." He paused, grinning darkly. "Plus, I have a score to settle with 'Prince Hussack' and his son. I suppose it is time to repay it."

"So," Euleilla sighed, settling into bed next to her husband. "Off to war we go."

"We set out at dawn," Maelgyn said. "And, while I like our chances to succeed, things will be very difficult. We're going to be outnumbered – how heavily, I don't think anybody knows just yet. We're going to be overpowered – we have nothing that can match a Black Dragon in our forces at the moment. And... we're going to be separated."

Euleilla sighed, pulling him into her embrace. "I know... and this time I can't argue against it. The two most powerful mages in our army must be on our flanks, and you and I are the two most powerful mages here. I just wish Wangdu were present – he could take one of the flanks, and leave me to support you on the other one."

Maelgyn shifted slightly to look at her. "How is your *schlipf?*" he asked. "Where is he in his development?"

Euleilla cocked her head. "She, not he. And... well, she'll be able to help me sense danger, as before, I think. She hasn't talked with me since your duel with Paljor, only giving me occasional warnings of danger and helping me 'see' while shipboard. I get the feeling she's putting most of her energy into maturing faster."

Maelgyn sighed. "Sekhar's not talking, much, either. I asked him about it last time he was feeling 'chatty' and he said he's waiting for me to heal. The fact that both of our *schlipf* are keeping quiet is disturbing, though. I am worried about their ability to help us in the coming battle."

Euleilla gave him a reassuring squeeze. "It'll be okay – I'm not worried. I was able to fight long before I gained my *schlipf*, and so were you. But I'm not worried about their loyalty, either – they'll help us."

"That's not my concern," Maelgyn said. "I'm worried about you. I've seen you in combat – you're a powerhouse, and no-one disagrees with that, but you also get yourself in over your head. You burn through all of your magic so quickly that you pass out before the battle's won, leaving yourself vulnerable to attack. You need someone – whether it's me or it's a *schlipf* – to rein you in."

Euleilla tucked her head into his shoulder. "I know. I'm sorry, but I don't know any other way to fight." She paused. "And I am worried about you. You will be going into battle already wounded, and you are taking a great burden on yourself by assuming command." She paused. "And you might have a *schlipf* with you, but I don't know what *either* of us will be able to do if there really are Dragons to deal with."

"They most likely aren't being kept with the rest of the siege camp," Maelgyn said, trying to alleviate her fears. "While it is possible to tame Black Dragons, they aren't exactly safe to leave in a camp with thousands of people around them. They're much larger than Golden Dragons, and don't appreciate crowds. More than likely, the reason we haven't seen Sho'Curlas' Black Dragons before now was that they had to build a Dragon pen close enough to the front that they didn't have to stay with the army when they were resting. That should give us a chance to break the siege before the Dragon Riders can be summoned."

"Our biggest advantage will be speed. Wolf Riders, Nekoji, and Cavalry all can move much faster than your basic infantryman or siege engineer, and we must move with speed in order to raise the siege before the Dragons can be summoned." Euleilla paused. "We have to hope we move fast enough that they can't use their full power, in other words."

"I know," Maelgyn sighed. "But they have powerful forces outside of those Dragons, as well. In addition to having some of the best-trained swordsmen, spearmen, and archers in the world—"

"Which I'm sure our own soldiers can match," Euleilla interjected.

"—their siege camp will likely be entrenched. They have numbers, a number of good officers, and they will likely have some siege weapons that could be brought to bear. And... they'll have Hussack."

"I've heard you talk of him, before," Euleilla said. "He is another mage?"

"A powerful one," Maelgyn said, pulling her close. "Very experienced, and ruthless. When he killed Sword King Gilbereth, he used his magic to rip a necklace from the neck of my tutor – breaking his neck in the process – and flung the shards into Gilbereth's body without pause. He is undoubtedly more skilled than either of us, and might even be more powerful than you are...."

"I'll be careful," Euleilla said, soothing out his concerns as best she could. "If he approaches me, as powerful as you describe him, I'll know. I won't try to fight him, just to hold him off until you arrive. Just how powerful is he, though? You said he was stronger than me. You sound like you think he's stronger than you, though I'm sure you have grown in power since you last met him. Is he stronger than Paljor?"

Maelgyn frowned, considering. "More powerful? I doubt it. Paljor was a genuine High Mage, without question, while Hussack is only a fully-matured First Class. But Hussack is far more in control of himself, which may make him more dangerous – I met him frequently while we were both at the Royal Castle, and I never quite felt... comfortable around him. Even before I knew he was a mage, I could tell he was powerful. Add magic to the mix... well, I'm more afraid of him than I was of Paljor."

"You're stronger than when you first knew him," Euleilla repeated. "Your magic has improved by leaps and bounds just since I first met you, and you still haven't fulfilled all of your potential. Your sword fighting skills have improved considerably, thanks to your training with Wangdu." She paused. "And you won't be alone. You have become very important to the people here, and you will be well protected. As will I... we will win this battle. And Hussack will regret ever coming to Svieda."

Maelgyn smiled at her words, but knew that was all they were. He suspected Euleilla even believed them... and it was possible that some of what she said was true. He was stronger, and he would be protected. But he knew that it would not be easy. And he wasn't exactly worried about himself.

"But that's enough of that discussion," she added, sounding almost exasperated. "More than enough." Maelgyn turned to Euleilla in surprise as she wriggled out of his grasp and stood up.

"We have something more important to deal with tonight. Something we've put off far too long. And you're not going off to war again before we do." Slowly and deliberately, she loosened the fastenings of her nightdress, and let it fall to the floor.

And after consummating their marriage for the first time, they made love a second time. Then a third. It was some time after the fourth that they finally went to sleep.

The Camp was a scene of complete chaos. Volunteers were lining up to join the mission to free the Royal Castle in droves, and it was hard to pick and choose which ones to take.

The difficulty came because it took time to properly decamp, and they weren't taking that time. Only packs and horses that were able to leave at a moments notice were being brought along, and only people with a full set of equipment were being allowed to volunteer. This was why, even though there were tens of thousands of Human cavalrymen present, only six thousand would be coming on the expedition.

All over the camp, various mentors – leaders, teachers, or masters of tradecraft – were giving last minute instructions; those departing to the ones left behind so that their work could be carried on in their absence, and those staying to the departing so that their lessons would be fresh. It was no surprise, then, when Maelgyn found his servant, Tur'Ba, talking to his Dwarven Axemen trainees.

"...and while I realize you haven't exactly become experts at this, yet," the young Dwarf was saying. "Most of you already have a good grasp the basics, which is all I had to develop the skills I have now. All I had to go on were the half-forgotten memories of an Elf, and you have all seen what I've been able to rebuild from that. If I don't make it back, Wangdu should be able to help you finish your education – don't be thrown by the fact he's an Elf, as he is the only person I know who has ever seen one of the Dwarven Axemen of old in action. Keep practicing, and remember our lessons. If I don't come back, Tur'Ka, Tur'Tei, the two of you will have the most important job of all, as I expect the two of you to finish my work. Now, farewell, and remember me fondly."

"Yes, sensei," the class chorused back before scattering to help prepare for the cavalry's departure.

Maelgyn approached Tur'Ba. Despite the tension in the air over the upcoming battle, his night with Euleilla just had him bubbling with happiness. He couldn't help but be amused at his young servant. "And just where do you think you'll be *going* that you might not come back from?"

"Are you trying to tell me there isn't any chance I'll be killed during this mission, sir?" Tur'Ba replied uncertainly.

"No, there isn't," Maelgyn said. "Because you aren't coming with me on it. You aren't a Wolf Rider, this isn't a defensive mission, and you don't have any role in this upcoming battle."

"But I'm to be at your side!" Tur'Ba insisted. "My father's agreement with you—"

"Doesn't include taking you into battle," Maelgyn replied, breaking in before Tur'Ba could get started. "You aren't ready for this kind of pitch battle. You aren't even able to get there."

Tur'Ba sighed, his eyes clouding in desperation. "How about a challenge? If I can do any reasonable task you can think of to set for me, you'll take me along?"

Maelgyn wasn't quite sure how to deal with this. His intention was to convince Tur'Ba to stay behind, since he viewed the Dwarf as a liability as he was. The Dwarven servant was so insistent, however, that it didn't look as if there was much chance of convincing him to stay behind.

Still, he had to try something. "If you fail this task, will you promise to stay behind, no protests and no further arguments?"

"Of course, sir!" Tur'Ba chirped, brightening.

Maelgyn glanced around him, looking for inspiration. Seeing one Dwarf leading his lupine mount down the road to the green at which the Wolf-Riders were assembling, he had an idea.

"For this battle, we need speed more than anything else. That is a big part of why we're only taking the cavalry and the Nekoji – they give us speed. However, you have no Wolf to ride, no Nekoji will be able to carry you, and Horses generally don't like Dwarves. I will be taking no carts or wagons on this journey, and there are no other ways I can think of for you to join us. If you can find a way to keep up without slowing us down, I will allow you to come."

Tur'Ba froze for a moment, his eyes widening, but then he slowly grinned. "I'm afraid, sir, you are a bit mistaken about something."

Maelgyn paused. What did the Dwarf mean by that? "Oh?"

"Horses may not like Dwarves, but we can still ride them," Tur'Ba explained. "We just need a Human to partner with... such as you, sir. I could ride on your horse with you."

Maelgyn was a bit surprised at that solution, though it was obvious when he thought about it. He was also annoyed – he didn't want Tur'Ba to get in over his head. He liked the young Dwarf, and was worried for him in the coming battle... but he'd made a promise, and so he would keep it. And maybe he could ease a fear that had been growing for a while.

"Very well. But I don't want you to ride with me – if you're going to share a horse with someone, I have another job for you to do...."

Chapter VII

It was morning, a week's worth of hard riding later, and men scurried about the night's camp near the edge of a forest they would soon need to traverse, making their final preparations before battle. Soldiers inspected their swords for defects that could be honed out, archers checked the fletching on their arrows, and workmen broke down tents for travel. Euleilla trudged through the dirt where many boots had worn paths in the grass and underbrush, seeking the makeshift horse paddock.

During the journey, Euleilla had been riding on the same horse as Maelgyn, using her magic to help him heal faster despite Wodtke's warnings against that. It was Euleilla who had removed the stitches when they paused to rest their horses and eat a meal on the first day, and it was Euleilla that was doing everything in her power to ensure he didn't stress his just-healed body too much.

Today, however, she would need a different horse. She and her husband would have to ride separately. Euleilla would be needed in a position on Maelgyn's opposite flank if his plan was to have any hope of success, and this was the day they would be riding to battle. She had waited by his side until she was sure he was securely on his horse, but then she had to leave and find her own steed.

She found Tur'Ba grooming the horse that was to take her into battle. Sir Leno had been in charge of driving it with the army, and the young Dwarf had been in charge of caring for it when they were encamped. Both had been sharing a different horse – a more even-tempered chestnut gelding that had been trained and disciplined as a war horse. This stallion was far less trained, but would be suitable for her needs.

"Thank you, Tur'Ba," Euleilla said, patting the horse she was about to mount. "Now, hurry back to Sir Leno. You don't want to hold him up, do you?"

Tur'Ba hesitated. "I'm not going into battle with Sir Leno, milady. I'm going into battle with you."

Euleilla froze for just a split second, but then with long practiced ease shrugged her dismay off stoically. "Was this your idea?" she asked, climbing onto the back of the horse.

"Master Maelgyn wants you safe," the young Dwarf explained. "And I wished to be in the battle. I volunteered to be your bodyguard, again." He looked down at his feet sadly. "Truthfully, he didn't want me on this trip. He felt I would slow us all down unnecessarily. I think he feels I just get in the way."

Euleilla clucked her tongue, holding back from answering at first. All of her initial responses would have only reinforced the idea that Maelgyn viewed the young Dwarf as a burden, which she didn't believe. Maelgyn would not have wanted Tur'Ba in this battle for a variety of reasons, but none of them would have been so insulting – her husband had confided in her that he was actually rather fond of Tur'Ba. He knew Tur'Ba was developing rather quickly as a Dwarven Axemen, but he didn't believe that training was complete.

Then there was the concern that the skills an Axeman brought would be useless in a cavalry charge. Euleilla had to agree on both parts, and Tur'Ba probably would as well if he had thought it through. He was best off on foot, defending fortifications or protecting important people. But then, that was why Tur'Ba said he had been assigned to her, after all.

"He would not have entrusted my care to you if he felt that," she said. "He worries about me constantly, and knows that I can get a bit reckless on the battlefield. I suspect that played no small part in his decision. Should I overdo things, I am pleased that there will be a great defender there to protect me... just as that defender protected me on the Borden Isles more than a month ago."

Tur'Ba grinned shyly up at her. "Thank you, my Lady. I will protect you from any danger you encounter."

It was next to impossible to maintain a stealthy approach when you had tens of thousands of soldiers, wolves, and horses to deal with. Masking their presence up until they emerged from the woods less than a mile away from the Sho'Curlan siege camp took a minor miracle, in itself.

The soldiers of Sho'Curlas went into a full-on scramble upon sighting them. While they were ready for a sortie from the castle itself, they evidently hadn't considered the possibility that significant reinforcements would arrive this quickly, and they had failed to establish an effective rear guard.

Maelgyn's forces advanced as Sho'Curlan archers scurried to man the partially assembled siege towers scattered throughout the camp, hoping they would act as adequate platforms from which to shoot. Many swordsmen started forming a line and ranks, trying to protect themselves from the assault, but only spearmen could hold off a proper cavalry charge, and while there were spears in their stores they had not yet been issued to the soldiers.

Sir Leno had been surprised to learn he would be in the center of the attacking charge. After all, out of Maelgyn, Euleilla, and himself, he was by far the weakest mage... but they needed the more powerful mages on the flanks. He was almost just a decoy.

Riding well behind each of the three mages were two groups of archers – Wolf Rider bowmen flanking out to one side and a large number of Nekoji archers moving to the other, a smattering of Human horse archers in both groups.

As the two armies closed in to face each other, those archer units sent an orchestrated wave of arrows, flying high into the air. The few Sho'Curlan archers who had been able to get into position tried to return fire, but they weren't in position to or organized enough to make a dent in the charging cavalry. Horses, wolves and Nekoji infantrymen charged forward steadily, their lines breaking only slightly as they picked up speed. To the Sho'Curlan forces, it seemed as if they were racing the arrows into the enemy camp... and that the arrows would overshoot their targets.

At a predetermined point, Maelgyn, Sir Leno, and Euleilla started gathering all of the magic they could together. And not just them – they had scoured the Happaso campsite, looking for any cavalry riders who might be considered even fifth rate mages. Even Onayari, charging into the teeth of the enemy at Sir Leno's side, decided that this was one moment where she could attempt to use her largely uncontrollable powers freely.

In mid-air all of the thousands of steel-tipped arrows that had been launched stopped, changed directions, and angled into the rear of the Sho'Curlas line. Every shield was facing the wrong way, and most of the arrows were traveling faster than a normal bow shot. A few small spots showed magical deflections of the arrows, and the mages on Svieda's side were quick to pick up where those were: It would take a mage to counter a mage properly, and that first strike revealed where most of Sho'Curlan mages were.

Just as the rear of the Sho'Curlas line was decimated by the unexpected barrage of arrows, the fastest of Svieda's cavalry – mostly Dwarven Wolf Riders – hit the front. The wolves tore into their enemies with tooth and claw while the Dwarven riders swung swords and naginata to strike with more precision.

Armor made of brass or rawhide – designed to protect against a mage's powers – wasn't capable of standing up to the claws of the beasts, and all types of armor were vulnerable at the joints. Steel armor was vulnerable to the mages who were attacking from the rear. The Dwarves were sweeping through the enemy forces with such destructive power that there wasn't much left for the Nekoji or the Human cavalry to finish off.

However, that initial success would not last forever.

The advance into the camp gradually slowed, but it didn't stop. In certain areas, however, the line was pressing forwards faster than others – especially the ones centered around Maelgyn and Euleilla.

The initial plan was for the two 'flanking' wings of the army to cut deeper into the enemy force, before swinging around to meet and encircling the bulk of the Sho'Curlan army. A force composed primarily of the archers and soldiers on slower mounts had been held back in reserve, hoping to move in and guard their new flanks, while the encircled enemy army was cut down. To say that things were going exactly according to plan would be a mistake – El'Athras' spies didn't tell them about the siege towers or other improvised fortifications, and the Dragons were thought to be the bulk of the Sho'Curlan siege engine. The Dragons were still being held back, and perhaps were thought unnecessary at this stage of the battle, as it appeared a more traditional effort to capture the castle was being organized. Setting this gear up had reduced the amount of time the Sho'Curlans had to fortify their rear guard, but it also gave them ideal platforms from which archers could try to pick off Sviedan leaders.

Somewhere along the line Euleilla's horse had been shot out from under her. She, with perfect balance, was able to land on her feet after using the butt of her spear to vault over the dying animal. Tur'Ba hadn't been so lucky, tumbling off and landing on his head, and he found himself unable to keep up. The blow on his head left his vision unfocused and his head hurting, but he still stood and chased after the woman he had sworn to his master that he would protect.

Nevertheless, the plan was working. Perhaps a bit too well, in some cases.

Euleilla seemed to be moving faster without her horse than with it – now that the initial charge had settled down, it was growing difficult for the horses to move forward. She was using a naginata, and her fighting style was best suited for the ground. She was practically dancing her way through the broken enemy lines, leaving paths of the dead Sho'Curlan soldiers in her wake.

Maelgyn knew she was not conserving her magic like she should have – there was no way she would be outpacing him like she was if she weren't. He hoped to convince her to slow down when he caught up with her, but that proved to be impossible.

By the time Tur'Ba was able to rejoin Euleilla's side, she was clashing with another mage. To make matters worse, he saw another man dressed as a mage approaching from her flank. She seemed capable of handling the first mage, but he suspected that even if she could handle both, the second would start to exhaust her magic. Tur'Ba turned to deal with the newcomer himself.

The oncoming mage was stopped by an axe in his head before he was even aware that the young Dwarf had thrown it. Almost at the same time, Euleilla finished off the first mage with a well-placed spear to the gut. For a moment, they had a breather, as no-one dared approach the pair.

"Thank you," Euleilla huffed, adjusting her Golden Dragonhide armor slightly. It didn't fit quite right, having been designed by Paljor's armorers for a young man rather than a young woman, but it did the job of protecting her better than the rawhide scraps she was used to.

"My pleasure, milady," the Dwarf replied, bowing his head as much as he could afford to while retrieving his axe.

"Shall we continue, then?"

Knowing that there was only one answer she'd accept, Tur'Ba nodded. "Of course, milady. But please... allow me to lead, this time."

Prince Hussack was no fool. He knew, from the moment he heard the alarms, just what was going on outside of his tent – somehow, news of their attack had reached the enemy in time to respond before he had completed setting up his defenses. He had even guessed that the only force that could make such an attempt was an all cavalry force (as he was unaware of the presence of Nekoji in Svieda's ranks, he was only partially correct on that guess), for there were no infantry forces large enough to cause such a commotion nearby. The army gathering in Happaso was too entrenched to get here this quickly unless it sent the cavalry on ahead.

Not that there weren't the numbers in the so-called "Royal Province" to break the siege. When Svieda reclaimed its Royal Castle, he returned to the front. After going to all the trouble to claim the city for himself in his initial strike to open the war, he felt it important that he personally reclaim it.

Hussack's strategy (this time) had been to send an advance force of several raiding parties, hoping to simultaneously capture multiple strategic targets that the Sviedan front-line army would be forced to respond to. Once the bulk of the Sviedan army had been scattered in their efforts to protect those areas, the bulk of Hussack's army would strike at the castle. Spreading Svieda's army so thin made breaking the siege impossible without abandoning those targets, and his use of the Black Dragons would allow him to take the city before they could re-organize themselves even if they were willing to do so.

The forces in Happaso were the only uncontrolled element, but his intelligence had said they were too disorganized and ill-equipped to respond in time. They could deploy a few thousand poorly equipped horsemen, at best, and the leaders of that reserve force were all too heavily wounded to lead such an effort.

Sho'Curlas' army would outnumber the horsemen five to one, even if there was someone unexpected in the camp capable of leading a cavalry attack. They would be poorly equipped at best, and anyone with real military experience would know it was a lost cause. Even that snotty whelp, Arnach, should have known that he stood no chance of breaking the siege with what was in Happaso. He would be better off conceding the Royal Province and using that reserve force to better fortify the borders of Happaso and Glorest, and try and recover the scattered remnants of the Sviedan army before the province was fully overrun. That was why he had put more priority on setting up the siege engines than fortifying their rear guard – taking the castle fast was strategically more important than the minor risk that Arnach would order a futile cavalry charge.

The soldier who reported that obvious bit of news – that Arnach's reserve force indeed was attempting that futile charge – very nearly had his head cut off for wasting his time. He saved it by immediately going into detail about just who was attacking them.

"Nekoji? Dwarves?" Hussack repeated, startled. "I had heard that part of Svieda's response to our war was to annex Mar'Tok and Caseificio, but how did they manage to assemble an army of Dwarves and Nekoji that could get here so fast?"

The soldier, eying his half-naked commander and the nude young prostitute making no effort to cover herself up on his bed, shifted uncomfortably. "I don't know, sir. I do know, however, that there are several powerful mages in their force, as well. At least three of them are much stronger than the 3rd and 4th Rate mages assigned to our infantry units. They... well, they are strong enough to make me feel uncomfortable, and I'm trained and equipped to fight mages."

Hussack snorted dismissively. "Well, let me get my armor on and I'll deal with it. Have someone send up the signal summoning the Dragon Riders and I'll be right there."

It didn't take too long for Hussack to ready himself. The dragonhide armor he had taken off of Nattiel, the now imprisoned

"Sword Prince of Svieda and Duke of Rubick," was in fine condition even after the battle that took the Royal Castle the first time. It was designed to be rapidly equipped, and to be easily customized to many different body types. The sword he donned was also a piece of Sviedan Royal gear – one of the ten Swords of Svieda. Even those with the proper blood ties to wield one of them rarely used such a blade in battle, they were so valuable, but they were magnificent weapons... and as he wasn't Sviedan Hussack had no issues of sentiment with using them.

"Hussack!" the young prostitute called, still unclothed, right before he left the tent.

He spun around, annoyed a the delay. "Yeah?" he grumbled.

"You'd better come back safely, do you understand me?"

Hussack was astonished. Was that really concern he heard, coming from a lowly girl he was paying to keep his bed warm for him at night? Maybe he'd been using this one too long, and it was time to pick a new girl. Still, form dictated he reassure her.

"Don't worry about me," he said, snorting. "I doubt there's anyone in all of Svieda who is a threat do me."

The prostitute gave a lazy, seductive grin. "Well, good. Because I'm still waiting to be paid, you know."

Hussack rolled his eyes – perhaps it wasn't concern after all. He stepped out of the tent, and was a bit surprised to see just how much chaos his camp had descended into.

"I'm pleased to see you, your Highness... finally," his personal guardsman said, bowing appropriately despite the rebuke whispered under his breath. "We are ready for battle."

"I was told there were powerful mages attacking us," Hussack said without preamble, ignoring the remark he wasn't supposed to hear. He glanced around. It was obvious that their rear guard had crumbled before much of a defensive line could be organized, but that was of little significance – the numbers were still on his side. Field commanders were starting to organize new lines, from new defensive positions, and Archers were behind fortifications. The battle was far from lost... though if the castle decided to launch a sortie before his army finished settling itself down, things would get ugly. He could understand why the guardsman might have been a little impatient with him. That wouldn't stop Hussack from punishing him later.

He needed to deal with the serious threats, first, though. "Point out where they are."

The guardsman was expecting the request and knew exactly where to direct him. "In the center is the weakest of the three. From what I can tell, he can't be higher than a second rate, but that is still stronger than most of the mages we have at our disposal."

"Not a great concern to me, however," Hussack sighed. He was bored of fighting underpowered mages. "Next?"

"On the far side, there appears to be a stronger mage, though what rate he would be I cannot judge – he has been fighting using things more dangerous than magic. I'm told he bears an Elven weapon, a *schlipf*, and yet his sword skills are also unparalleled. He may be one of the Swords, himself, for he wields two of the finest katana we have ever seen."

"Hm. Interesting." Hussack smiled, glad to hear that there may actually be a challenge for him after all. "And the third?"

"Female mage, likely a First Rate, wielding a spear with unorthodox style but great effectiveness. She is on the near side, and is closest to us."

The prince smiled even wider. "A First Rate, huh? Well, now, this sounds like an interesting challenge."

Despite Tur'Ba asking her to follow him, he was still struggling to stay close to his charge. Euleilla was plowing through their enemies with ease – in fact, with too much ease, as she was leaving both him and much of the front line behind. He was barely able to keep pace with her, much less guide her to safer paths. He was worried that she would soon run out of the magical energy to keep her attacks going, but she didn't seem to be straining her abilities just yet. He needed to warn her to slow down, though, so that the rest of the army could catch up at the very least. She may have learned a lot about combat and tactics from her foster father, but she seemed woefully inexperienced when it came to fighting against such large armies in battle. Tur'Ba was, as well, but while he had been taught to fight as part of a unit, she had been instructed in how to fight by herself. It was something he made a mental note to mention to Maelgyn as soon as he could, provided they could just get out of this situation.

She had just passed him once again, and was starting to put some distance between them when he noticed a commotion behind the Sho'Curlan lines. Someone with very powerful magic was approaching, and for a brief moment Tur'Ba allowed himself to hope that it was Maelgyn, but that hope vanished rather quickly.

Rather, another Sho'Curlan was coming through... someone who was rather casually using magic, himself. Was this man coming to challenge Euleilla?

His answer came quickly enough as the crowd parted, allowing the newcomer to show himself. He was dressed in dragonhide armor, himself – Red Dragonhide as opposed to the Golden Dragonhide Euleilla had taken from Paljor's stores – and wielded a fine looking katana. It looked like one of the Swords, but Tur'Ba could not be certain.

The middle-aged man easily towered over Tur'Ba. He ignored the Dwarf, however, and went straight for the princess.

Euleilla's face was well schooled, moving herself clear of the enemy and falling into a deceptively casual stance, but Tur'Ba could tell that she had noticed the newcomer and was worried. Her face had paled as her finger sensed, tighten her grip on her spear. The Sho'Curlan soldiers were staying back, as well, many of them watching the upcoming confrontation with awe in their faces. "Hussack," she hissed dangerously.

A smile quirked itself up on the Sho'Curlan mage. He taunted her with a sketched bow, taking on the arrogant air of someone who wanted to 'play' with his opponent. "You have me at a disadvantage, my Lady."

Tur'Ba wasn't sure how Euleilla would respond. Announcing herself would inform the Sho'Curlan that a valuable prize was in their midst. On the other hand, it would make them more interested in capturing her than killing her: A dead princess was of no value, but a live one made for excellent ransom material, and a powerful bargaining chip in future negotiations.

After mulling over possible responses, the girl finally settled on one that seemed to be a compromise of sorts. "Euleilla," she answered slowly.

"Euleilla, is it?" Hussack shot back. "And am I supposed to have heard of you, girl?"

The color returned to her cheeks as she bantered, and Tur'Ba realized she was trying to delay the man. Perhaps she wanted enough time to recover some of her magical strength, or perhaps she was hoping for some other sort of intervention, but he was able to read that in her body language – something someone less familiar with her might not have noticed. The slight rest was hopefully doing her some good, but Tur'Ba was afraid it might not be enough. He slowly shifted to take a supporting position around her.

"Maybe," she answered confidently.

"Is that so?" Hussack growled. "And just how would I have heard of you?"

"I'm royalty," was her answer, polishing the head of her spear nonchalantly. Only Tur'Ba caught how that answer was an indication of her fraying nerves – if she was nearly as cocky as she appeared, she would have managed that answer in only one word. He tensed – the battle was sure to start soon.

Hussack was not completely ignoring the lone Dwarf accompanying this 'Euleilla,' even if he didn't think the creature was much of a threat. He noticed that this one seemed especially concerned about the woman who was telling what seemed to be such an obvious lie – in fact, it was only the Dwarf's behavior that gave him even the slightest of doubt that she might be telling the truth. With the corner of his eye on the Dwarf, looking for hidden signs of an imminent attack, he shook his head. "Liar. I know the name of every royal in Svieda, Sword or not, and your name is not among them. How do you claim royal status?"

"Consort."

That caused Hussack's eyes to widen. Mages as powerful as Euleilla were rare, and when someone found one it made plenty of sense to marry them into another magical line – powerful mages tended to have even stronger mages as children, after all. He never heard of a 'Euleilla' in any of the noble families of Svieda, but he didn't doubt that one would have used her magical skills as a bargaining chip towards marrying into the Royal line.

Which meant she was a very, very valuable person.

"If you know my name, you surely know what I am capable of," Hussack said, his voice hardening as he decided to end the verbal game. "Do you wish me to beat you unconscious in a fight, or would you like to save us both the trouble and surrender right away?"

The ever-present magical dust surrounding Euleilla started swirling at a speed Tur'Ba had never seen before. "No," was all she said in response.

The next move was felt all across the battlefield.

Chapter VIII

Maelgyn was finding combat easier than he had expected, considering his wounds. In fact, he was finding it was difficult not to rush ahead of his supporting force as he trounced Sho'Curlan footsoldiers almost effortlessly. He was only using one of his swords at this point, freeing his *schlipf* to act as both spear and shield when needed. He had encountered at least two opposing mages, but they were both fairly average, and he had yet to find anyone who could present a real match for him either as a mage or a swordsman. In effect, he was just plowing through the enemy as if they weren't even there.

Not that there weren't casualties on his side, too. He had started the fight with a pair of Nekoji to act as his personal guards, but one of them had taken a spear to the gut early on. Worse, three Wolf Riders on the far end of his flank were hit by arrows – an unusual way for them to die. As the wolves were typically too nimble to be hit in unarmored spots, they were rarely troubled by archers. Perhaps, in the crush of battle with the infantry, they were slowed to the point of vulnerability, but Maelgyn still wondered if there was another mage among the Sho'Curlan archers they had yet to identify. Perhaps, if the Dragonriders didn't show themselves soon, he would investigate.

The line behind him was at least making some progress pushing through the Sho'Curlan infantry, even if they weren't going fast enough for him. Quite frankly, the battle overall – and not just his own part in it – was going far better than Maelgyn felt he had any right to expect. He was starting to hope they would be able to break the siege before the Dragons could arrive.

He was worried, though, that Hussack had not been identified during the initial arrow bombardment they had used to find the other mages. Maelgyn wanted to fight the assassin of his king and the captor of his father, himself, and was sure he was on the battlefield somewhere. But that wasn't the only reason he wanted to be the one to fight Hussack – he was fairly confident that he was the only person (with the possible exception of a well-rested Euleilla) who had the magical strength to match him.

The other concern came from the Nekoji personal guard that was still fighting on his right.

"Your Highness, why haven't your people organized a sortie from the castle, yet?"

It was a crucial part of the plan. Arnach knew that there was a significant force of men still inside the castle walls, and that a sizable sortie could be launched without risking the surviving defenses. The hope was that Maelgyn's strike from the outside would pull enough men away from the siege that the castle could launch one, completely surrounding their enemy and utterly destroying this part of their army. The Brode that Maelgyn knew would take decisive action if it was warranted, yet the castle didn't even seem to notice it was being rescued.

"Maybe they're just waiting for us to draw off more enemy soldiers," Maelgyn suggested, though he didn't believe it. He casually grabbed one enemy with Sekhar's vines around his neck, tossing him into a trio of charging Sho'Curlans before finishing them all off magically with the metal tips of their own spears. He then used his magic to 'bounce' a charging attacker away from his Nekoji guard.

"But that would only make sense if... what is *that?*"

Maelgyn turned to glance at where the Nekoji was pointing and froze. Even his heart stopped for a split second, and the rest of him was unable to move. In the middle of the forces on Euleilla's side of the battle, there was a disturbance – a visible shimmering in the air, with dust and colors and lights like the auroras sometimes seen late at night in parts of the world. He had never seen such a phenomenon before, but he had heard of it... and he knew there could be only one possible explanation for its presence.

His duel with Paljor never allowed either mage the chance to properly exert the full force of their magic against each other – Paljor was dividing his energy among more than a dozen people, while Maelgyn was first more worried with increasing the speed and strength of his sword arm and then with holding his wounds together. However, it was said that should two First Rate mages go into a purely magical duel with one another, light itself would bend and flicker around them as their powers crashed. They were sometimes described as "auroras," after the phenomenon occasionally seen in the far north. After fighting Paljor, Maelgyn was uncertain that such rumors were true, but now... now, he knew.

His wife was fighting Hussack. And, looking where the aurora was coming from, he suspected she was doing it alone. If she had exhausted too much of her magic prior to the meeting, as he feared, she could not win.

"I have to go on ahead," he warned the Nekoji guardsman. "Keep pushing the line forward. I'll try and come back to you if I can."

"You shouldn't go alone, your Highness," the Nekoji said. "I shall accompany you."

"No, you won't," Maelgyn replied. "You won't be able to keep up. You want to protect me? Keep pressing the enemy."

It was obvious the Nekoji wanted to protest more, but there wasn't time to discuss it. "Very well, your Highness."

Maelgyn turned away from him and started pushing his way through the enemy. He had been holding himself back to stay with the Sviedan line, but now he was able to cut a path through the enemy forces with deliberation. He was shrugging attackers over with just a flick of magic, cutting people down with magically powered swings of his blade, and when that wasn't enough Sekhar would be unleashed to rip through enemy resistance.

The *schlipf* proved invaluable as shield, spear, and whip – he could grab a person with a vine and pull him into the spear-like thorn that would suddenly sprout out of Maelgyn's wrist. Further vines would form into a shield to deflect any wild swings sent by the victim...

and then Maelgyn's hand punching forward and the motion of the thorn retreating would dislodge the body. It was a bit gruesome, but given that they were in the middle of a battlefields where swords were swinging wildly and hacking at bodies and limbs, it wasn't the bloodiest thing that day.

His injuries from the fight with Paljor hadn't bothered him at all that day... until he made that push. Muscles were strained, scars that only yesterday were held together by stitches were pulled, and his breathing grew labored. Despite this, it took less than a minute for him to push through the enemy lines and into open ground.

Euleilla was still on the other side of the battlefield. She was holding her own for the moment, but Maelgyn knew he had to hurry. He dodged or magically deflected several arrows with the help of Sekhar. About half-way across the ground, however, the schlipf became suddenly anxious.

Down! Now! Sekhar thought to him, harder and louder than the living weapon had ever spoken before. Without thought, Maelgyn obeyed, jumping to the ground and covering up.

The fireball missed him by inches. Had it hit him directly, he would have died instantly. It was only thanks to the Nekoji fur cloak he had received a few months before that several of Maelgyn's extremities were only blistered by the heat instead of seared off. When the blast subsided, he rolled over to see what was attacking him.

"Oh... damn," he said, as at least five Black Dragons banking away to ready themselves for another pass. He slowly stood up on his feet, tracking them with his eyes. Then he glanced over to where the aurora of Euleilla's battle with Hussack was still showing, then back at the Dragons. He was torn.

Your mate can handle herself, Sekhar advised, sensing the internal debate. *She is a powerful warrior, and you arranged for an excellent protector to stay at her side. But there isn't anyone else in the Sviedan line who even stands a chance against those Dragons, and you know it.*

Yeah, Maelgyn sighed mentally. *But it's not like I stand much of a chance against those Dragons, myself. I guess today is the day I prove my 'High Mage' pedigree in the 'traditional' way. But that challenge is for fighting one dragon, not five.*

You must try, Sekhar replied. *There's no-one else who can.*

I could save Euleilla first, and then go after the Dragon Riders, Maelgyn argued.

At the cost of thousands of your soldiers? Sekhar moralized. *What choice do you think she would want you to make?*

Maelgyn shook his head, turning to look at the dragons as they wheeled around in mid-air. Aloud he said, "Damn. Now how am I supposed to get up there to challenge them, anyway?"

Tur'Ba felt himself being pushed back as the two magical titans clashed in front of him. He was not alone – all of the soldiers surrounding the pair were being forced back. However, he was better able to hold his ground. As magic could effect Human blood but not Dwarven blood, the only reason he couldn't get close to them was his axe. At least at that moment – it was getting easier to stand his ground as time went on.

Euleilla wasn't going to be able to keep the pace much longer, he feared. Her contribution to the maelstrom of magic was visibly weakening, as even the magical powder she wielded was scattered over the battlefield carelessly. In addition to the magical struggle, both were engaged in a duel of sword versus spear, and Hussack was winning that as well.

She had expended a lot of her energy before Hussack's entrance and now she was pushed to her limits just to match him. Her stamina had been on Tur'Ba's mind since the start of the battle, and it was obvious her magic was about to fail.

It would be his job to protect her until she could recover, but Tur'Ba wasn't sure what he could do against someone like Hussack. He might be able to make himself a distraction, to give Euleilla a few critical moments of time, but his axe was keeping him out of the fight. The steel edge that was designed to break through the bronze armor of his regular foes was keeping him from his duty.

Well, Tur'Ba thought to himself. *If my axe is holding me back... I guess I just need to drop it.* With that, he slowly struggled to raise the weapon over his head, and then just let it go. A satisfying thunk told him that the blade of his axe had hit one of the Sho'Curlan soldiers behind him, but he didn't need to confirm that – Hussack was more important. With the axe gone, there was practically nothing that the magic could affect on his person. It was time to act.

Euleilla knew from the moment their magic clashed that she was in over her head. Her magic had been largely exhausted prior to this encounter – her mistake, she knew – and Hussack was an opponent she could only hope to match when she was at her full strength. Even then, she would probably be at a disadvantage.

There really was only one person in the army that could match him, she believed, and that was Maelgyn. She had sensed her husband running to join her, much to her relief... until the Dragons attacked and drew him off. She would have to win this battle with her own flagging strength. At this point, just to avoid passing out and defeating herself, she'd have to concentrate on being more conventional than her usual tactic of magical onslaught.

Once it became clear that Maelgyn wouldn't be able to join her, being 'conventional' no longer became an option. Euleilla changed tactics from a safe and defensive holding action to a far riskier offensive one. Hussack was better with a sword than she was with a spear, but much of that advantage disappeared when she awoke her still nameless immature *schlipf* to help co-ordinate her defense. The living weapon had been silent for the entire battle, but now it was letting her know exactly where every attack was coming from and pointing out holes in his defense.

Using this advantage, she managed a masterful parry, using the butt of her spear to deflect his sword before spinning around inside of his guard. The opening only worked for a split second, but it was enough to strike out with the sharp end of her weapon, pushing much of her ever-dwindling magic into her arms to make the blow stronger.

Hussack stumbled back and coughed, his arms flailing slightly, but he regained his balance quickly with a laugh. "Dear girl, my armor may not be golden dragonhide, like your own, but it is still dragonhide. No matter how hard you strike me, something that dull won't get through."

Euleilla was confused until a quick magical probe informed her just how dinged and dented the point of her spear had become on the armor of the soldiers she had been plowing through prior to Hussack's arrival. As good as this last, desperate attack had been, she may as well not have had a point at all on her spear. It would have been a close thing to pierce that hide with a sharp spearpoint, but

Hussack was right – nothing that blunt could possibly get through. Her only chance had been to strike through a joint, and the opening she had exploited didn't offer that chance.

She was in too close for Hussack to counter with a sword attack, but a backhand from his gauntleted fist was still devastating. She was sent flying back, collapsing in a heap several feet away. She tried to roll over and stand up, but her head was aching and her energy was almost gone. She had no useful weapon, her magic had been too expended even to let her 'see' around her, and even her *schlipf* seemed unable to speak to her.

I'm sorry, my husband, she thought to herself, the world fading around her. *We should have had more than one night....*

Hussack couldn't believe she had struck him, much less delivered a blow as hard as she did. It was only luck that left him alive... but, fortunately for him, that was the end of her strength, and his counter-attack ended her assault.

She might be unconscious, but she could still be dangerous – and the way things were going, it would be too much of a risk to leave her alive. "Such a pity – you would be a great prize for us, perhaps as valuable as that Sword we captured." He straddled her, preparing to drive his katana deep into her back. "But be honored to know you were a greater challenge to me than any I have faced before." His arm began its downward stroke.

Suddenly, he was no longer standing over the girl, but instead found himself flying twenty feet away, the breath knocked out of him from a second blow to his chest.

It was a powerful blow, and on top of the girl's strike it might have even cracked the armor – Hussack would have to check on that later – and at the very least his breath was knocked out of him. He was able to catch himself before he collapsed to the ground, but he struggled to make sense of his surroundings for a moment. He was dry heaving, and couldn't stand straight up right away. Hussack had to take a moment to recover before pulling himself back to his feet.

That was a good hit. But again, there was no follow up. Hussack would prove to his attacker that not killing him when he had the chance was a mistake.

Adjusting his helmet, Tur'Ba stood defensively over Euleilla's unconscious body. "So that's why the old helmets had those horns," he muttered to himself.

"A Dwarf?" Hussack snarled incredulously. "A lone Dwarf thinks he can challenge me?"

Tur'Ba glanced down at Euleilla, then back up at the Sho'Curlas Prince. "No, I don't. But I have to try. I can't allow you to harm my master's wife any more."

Hussack advanced slowly, still trying to recover his breath. "And just how do you plan to stop me? One lucky blow from my blindside won't be enough, and you don't appear to be armed. Are you even a warrior? You sound like a nursemaid."

"I'm the Duke of Sopan's aide-de-camp," Tur'Ba said, stalling for time. "And the personal bodyguard of his wife. I did lose my best weapon thanks to all that magic the two of you were putting out, though."

"My humble apologies," Hussack sneered, mock bowing. "But, warrior or not, you're going to be at a serious disadvantage without a weapon."

A slight smile curved its way onto Tur'Ba's face. "I did not say I was unarmed, just that I lost my favorite weapon. But what remains on my person will probably be more useful to me in this battle than the one I lost would have been."

"How so?" Hussack asked, amused.

"I guess it won't matter if I tell you or not," Tur'Ba said, reaching behind his back. He pulled the bag he wore on his back around to in front of him, and started fiddling with something inside. "It's a bit of a long story, though."

Hussack couldn't see anything more than a flash of wood, but he didn't see any possibility that the Dwarf could have anything inside it that would be a threat. It was much more amusing just to hear the Dwarf out. Soldiers of both sides were now avoiding the area that had been cleared from his battle with that princess-mage, and the Black Dragons' arrival should turn the tide of battle in his army's favor without his intervention. He could afford the time for a bit of amusement.

"Go ahead," he said, cackling. "Tell me everything! It will give you one last chance to amuse someone before you die."

Tur'Ba continued working with the object in his bag, but his eyes didn't leave Hussack's. "Much of what I'm about to say, I'm sure you already know. The Elven mentor I learned if from, however, insisted that it needed to be said whenever I was asked to explain."

Elves? Hussack echoed mentally. He knew of Elves, of course – the rumor was that one consulted with the Sho'Curlan King on a regular basis, though Hussack had never seen him or any other Elf that he could recall. Given their history, he was a bit surprised than any Elf would associate itself with a Dwarf, even though all the Elf-Dwarf wars having ended centuries before. What did they have to do with anything?

"Dwarves have long been the weakest of the major races, militarily," Tur'Ba continued. "Components of a great army are there. We have what may be considered the greatest light cavalry in the world, satisfactory archers, and unsurpassed engineers. But, when it comes to a sustained campaign, we have a bunch of incomplete parts that make it nearly impossible to hold our own for very long. This, however, has not always been true.

"Long ago, the Dwarves had an elite class of warrior – the kind of warrior class whose abilities were so great that their disappearance shifted the balance of power in the world. They were the Dwarven Axemen, and they were the pride of my people. Stories among your kind told of how a single Axeman could defend the entrance to our caves standing alone against a hundred men... but those were not just stories. They were truths... and understated truths, at that, if the Elves are to be believed. We sadly made a foolish mistake, however, and the ways of the Dwarven Axemen have been lost to us for almost a thousand years... but recently a certain Elf was willing to teach me my people's lost art, using records that have been lost since ancient times, and now we're starting to discover just what made them so powerful."

"And what is that?" Hussack asked derisively, though he was genuinely intrigued by the story.

"The Dwarves of the time fought in many wars, and in those wars the enemies were one of several races: The Elves, against whom the axe is a particularly potent weapon – most of their weapons were and are based in dead wood and live plant, which an axe is well suited to combat. The Elves' Ancient Enemy, who none speak of now. And finally, the Humans.

"It is against the Humans that the Dwarven Axemen earned their reputation, most of all. Regardless of our enemy's numbers, we could stop any incursion into our caves with ease – our axes and techniques were ideal for defending an enclosed position such as a cave entrance. So, the Humans decided to bring out the secret weapons they had been gradually molding in the churches and temples of the day: Mages.

"It turned out, however, that the Axemen were able to handle a Mage just as easily as they could handle a normal Human. Dwarves just aren't vulnerable to Human magic, and... well, we had techniques that would compensate for just about everything else a mage could do."

Hussack laughed, not believing a word of it. "I see... but what does this have to do with you? Even if, as you say, you have rediscovered some of these 'secrets,' just what do you think this training will help you accomplish? Especially since, well, you no longer have an axe."

Tur'Ba grinned darkly. "I did lose my favorite steel axe, it is true. But the original Dwarven Axemen knew that Humans could use steel against them, so they had a different weapon for battling Mages." He slowly pulled the handled weapon out of his bag. "We fought Mages not with steel... but with stone."

It's one thing to decide you're going to go off and attack five Black Dragons by yourself, Maelgyn mused. *It's quite another to actually figure out how you can actually do it.*

Black Dragons were significantly larger than their more intelligent golden-skinned cousins. While Gold Dragons were about the size of small horses, Black Dragons could be thought of as elephants. They, in turn, were smaller than the Red Dragons which still inhabited the wastelands to the west and mountains to the north of Oregal – Red Dragons were usually even larger than the whales, and were easily the largest creatures of any kind in the known world. Fortunately for the rest of the world, they rarely left the wastelands or the mountains they inhabited. Unfortunately, despite their difference in size, the Black Dragon was thought to be the more dangerous of the two species.

Black Dragons were more powerfully built than Reds, their skin was harder to penetrate, and their intelligence was much greater. Even their fires burned hotter, according to the Elves, though no-one alive now knew how that could be tested without killing the tester.

Fighting a dragon of any breed in single combat was talked about in many stories... but usually only in fables, to teach children not to bite off more than they could chew. Often, those stories ended in a rather gruesome fate for the hero of the piece, though likely not as gruesome a fate as the one likely suffered by anyone insane enough to attempt it.

Maelgyn was planning to engage not one, but five Black Dragons in battle alone, drawing all of their attention to him and giving his army the opportunity to win without draconic interference. Maelgyn wondered if 'insane enough' was an adequate description for himself.

Stop complaining, Sekhar groused. *I don't have the time for it, and you need to pay more attention. Here, one is coming in now!*

Maelgyn saw a low-flying dragon about to pass overhead. His hand shot up, and with it one of Sekhar's vines. He felt his arm nearly wrench itself out of its socket as he was lifted into the air.

This wasn't as good of a plan as you made it sound, Maelgyn protested, feeling some of his wounds split open with the strain..

Sekhar, slowly pulling Maelgyn up to the Dragon by recalling his vines, was slightly apologetic. *I admit, I thought it would be easier than this. Your wounds must still be worse than I thought.*

So, what do I have that can actually hurt this thing? Maelgyn asked as they got close to the Dragon's underbelly.

You're only thinking of this now? Sekhar thought back, annoyed. *Many of the idiots who go after Dragons don't have anything that can pierce dragonhide, but you're lucky enough to have several different weapons that will work on him.*

"And those are?" Maelgyn asked impatiently, forgetting momentarily that he only had to think the words.

Well, me, for one, Sekhar replied, nonplussed. *I figured you'd have realized that. And keep your voice down – the Dragon probably knows we're here, but he isn't likely to react unless his rider does. If your voice carries....*

Sorry, Maelgyn apologized.

Don't apologize – just keep quiet! Sekhar cautioned. *Both of your swords were bathed in Dragon's blood as they were tempered; that gives them special properties that might allow them to cut through dragonhide. Maybe. At the very least, you won't dull its edge if you try. Finally, you should be able to enhance your strength enough for your armored fists and legs to be as effective on a Dragon as unarmored and unenhanced hand-to-hand is on a normal Human.*

Well, that's something, Maelgyn replied.

There is one more weapon you might want to consider, Sekhar added. *And that is gravity. Dragons are like bats and birds, in that they need wings to fly. But they are also too heavy to fly by wings alone, and must rely on their own internal gasses. Both are required for them to fly, and both present a weakness for the dragon – the gas can sometimes cause them to explode should they crash into the ground, and without their wing they will still drop like a rock. While they have strong bones, blood with unusual properties not otherwise found in nature, and skin stronger than the strongest steel armor, their internal gas sacks can rupture during a sudden, uncontrolled fall. Even if they don't, while the Dragon may live for a short time following that type of fall it will be but a short reprieve before other injuries end its life.*

Maelgyn felt his stomach go a little queasy. He rather liked Dragons, especially after meeting the likes of Khumbaya. That particular idea felt like a cruel and inhumane way to kill them... but it was something to keep in mind if he grew desperate.

He reached the Black Dragon's hind leg, and once he was holding onto it securely Sekhar released his vine. His grip seemed to irritate the dragon – it tried swinging its leg to dislodge him – but it quickly stopped when it started wobbling in mid-air. Much more cautiously, it reached over with one of its other legs, trying to scratch Maelgyn off with its claws. It was all Maelgyn could do to hang on, much less free a hand to attack.

Okay, I'm here, he thought. *Now what?*

Sekhar didn't have a chance to respond before the Dragon banked, taking an angle of attack on Maelgyn's army. The target appeared to be a cluster of Nekoji attempting to storm one of the siege towers, and the Dragon was closing in fairly rapidly. With no more time for thought, Maelgyn acted.

He reached his arms out and grabbed the Dragon's tail, using it to swing up to the top of the creature. He then tried to run up – or rather down, as the Dragon was tilting towards the ground – its back, hoping to make it to the rider in time to prevent the attack. Walking on the Dragon's spine proved to be more difficult than he imagined, and he stumbled several times before falling onto his hands and knees. He couldn't move fast enough crawling, however, and it didn't look like he'd have enough time to stop the strafing attack on his Nekoji allies.

Kick the tail to the right, Sekhar suggested frantically. *It's like a rudder – if you turn his tail right, he'll spin out left.*

Maelgyn grasped the idea and summoned the magically enhanced strength necessary for wrestling with a Dragon's tail. However, he didn't make his move right away.

What are you waiting for? Sekhar demanded, sounding almost panicked.

Maelgyn watched as the Dragon lifted its head, a sign that its jaws were about to open and a fireball was being prepared. At the last second, he heaved with all of his strength.

Wrestling with a Dragon required more magical enhancement of his muscles than he had dreamed possible, yet it was enough. The tail turned, and the Dragon turned with it. The fireball it had been preparing flew off course... and right into the tail of another Black Dragon.

While these Black Dragons were tamed, they were still animals... and they lacked both the intelligence and the discipline to know that this wasn't a time to clash over an accidental tail singe. The offended dragon ignored its rider's direction, charging at Maelgyn's dragon with a mighty crash. Claws, fireballs, and teeth flashed everywhere, from Maelgyn's perspective. Unable to hold on against all of the bucking and the thrashing, he felt himself sent flying off.

Despite how much magic could enhance his strength and durability, he would never survive a fall from this height, and he knew it. Maelgyn was at a loss – what could he do now? Fighting down panic, he tried to think of some way to stop his fall. He saw, from this distance, a fallen figure – Euleilla. The Sho'Curlas warriors were largely avoiding her and the area around her, and she didn't seem to be wounded... so she must have passed out. Tur'Ba was running off at something, surrounded in dust, but that was all he could see in that instant before a memory struck him.

As Euleilla had done for him many months ago, he found the iron in his own blood and used his magic to lift himself up. He couldn't make himself fly – at least, not for long – but maybe he could slow his fall.

As his skin reddened, blood vessels deformed, and blisters formed, he remembered just why he never tried practicing the technique after Euleilla had shown it to him.

This is going to hurt, he thought, moments before he hit the ground.

Chapter IX

Tur'Ba glared defiantly across the battlefield, staring down – or rather, given their relative statures, up – at the grim face of what he knew was one of the most powerful mages in the world. He had made his statement, biding his time long enough to fix the dark stone head of his axe to its handle. This particular type of axe, known as an *ichiono* in his native Dwarvish tongue, was what had made his kind so powerful in the heyday of the Dwarven Axemen. According to Wangdu, his people moving away from these stone axes to steel ones was part of their downfall – steel axes were unable to defend against mages. Every Human army had a mage in it, and every Elven army would hire Human mages as mercenaries in their wars against the Dwarves. The mage was the downfall of his people, but it was the steel axe that made them vulnerable to mages. Without that axe, they were far less vulnerable than the other great races of the world.

That said, he wasn't exactly a fully trained Dwarven Axeman. He hadn't even been a warrior before leaving with Maelgyn on his journey – just an innkeeper's son who liked to run around and explore the countryside. While he had learned all of the essential techniques, according to Wangdu, he lacked the physical strength and stamina of the true Axemen. Most of the moves required for this type of battle needed great strength – and while he knew he could perform each of them when well rested, he had no idea if he had the energy to do them now, in the middle of a real battle.

The corner of one of his eyes caught sight of his Master swinging from what looked like a rope tied around the foot of a Dragon. The corner of the other caught sight of Euleilla, lying motionless in a heap only a few feet away from him. He didn't have a choice – his Master, who appeared to be literally taking on Dragons on his own, shouldn't have to give up his mate so early in their life together.

Hussack twitched, causing the young Dwarf to flinch. The twitching continued until a low, largely suppressed chuckle escaped from the Sho'Curlas prince. "For a brief moment, there, with what you were saying, I thought you might actually pose a threat. But seriously – you expect me to be worried because you're using a stone axe?"

"No," Tur'Ba snorted. "I'm expecting you to be too arrogant to know just how big a threat one can be to you."

Hussack shook his head resignedly. "You won't even get a chance to use it," he said. Sheathing the high-quality Sviedan Sword he used for dueling, he reached out with his off hand towards one of the discarded steel blades lying on the battlefield. It flew into his grasp, and he brought it in front of him, the flat of the blade facing parallel to his eyes. With a slow grin at the Dwarf, he performed a magical combat technique that had been used with brutal effectiveness since magic was first applied to combat: He shattered the blade and sent the shards flying at Tur'Ba with lethal speed.

Tur'Ba dodged the first wave of metal shards before beginning his counterattack. Counterbalancing the blade edge of the stone axe was a rather unusually carved hammer head. While it would work well as a hammer, if blunt force was desired, it also had a bit of a scoop wedge carved into it. Tur'Ba slammed this side of the axe into the ground with enough force that it made a divot. Dragging the scoop-edge of the stone head behind him, Tur'Ba charged at Hussack, ripping his axe out of the ground at the last moment.

The purpose of the scoop edge became clear when Tur'Ba's swing sent a cloud of dirt and grass into Hussack's eyes. Unable to see the Dwarf, all Hussack could do to avoid being hit was to step back out of range.

Only to be tackled by Tur'Ba as the young Dwarf charged at him with impressive speed. Again, the armored head to his gut sent Hussack flying back, though this time he was able to catch himself before going too far and land on his feet. He didn't have time to draw his regular sword before he had to dodge, himself, just seconds before a stone axe would have buried itself into his neck. Outside of a little surprise, he was unhurt by the blows he had received – the dragonhide armor was absorbing most of the impact of Tur'Ba's head-butts, and it was rather unlikely that anything made of stone would ever penetrate dragonhide – but he was growing quite winded.

Hussack was desperate for a moment's breather, but now he saw the reason for the Dwarf's stone axe – with stone and not steel, there was absolutely nothing for his magic to grab on to with the Dwarf. Even the buckles on his shoes were made of wood, not metal, and Dwarven blood was immune to magic. He was too busy dodging axe swings to build up the concentration needed to use magic, anyway.

Tur'Ba was going wild with his swings. He was using his own body to counterbalance the stone head's weight as he swung in complete circles – horizontally, vertically, and diagonally. There was no way to judge which direction he would go until the swing started, and he was moving too fast for Hussack to take advantage when his back was turned. Every now and then, a kick was thrown in, too – flipping over the axe so that both his feet could strike. Usually, these kicks only hit armor, but even so they were forcing Hussack to react with more speed than he could handle.

The onslaught, however, couldn't last forever. Tur'Ba lacked the energy and endurance of his ancestors, and it showed as his speed started to slip. It didn't drop by much, but it was enough for Hussack to finally take an action other than dodging.

With a vicious, magically enhanced palm strike to the chest, Hussack slipped inside of Tur'Ba's whirling axe and knocked the Dwarf back several feet. The blow knocked the breath out of Tur'Ba and sent him to the ground, but Hussack's momentary success was tempered by the knowledge that he'd hurt himself – sharp pains in his elbow warned him that he'd strained his arm a bit too hard, and that pain would make it harder to use magic. Not that magic would be of much use, it seemed – he would have to finish this Dwarf off the hard way.

With that in mind, Hussack drew the Sword he had captured when he first took Svieda's Royal Castle. The pain in his elbow was bothering him enough that, if he wanted to enhance his strength and speed with magic, he would have to fight with one hand. It could be a serious issue, but not an insurmountable one.

"Perhaps I underestimated you," Hussack breathed out, hoping to gain a moments rest, himself, with a little battlefield banter. "But that axe of yours is *still* useless against my armor... and now that I have my own weapon ready. The element of surprise is no longer on your side, and your speed has dropped to where I can start to match it. You are getting weaker as this fight progresses, yet I have exerted little strength defending myself. Even at your best, I can still wear you down through attrition, and you are no longer at your best. How can you hope to defeat me?"

Tur'Ba slowly rose back to his feet, positioning his axe defensively. While gasping for air, he was otherwise unphased by Hussack's declaration. "I suppose it's time for round two, then, huh?"

His knees weren't working properly, his skin was flushed and burning, and his whole body was in pain, but at least Maelgyn knew he had survived. He was lying on the ground, unable to stand up and barely conscious. With an odd detachment, he found he had a good view of the two Black Dragons fighting one another above him, and it was plainly obvious that neither would live long once their fight was over. He would have been content to lie there and just watch then battle it out.

Someone, however, was annoyingly reminding him that there were more important things happening.

Get up, Sekhar demanded again frantically. *There are still three more Dragons to deal with out there!*

I need to rest, Maelgyn insisted. In his dazed state, his mind was retreating to a night not too long ago, where everything was blissfully happy and Euleilla was in his bed. It was so fresh and new. He wanted to go back to that night. He wanted ten thousand more just like it. *A few minutes, at least....*

You don't have a few minutes! Your wife needs you! She's injured, and—

That snapped Maelgyn out of his stupor. *Injured? Huh? What? Euleilla! Quick, where is she?* His knees weren't working right naturally, but his magic could get them to move, and with that in mind he pulled himself to his feet.

You have the Dragons that need to be dealt with first—

No! Maelgyn snapped back. *The Dragons can wait. If Euleilla's injured and battling Hussack, she can't. Now, where is she?*

Sekhar would have sighed if he was capable of the feat. However, *schlipf* didn't have proper lungs, and so that was impossible – instead, he gave in to Maelgyn's demand and pointed with his mind. *I suppose, since you're insisting we deal with her first, you'd better hurry.*

Maelgyn didn't need the encouragement, as he was already forcing himself to run towards the crowd that was apparently forming around his wife. He was disoriented – not sure where he was in relation to the rest of his army, the Dragons, the castle, or anything else – and his legs were useless without magic, but he didn't care. He knew where Euleilla was, now, and nothing was going to stop him from getting to her.

Well, nothing, perhaps, other than the larger-than-average Black Dragon which just landed between them.

Oh, great, Maelgyn sighed in resignation. *Seems like I still have to take down one more Dragon, first.*

'Round two,' as Tur'Ba had called it, wasn't going quite as well for the young Dwarf. The Dwarven Axemen of old employed tactics designed to break swords, but Hussack's weapon was unbreakable. The stone head of his axe would break before piercing Hussack's Dragonhide armor. Worst of all, Hussack had been right – he was getting weaker while Hussack seemed unphased by just about everything he did.

Tur'Ba had been able to press the attack so fast that Hussack couldn't defend himself in the first part of the battle, but the now magically enhanced speed and strength of Hussack was reversing that. The handle of his axe, which he was using to block some swings of the Sword, was now rather pitted and splintered. The spinning, whirling, twirling moves he had been taught – which used the momentum of his axe to increase his speed exponentially – were utterly useless in this situation, and unless something changed, soon, all he could do was delay his inevitable defeat.

Hussack started slowing down, himself, and when Tur'Ba started to catch up he changed tactics. Reaching out with his injured off hand, he was able to hook Tur'Ba's axe as he blocked a swing from the other side. Hussack threw out his sword arm, still holding his weapon, and used the momentum – and some magical strength – to toss the Dwarf as far as he could. Unprepared for such a move, Tur'Ba went flying nearly forty feet before catching himself. It was like he had been flung from a catapult. Was magic really able to increase a man's strength this far? Maelgyn was an even more powerful mage, but Tur'Ba had yet to see him even attempt such a feat.

He rolled back to his feet, hoping he could raise his defenses for the expected attack to come. No attack was coming, however, as the Sho'Curlas prince was seemingly more interested in something to his right. Cautiously, Tur'Ba spared one eye to follow his gaze.

Several Sho'Curlas soldiers were surrounding Euleilla, poised to strike if she moved. One of them seemed to be glancing at Hussack, awaiting orders.

"Your highness?" the soldier began. "Is she a worthy prisoner?"

Not knowing what Hussack would say, Tur'Ba quickly decided to make it obvious Euleilla was worth taking a prisoner before there was a chance for him to give an order. If they wanted, the six soldiers surrounding her could kill the young woman before he had a chance to move; as a prisoner, she could always be rescued.

"That is Euleilla, the Princess Consort of the Sword of Sopan," he declared with a forced bravado. "Touch her Highness, and I will kill you all!"

Hussack considered this for a moment. The Dwarf was obviously very protective of the lady, and he was quite... troublesome to deal with. Perhaps, with a hostage, it would get easier. "Take her prisoner, but beware; she is a powerful mage. If I do not make it out of this battle alive, execute her immediately, as I will be needed to ensure she stays a captive."

"As you say, your highness," the soldier agreed, directing his men to pick the young woman up and carry her off. Tur'Ba could only watch, helplessly, as Hussack moved to stand between him and the departing troop.

"So, young Axeman," Hussack asked, holding his sword out in a deceptively lazy low guard. "What are you going to do now?"

Tur'Ba took a few deep breaths, trying to think of what he could accomplish with the restrictions now imposed upon him. Until she was freed, a death sentence hung over Euleilla should Hussack be killed... but if Hussack wasn't killed, Euleilla would remain a captive. "If your death is now off the table," he finally said, his fists clenching around the battered handle of his axe. "I can still cripple you!"

It was a final, wild charge that Tur'Ba decided to end this battle with, for good or ill. Dwarves may have looked stocky and slow, but that was an undeserved reputation... and Tur'Ba was a very fast runner. He charged in with unprecedented speed, his axe trailing behind him as he prepared to deliver at least one successful blow.

Hussack had time to react, however. Not much time, but enough to raise his sword to block, and to call his magic to action. Several shards of metal from various broken weapons strewn across the battlefield were pulled to his defense, all concentrating into a barrage of shrapnel directed into the body of the charging Dwarf.

Tur'Ba didn't even feel the blows. This was, as planned, a berserker-style charge that required he focus entirely on the attack – in this mindset, even mortal blows could be and were shrugged off. As he entered into range, he swung his axe as hard and fast as he could. It collided with the unbreakable steel of the dragon-blood tempered Sword Hussack wielded... and broke it.

Hussack's eyes widened in disbelief as an axe made of stone ripped through first his steel weapon, and then his dragonhide armor before crumbling into fragments, the wooden handle snapping in two behind it. The Sword fell in two pieces and several scales of the dragonhide were dislodged, leaving a large and vulnerable hole underneath. He took a glancing blow to the shoulder, as well, though by that point the stone axe was chipped and blunted enough that it merely broke bones and not skin, but it was a significant injury nonetheless. He glanced up into the Dwarf's eyes.

His heart and lungs both pierced with the remains of multiple steel blades, Tur'Ba could no longer speak. The Dwarf wasn't looking at him, initially, but rather behind him. A bitterly triumphant grin rose on his pain-etched face, as he mouthed out the last word he wanted to say but could not speak... before collapsing into death.

"Gotcha."

It should not have been possible for him to even stand, much less walk. As much pain as he was in, it should not have been possible for Maelgyn to wield any magic at all, much less enough to force his severely damaged legs and knees to move. However, as the battle had raged on and as Maelgyn constantly found himself using more and more magic just to keep going, it had been getting easier to use. Not only could he feel magical reserves he had never tapped into, before, but his control seemed greater.

Maelgyn had earned the title of 'High Mage' when he bested Paljor in their duel, but he had never felt he'd earned it. It was Sekhar, not he, who had delivered the fatal blow. It was Sekhar, not he, whose senses gave his reflexes enough warning to match the speed and power of the other High Mage. It was his friends and companions who had distracted Paljor enough for him to even move against the wave of magic pressing against him in that fights closing moments.

But a neutral observer watching the battle would have no question of it, now. His magic was helping him not just move, but move with more speed and strength than he would normally wield.

He noticed, but it was more subconsciously than anything. He was too focused on his goal to pay attention to how impressive his magical feats were; there was a Dragon between him and his wife, and he would burn whatever magical strength he had inside him to get to her.

Dragons may have been able to fly, but that was not their greatest strength. In fact, instinctually, Dragons avoided fighting in the air when it could be avoided. Human riders almost had to force their Black Dragon mounts to attack targets from the air. Griffins (another flying mount Humans and Elves had used in the past) and many other flying beasts were much better at mid-air combat than Dragons were, despite none of the others being able to shoot fire or having nearly unbreakable skin. On the ground, however, a Dragon was superior to just about any creature they came in contact with.

All of which meant that the Dragon standing in front of him was even more of a danger to Maelgyn than it could have been were it flying. *This is not going to be easy*, he said mentally, not particularly caring if Sekhar could hear him.

It was very rare that a single person would try to take on a Dragon by himself, but with his army so busy there was no way for Maelgyn to call for any additional support. In those rare instances history recorded it happening, stealth was always the greatest weapon the Human could have. It was unheard of for a single individual to go charging head-on into the teeth of a dragon, as Maelgyn was doing now.

Dragon and rider were both too startled by the unprecedented tactics to immediately respond. When the dragon came to its senses, it erupted with a stream of fire in Maelgyn's direction. Maelgyn ducked and rolled under the blast, narrowly avoiding incineration, before continuing to charge forward. The rider struggled to maintain his seat when the dragon reared unexpectedly, furious that Maelgyn was getting too close. It first tried stomping on him, and he barely weaved his way around those frantic feet. It was a near thing, and one claw snagged his Nekoji cloak. Within moments, the only protection he had from the dragon's flames had been shredded into ineffectual pieces.

Maelgyn attempted to hamstring the beast, slicing across the back of its hind leg, but while his Sword was able to cut through the tough hide it only scratched the surface. A stab attempt to the supposedly soft underbelly proved futile; Maelgyn had to extend his reach as far as he could just to hit the 'vulnerable' spot, and without more leverage he would be unable to penetrate even that thinner bit of hide.

Dragon and mage danced around each other, neither able to land a telling blow. The longer it went on, the more panicked the Dragon, but Maelgyn knew he was running out of time and energy himself. He only had a finite amount of magic to use before he had to rest, and that would expire before he could reach Euleilla at this rate.

A quick glance to check on Euleilla proved to be a misstep – literally. Trying to move one direction while looking another caused him to miss a rock, and he stumbled. Before he could recover, he was being pinned to the ground by a Dragon's foot.

Had any of the Dragon's claws been in position to stab him, Maelgyn would have been dead instantly. Fortunately, the razor-sharp fingernails of the beast had missed him completely. His armor was strong enough to keep him from being instantly crushed, but it wouldn't last long if he couldn't get the Dragon off him quickly. To make matters worse he had dropped both of his swords and couldn't sense them to summon them. He was pinned, face-down, with

Sekhar caught between him and the ground.

How the hell do I get out of this one? Maelgyn wondered, as his bones were slowly compressing. Much longer and he'd be dealing with cracked ribs.

Make him flinch, Sekhar suggested. *Stab his foot, and make him lift it away from you.*

How can I do that? Maelgyn asked. *I don't have a sword, and you're pinned down as much as I am.*

Before Sekhar could answer, however, something grabbed Maelgyn's attention despite the situation he was in. There, right in front of his eyes, a group of seven or eight men were carrying his wife off the battlefield... and straight into the heart of the enemy camp.

"Euleilla!" he called – or tried to. Expelling the air in his lungs to shout nearly proved the death of him, as his ribs started to crack. *Enough of this,* he thought angrily. *Euleilla needs me, so I need to get out of here!*

With all of his strength, he started to push up from the ground. At first, nothing happened, but then he started to lift the Dragon's foot with his back. After a moment the Dragon staggered back, and Maelgyn was free. Maelgyn, after rolling to his feet, slammed his strongest punch into the Dragon's head. If that punch stunned it or not, he didn't care – it was no longer a concern of his. Euleilla was the most important thing.

Maelgyn stumbled slightly as reached down to pick up his swords, exhaustion from the overuse of magic beginning to overwhelm him. Red and black circles in his vision warned he was about to pass out, but he shook his head and managed to clear it. Fighting unconsciousness every step of the way, he ran after his wife. He wasn't sure what he would do when he got there, as little strength as he had left, but he had to save her. That was the only thing still running through his head.

His path was blocked, however, when Prince Hussack, the assassin of Maelgyn's King and the apparent leader of Sho'Curlas' attacking army, limped into his path. His armor was cracked, he had a limp, and one of his arms was hanging at his side uselessly, but he was in better shape than Maelgyn. "You," Hussack snarled, reaching for a sword on his belt that wasn't there any more. "I remember you."

"Out of my way, Hussack," Maelgyn snapped, unwilling to deal with the man at the moment. "I have bigger concerns than you. You are in my way, and I'll destroy you if you don't get out of it."

"I imagine you do," Hussack laughed. "My men are taking the 'Princess Consort of Sopan' away. You were due to be the Duke of Sopan. You are the one who married that woman, correct? She is my... hostage. If I die, she dies – my men know this."

Maelgyn didn't say anything. Instead, he tightened his grip on his swords and started running towards Hussack.

"Oh, dear," Hussack sighed mockingly. "Dragon Rider!" he called.

"Yes, your Highness!" Astonishingly, even though his Dragon had reared like a horse being broken, the rider managed to stay on. A quick glance showed the Dragon itself was still a little dazed, however.

"That team of men over there is carrying away a young woman who is of some value to this young man. And I, apparently, am standing between them, yet he cannot kill me. There are two solutions to this problem – he can try to remove me without killing me, or we can remove her." He grinned darkly. "Go 'remove' her from existence, will you?"

Unseen by either prince, the rider rolled his eyes – Hussack was well known for pretentious showmanship. Still, it was best to follow orders. "Of course, your Highness."

Maelgyn gawked as the black dragon leapt into the air. He had to wonder just what it was he could do to keep Euleilla safe. At this point, his magic was keeping him standing by force of will alone, Hussack was between him and his wife, and now a dragon was about to destroy her.

Obviously, Sekhar sighed. *We have to kill the dragon before it reaches her.*

And just how are we supposed to do that? Maelgyn asked. *Even if I were a match for it one-on-one, it's not like I could fly up there to fight it.*

Well... you could always bring him down, Sekhar pointed out.

That suggestion, Maelgyn decided, had some merit, but he wasn't about to admit that to Sekhar if he could help it. Of course, the obvious question was – how does one bring a dragon down? He thought back to the stories – the supposedly true stories, and not the myths and legends – of how dragons were defeated in past battles. The difficulties of fighting fire-breathing creatures that were larger than an elephant and could fly were boundless, but the greatest of those problems had always been how to keep the Dragon from flying away if it was starting to lose.

One theoretical way to stop them – which had never been tried, for there had never been anyone with a strong enough arm to attempt it – involved little more than a thick rope. The idea was to tie the rope into a lasso and then throw the lasso around the dragon, pulling him down. Maelgyn's sore body from his last lassoing attempt of a dragon proved how spectacularly useless that plan was, however.

Or did it?

If the rope in question was strong enough not to break.... if he could anchor himself to the ground... if he could find a weapon that could pierce a dragon... if he could find a rope....

He didn't have any rope... but he still had a *schlipf.*

By the time a plan started forming in his head, the Dragon had finished its climb into the sky and was circling around to the best angle of attack on Euleilla. He had to act, and immediately, regardless of what plan he chose.

With that in mind he raised his arm, and with a mental command to Sekhar sent a *schlipf*-vine sailing up into the air. He had just the one option left.

Buried deep underground – very deep – every mage was aware that there was tons and tons of molten iron. Normally this iron was – from the perspective of a mage – useless. It was way too deep for the average mage to do more than remotely sense – hard even for stronger mages to sense reliably – and a low-grade field of magical disruption similar to that of a lodestone seemed to surround it most of the time. However, it was there. When nothing else was available, it made for a usable anchor should, for example, a high mage not want to be lifted from the ground after attaching himself to a dragon.

Maelgyn was paying a heavy price for his reluctance to go airborne again. It felt as if his entire body was being pulled apart at the joints, muscles and tendons stretching to their limits while Sekhar screamed as he was nearly torn out by the roots. However, Sekhar, Maelgyn, and the magic keeping them both in one piece survived long enough to hook the dragon. By sheer stroke of luck, they had grabbed on to a foreleg. The Dragon's momentum jerked to a stop, pivoting around over the leg and flipping head over heals.

Now upside down, and jolted out of flight, it tumbled to the ground with a resounding crash. The dragon survived the landing for a brief moment, as it struggled to right itself, but it wasn't long before its belly started swelling. With an astounding rain of burnt flesh and bone, the dragon detonated into thousands of pieces.

The fury of the blast echoed across the entire battlefield, and people from both sides of the battle stopped to turn and watch the destruction. Maelgyn was thrown back hard, and his body lacked the capacity to resist or to even protect himself from the fall, with magical assistance or without it. Hussack, however, stood unphased.

In fact, Hussack was smiling as he watched. Maelgyn was barely able to move his neck to see why. Out of the corner of his eye, however, he noticed the two remaining dragons were moving in to kill the man who had destroyed three of their brethren, and Maelgyn didn't have the strength to do anything to stop them.

Maelgyn knew it was over – he was about to die, Euleilla was as good as dead, and there was no telling what would happen to his soldiers once he was gone from the battle. In a brief moment of surrender to the inevitable, all he wished was that he and Euleilla could have had a little more time together. Maybe that he could see her one last time... but the large beasts that were his doom were all that filled his vision. Their mouths opened wide, and he was sure fire was gathering in their mouths

Several flashes of dull gold slammed into those black creatures, just as the spark of ignition filled in the lead dragon's mouth. Those flashes resolved into an army he had spent the last several months of his life trying to recruit – the collective might of the Golden Dragons.

Hussack's glee turned to horror, but he refused to be denied his victory over the young man he knew as a royal delinquent from their days together in the Royal castle. He summoned a new sword from a nearby corpse, and started to run at the young prince.

Khumbaya landed between him and Maelgyn, snorting steam out of his nose. "Halt, and advance no further, lest I slay thee!" he snarled.

That stopped Hussack in his tracks. Khumbaya started to advance on him anyway, but Maelgyn mustered up the strength to speak. "Stop!" he called.

Khumbaya turned to stare at Maelgyn disbelievingly. "Why? We both know the best enemy is a dead one."

"Perhaps," Maelgyn replied. "But if he dies my wife dies. Instead, we will use him as a messenger." He paused, and astonished even himself by getting to his feet to stare the hated man down. "Prince Hussack, I believe you know what the entry of the Golden Dragons into this war means." He took a step forward, despite all the pain and agony it took. "You have my wife as your hostage. You had best keep her safe until I win her return. If one hair on her head is harmed, I will dedicate my life to tracking you down and killing you."

"You can try," Hussack replied haughtily, though his eyes were shifting nervously. "But this battle has left you in much worse health than I."

"I may be wounded," Maelgyn replied, reaching out one hand dramatically. "But I am not toothless."

Maelgyn's hand closed, and the last of his magic reached out around Hussack's already-injured arm. Hussack sensed the attack in time to set up some counter-magic defenses, but they proved utterly useless. In a matter of moments, the muscles in that arm were squeezing his bones into powder, before those same muscles squeezed themselves into mush. No doctor would ever be able to heal that sort of injury.

Hussack screamed in pain, collapsing to the ground. The fear on his pale face was greater than Maelgyn could ever remember seeing in him, before, and all he could do was stutter in shock, "H-how..."

"Remember," Maelgyn snapped. "I will heal. And when I do, my wife had better be alive and unspoiled... or else that fate awaits the rest of you."

Hussack had just enough time to stagger off, a lick of steam from Khumbaya's nostril chasing him, before Maelgyn's exhaustion – both physical and magical – claimed him.

The darkness was welcome – he could still dream of Euleilla, even if she wasn't there.

Chapter X

Once the Golden Dragons arrived, the battle was quick to end. Hussack fled the battlefield, taking a portion of his surviving army, and the remaining Sho'Curlan forces were quick to surrender. On paper, it was a victory of unprecedented proportions – five Black Dragons down, tens of thousands of enemies killed, tens of thousands captured, and the rest scattered. It would take Sho'Curlas months to recover from this defeat.

The 'victory' left behind a lot of battlefield confusion, however. Euleilla was captured and Maelgyn incapacitated, leaving Sir Leno as the highest-ranking officer in the chain of command, though perhaps one of the Nekoji or wolf-riders were technically of equal or better rank.

Rumors sprang up from soldiers in the aftermath. They went everywhere from 'Maelgyn is dead' to 'The war is over and we've won.' Every one of those rumors was wrong, and most of them only led to more confusion. Someone at the top needed to quell those rumors, but there was some question as to who that might be.

Sir Leno was trying to restore some order among his forces when a summons came from the Royal Castle: The leaders of the relief army were ordered to attend Sword King Brode at once. With the doctors rushing to save Maelgyn's life, that left him to answer the call.

But there had been no meeting even after Sir Leno abandoned his soldiers to answer the summons. Brode was waiting for Maelgyn, himself, according to his majordomo, and would only meet with him. One of his 'underlings' wasn't enough. Hearing that, Sir Leno planned to rejoin his men, but the guards wouldn't let him leave. While Maelgyn's survival was still in question, he was still the ranking soldier from the battle – if Maelgyn died, he would then have to have that audience with the king. If Maelgyn lived and met with the king, Sir Leno would be permitted to leave. Until one of them met with the king, however, he was not permitted to leave the castle.

Sir Leno had practically been imprisoned in the two weeks since. He had brief meetings with some of the officers of the Royal Guard, but he wasn't being allowed to leave the Castle to attend to his duties. He was hoping that Onayari had taken command of the soldiers outside of the Castle walls in his absence, but these guardsmen couldn't even tell him that.

Until Gyato entered his suite at the castle just a few minutes ago, he'd received little in the way of accurate news at all, or answers to any of his questions. He brought Onayari with him, and Sir Leno was glad to see both of them. Finally, he might learn what was going on.

"Where is Maelgyn? What of our forces outside? Why did the king insist I grant him an audience if he won't see me? Why didn't the army inside the castle even attempt a sortie when we struck? Who—"

"We have all been asking these questions and more," Onayari interrupted. "So far, we have very few answers."

"The Sword King is seeing none of us," Gyato snorted. "I did receive a letter from El'Athras today, saying that he and his wife are on their way here with some 'information.' I would like you to be there when he arrives."

Sir Leno sighed, taking a seat. "And why is it that this is the first time I've seen you since I was summoned here?"

"We weren't allowed into the castle," Onayari snarled, letting a little of her own anger into her voice. "Nor were any of our Dwarven or Nekoji soldiers. I sent our Human cavalry back to Happaso, but the rest of our soldiers are now making camp outside of the Castle walls. We are trying to set up additional temporary fortifications to last until we are either relieved or allowed inside."

"They refused me entry until 'my identity could be verified,'" Gyato added, not sounding nearly as upset as Sir Leno imagined he would be in that sort of situation. "The Royal Court finally acknowledged the treaty Maelgyn signed with Caseificio and Mar'Tok, however, and as of last night acknowledge me as the 'Count of Caseificio.' I immediately set about arranging for El'Athras' and the Lady Wodtke's arrival. According to their message, they will be here any moment."

"We're here already, actually," El'Athras said, walking in the door with Wodtke behind him.

"You had no troubles gaining entry?" Gyato asked.

"Not especially," El'Athras said.

Wodtke snorted. "Only because he posed as my assistant instead of my husband or as the Count. The guards didn't seem to think it all that strange that the Duke of Sopan would have a personal physician, nor did they think it strange that a physician might need a strong man like a Dwarf to help her."

"Posing as someone less important than I really am is just spycraft," El'Athras said. "I am a spymaster, after all."

"Good. If you're a spymaster, you must have some answers," Sir Leno said.

"I have a few suspicions." El'Athras started grabbing chairs, arranging for everyone to sit down. "And a few pieces of news. First, though, where is Wangdu? Last I heard he was heading here."

"He was?" Sir Leno replied, startled. Even Gyato and Onayari seemed taken aback. "When? Why hasn't he visited us, here?"

The two Nekoji glanced at each other. "We have yet to see him," Gyato said.

"That's odd," El'Athras said. "He was supposed to be checking on some information in the Royal Castle's libraries, hoping they had been unspoiled in the earlier siege – where is he?"

Gyato sighed. He stepped to the door, and pointed to something outside it. After a moment, a soldier stepped in to join the five people. "Yes, your Lordship?" the soldier asked.

"We have word that an Elven companion of ours is here, but we have yet to see him. Do you know where he might be?"

The soldier immediately looked suspicious. "Well, there was an

Elf who visited shortly before the siege began. He was arrested by order of the Sword King himself! He is suspected of being the traitor who lead the Sho'Curlas army through our outer defenses."

El'Athras barked a laugh. "Give me a break. Sonny boy, I know one should never trust an Elf, but when you don't have any outer defenses to be lead through, it's pretty ridiculous to accuse someone of betraying them to the enemy. I'm not sure if the Elf you have in your prison is the one we're looking for, but if he is he's one of Svieda's most important allies."

A confused look replaced the suspicious one. "No outer defenses? But... we were told we had large armies around the castle, keeping watch on the enemy approach."

"The only large Sviedan army assembled outside of this castle is the one we left to reinforce you," Sir Leno said. "There aren't enough soldiers in Svieda to man those so-called 'outer defenses' and keep that much of a reserve force in Happaso province. Someone's lying to you, son."

The soldier swallowed. "But... the king—"

"I'm not sure that man is your king, sonny boy," El'Athras said. "Would the real Brode have left Arnach as estranged as he has? Would he have done nothing while his cousin Maelgyn was taking on five Black Dragons by himself? Again, someone is lying to you."

The guard wasn't the only one surprised by El'Athras' words. Even Gyato looked a bit startled at the implications of what was being said.

It took a moment, but the guard finally made a decision. "You... raise very interesting questions. I can take you to the Elf if you wish."

"Thank you, sonny boy. What's your name?" El'Athras replied, much more cordially than before.

"Vihanto, sir," the soldier replied, nodding to the Dwarf. "If you'll follow me?"

"Actually, I would prefer to check on his Highness, the Sword Prince Maelgyn," Wodtke spoke up. "I have been his court doctor since he was confirmed as the Duke of Sopan, and if his injuries are as severe as I've heard I'm worried about what can be done for him."

Vihanto nodded. "Of course, ma'am. I'll have one of my subordinates take you to him. If the rest of you will follow me?"

Euleilla awoke slowly, confused and disoriented. Magical fields were surrounding her everywhere, making it impossible to grasp where she was, and her *schlipf* was once again dormant and unable to help her. Her hands were bound behind her with a scratchy twine, but that wouldn't be an issue once her magic came back to her. Her head ached, however, making the concentration necessary to use magic nearly impossible.

"...drugged?" she heard. The voice was speaking in heavily accented Tel'Curlas, but despite her massive headache she was able to focus enough to understand it.

"Well, she's a First Class mage," came the reply, this voice speaking in a much clearer form of Tel'Curlas. "And all we gave her was a very strong form of Dwarven rum. She'll be fine in a few hours, but we can't allow her to use magic. The headache that brew gives Humans has been proven to disable a mage's powers for hours after they awaken."

"And why hasn't she been stripped and searched?"

Euleilla swallowed. If her magic was gone – and she was pretty sure the voices she was hearing were telling the truth about her magic being disabled for a time – there was little she could do to stop these people if they intended something... unpleasant for her.

"We had a mage do a quick scan to make sure she was fully disarmed. Any metal on her has been removed already, as have any obvious weapons or armor. As far as stripping and searching her goes... well, unless we are searching her for something specific, that isn't necessary. We felt it important to allow her to keep her dignity – Prince Hussack's orders were very clear: She is a valuable hostage and is not to be harmed or spoiled. I'm not sure of all the reasons, myself, but he was adamant on that. It was his last order before heading off to meet with High King Fitz. He was distressed about the injury to his arm, and wanted to see someone to try and save it, so I didn't question him."

"The king? That's quite a journey! Why didn't he come here, first? We have a very good doctor."

"The wounds aren't such that a normal doctor could heal him," a third voice noted gravely. "My father hopes that there may be a treatment in the ancient archives that only our High King has access to. He hopes to find one and return soon, and will decide her fate then. If he is unable to leave due to treatment after a few weeks, he will send a courier with orders for this woman's... disposition."

"Your father's arm looked beyond any hope to me, Prince Mussack," the second voice proclaimed. The name struck a chord in Euleilla's memories – the similarity to the very Prince Hussack she had battled, and stories about a childhood enemy of Maelgyn's, rattled around in her head. Mussack sounded a bit rattled about his father's injuries, whatever they were. To the best of Euleilla's knowledge, however, Mussack had not been at the battle.

"Don't say it!" Mussack screeched. "My father is the most powerful warrior our kingdom has ever known. Those ancient texts have allowed our kingdom to thrive for hundreds of years – they can restore his arm, and make him even stronger than he was before."

"If you say so," the second voice replied dubiously. "At any rate, it was his order that this woman be treated well. I believe he intends to trade her for something big, and her value would be diminished if she were spoiled."

"But as a First Class mage—" the first voice began.

"She is also the wife of one of the Swords," the second replied. "As far as being a First Class Mage is concerned... well, that's why they sent her here. The dungeons of this castle were built especially to handle mages of all classes. Prince Hussack inspected our cells to prove that, himself, before leaving her with us."

"Of course, of course." Whoever the first speaker was sounded nervous, but Euleilla couldn't determine why. At least, from what she could tell, they hadn't really searched her – if they had, they would have noticed her eyes, and they would be talking about them.

It was an advantage, albeit a small one. As long as they didn't know that she could not see, she could conceal at least one weakness from them. She'd take whatever she could. "However, we have an overcrowding issue in our prisons, thanks to the sacking of Sycanth and Svieda's Royal Castle. We only have one cell equipped for a first class mage, and there is already a... prominent person in that cell, one who we cannot move."

"Then they'll have to share. Unless there's a chance this other prisoner might, ahem, spoil her?"

"Very unlikely, but it will be difficult to manage with the both of them. We'll have to prepare the room, first. He has been given certain amenities, in accord with the laws of war, that will have to be replaced with non-magically reactive items."

"Do it," Mussack snapped. "And then I want to see your commanding officer. Thanks to our recent defeat, and the arrival of the Golden Dragons on Svieda's side, we have been forced to change strategy. Lord Knold is currently repairing the ruins of Sycanth Castle, making it defensible enough to be a permanent headquarters for our war effort's command. I have been deemed too valuable to risk, however, so I will be taking charge here until his work is done."

"Of course, your Highness," the first voice said. "I should point out that we have a visiting dignitary from the Merfolk here, discussing our recent treaty with the Oden City-State. It would be wise for you to visit with him as a courtesy."

Mussack sighed. "If you insist. But first, take care of this prisoner...."

Euleilla's head swam as she was picked up. She blacked out before she could hear any more.

"Through those doors, ma'am," Vihanto's page said to Wodtke, gesturing. He was very young for an escort, but that suited her just fine. "I am not allowed inside because I am not a doctor, but I will gladly wait out here and be your guide when you are ready to leave."

"Thank you," Wodtke said, nodding to the young man before passing through the doors, closing them behind her. She saw Maelgyn, but the doctors treating him were behind a privacy screen of some sort, and it sounded as if they were sharpening their scalpels. She immediately stepped up to see just how bad off he was.

Maelgyn was a complete mess. Every joint was swollen, his body oddly flushed and feverish, and a quick magical scan showed a number of cracked and broken bones. Detached tendons, torn muscles, and worse were revealed as her diagnosis continued. He was unconscious, but there was something odd about the way his magic seemed to be swirling all through him – it was acting in a way that shouldn't be possible unless he was awake.

A doctor and his assistant appeared from around the screen, holding various medical implements of a sort Wodtke recognized as being rather... dated. "Who are you? What are you doing here?" the doctor exclaimed, sounding alarmed.

"I'm Wodtke, the court physician for Sword Prince Maelgyn," she said by way of introduction. She was actually much more – the de facto wife consort of Count El'Athras, a member of Maelgyn's inner council, an informant for El'Athras' spy service (in fact, that was how she first met him, though she was largely inactive in that job now), and thanks to decades of practice could now call herself a Third Rate mage. However, El'Athras has been careful to caution her about just using her title of court physician until he had confirmed or refuted certain suspicions he had formed. "I just arrived, and was examining his Highness. I have been vouched for, but you may confirm my words at your leisure."

The doctor seemed to nod reluctantly at that. "I will accept your word, for now. I am too busy – I was just preparing myself for surgery."

Wodtke's eyes flickered, but she replied with only the slightest of inflections coloring her fears. "Isn't it a bit premature to go in and repair the tendons and muscles? The swelling is too severe at the moment, and that should be treated first."

The doctor blinked. "Tendons? Muscles? What are you talking about? This is to treat the swelling. And, perhaps, it will allow us to see what other damage is inside."

That sent serious alarms blaring through Wodtke's head. This doctor was a quack. She didn't immediately believe he knew he was a quack – he was probably trained in the older tradition, which employed techniques that were centuries out of date – but he would be doing more harm than good if she let him operate. He clearly did not have magic, or at least any training in using magic to make a diagnosis, and from his reaction didn't even know that such a diagnosis was possible. Which made him very dangerous – instead of just being a fraud who knew he might be wrong, like most quacks, this doctor believed he was right.

"Um, in addition to being a court physician, I am also something of a mage," Wodtke said, hoping the man would understand what she was about to say. "I can use magic to examine his injuries. He has significant damage to both tendon and muscle all over his body, which is causing the swelling. Rest and some medications such as willow bark tea can bring down the swelling to the point that those injuries can be repaired, but I fear surgical relief of the swelling may prove counter-productive at this point."

The doctor shot her a sour expression. "If what you say is true, then he needs help for his tendons and muscles as quickly as possible. Relieving the pressure—"

"Is a flawed technique," Wodtke replied. "Best used when the trouble is fluid on the knee, but that's not evident in this case because—"

"It is a technique that has been successfully employed since the Porosian days!" the doctor snapped. "It is not flawed!"

Wodtke rolled her eyes. Not one of these guys.... "You are aware that medicine, like most sciences, makes new discoveries every day? The technique you intend to use works, yes, but only in certain cases. This is not such a case."

The physician's hands tightened around his scalpel. "Then what do you suggest, doctor?"

"Well, I already mentioned willow bark tea. Beyond that, fill some goats' bladders with hot water, wrap them up for cleanliness sake, and lay them on the swollen joints. If such bladders are unavailable, find some rags – clean and absorbent ones, mind – and soak them in very hot water. Squeeze out most of the water leaving them merely damp and still quite hot. Wrap those rags around the swollen areas," Wodtke said. It was almost a word-for-word quote from a text she read when she was studying to become a doctor – if he had learned any of the techniques developed in the past century, he would know this much.

The other doctor looked horrified. "Applying extremes in temperature to the joints? But that causes rheumatism!"

That might have been true. As far as Wodtke knew, no Human doctor alive knew for certain what caused rheumatism. It was not something the best of medical science could determine, despite the leaps and bounds that medicine took when people started exploring the benefits of using magic for medical purposes. Magic as medicine was still in its infancy, old stigma from magic's days when it was inseparable from religion long preventing that kind of use.

Wodtke stayed his hand before the scalpel started to make an incision along Maelgyn's knee. "It may be a cause of rheumatism, but this is an extreme case where the risk is justified. Your over-enthusiastic carving of his flesh, however, will only worsen the symptoms, and *still* may cause rheumatism. That, again, is a point of debate in our professional community, which you would know if you ever bothered to follow the recent texts on the subject."

"The Sword King himself has made me personally responsible for the health of this man," the doctor insisted. "I will not turn over his care to someone who obviously doesn't know the basics of Porosian medicine!"

"Of course I know the basics of Porosian medicine!" Wodtke snorted disgustedly. "I also know that Porosian medicine is horribly outdated."

"Forgive me for interrupting," a gravelly voice "But can I have a say in my own treatment?"

"Maelgyn!" Wodtke started. "I... are you alright?"

"No," Maelgyn replied, struggling to lift his head and look around. "I think I'd rather avoid Porosian medicine, if I can avoid it, but perhaps there is a better treatment than even yours, doctor. Wangdu is here, yes?"

"I... I don't know," Wodtke replied. "We think he may be in the castle, but we weren't sure."

"If he is, bring him to me," Maelgyn said, letting his head fall back down. "Do nothing until then."

"But—"

"Those are my orders," Maelgyn replied, his eyes closed. "Obey them."

Both Wodtke and the castle doctor nodded. "Of course, your Highness."

El'Athras followed Vihanto down into the Royal Dungeons. If he were honest, he didn't like what he saw – they were built sturdy enough for regular humans, but someone like Wangdu, or even a sub-par mage, could escape from them easily. Despite that, it was oppressively dark and dismal. Burns on the wall and old stains where sconces once held candles made it obvious this wasn't always so – and the shape of the stains made it obvious that the change was recent.

By the time they reached Wangdu's cell, the light was so dim that even El'Athras' Dwarven eyes would have strained to see through it, were they not carrying torches. The Elf was looking somewhat ragged as he lay on his cell bunk – evidently the theory that Elves needed light to survive, or at least to stay strong, was correct. El'Athras had a strong suspicion that the lights had been removed specifically to help imprison an Elf.

"Gyato? Onayari? El'Athras? Sir Leno?" Wangdu's hoarse voice echoed across the room. "I was starting to fear... well, no matter. Where is Maelgyn?"

"His Highness was severely injured in the battle. His doctor and the Royal physician are looking after him as we speak," Vihanto said. He glanced over at Sir Leno. "I take it this is your Elf?"

El'Athras nearly sputtered at the implication an Elf could belong to anybody, but he knew the young guard didn't mean it that way. "Aye, that's Wangdu all right."

The Elf's identity confirmed, the two Nekoji left the room to watch for potential eavesdroppers. Sir Leno took one of their two lights and started using it to look for a key. The light of the torches made Wangdu's stare all the more intense. "You know, you do, yes?" he asked.

El'Athras nodded. "Well, I suspect... but that's more than any of the others know. I was about to tell them when we learned you were down here."

Wangdu glanced at the guard briefly. "Well, don't say anything just yet. There's more going on here than I realized."

Vihanto frowned, but walked over to a desk El'Athras hadn't seen before and grabbed a set of keys from it. "Come on, let me commit my treason for releasing you before you leave me in the dark."

Wangdu laughed – or tried to. His voice was so hoarse it came out more as a coughing fit. "I mean no offense, I didn't. I'm worried about discussing this with my known friends, as well, I am."

"Just tell me this, then," Vihanto said, putting the key in the lock. "Is it that my king is an impostor, or is he merely not in control of himself?"

Wangdu was so startled he didn't even walk through the gate as the door opened. "Athy? I thought you said you did not say anything to anyone, you didn't!"

El'Athras gritted his teeth. "Well, I might have implied one or two things. But call me 'Athy' ever again and friend or not, super powerful Elf or not, I will end you."

Wangdu pouted playfully. "You let Wodtke call you that, you do."

"It is physically impossible for you to do the sorts of things that are required to earn that same privilege."

"You may be surprised, you might, but fair enough." Wangdu turned back to the guard. "I'm afraid the answer to your question is 'we don't know,' it is. We have suspicions, we do, but I'm afraid to voice them – someone might take action before we're ready, they might, and that could be disastrous, it could."

"What do you mean?" Vihanto asked.

"The evidence fits both the 'impostor' and the 'controlled' theories, it does." Wangdu said. "But I believe the real Brode can be recovered, he can, whichever is the truth, it is. If we guess wrong and act hastily, we do, Brode may be killed, he might... or worse, if he is 'controlled,' he is, he may never escape that control, he might not, forever trapped inside the mind of someone else."

"I've already sent for Arnach," El'Athras said. "Maelgyn is too badly injured to play that role, so our options are limited. Once he gets here, we can act."

"Role? What role?" Sir Leno asked. "If you just need someone with the right rank, perhaps I—"

"It must be a blood relation, it must, and the closer the better," Wangdu said. "Arnach is Brode's brother, he is, which is about as close as you can get with their parents both dead, it is. Saving Brode will take a little Dwarven know-how and a lot of Elven magic, it will. Speaking of Dwarves, is Tur'Ba here, is he?"

Sir Leno winced. "I... no. The battle to break the siege was intense. Euleilla was captured, and Tur'Ba was killed protecting her. Prince Hussack killed him."

Wangdu's smile fell. "Damn. I'll have to start over, I will, and I do not know enough Dwarves, I don't. El'Athras, do you know any trustworthy types, do you? You know it will take two of you to get it done, you do."

El'Athras was slightly offended on behalf of his people, but laughed with bravado anyway. "Hah! I know a lot of trustworthy types. Tur'Ka and Tur'Tei will be traveling up with Arnach, though, and they would be the best two to help. Tur'Ba was grooming them as Dwarven Axemen with some success."

"Dwarven Axemen?" Vihanto repeated curiously. "Are there any other myths or legends I should be watching for?"

"Actually, ye—"

Before Wangdu could finish, Onayari burst through the door. "That page who was escorting Doctor Wodtke is here. Maelgyn is awake... and he wants to see Wangdu."

"He wishes to see me, he does?" Wangdu said, startled. "How did he even know I was here, did he?"

"I don't know," Onayari said. "But the boy was most insistent."

Vihanto sighed. "Just when I thought I was about to get a straight answer or two. Come on – I know a path that will get us to Maelgyn's current suite unseen. Since it'll mean my head once the king learns I let you out, my new Elf friend, I think you should follow me."

When Euleilla awoke for the second time that day, she found her head still spinning and her magic still impossible to summon... but at least she was lying on a makeshift bed of some kind instead of a cold stone floor. Her *schlipf* seemed somewhat woozy, as well, but it was able to communicate that there was only one other person in the room, who was also asleep. That would give her some time to make an assessment of her chance to escape... if her head ever stopped pounding, that is.

She rolled to a sitting position, finding herself on a fur-covered stone slab about two feet off the floor. She was undoubtedly in a "mage-proof" cell, but depending how much the designers relied on lodestones it might not be as "mage-proof" as they thought. Lodestones were a good defense against the average mage, but for someone of her level they were a distraction at best. Give her a little time, she might even be able to turn those lodestones into something she could work with to escape.

But that determination would have to wait until her magical senses were working better. For now, all she had was her groggy *schlipf* and her four functioning natural senses. And the stone slab she was resting on meant that the builders of this cell were at least smart enough not to build the bunks using iron nails.

She slowly stood up. Her *schlipf* was aware enough to give her a rough idea of where the walls, window, and door was, but that was it. Unsteadily, she reached one wall and started tracing it with her hand. It was stonework, so everything was as expected there. She slowly made her way to the door, running her hand over the stones all the way. Perhaps there was some weakness in the mortar that could be exploited, later, if she could gather enough iron together.

The door surprised her when she finally got to where she could examine it. Wooden bars – one of those particular types of hardwood known as 'ironwood,' if her guess was right, though there was no iron in them. The hinge was metal, but nothing she could touch magically. Copper or bronze of some form, perhaps, but nothing magically reactive.

She tried to cross the room to check on the window, but her *schlipf* wasn't sensing the dangers around her well enough to spot uneven flooring. Her foot tripped over a raised stone and she found herself tumbling to the ground. She tried – unsuccessfully – to turn her fall into a roll, but she managed to avoid further injuring herself, thankfully.

The clatter of her nearly completing an accidental somersault awoke her fellow prisoner, however. "Huh? Who goes there?"

Euleilla took a moment to regain her composure before answering. She had no idea who this was, other than that he was supposed to be a high ranking Sviedan who Sho'Curlas was holding captive. Of course, that might just be a ploy to gather intelligence from her... so her best bet was to give as little information as possible.

Perfect.

"Euleilla," she said. The Sho'Curlan's already knew her name. Anything they already knew was safe to mention... as long as she refused to elaborate any further. Just her specialty.

"You aren't some whore they brought in for my benefit, are they?"

"No," she replied, not allowing herself any physical response to the unpleasant suggestion.

"Good. Because I don't care what they bribe me with, I'm not betraying my people or my family," the other prisoner said. Euleilla heard him moving around, but couldn't really tell what he was doing, so she decided to continue her exploration as if he wasn't there. She felt the bars on the window – ironwood, just like the door. And too small even for her to crawl out.

Her exploration complete, she went back to her bunk and sat down, taking a meditative position. Her head wasn't hurting quite as bad as when she first woke – perhaps some mental exercises could help her focus enough to regain her magical senses.

"I don't suppose you have any news of the outside world?" the other prisoner asked. "They don't tell me much, in here."

"Nope," she shot back, not letting him break her concentration. She supposed she could have safely regaled him with talk of the latest battle, but better not to say anything.

The old man huffed in annoyance. "Great. Well, how did you come to be put in this fine Sho'Curlan establishment? I figure we can trade war stories, at least."

Euleilla shrugged. "Captured."

"Well, I figured you were captured, but where? When? Heck, why? And why did they send you here – there must be prisons closer to the front lines than this old castle."

Stretching out her senses, Euleilla found she could sense the other prisoner when she focused. It wasn't coming quite as naturally to her as it usually did – whatever they drugged her with, it was effective.

"Mage," she explained, continuing the one word game. Her *schlipf* was giving her no significant danger warnings about this person, so perhaps he wasn't a spy. In fact, even though she was certain she had never met the man before in his life, there was something... familiar about him. Still, none of her senses were working quite right, so she decided to keep the one-word game going until things cleared up some more.

That seemed to anger her fellow prisoner, but he calmed down quickly enough. "Well, that was abrupt... but I suppose no more abrupt than I have been. You gave me your name, but I have yet to give you mine. Perhaps then you'll tell me something about what's been going on outside this jail cell."

She shrugged noncommittally. "Perhaps."

"Allow me to present myself – I am Nattiel, Sword Prince of Svieda, Duke of Rubick, Captain of the Guard of the Sviedan Royal Castle, and very briefly acting as the Royal Regent of Svieda."

Euleilla nearly fell off her furs. She detected no lie in his voice, and her *schlipf* was insisting that he was telling the truth as well. Perhaps the one-word game should end, after all... for the moment, at least. She still wouldn't tell him everything.

"Well," she began. "In that case, I *might* have a bit of news about your son...."

Chapter XI

Doctor Wodtke wasn't entirely sure what Maelgyn was hoping Wangdu could do for him. The Elf was wise, and had more years of education than any Human, but he was not a doctor. Since it would take Wangdu some time to arrive, she had at least convinced everyone present to allow her to brew and administer some willow bark tea – they all agreed that couldn't hurt anything. She had also talked Maelgyn into allowing her to start her hot towel treatments.

"Anything that won't slow Wangdu down is fine with me," Maelgyn had said, even after the so-called "Royal Physician" objected.

"Slow Wangdu down from doing what?" she had asked.

Maelgyn refused to say. So, after setting the physician and his apprentice to work on brewing the tea (thankfully, the use of that medicine was taught even in the classic Porosian school that they had studied under), she went off to heat some towels.

When she returned a few minutes later with some clean towels and a large scrubbing bucket full of hot water to find the room filled with people and the physician being held against the wall at Sir Leno's swordpoint.

"What's going on here?" she asked fiercely. "This is a hospital!"

"Sorry, love," El'Athras said, stepping out from behind the room's privacy screen carrying the pot the doctor had been making his batch of willow bark tea in. "Your doctor friend, here, was about to run out of the room screaming that the prisoner was escaping, and we figured this was much less distressing for Maelgyn."

"Prisoner?" Wodtke asked.

He gestured over at Wangdu with his thumb. "For some reason, Wangdu was arrested for the high crime of reading books in the Royal Archives."

"It was more for the crime of catching the supposed king trying to sabotage the Royal Archives, it was," Wangdu said. "I've taken steps to prevent him from trying again, I have, and he was not going to release me until I allowed him to do so, he wasn't."

"Lies!" The doctor cried. "Why would the king try to sabotage his own Archives?"

"Because he isn't the king," El'Athras said. "Or, if he is, he's not in control of himself."

"What are you talking about?" the doctor asked. A glare from the old Dwarf shut him up.

Maelgyn slowly lifted his head, much to Wodtke's distress. He wasn't supposed to move – in fact, should not have been able to move – for some time. "Does this have something to do with that... incident in Sopan's libraries?" He didn't sound surprised.

"It seems likely, it does," Wangdu agreed. "But the culprit was not an Elf this time, he wasn't."

Maelgyn sighed, dropping his head back against the pillow. "Well... I should have expected it. They have long-term plans, but I knew they hadn't touched the Royal library before this war started; this is too good an opportunity for them to pass up. Well, if it really is them, do you think we could get fake-Brode to make sensible decisions on behalf of the kingdom, if for no other reason than to keep up the appearance of being who he claims to be?"

"You do not seem surprised that Brode might not be who he says he is," El'Athras noted.

"Of course it's not the real Brode!" Maelgyn snorted. "I've known *that* since we got back from the Borden Isles. The real Brode would not have let the reserve camp fall into the state it's in. The real Brode would have been glad to have allies wherever he could get them, not exiled them just because they were Dwarves or Nekoji. The real

Brode would have ridden out of the castle in a sortie once it became clear that we were there to break the siege."

"And you said nothing?" Wodtke asked, a little surprised.

"Well, no-one else said anything," Maelgyn said. "Even though it should have been blatantly obvious even to those who didn't know him intimately."

"I wasn't sure. I'm still not," El'Athras said. "I was getting before and after reports contrasting Brode's behavior now with what it was before he became king. The difference was too great to be normal, but only the Merfolk have enough talent for physical impersonation to fool all the people who have seen him since he ascended to the throne. Given my past experience with them, I wouldn't think a Merfolk capable of the basic language requirements needed to impersonate someone for this long."

"The only time I spoke directly with one of their kind, he sort of sounded like me when I try to speak Elvish," Maelgyn admitted. "I can understand Elvish well enough, when spoken, but I never could grasp the concept of bifurcated verbs well enough to conjugate them properly."

"That is a common Human failing, it is. But many Merfolk can speak Human tongues far better than they let on, they can," Wangdu said. "They pretend to speak poorly when in their true form, they do, but most of their warriors and spies are fluent in many languages, they are. They are even good with Elven languages, they are, and don't seem to have a problem grasping those bifurcated verbs, they do not."

Wodtke chuckled along with everyone else, but she and all the Humans in the room looked decidedly uncomfortable. She couldn't get a grip on those bifurcated verbs, either.

"Fortunately, Svieda's fate does not depend on a Human's ability to speak Elvish," Maelgyn said. "Back to my question – do you think fake-Brode will make rational decisions?"

"Eh... depends," El'Athras said, pouring the willow bark tea into a cup. "If he really is a Merfolk pretending to be a human, he might if he could be made to understand why it is a rational decision from a Human perspective. His existing policy of isolationism to the point of insanity fits with that mentality, come to think of it – it's not like the Porosians ever really cared who their allies were in the past, after all, and the Merfolk frequently work as mercenaries, but never as allies."

Maelgyn looked like he wanted to say more, but was stopped when El'Athras started helping him drink his medicinal tea. That prompted Wodtke to remember that he still needed treatment. She started soaking towels in the basin's hot water and applying them to his joints.

But Maelgyn wasn't the only one with questions. "What makes you think the king is a Merfolk?" the doctor asked, still pinned to the wall by the point of Sir Leno's blade. "I mean, that's the sort of thing I think I would have noticed in my position."

"Just how have you examined him, have you, that you would have noticed, you would?" Wangdu asked, taking a close look at Maelgyn's injuries.

"Well... just the routine services that a court physician would normally grant his king," the doctor admitted. "I... I've never performed surgery on him or anything like that, but I examined his hand when it was injured. Broke a knuckle and three fingers, he did."

"He wasn't bleeding?" Sir Leno asked, curious. "Have you ever seen him bleeding?"

The doctor hesitated. "No... I can't recall ever seeing him bleed. Not even a small cut, come to think of it... but most small cuts would be cleaned before I saw him, as frequently as... he... bathes. You know, he might really be a Merfolk in disguise! He takes at least three baths a day, which is far from normal. But he breathes as normal as a regular Human, and he has a Human pulse."

"Merfolk can mimic human breathing, they can," Wangdu said. "But they need to soak in water to maintain their transformative abilities, they do."

"Well, it doesn't matter whether he is or not," Maelgyn said, having finished his tea. Wodtke was applying the last hot compress. She took the basin to the small section of the room behind the privacy screen, where a small fireplace was available to re-heat the water with. "He isn't the Brode I knew, and that's enough for me to worry about the real Brode. And it appears the kingdom is being run by a foreign power, which would normally be our top priority. But... but I don't think we can afford to do anything about it, right now."

That statement drew a large chorus of "What!" from everyone in the room. Even the Royal doctor looked surprised.

Maelgyn sighed. "It's hard to understand, I know. Trust me – if we took action against him now, we'd leave Svieda open to conquest from within."

"What do you mean by that?" El'Athras said. "It seems to me that as things are, Svieda has already been conquered from within."

"Not really – right now, all we've got is an interregnum," Maelgyn said. "The rest of the country just doesn't know it, yet. If fake-Brode were to die, now, the country would return to the rightful heir to the throne, and all of the damage he's done can be reversed... assuming we last long enough in our war against Sho'Curlas to fix things, that is. But if we were to take action now, the Law of Swords will have to be rewritten... and I'm fairly confident fake-Brode has put people in place who would rebuild it to match the goals of the Porosian Conspiracy."

Sir Leno pulled away from the doctor long enough to look at Maelgyn in confusion. "The Law of Swords? I'm as familiar with them as most Sviedans, your Highness, and even I don't understand that one."

"Look... Onayari and Gyato are standing guard outside, correct? Let them in – I don't want to have to repeat myself. This is giving me enough of a headache as it is."

Wodtke, who had just walked back around the privacy screen, was the first to the door. She beckoned Gyato and Onayari inside, and they were joined by the young guard who had helped them find Wangdu. The door closed behind him, and she thought she heard it lock after them.

"What are we needed for?" Gyato asked.

"His Highness is just about to explain how removing an impostor from the throne of Svieda will somehow destroy the kingdom because of the Law of Swords," El'Athras said. "He thought you should hear it."

Gyato looked a little startled at that one, and he glanced over at the native Sviedans in the room. None of them seemed to know any better than he. "I... don't know what to make of that one."

Maelgyn laughed. "Look, I understand. Most of you are at least vaguely aware of what the Law of Swords entails, but I'm fairly certain none of you have ever been forced to memorize the entire thing. Even if you have, none of you have ever been given several years of instruction in it, complete with exercises in figuring out what happens in various 'what-if' scenarios. Thanks to poor old Troubuxet, however, I did... and I suspect whoever put fake-Brode on the throne has figured it out, too."

"Your Highness," Vihanto said. "While I have not studied things as much as you must have with the late Royal tutor, I have read the entire law a time or two, yet I cannot see where you are going with this."

"I know," Maelgyn said. "That's why it's so clever. Look – how many of the Swords who, before this war started, could assume the throne are now unable to?"

"Um..." Vihanto said, not sure how to answer that one.

"The king and his sister are dead, so that's two," El'Athras said. "Your father has been captured. Idril and Ambrosius are missing. Hm... I think that's it."

"It's enough. Of the ten, five are unavailable. One – the Sword of the Borden Isles – was vacant. That leaves me, Arnach, Wybert, and Brode. We depose fake-Brode without finding the real Brode first, and he's gone, too."

"That still leaves three," Vihanto said. "But—"

"The Law of Swords is a complicated document," Maelgyn said. "Designed to ensure the line of succession would always be clear, smooth, and peaceful, it was written with contingencies for contingencies for contingencies. Unfortunately, all of those sections devoted to preventing infighting among the Swords will work against us, in this case."

"Surely, in all of those contingencies, there was a method for deposing of an impostor on the throne," El'Athras said.

"There is," Vihanto agreed, frowning. "If I remember correctly, any of the Swords may make the challenge that one of the other Swords is an impostor."

"And if you make the challenge without presenting the real Sword as proof?" Maelgyn prompted.

"You... sacrifice your own Sword."

"Correct. If I challenged fake-Brode's bonafides, I lose my status as a Sword," Maelgyn said.

"A costly sacrifice, to be sure," Gyato said. "But you implied this could bring about the downfall of Svieda. As important as we all know you are on the battlefield, surely there is more to it than this."

"Of course there is," Maelgyn said. "I am not that self-centered. No... it's more than that. Think to how Brode was named the Sword King – who vouched for him? Arnach, right?"

"Vouched?" El'Athras said. "I don't think anyone thought him a fraud before he took the throne, so I'm not sure why anyone would need to have vouched for him."

"The Law of Swords strikes again," Maelgyn said. "Remember how, when I took the title of Duke of Sopan, I had to be confirmed by Duke Valfarn and Sopan's parliament?"

"Of course," El'Athras said.

"The Law of Swords includes several layers of contingency plans in the event that a Sword is not capable of fulfilling his duties. They must be judged fit to rule, by with standards written by each provincial government, or else a regent takes their place. The Law of Swords, however, dictates what those standards are for the Sword King. Namely, the Council of the Royal Province of Svieda must confirm him after a majority of delegations from Svieda's nine other provinces vote to accept his leadership, and then the regent surrenders the crown. If the Royal Regent believes the Sword King candidate to be incompetent, he may appeal the Sword King's right to rule, at which point the remaining Swords, themselves, must come to the Royal Province to vote on the matter personally. None of this could have happened, as the Regent was captured, the Council of the Royal Province of Svieda was destroyed with the fall of the castle, and none of the provinces has had the time or ability to send a delegation to the castle."

"Then... Brode was never officially the Sword King?" Wodtke asked hesitantly.

It was Sir Leno who answered that one with a shake of the head. "There are always contingencies in the Law of Swords. Let me see... if, due to pestilence or war – which this certainly qualifies as – the provinces are unable to send their own delegations to the Royal Province, the Council may act alone in appointing the Sword King... provided he is vouched for by one of the other Swords in person. But, as his Highness said, the Council was destroyed, so...."

"So there must have been a makeshift council in place at the time," Maelgyn said. He turned to the Royal physician. "Correct me if I'm wrong, but no permanent council has been seated since Brode was placed on the throne, yes?"

The doctor hesitated. "I... no, the council has not been seated. We've kept the members of the makeshift council on for now, but—"

"But the permanent council hasn't been formed, yet," Maelgyn finished. "Thought as much."

"What does that have to do with the Law of Swords?" Vihanto asked. "A makeshift council can rule for years without causing any crisis. The only thing you require a permanent council for is determining where the lines of succession go to replace the dead Swords."

"I'm getting there," Maelgyn said. "Now, what are the consequences if one Sword successfully challenges the right to rule for a vouched Sword King?"

"Well," Vihanto said, squinting as he tried to remember. "That's an obscure one. I think, if a vouched Sword King is deposed by a challenge, then the challenger, the Sword King, and the Sword who vouched for him are all ejected from the line of succession."

"Assuming Arnach vouched for him—"

"He did," the doctor said.

"—if we were to depose fake-Brode, Arnach would be ejected from the line of succession, too. That leaves old, legless Wybert as the only Sword who can take the throne. It would be a simple thing for an assassin to kill Wybert, at that point. At this point, without a permanent council, there would be no-one in line for the throne after him."

Vihanto's eyes widened. "The Law of Swords would be abrogated! And without a permanent council ruling Svieda, there is no legal way to declare who would be next in line for the throne. We would have to look through the Royal Archives to find the older laws in order to restore the line of succession."

"A job for the Royal Archivist," Maelgyn said. "I'm guessing that position was one of the first that fake-Brode filled upon assuming the throne?"

"Yes," the doctor said. At this point, even though Sir Leno's attention was elsewhere, he was still slumped against the wall. He looked to be in a daze. "Yes, though I've never met the man."

"My guess is that the current Royal Archivist is one of the members of the Porosian Conspiracy," Maelgyn said. "With such a man in charge, he can replace the historic laws that no-one has bothered studying in hundreds of years with fake documents, like they were doing in Sopan, which could be the beginning of the end for Svieda."

"Damn," El'Athras said. "So... what's the solution?"

"The ideal solution would be to find the real Brode and put him on the throne," Maelgyn said. "Replacing the impostor with the true Brode will eliminate all of the consequences for myself, Arnach, and anyone else."

"And the less than ideal solution?" El'Athras said.

As Maelgyn answered him, Wodtke checked the state of his hot towels. They were cooling quickly, so she started to remove them. "We do nothing until fake-Brode dies naturally, trying to preserve the archives and restore the other Swords to power once he's gone, or do it all anyway and let the Porosian Conspiracy begin its slow march to victory. Poros would be a better choice of master than the Sho'Curlans, at least."

"I would not be so sure of that, I wouldn't," Wangdu said. "Not as long as there are Elves at the heart of the conspiracy, there are."

"I'd rather not have either as a master, myself," El'Athras said. "Once we've confirmed to ourselves that the Brode on the throne is an impostor, I'll set about to find us the real Brode to rescue."

"Do that," Maelgyn said. "But in the meantime, there's something else I want you to do."

"And that is?"

Wodtke removed the last of the hot cloths, but a look of extreme pain erupted on Maelgyn's face when she did. It took his next words to see that this pain had nothing to do with her ministrations, and there was nothing she could do for this pain.

"I do not know if I can convince a Porosian agent with the mindset of a Merfolk of the need to exchange Sho'Curlan prisoners for our own," he said. "Which means the only way to get my wife back is to go and rescue her. Find my wife, spymaster El'Athras. I don't believe I will get her back unless we go and save her, ourselves."

"...and now you tell me that my son married some commoner witch? By accident?" Nattiel said, summarizing what Euleilla had just told him.

She had been very careful not to reveal too much. She still wasn't certain that it was safe to reveal any secrets to the man, but there were plenty of things she could say that were public knowledge outside of the prison. She had also been careful not to reveal her own relationship with Nattiel's son, instead glossing over that part of the story by referring to herself in the third person.

"I suppose that's one way of looking at it, yes," she agreed.

"And she's a mage, too," he sighed. "I told him not to get involved in magic, but he never listens."

Euleilla cocked her head. She was unaware of any strife between Maelgyn and Nattiel before this, though she did recall him saying something about how his father had abruptly ended his training as a mage, at one point. "Is there something wrong with mages?"

Nattiel shrugged. "They're – I mean your kind are fine people, I'm sure, but Maelgyn... my son is a Sword Prince of Svieda, the Duke of Sopan! Magecraft is useful if you're a common soldier or you're mass producing some sort of metalwork. It really isn't useful for much more than that. Maelgyn is not going to be a common soldier or some sort of tinker – magecraft is a completely worthless skill for him. He needs to know the fine arts of diplomacy, politics, bureaucracy, history, the law, that kind of thing. Whenever he studies magic, he loses the time he desperately needs to learn those things."

"You don't seem to have suffered by becoming a skilled swordsman, if what I've heard is to be believed." Euleilla didn't actually know if Nattiel was a good swordsman, nor a good Sword Prince, but after holding the Sviedan capital as long as he did it made sense.

"Do you know how long it takes to train someone in magic?" Nattiel said.

If she had working eyes, she would have shot him an incredulous glance. "I... might have some idea, yes."

"Years! And I don't just mean for a one-hour class now and then. Children are stripped away from their parents for years to undergo Mage training. Learning the sword takes a few hours a day, but it doesn't require anything close to the amount of time a mage spends." He paused. "You're said you were a mage, didn't you?"

"Yes."

"And how long each day do you have to spend training?"

Euleilla frowned. "When I was very young, several hours a day. But after using it on a regular basis for as long as I have, my magic has now become instinctive – I don't spend any time in actual practice, unless I'm trying to learn something new."

There was a long moment of silence. Euleilla wished she could see the man's face – this sort of pause could mean anything – but she couldn't. She could sometimes use magic to read the emotions on a persons face as easily as some people could by watching them, but her magical senses were still too 'blurry.'

"How long did it take you to get to the point you didn't need to practice regularly?" he finally asked.

"I was about ten or eleven years old, I'd guess," Euleilla said, considering. "Maybe a bit older. I had some pretty strong incentives to learn quickly, though – most mages don't get to that point before they're fourteen or fifteen. But all mages – and I am no exception – have regular schooling in a number of other subjects while we learn magic. You can only practice so much in one day before you risk overtaxing your magical reserves."

Nattiel gave a long sigh. "My late wife, may her soul forever find peace, was a mage. I don't think she ever reached that point, and she was in her thirties when she died."

"How did she die?" Euleilla asked. The question was a delaying tactic – something from Nattiel's story wasn't adding up.

"No-one really knows," Nattiel said. "She was alive one day and dead the next – stiff as a board, too. At first I thought she might have been poisoned, but our doctors never could find any proof."

"There are poisons that even the Elves cannot detect," Euleilla said. Most of those poisons were made by the Elves, themselves, but she wasn't going to mention that. "So, Maelgyn's mother was a mage. Maelgyn is a mage, as well. From what I gather, it is one of the only traits he shares with his mother... and you object to him learning magic for what reason?"

"I let her put him in that damned magic school as a babe, didn't I?" Nattiel snapped. "I don't object to him knowing magic at all – just to the amount of time he would need to focus on it. If he married another mage, though, he's probably changing his attention back to magic, again, instead of his studies, like he should."

Euleilla almost laughed. "Yes, he's probably focusing on his magical talent again. There are rumors going around that his magical skill has reached legendary levels. People are calling him a high mage."

"Oh, great – more distractions for my son. And you? Would you call him a 'high mage?'"

It was fun, pretending she didn't actually know Maelgyn, but Euleilla considered revealing herself to Nattiel right then. He still seemed hostile to the idea of Maelgyn marrying a mage, however. Until she broke down the real reason why that was, she would play it coy.

"Well, he fought a magical duel to the deal with Sword King Paljor while reclaiming the Borden Isles and won. Paljor was definitely a high mage, as he killed a Golden Dragon by himself, with magic alone. I suppose Maelgyn would qualify, yes."

"That's exactly what I'm talking about!" Nattiel said, sounding frustrated. "As a Sword Prince, Maelgyn's role should have been as an ambassador – he should have used his words, not done deeds, to win the Borden Isles. If action needed to be taken, that's what he has nobles for! Instead, he went in as some sort of magical warrior – something I know my boy doesn't have in him – and fought a duel with their king."

"We *did* win the Borden Isles back in that duel," Euleilla reminded him, trying to keep the incredulity out of her voice and not quite succeeding. "That should count for something."

Nattiel didn't bother to argue, he just snorted. "My boy should not be frivolously playing at being a mage. This is war time – he needs to act like a leader. Mages are servants, not leaders."

Euleilla paused, again uncertain where this was coming from; it certainly did not fit her understanding of Svieda's traditions. "Milord... you are aware that the laws of Svieda were written to ensure that the nobility would provide a large supply of mages to our armies. Surely you aren't saying the nobility are all servants?"

"The nobles, sure! And if it had been a noblewoman Maelgyn had married, and she was coincidentally a mage, that would have been one thing. But Maelgyn is more than a noble; he is a *royal*, and that means he can't afford the time for that sort of thing."

Euleilla's temper flared briefly. "And yet the symbols of royalty in Svieda are *Swords* for a reason, milord; our kings and princes are *required* to take up arms in defense of our country, and not just with words alone. As you yourself must have done in the castle, to uphold your oaths."

Nattiel said nothing. Euleilla could not tell if her words struck a nerve, or if Nattiel was simply incredulous at being called on the carpet by a commoner, but she continued. "If it helps, I heard his wife was made a baronet in Sopan after they arrived," Euleilla said. She hadn't really thought much about the title, but it would hopefully be a sop to people like Nattiel who thought she was too 'common' to be the spouse of one of the Swords.

"That's just a publicity stunt," Nattiel snorted. "No, the reason a noblewoman would have been acceptable is that she would have inevitably had training in the fine arts of politics and diplomacy – skills she could have helped Maelgyn with. A commoner is incapable of learning such skills to that level, however."

"I see," Euleilla said.

She still wasn't sure what Nattiel's real issues were with her and Maelgyn. He seemed strangely hypocritical about the whole thing – he had married a mage, himself. He spent a great deal of his time learning skills with the sword instead of the so-called fine arts of politics and diplomacy. Yet still he condemned Maelgyn, who used his magical skills to take back the Borden Isles – an action Svieda had been unsuccessfully trying to accomplish for almost a century, using fleets of ships and armies of men.

She lay back down on the furs, no longer really listening as he continued to rant. She had a lot to think about. What was the story behind Maelgyn's mother? Why was Nattiel so hostile towards Maelgyn's magical studies? And what could she do to soften the blow when Nattiel learned who she really was?

And then she had to plan her escape. Maelgyn was probably worried about her, after all.

Chapter XII

Treating Maelgyn's condition was monotonous work. Wodtke still wasn't sure why he had asked for Wangdu, though she caught them chatting quietly a few times as she worked, but he'd allowed her to treat him as if her plan was the only way to proceed.

The heat from the towels wasn't lasting. This wasn't like in Mar'Tok, where they had perfected a method for running hot water directly into your home – she could not close the doors, run the hot water, and make things warm and steamy enough that the hot towels kept their temperature for a while. Instead, she was constantly boiling water in a kettle, either fixing willow bark tea or re-heating the hot towels that she was constantly changing.

She considered just asking for a bathing tub to be brought into the room, allowing Maelgyn to relax in hot water instead of constantly changing hot towels, but there was a problem of logistics: Wangdu was still hiding in the room, and the Royal Physician was still their prisoner... though he seemed a lot more sympathetic about their cause ever since they made their convincing argument that Brode was an impostor. It would take a team of servants to bring a bathing tub in and fill it with hot water, and they couldn't keep their secrets with that many people wandering in and out of the room.

Trying to make herself busy in between refreshing the hot towels, she sat down at Maelgyn's bedside and started examining the one area he absolutely refused to allow her hot towel treatment to be employed: The wrist in which his *schlipf* was implanted.

To her surprise, that wrist was less damaged than any of his other joints. The skin was a still a mottled red, but there was little or no inflammation remaining. Even the knuckles in that hand, which often showed the most swelling, seemed relatively normal. The only oddity was some dark markings she couldn't identify deep under his skin, centered around the worst of the red mottling.

"That's Sekhar's doing," Maelgyn said as she was examining them.

Wodtke was surprised Maelgyn was even awake – many of their companions were still setting up bunks for the night, but it was time for them all to sleep, and he needed his sleep more than most. Even his eyes were closed, but he still must have been awake.

"Excuse me?"

"My wrist and hand? My *schlipf*, Sekhar, has been healing the damage, himself. It hasn't been comfortable, but he can treat the areas his roots expand into. He can't safely push his root system much further up my arm than the joint of my elbow, however, so you'll have to keep working on the rest of my joints for now."

Wodtke was a little stunned. While they were all in Sopan, she had read up the available literature on *schlipf* abilities. The ability to extend or shorten a Human's lifespan was mentioned (though most of what she read focused on the shortening), but there was nothing mentioned regarding any healing talents one might have.

"I see," she said.

"So, how soon before I can walk again?" he asked.

It took a moment for her mind to shift topics from the *schlipf* to his knees. "It depends on how long it takes for the swelling to go down," she said. "I have to warn you, though – as badly damaged as your joints are, don't be surprised if some things never fully heal."

His reply to that was so long in coming that Wodtke wondered if he might have fallen asleep, after all. "I'm sure you would normally be right... but I have no choice. My body must heal, and soon."

"I don't think it's a choice at all," Wodtke argued. "I'm doing whatever I can, but I'm not sure there's all that much I can do, so—"

"I will heal," Maelgyn insisted. "The more you can do, the better –

the less painful things will be in the end. The faster I can get walking and exercising, the better."

Wodtke nodded, though she wasn't entirely sure what he was talking about. "We don't want your muscles atrophying, like they started to when you were first adjusting to that *schlipf*. Exercise may even help with the rheumatism I fear may result from all of this swelling in your joints, but you *must* rest first to let that inflammation go down."

"I suspect I'll always know before it rains, after this," Maelgyn laughed. There was another long silence, and again Wodtke started thinking he had fallen asleep. "Doctor... my wife and I... we only had one 'time' together. It was only days before the battle. What are the chances that she is... is..."

Wodtke's eyes widened. To be honest, she thought they had been together many times, in that way, since they arrived in Sopan. But he was asking about the possibility of Euleilla being with child, so....

"It is possible," she said. "I would not dwell on it – the chances are not all that high after just a single... encounter. Things have been very stressful lately, and that tends to reduce the chances of that sort of thing happening. But even if it did, Sho'Curlas – for all its faults – keeps to the International War Accords; they will not harm a prisoner-of-war if she doesn't give them cause to. The accords say that if she's pregnant, they must release her to us should she swear out a parole."

"They kept to the International War Accords when they were our allies, true," Maelgyn agreed. "But then they kept to our treaty of alliance, too, until the day they stormed the borders at Sycanth and murdered my uncle, the Sword King Gilbereth."

"Don't borrow trouble, your Highness," Sir Leno said, stepping over to the bed. He had a set of heavy furs with him, and a bronze pan that reminded Wodtke of....

"Is that a bedwarmer?" she asked incredulously. They were almost unheard of in Mar'Tok; they had been increasingly unnecessary since the development of hot running water allowed people to heat their homes even without a fire. Honestly, Wodtke hadn't even remembered they existed until Sir Leno showed up with one.

"I've seen how difficult things are for you, trying to keep Maelgyn's joints warmed," he said. "I know you want moist heat, but I think that we can rig something up between those wet towels and this thing that will allow you to get some sleep, tonight."

"Thank you, Sir Leno," Wodtke said, bowing. "I have to admit, I wasn't looking forward to staying up all night just to keep the water warm."

Sir Leno handed her the bedwarming pan with a nod. It was cold, but she had an ember-filled fire going that would warm it up quick enough.

"I couldn't help but overhear," he said, turning to Maelgyn. "Your Highness, you have enough troubles to worry about. Your wife would not be happy to learn you lost sleep *fearing* the possibility that she might be with your child. You should not borrow trouble."

"You're right," Maelgyn said, releasing a deep breath that Wodtke never realized he'd taken. "On all counts. But I have a hard time letting go – my dreams have turned the happy occasions of my time with her into nightmares. It would help if I just knew where she was – if I knew, for a fact, that she was in one of the nearby prison facilities they have, and wasn't being transported deeper into Sho'Curlas where Hrabak might decide to experiment with her or Hussack might decide to do... worse. I don't trust Sho'Curlas to keep to the Accords."

Sir Leno nodded. "El'Athras is your spymaster, and he is on the job, your Highness, but it will take him some time to find that information. If you would like, however, I can question some of the soldiers here in the castle – if Sho'Curlas is violating the Accords, they very well may hear rumors even before your spies do."

"Thank you, Sir Leno," Maelgyn said, yawning. A few moments later and a soft snore could be heard.

Wodtke stood, once more walking to that section of the room hidden by the privacy screen, carrying the bedwarmer over to the lone source of fire in the room. Sir Leno, after taking a moment to add some furs to Maelgyn's bed, followed her.

"He's going to have a rough time of it," he said, watching her add coals to the heating chamber of the bedwarmer. "And I'm not just talking about his injuries."

Wodtke nodded. "He seems cheerful enough, but there's something off about him. It's almost like he thinks he can just heal himself in an instant, but that he's waiting for something first –

maybe to hear that Euleilla is safe or something like that."

"Maybe," Sir Leno said. "I know if my wife had been captured in battle, I wouldn't feel like I could do anything right until she was back with me. Well, if I were married, that is."

"I just hope he isn't going to try using magic to wish all his injuries away. It doesn't work like that, and he could do himself far more harm than good by trying," Wodtke sighed. "He's a difficult patient, especially without Euleilla here to keep watch on him."

"I don't think that's his plan," Sir Leno said. "He's clearly been using his time laid up in bed to think – I'm still surprised how much he'd thought through the possibility of replacing fake-Brode – so I don't think he'd do anything that hot-headed. I've been practically locked up in my room for a week, myself, and I didn't think through any of what he's come up with."

"Well, he's got something in mind," Wodtke said. "I just wish I knew what it was."

Arnach read the missive from El'Athras with some hesitation. There was something wrong with Brode, no question about that, and somehow his presence was needed to figure out which of the possible things that could have happened to him had happened.

"Is something wrong, cousin?" Wybert asked, stomping into the tent on his two pegs.

"Possibly," Arnach said. "No, actually I'm pretty sure there is – I'm just not sure what I'm supposed to be able to do about it."

"Well, then... talk to me," Wybert said. "I've got less to do, here, than you do – I could use the distraction."

Arnach waved the letter he'd just read at Wybert. "Not for long – I'm about to leave camp and put you in charge. I've been summoned to the Royal Castle."

"Huh. Well, not that surprising, now that it looks like things will be safe there for a time," Wybert said. "So what troubles you?"

"Brode isn't the one who summoned me," Arnach said, handing Wybert the letter. "And it sounds like things are going to be real complicated when I get there."

Wybert quickly scanned over the message and let out a slow whistle. "I sort of suspected something when I got here, but..."

"They don't have any proof, really," Arnach said. "Not when they sent that, at least – that's what they need me for."

"They need you to straighten things out," Wybert said. "So you'll have to go, of course."

"Of course," Arnach said, fists clenching. "But... look. You weren't here, so you wouldn't know – I had to vouch for Brode."

The letter slipped from Wybert's hand. "Oh... oh, cousin, I'm sorry. But maybe he's really who he says he is – he... I don't know. Maybe someone's blackmailing him or something?"

"Do you really think there's anything someone could hold over Brode's head that would make him act the way he has these past few months?" Arnach asked. "If things go the way I fear they must, either you or Maelgyn will become Sword King... and I will be ejected from the family."

"Only from the line of succession – never the family," Wybert was quick to counter. "The law can't compel us to kick you out of the family."

"Idril and Ambrosius are missing. Nattiel's in enemy hands. With just two surviving Swords... how will Svieda survive? The Royal Province is nothing but a battleground, right now – there is no way to restore the council to permanent status without circumventing the same Law of Swords it is in place to enforce. That means there is no way to determine the line of succession without going to the old laws. Under those, that Nekoji friend of Maelgyn's – Gyato, I think his name was – would become our king, as he has ruled over his province continuously longer than any of the surviving regents or Swords."

"Arguable, though I'm not sure the laws would consider being the Emperor of the Empire of Caseificio and Count of County Caseificio to be the same position," Wybert mused. "One is ruler of a foreign empire, the other is ruler of Svieda's newest province. Actually, under the old laws, your claim to the throne would be re-instated, and I think it would go back to your hands – you've ruled Happaso for exactly two months longer than I've ruled Largo."

"Don't joke about that," Arnach snapped. "The Law of Swords has kept our family intact for far longer than any other dynastic government. Poros, which our old laws were based on, was destroyed by familial infighting over the line of succession, and Oregal seems to break out into a civil war every fourth or fifth generation because they never seem to know who rules when the latest 'Hereditary Dictator' dies. Going back to the old laws, now, would be devastating."

"The Law of Swords only worked because our family was always so large," Wybert mused. "If we couldn't easily figure out who the king and the nine people closest to him in succession were, things would be a lot more difficult for us. Well, guess what? Our family's taken a pretty big hit, these past few months. I'm not saying the Law of Swords should be significantly altered... but if it collapses, something will need to be done to fix it. And under the old laws, you'd actually have the power to make those kinds of changes."

"Changes?" Arnach said incredulously. "What sort of 'changes' should a person like me make to a document the likes of the Law of Swords? I... I wouldn't feel right doing that, and even if I did I wouldn't know where to begin."

"Well, the Law of Swords is sometimes known as 'The Big Book of Contingencies,'" Wybert pointed out. "And most of it was written in the early days by people thinking up ways to break it. If it comes right down to it, this whole situation is a contingency that the writers of the Law of Swords never thought of. So, we should figure out a change that would take care of the immediate contingency and plug it in." He paused. "You know, if Maelgyn takes action before you get to the castle, I'll probably be made Sword King. I'd suspend the Law of Swords, with the approval of the makeshift council, and re-write things so that you two were brought back into the line of succession. I don't think we should get rid of it, entirely, but with things as they are now... it's doing us more harm than good."

"You can't suspend the Law of Swords without the unanimous approval of all the other Swords!" Arnach said.

Wybert laughed. "Well, considering I would be the only Sword left, that might not be so hard to come by."

"Idril might still be alive." Arnach almost added Ambrosius' name, as well, but decided that he'd rather not encourage the idea that their drunkard of a cousin might somehow claim the throne, himself.

"We are already under martial law. If, when the country is under martial law, the sitting Sword King decides that one of Svieda's founding laws – such as the Law of Swords – must be suspended, a summons will go out. Any Swords who do not appear after a period of three months will not have a vote," Wybert pointed out. "I'm not sure how Idril will hear the summons, though, since she is neither with her army nor at her castle. And if she does somehow show up, I think I can convince her of the need."

Arnach frowned. "I suppose that makes some sense. I wonder where she has gotten herself to, anyway?"

Wybert shuffled through his pockets, eventually finding a map of Svieda that he unrolled and placed on the table. Gesticulating fiercely with his finger, he started explaining what he knew. "The steward of her castle in Stanget said she was with the army, which he claimed was on its way to this encampment. The general of her army, who was actually moving to assist with the evacuation of Rubick, said she was with her regent meeting with the Sword of Leyland. Her regent, who actually *was* in Leyland, said that she had been there to meet with Ambrosius shortly before he left for the front, but then she departed when a so-called 'potential ally' had sent a messenger for her And that's the last anyone – including Maelgyn's Dwarven spymaster – saw of her."

"She went with this messenger, then?" Arnach said, alarmed. "Are we sure she isn't a captive, somewhere?"

"I think either our spies or the Dwarves' spies would have heard by now, if she was," Wybert said, pausing. He glanced down at the map again. "I asked her army's general to take position with the second line Maelgyn was organizing once he was done in Rubick. I honestly didn't think the Royal Province would hold as long as it has, and the camp here was in no state to receive them. With the Golden Dragons here, though, I'm wondering if I shouldn't have asked them to join us."

Arnach studied the map and whistled. "The middle third of our country really will be undefended, then. Well... perhaps sending them to Maelgyn's line will work. With so much of our army concentrated here – in the Happaso, Glorest, and Royal Provinces – there is no way to defend Rubick, and without Rubick no way to defend Stanget or Leyland... but Largo and all parts westward could be saved, if they were prepared well enough."

"If someone hits us in Rubick, we're pretty much done for," Wybert snorted. "We can't fight a war on two fronts, one of them against the largest army in the world, using the resources of just three provinces."

"That's my point, actually. With Stanget's army to reinforce them,

Maelgyn's line is a powerful force. We might have to fight on two fronts, but so would any invaders coming from that direction. With luck, maybe we could convince them to focus their attention on that front, instead. We go purely defensive, here, until the army in Largo can defeat the invading army and reunite the country." Arnach said.

"The country would be split in two," Wybert protested. "And who would lead the armies in Largo? All the Swords are here."

"I don't know. Let's just hope it never comes to that – we've got enough trouble with just one border to defend."

Hussack came to awareness suddenly, as if startled awake... except he was fairly certain he had not been asleep. He was in too much pain to sleep – every movement jarred his shattered arm. It was as if someone had shattered a glass bottle under his skin, and each time the cart he was traveling in hit a bump those glass pieces dug further in.

Except he wasn't in that cart, any more, it seemed – he was lying on a table of some sort, covered in furs, in a poorly lit room that was being warmed by a fire somewhere outside of his vision. A sanatorium of some sort, from the smell. Perhaps the last time he threw up from the pain had made him pass out, but he couldn't remember for sure. Everything was foggy – memories, vision, even the soreness in his arm now seemed as if it was being filtered through a veil of some kind.

"Ah – you're back with us, I see," someone said. Hussack looked in the direction of the voice, and saw someone whose face he didn't recognize. There was another man in the room, as well, though he couldn't make out any features of that person.

"What— who?"

"Yes, I'm not surprised you're disoriented with that fever. I'm afraid your arm has become severely infected and will need to be removed... not that we could have saved it, even if gangrene wasn't setting in."

Hussack looked down at his arm and noticed for the first time that he was naked. His injured arm really looked terrible. It was misshapen and wrapped in bandages, some of which appeared to be soaking through with blood. A tourniquet up near his shoulder joint was cutting off further blood flow, and through the bandages he could see darkening skin, bone fragments, and what little blood that remained seeping through.

"Damn. Didn't know the little bastard had it in him," Hussack muttered.

"Whoever it was who did this was very careful," the man said, using a stick to peak under one of the bandages before deciding to tighten the tourniquet some more.

"Careful!" Hussack exclaimed incredulously.

"Yes, careful. Your muscles and tendons are torn and bones shattered. You would never have been able to use this arm again even with treatment, had it healed... but prior to your little cart-ride up here, you would not have died from these injuries. That ride jostled your arm so much that it aggravated the wounds until, well, here we are. He wanted you to live, for some reason."

"His wife is our prisoner," Hussack said. "She would have been killed had I died."

"Well, fortunately for you and her, you should live if we amputate quickly. I'm just waiting for the bone saw to finish being boiled clean, and then I'll be right with you. In fact, I had better check on that."

The man – a surgeon, Hussack assumed – left after that... but the person in the shadows remained.

"It's a shame," the shadowy figure said. "You are the most naturally powerful mage I have encountered in a very, very long time. Even young Paljor didn't have your potential. With this injury, though...."

"Who are you?" Hussack demanded. The moment this stranger opened his mouth, shivers crept down his spine. This was someone horribly dangerous, and Hussack was more vulnerable than he had been since he was a babe.

The stranger didn't answer, though now that he stepped closer there was something familiar about him. "You were beaten by a high mage. A naturally occurring one – I wasn't sure if I would ever see one of those. A rarity, to be sure... but I could make you even more powerful, if you desire."

"I don't need a tutor," Hussack snapped, though he instantly regretted it. He couldn't tell what it was, but there was a terrible feeling of intimidation emanating from this person.

"You don't need any more training. Well, not in magic, anyway. No, I merely propose to strengthen what you already have – to double, or even triple it. And there are other things I could offer...."

Hussack didn't want to take anything from this man, but felt compelled to ask anyway. "Such as?"

A bundle was pulled out from... somewhere, Hussack wasn't sure where. It was long and thing, and the stranger slowly unwrapped it to reveal... was that an arm?

It must have been, though it wasn't human. There were talons on the fingers, and feather-like scales adorning it from about halfway down the forearm. It was fairly well muscled... and not attached to anything.

"This belonged to one of what my people now call the 'Ancient Enemy.' They were known as the Tengu, and they fought my people for centuries of unending war before the Dragons ultimately wiped them out – we could not, for our strengths were too similar and they were better with them. I have made a few... changes to it. Changes that make it more adaptable to my people. At one point, I thought to use it to replace one of my own arms, but that always seemed a bit drastic. Plus, even with my changes I suspect it would fight me. You, however... it would adapt to you quickly enough."

"I... are you suggesting you can just sew this arm on in place of my old one, and it'll work?" Hussack asked.

"It won't be that simple, no," the stranger laughed. He stepped forward again, touching the tourniquet with a finger. As he bent over, Hussack could see Elven ears on him – an oddity, as he spoke like no Elf he had ever encountered, before. "I must use my magic to graft it onto you. It will not be a pleasant process, and you will be in pain for some time until it takes. Then there will be a period of adjustment... hm. At best, I would say you can use this arm in about three years."

"Three years!"

"Three years of excruciating pain," the Elf laughed. "But I will work on your magic during that time, as well. When this period is over, you will be more powerful than any Human, Dwarf, Elf, or Tengu."

Hussack was no coward, but that was a bit much. "I am not going to endure three years of agony just to become an Elven experiment! I am Prince Hussack, and I refuse to accept—"

The Elf laughed again; it was not a sane laugh. "You act as if you have a choice. Allow me to introduce myself – I am Hrabak. Yes, the same Hrabak you might know from the stories in your youth, the ones your father assured you were pure fiction. But I am very real... and not even your king can refuse me."

Chapter XIII

With the cavalry of all sorts gone from the camp at Happaso, Arnach had a difficult time locating mounts suitable for himself and the two Dwarves accompanying him to the Royal City. Almost all of the horses remaining were pack animals, and the few remaining were not able to handle the Dwarves. Even the trained wolves of the Wolfriders had been taken... not that any of the three of them knew how to ride those dangerous beasts.

Eventually, someone came up with a solution, of sorts, though it was somewhat undignified. One of the less savory sorts from the less disciplined part of camp had come up with the idea and made the arrangements, but Arnach was not one to look a gift horse in the mouth. A would-be bureaucrat had made some fancy deals, locating an oxcart that all three of them could ride in. It was not exactly a dignified way for a Sword Prince to visit the Royal City, but considering Arnach's injury it was forgivable. He certainly wasn't traveling on foot.

The oxcarts of Svieda were, as one might imagine, typically pulled by oxes, just as mulecarts were usually pulled by mules. Arnach's oxcart, however, was being pulled by team of mules, as they had no mulecarts available.

Arnach did not know, and probably would not have cared, about the differences between the two types of carts. Just about any farmer could have told him it was the type of yoke and harness that each was equipped with. A layman wouldn't have known the difference, but there was one.

This oxcart had been bought from someone who never used it, and it was sold to someone who didn't know any better. The mules were procured by soldiers, not people who knew mules. The person who matched the mules to the carts did not know what he was doing at all, resulting in very ill-fitting yokes and harnesses.

Arnach would have been better off if he had known and cared, however. Especially when the mules were startled by a charging Nekoji. With beast and equipment matched in a way that only the ignorant would have done, the mules were able to brake free from their ill-fitting yokes and send him flying out of the oxcart.

Fortunately, it was a friendly Nekoji with prodigious strength and the reflexes expected of his people who had startled Arnach's mules. A large, furry hand reached out and snagged him out of mid-air.

"Whoa, there, your Highness. There aren't enough Swords left, as it is – I'd hate it if I accidentally snuffed one of them."

It took Arnach a moment, as he was hanging upside down from his (good) ankle, but the voice helped him recognize the Nekoji holding him as Gyato.

"Well, I'm rather happy not to be, uh, snuffed, Count Gyato," he said. "But could you, perhaps, set me down?"

"Of course," Gyato laughed, using his other hand to help get Arnach on his feet before releasing him. "I might even be persuaded to help you collect your mules, if you'd like."

"Oh, the mules," Arnach muttered. "Yes, someone had better get those, or else I'll have to spend the next few weeks walking the rest of the way to the Royal City."

"We'll do it!" Tur'Ka said, pulling his companion Tur'Tei off of the cart's floor. "Just wait for us."

"You exaggerate," Gyato said, watching them run off. "Even for your slow-legged Dwarves it's only a few day's walk out, not weeks."

"Not with this bum leg," Arnach pointed out, tapping his thigh. "So... what brings you out of the castle in such a hurry?"

"I am actually returning to the castle, not leaving it. Maelgyn has been getting increasingly antsy for word of his wife's whereabouts," Gyato said. "And 'Brode' has been of no help. El'Athras is working his network of spies, but it will be some time before he has any word. I thought things might go faster if I went to the commanders of the local Sviedan armies and see if any of them knew where Sho'Curlas was keeping their prisoners-of-war."

"Anything helpful?" Arnach asked. He had liked Euleilla, for the brief time that he knew her, and knew his cousin would be devastated by her capture.

"I believe so, yes," Gyato said. "But we'll still have to see if there's any way to get 'Brode' to do anything with that information."

Arnach sighed. "I probably shouldn't say this, but I'd rather we had news on Brode. I know Maelgyn is worried about his wife, but I am worried for our entire kingdom. Knowing where Euleilla is won't help us unless Brode signs off on a rescue mission, and right now..."

"Right now, 'Brode' is more likely to say 'good riddance' to the commoner who married into the family rather than try anything to help her." Gyato smirked. "At the moment, Svieda's armies are far more willing to follow Maelgyn into battle than 'Brode.' Only a loyalty to the supposedly infallible nature of the 'Law of Swords' prevents some of your people from declaring Brode a fraud, already, and replacing him with Maelgyn. They still might, but they know what doing so would do to you."

Arnach grimaced. "Yes, revealing the deception may very well end my being one of the Swords. It is a sacrifice that must be made, however – to end the stain on the name of the real Brode as much as to save our kingdom."

"Not if we find the real Brode, first," Gyato said. "Maelgyn doesn't believe we should take action until we've at least made an attempt at that – he fears that the loss of that many Swords could overturn the Law of Swords, which would also make Svieda vulnerable to an attack from within. I've heard his justification – it's pretty convincing."

"He wants me to hold off on it, then?" Arnach said, almost unable to believe what he was hearing. "That doesn't sound like him. Are all of my relatives going to be replaced by impostors the moment they enter that castle?"

"I assure you, it was the real Maelgyn who was speaking," Gyato said. "At least you should talk with him, first. He does have real concerns that make his decision on this reasonable... unlike some of the decisions 'Brode' has made."

"Well, if you aren't planning to replace this impostor, then why did you summon me?" Arnach asked warily. He was starting to feel as if he was being played like a pawn, and he didn't like it.

"The summons went out before we had any discussion with him," Gyato explained, a low purring rumble deep in his throat. It was strangely soothing, and made some of the anger slip away from Arnach. "But we still need your help. We cannot replace 'Brode,' yet, so instead we have to work with him. So far we have had little success, but Maelgyn has not been in any condition to speak with 'Brode' personally. Perhaps your presence will be enough to convince him to take certain actions, as long as they do not go against his long-term plans."

"His 'long-term plans?'" Arnach repeated. "But... surely his long-term plans are our defeat at the hands of Sho'Curlas. How can we get anything beneficial done with such a man in charge?"

"We aren't convinced that those are his long-term plans," Gyato said. "And we're not sure he knows just how much damage he is doing, right now. At least in regards to the war effort."

"Why else would Sho'Curlas have replaced Brode with an impostor, then?" Arnach said incredulously.

"Ah, that goes into why we think replacing 'Brode' might be a bad idea. We suspect the impostor has loyalties to a different power – a third player in the game, if you will."

That brought Arnach up short. He could only think of one other country that might care, and if they were taking an interest in this war that couldn't be a good thing. "Oregal?"

"Fortunately, no," Gyato said. "Unfortunately, it may be even more serious than that. We—" He opened his mouth to say more, but a mule's bray interrupted them. They both turned to see the two Dwarves leading a group of mules back to the road. "I'll explain later. Let me help you get your cart settled, and I will ride with you back to the castle. Along the way, I will tell you everything I know...."

Euleilla rested on her stone bed as she had for several days now. She was meditating, which proved useful in many ways: She was healing from her injuries, she was restoring her magical abilities, and she was tuning Nattiel out.

She had yet to reveal her relationship with Maelgyn to Nattiel. In fact, since that original conversation, she'd been playing the "one word game" with him... and had yet to actually say that one word.

It wasn't as if Nattiel was silent in all that time. He had quite a bit to say... and most of it was to lambaste her (as Maelgyn's wife, though not as his fellow prisoner), her husband, or her magical talent in some way. Occasionally, when he spouted one of the less objectionable things he was apt to say, she would give a vague noise of agreement... but so far, even those moments had been few and far between.

She had never thanked her lessons in ignoring the outside world (a part of her magic training) more. As much as she wanted to get along with the father of her husband, his words were anathema to her. She couldn't believe that this was all there was to this man – so far, she saw nothing of Maelgyn in him. She also couldn't believe that his attitude towards magic was coming from nowhere – there had to be something behind it – but she wasn't getting any clues from his words. There simply was no point in engaging him. Not until she solved the puzzle behind his anger, anyway.

She had to know if he had always been like this, or if his time as a Sho'Curlan prisoner had made him crack. It would help if she could consult with Maelgyn on the matter – in fact, she really didn't want anything more to do with Nattiel until she could talk it over with several people who knew him best – but to do that, she needed to make her escape.

She was a little disappointed that Maelgyn had yet to rescue her. She would have expected him to be right on the heels of her captors, storming this prison and freeing her before she had even awoken. There were a number of reasons he might be delayed – one of those, his death, was something she refused to consider – but it was starting to look like she would be on her own to escape.

Her magic was still a little weak – either they were feeding her something that was meant to suppress it, or she had exhausted it further than she realized – but she was diligently working to restore her strength. She was also extending her magical senses as far as they would go.

There was iron in this facility, although all the pieces she could find were in the form of lodestones. Even in her reduced state, she could push through the disruptive fields of these lodestones and do something with the iron inside, but they were keeping them scattered and at a distance. She could probably grab a piece or two before the guards could do anything, but without a plan they would be able to subdue her before she was even out of her cell.

However, they probably wouldn't notice if a few filings the size of a grain of sand were removed from each of these lodestones over several days. By pulling just three grains of iron filings from each lodestone each day, she had now acquired about a tablespoon's worth of filings. Another two weeks and she could triple that... which might be enough to form a key for the lock on their cell, or a small weapon, or a similar small tool.

Of course, then there were the gates of the castle they were imprisoned in. They were massive, and heavy, and made of something similar to lodestone that was so powerful even she would have trouble getting through them. She could gradually pull iron out of them, but it would take time and she would need to almost be touching them to manage it. She would have to figure out how to get those gates open, first.

Euleilla? a voice sounded in her head.

It had been a long time since she heard that voice form actual words rather than mere impressions of danger, but she recognized it right away as her *schlipf.*

Talking to me again, are you?

My apologies for being so quiet, recently. I was not well, and it takes a lot of my concentration to speak.

I was not offended by your silence, Euleilla thought back. *I merely wondered if there was something wrong.*

Nothing you have done, the schlipf replied. *I am in the process of maturing, which takes much of my energy even when I am healthy. But I felt I should warn you of something, so I've gathered enough to speak with you now. But we should hurry – I cannot talk for long.*

Then speak, she prompted.

A schlipf does not have what you would call an adolescent period. We jump from seedling to fully mature plant in a matter of minutes, and are able to act as a weapon after only a brief period of recovery. You might call this a 'sprouting,' as it is when we first emerge from our hosts.

Okay, Euleilla thought. *Is your recent illness delaying this sprouting?*

It had been, the *schlipf* said. *But I believe that the delay will only strengthen me, in the end.*

Well, that's good news, Euleilla thought. *But then why the urgency in speaking to me?*

The sprouting will be sooner than I realized, when I first fell ill. Perhaps in two weeks time, when your current plans say you should be leaving this prison. While it will not debilitate you for weeks on end, as my sire did to your mate during their bonding, there will be some pain during the sprouting.

I understand, Euleilla thought. *I will wait until afterwords, then – it would be dangerous if I was found by our enemies, escaping, and the pain of your sprouting rendered my magic unusable.*

A wise decision, the *schlipf* agreed. *I do have one request, however.*

I am not in a position to grant you many boons, but I will do what I can, Euleilla thought. *What would you ask of me?*

It is... customary, according to the memories my sire granted me, for a volunteer schlipf to be granted their name before they have sprouted. I know you had been thinking about it at one point, but things have been so busy you seem to have forgotten...

Of course I will grant you a name! Euleilla thought, feeling somewhat ashamed that she had let that chore slip her mind. She used her magic to search for inspiration, but all she could find was Nattiel, taking a rest from ranting and now leaning against the wall of their prison.

While he was hardly a positive inspiration, she did what she could with it. She really didn't know much about him, other than that he was Maelgyn's father, and didn't like mages even if his son was one... and his wife. Euleilla didn't even know the name of her husband's mother, but there was that little fact.

And that was all the inspiration she needed.

How about Melka?

Melka? the *schlipf* repeated. *It sounds nice enough. What does it mean?*

I don't really know, Euleilla thought. *I only know it was my mother's name. I don't remember much about my mother – my father rarely spoke of her – but giving you her name would allow me to remember her. All children should have something fond to remember their parents by.* She glanced up at Nattiel. *No matter what else they might think about them.*

El'Athras was waiting at the gates when Gyato, Arnach, and

the two Dwarves arrived riding the repaired and re-muled cart. So far, things had been going surprisingly well: Wangdu had yet to be revealed, the Royal Physician had given – and, to date, kept – his word that their conversation at Maelgyn's bedside would remain secret, and Maelgyn himself was healing well. The swollen joints and similar visible injuries had slowly vanished; now all that was left was the torn muscles, strained tendons, and burst blood vessels that were underneath all that swelling. Wodtke had suggested a form of magical surgery that might speed his recovery time, some, but had so far been unable to get Maelgyn to agree to the procedure.

They did their best to take advantage of Maelgyn's slow recovery, however. His injuries were the perfect excuse for them to begin investigating for possible Elven intrusion. Wodtke was in the Royal Archives, ostensibly searching for medical treatments but really checking out those laws which pre-dated the Law of Swords for signs of tampering. She was also looking for information on how to fix a broken mage – something Maelgyn had requested on behalf of Onayari.

The female Nekoji was in the archives with her, looking for that same information as well as anything they could find on the signs you were dealing with a Merfolk impersonator. While a major race for at least as long as the Elves, with a recognized civilization pre-dating the Human, Dwarven, and Nekoji by centuries, not much was known about the Merfolk – they existed, almost literally, a world apart from the other major races.

Sir Leno and their new friend from the guard – Vihanto – were keeping an eye on Maelgyn's sick room. As Wangdu was hiding out in that room, for the moment, they were tasked with allowing no visitors outside of those people who already knew about the Elf's presence.

Surprisingly, no alarms had gone up after Wangdu's "escape." Either no-one cared, or no-one noticed. The old Dwarf wasn't sure which was the more disturbing thought, but he was happy they'd gotten away with freeing him. Well, sort of – the lack of information as to why there was no alarm was driving El'Athras crazy. The paranoia that came from being an old spymaster rarely allowed for him to let be truly "happy" when things were unexpectedly going better than anticipated.

Still, he would take what opportunities were given to him while he could, whether they came through incompetence or enemy design. So, when he saw the mule-drawn cart pulling through the gate, he was quick to run out the door to meet them He wasn't expecting to be ignored when he got there, however.

"...very disturbing, if what you tell me is true," Arnach was saying as Gyato helped him out of the cart. "But I think I now see where my cousin drew his conclusions from. I should go see him immediately." He saw El'Athras approaching and bowed his head politely in greeting. "I may be able to suggest a few options to deal with this crisis he would not be able to consider on his own."

Gyato, lifting Tur'Ka off of the cart, acknowledged Arnach with a nod. "I will join you momentarily."

"I'll he happy to see you." The newly-arrived Sword Prince sketched one more bow each, one to Gyato and the other – in the first sign he'd even seen the old Dwarf – to El'Athras. "I hope to see you there, as well."

El'Athras watched him go, Tur'Ka and Tur'Tei on his heels. As most of his kin were, the two Dwarves were delayed by the guards, but Arnach continued on inside without looking back. "Did I do something to offend him?"

"He was a trifle miffed that we summoned him ostensibly to challenge the rule of 'Brode,' but then decided to leave the impostor in place."

"Only for now. I would like to be able to act quickly when we do find the real Brode," El'Athras said. "So... you're back sooner than I thought you would be."

"I have news," Gyato said.

"I doubt you would return this quickly if you didn't."

"The local Sviedan armies are scattered about, trying to deal with too many smaller incursions with far too few soldiers. It would actually be better if a proper line of battle were formed, instead of the generals trying to counter each of these hit-and-run attacks, but I suspect this recent siege might make them think twice about allowing themselves to be drawn out like this again," Gyato said.

"As we feared," El'Athras said. "You wouldn't be here, though, if that was all you had discovered."

"No," Gyato said. "I was finally able to find one of the local provincial army's captains, and he had some intel that should make finding Euleilla easy. Sho'Curlas is known to place all of its prisoners-of-war in one of seven prisons or prison camps. Only one of these, however, is equipped to handle high-level mages."

El'Athras frowned. "And you know where this prison is?"

"Yes," Gyato said. "It is far back in the mountains, near the old border line between Sycanth Province and Sho'Curlas."

El'Athras took in a deep breath. "Did you tell Arnach about this?"

"Only that I believed I knew where they were keeping Euleilla; I did not say where I thought that was."

"Damn. Well, the cat's out of the bag, now," El'Athras said.

Gyato drew himself to his full height, glaring down at the Dwarf. "Is there something wrong with finding news that might allow us to rescue Euleilla?"

El'Athras shook his head. "No, I don't mean it like that. It's a good thing that we've found out where she's being held. But I'm not sure it's a good idea to let Maelgyn know... and Arnach is sure to have told him you know something, by now."

"Why should we hide this from him?" Gyato asked, his mane ruffling. "Surely he would be more interested in this than any of us."

"Because Maelgyn is a man of action," El'Athras said. "But he is currently not healthy enough to take that action. Wodtke thinks he needs six months, at a minimum, before he can even begin practicing with a weapon again. He should stay out of combat for a year or more. If he knows where Euleilla is, and we cannot convince 'Brode' to rescue her, I fear he may do something drastic in an attempt to rescue her, himself."

"What could he do?" Gyato asked. "He can't even sit up by himself. Or has he improved since I saw him last?"

"Who knows?" El'Athras said. "The truth is, after Paljor, he shouldn't have been able to go into battle yet... but he not only went into battle, he took on three Black Dragons by himself and then confronted the First Rate Mage that defeated his wife and killed poor Tur'Ba. During that confrontation, Maelgyn was able to reach out magically and cripple that mage for life."

"But—"

"Look, between the Borden Isles incident and that battle with the Dragons a few weeks ago, Maelgyn has made himself into a symbol –

that victory for Svieda is *possible*. By pushing his magical potential to the point that he can be called a High Mage, he has also become the greatest weapon Svieda has in this war." He paused. "Well, except possibly for Wangdu – I don't think we've yet seen what that Elf is capable of."

"Even among my people, the battle prowess of Elves is a thing of legend," Gyato agreed.

"Except for a very few, the Elves are overrated – they can and have been beaten in battle, even by my people. Those who've trained long in battle are a sight to behold, but not every Elf has the kind of motivation needed to learn all of those combat techniques. Still, one of Wangdu's caliber could do great damage to our enemies. But if Maelgyn, in a rash attempt to rescue his wife, were to permanently damage himself, what do you think would happen to the morale of Svieda's soldiers?"

Gyato looked off in the distance. If he had a tail, it would be flicking from side to side – the cat-like mannerisms of his people were evident as he considered El'Athras' words. Come to think of it, why didn't Gyato have a tail? Other Nekoji that El'Athras had met had them. Well, it was a question that could be asked after the immediate crisis was over.

"Maelgyn will learn that I have news for him," Gyato finally said. "And I will have to tell him – if we start keeping secrets from him and he learns that we know, he will leave us out of his future plans. We need him to trust us."

El'Athras nodded. "True. But you can see why I wish you hadn't told Arnach, yes?"

"We have no choice, at this point," Gyato said, ignoring the rhetorical question. "Convincing 'Brode' of the need to rescue Euleilla is a must. We might even have to remove him before we're ready, now, if we can't."

"Well, with Arnach and my two Dwarven compatriots here in the Castle, we have the ability to do that," El'Athras said. "But it would be best if we could delay Maelgyn a little longer. I'm still looking for the real Brode. He would be more likely to send out a rescue mission for Euleilla without raising too much of an argument."

"When you think about it, we need to prepare for two rescue missions," Gyato said. "It is likely we'll need some force of arms to recover both Euleilla and Brode, yes?"

"Well, perhaps," El'Athras said. "Depending on precisely how each of them are restrained, it may be possible for my spies to help them to escape on their own rather than risk the kind of battle required for a rescue. But you're probably right. I'll see if we can find any reliable information out on those prison camps you mentioned – a little information will make those inevitable battles much easier."

"You should try to confirm my... 'guess' about Euleilla's location, while you're at it," Gyato said. "In fact, that is how we will delay Maelgyn. My information is merely a starting point for you to begin the real search. But once it is confirmed, we will have to tell him right away – as you said, if we hold back information from him we will lose his trust."

"Then let's hope we find Brode, first," El'Athras said. "Because I can't see this impostor rescuing Euleilla no matter what we do."

"We might be able to convince him to make the effort," Gyato said. "If his loyalties are what we suspect, rescuing Euleilla will not conflict with his mission. Make a strong enough case for it, and he'll agree to rescue her just to keep his cover."

"Yeah... perhaps."

Neither of them believed that would be the case... but then, what alternative did they actually have?

Chapter XIV

Nattiel looked over at the strange girl he was sharing a cell with –
had she even given her name to him, yet? Yuleya, Euleia, something
like that – as she writhed in pain. He woke up when she let out a
whimper, and it was clear that whatever was causing her fits was
getting worse. At first, he wondered if she had been tortured while he
slept and was still recovering. They had yet to torture him, as it was
against the rules of war to torture captured royals or nobles, but this
girl was neither of those; she was just a lowly mage. A powerful one,
if they felt she had to be kept in *this* cell, but without the protection
of a royal or noble title she could legally be raped, tortured, or even
killed.

But the pain was clearly increasing for her, not fading – no,
something else was wrong.

"Say, girl – are you ill?"

Her head flashed up. He couldn't see her eyes through that hair,
so he wasn't sure exactly what she was looking at, but he could swear
that she was trying to see his voice. Then again, if her vision was
distorted by the pain, she might not be able to see him.

"No," she gasped. He wasn't sure if that was an answer to his
question, or just a protest as another wave of pain wracked her body,

but either way he wasn't likely to get a more specific answer.

"Is there anything I can do to help?" he asked. He doubted the answer would be yes. The girl was a mage – no matter what the situation, every mage he knew felt that they could handle whatever situation they were in without any outside aid. His wife had been that way, after all... and that attitude eventually ended her life.

To his surprise, she nodded in the affirmative. "Water," she said.

There was a clay pot full of water near her bed, in easy reach, so he wasn't sure why she was asking him to get the water. Still, he asked if he could help, so he might as well. With a wooden ladle and a prison-issue ceramic cup, he portioned out some water from his own jar and took it over to her.

"Here," he said.

The pain must have been worse than he imagined, because she wasn't even looking as she reached out out to try and grab the cup. With some effort, Nattiel managed to get it into her hand. She took the water and first swallowed a sip of it before pouring the rest over one of her wrists. That water washed away some old blood and dirt... but there was something else on that wrist. It looked like a spike or something, but it was green.

"What is that thing?" he asked.

The girl was still trembling, her face covered in a cold sweat, but she still gave him a wide smile... and then spoke the longest sentence she had uttered since she was first locked in his cell, several weeks ago.

"This 'thing' is what we need to escape."

She spoke no more, no matter what Nattiel said to her – at one point, he realized she had passed out – but her last statement left him with a ton of questions. Had the pain made her delusional? How would something that looked like a splinter help them to escape, and where did it come from to begin with? And just why was she in so much pain, anyway?

Still, it wouldn't do for the guards to come and investigate. He gently pushed the girl onto her back, then covered her with one of the furs. Then he did something he'd been hoping to do since he first saw her – he flicked her hair out of her face.

And immediately flicked it back down.

Now he knew why she would never look him in the eyes, at least.

*

For someone who could barely manage a slow limp, Maelgyn's pacing about the room was impressive. Wodtke had finally prevailed upon him to allow some additional treatment – perhaps not the full surgery she wanted to perform, but anything that could be managed through magical manipulation was fine. This amounted to most of what Wodtke wanted to do, anyway – she just was hoping to be able to see things with her eyes instead of her magic as she attempted more intricate work – and only a week later he was on his feet again. Not that Wodtke (or anyone else, really) wanted him back on his feet, at the moment.

"So we know where she is," Maelgyn said, glaring over at El'Athras first and Gyato last. "We've suspected it for weeks, now, but you've finally confirmed it. So why aren't we in the Royal Court right now, demanding that Brode – fake or not – send an army to free her?"

"We will, in due time," El'Athras said. "We have already requested an appointment. As difficult as it may be to deal with 'Brode,' we felt it best not to antagonize him needlessly. We'll keep to his schedule, at least until this meeting – we don't want to get him in a bad mood by forcing the issue during one of his 'bathes.'"

Maelgyn nodded. "All right – that makes sense. You two may go... for the moment. Wangdu!"

El'Athras and Gyato looked at each other uneasily. Maelgyn was giving in too easily, here.

"I'm here, I am, milord," the Elf said, coming into the room from... somewhere. Over the past several weeks, Wangdu's hiding place had undergone major changes. Now, none of them – save perhaps Maelgyn – knew how to find it. "Though I am not sure what I can do, I'm not."

"We have to work on our contingency plans," Maelgyn said. He glanced over at El'Athras and Gyato. "Why are you two still here? I thought I said you should go."

"Uh... of course, your Highness," El'Athras said, nonplussed. He almost had to drag Gyato out of there, himself, as the Nekoji seemed determined to remain planted where he was. Once they were out the door, it closed and locked behind them.

"That was... unexpected," Gyato said.

"I'll say... in more ways than one," El'Athras said, looking at the door. "He's using his magic, again, even though Wodtke said he shouldn't. His magic was the only thing in that room who could have locked that door."

"Come," Gyato said. "Let us gather the others and head to Arnach's suite. If we are to have any hope of convincing 'Brode' to do as we want, we must plan."

El'Athras stared at the door again. "I suppose. I guess I won't be able to figure out what Maelgyn's doing just by waiting at his door, anyway."

Now that Melka had finished sprouting, Euleilla could 'see' the room, again. She poured herself a cup of water from her own jar and took a long drink. Now that the pain was gone and her thirst was sated, she was surprised at how quiet the room had become. She extended her senses to find that Nattiel was awake, to her surprise, and he seemed to be staring at her.

"Thanks," she said.

"Er, what for?"

She gestured with her ceramic cup. "Helping."

"Well... who wouldn't? You looked like you were pretty desperate."

"Yes," she agreed. She had been pretty desperate, and Nattiel provided her with more help than just the water. She had woken up to find that she was covered in warm furs, and not just her own – he had loaned her the furs from his own pallet to help her keep comfortable in her distress. It was not the behavior she would expect from the sort of man who gave the rants she had endured over the past few weeks. Finally she had proof that there really was more to the man than his anger.

"So... you're feeling better, then?"

"Much." She was, indeed, feeling a lot better. In fact, now that the *schlipf* had matured, Melka could filter out the toxins from the drugs that the prison guards were putting in her food. In a short time, she would be back to full magical strength. She should probably try stretching her muscles out some, but she felt better physically than she had since the battle. And Melka was providing her own sense of strength.

"Good, good," Nattiel said. "So... what happened to you, anyway?"

She may have blabbed a bit more than she intended while under the influence of intense pain, but she wasn't about to give away everything, just yet.

"Secret," was all she said, a finger to her mouth in a gesture of silence.

Surprisingly, he didn't push for any hints. Instead, she sensed him nod. "Very well. But now, for the big question – you mentioned escape. How? When?"

She had to think about how to answer that one. The truth was, she could probably manage an escape right that minute... maybe. But every bit of the toxicity in her blood that could be filtered out, every grain of iron sand she could sneak off of the guards' lodestones, every moment she could spend refining her plan would increase their chances of success. They were being well treated, and the guards were (in a prison protocol that was common among anyone used to dealing with high-ranking mages) leaving them alone, for the most part. There was nothing pressing that demanded she escape as soon as possible.

Nothing except her husband, who she was sure was frantic with worry by this point. And she was worried about him – she knew he was the sort who would have tried to rescue her by now, if he was at all capable of it. There were certain reasons he might not be capable of it that would be... unwelcome. And a few others that she was refusing to think about. Maelgyn was alive, dammit!

"Hey, are we escaping or not?" Nattiel prompted, bringing her back to the present.

"Later," she decided.

"Later? That means yes. When?"

Good question. She still wasn't certain. She quickly checked to see how much of the iron sand she had been able to acquire over the past several weeks – a little less than she'd anticipated, but enough to form a key. Not enough to form an effective weapon, though – give her a little more time and she might be able to make a stiletto-style dagger from it.

"One week," she said. "Or sooner, if a better opportunity presents itself."

"Fine," Nattiel said. He stood from his bed and started stretching. "I'd better start exercising again, then – you shouldn't be expected to do this on your own."

"Okay," Euleilla said. She was happy about the attitude change in Nattiel... but what had prompted it? Was it merely the hope that soon they would be escaping... or was it something else?

In the end, once an appointment had been scheduled with the king, it was decided that only Maelgyn, Arnach, and Sir Leno alone should approach the fake Brode about sending an army to rescue Euleilla. El'Athras and Gyato would be sitting in the audience chambers of the royal court, but only those three would stand before the throne to make their case.

For Arnach, and undoubtedly for Maelgyn, it was a strange sensation to be in the throne room again. Many of the old accoutrements were no longer present – the Swords no longer were represented by their own chambers, their own tapestries, their provincial symbols, nor their own antechambers. Those had been removed, and in their place was now seating for nobles and other courtiers. It looked like a very different room... and yet it was the same place where they witnessed Hussack cold-bloodedly murder Sword King Gilbereth II... Arnach's father.

As they waited to be announced, Arnach idly wondered if the real Brode would have kept the old Royal Court chambers or if he would have moved them to a different room. There were several other ballrooms in the castle of sufficient size that could, and in some cases had, served in that role. In fact, this was the smallest of the rooms to have ever served that purpose.

Those musings ended, however, when the doors were opened by the guards to allow the king entrance. The man who entered was so perfectly identical to the real Brode that Arnach had a hard time believing he was an impostor, save that the body language was all wrong. Brode strode to the front of the throne and, after a formal gesture greeting the court, sat down. His posture was far too rigid for the real Brode, his eyes too unfocused and his mouth too hard. But beyond that, he was a perfect replica.

"We are here, today, to hear certain petitions brought forth by two of my kin," the fake-Brode said. "Please, come forward."

Sir Leno and Arnach both helped support Maelgyn as the Royal Herald ceremonially led them from the door to the base of the throne. It was an old form of the ceremony – Arnach's thrice-great grandfather had simplified things greatly, allowing the court to get business done faster, but fake-Brode had restored many of these time-consuming rituals.

When they were lined up before the throne, the herald announced them. "Your Majesty, may I present his Highness the Sword Prince Arnach, Duke of Happaso, his Highness the Sword Prince Maelgyn, Duke of Sopan, and the honorable Sir Leno of Sopan's First Archery Corps. Gentlemen, his Majesty, Brode IX, firstborn son of Gilbereth II, and by right of both birth and conquest the Sword King of Svieda!"

The fake-Brode surveyed them briefly before pointing to the floor. "Kneel," he commanded.

Kneel? It was unheard of. The Swords never knelt before one another – bowed, certainly, but kneeling? That was not a practice Svieda had ever endorsed, even prior to the implementation of the Law of Swords. Worse, with Maelgyn in his condition...

"Your Majesty, we are two of the Swords," Arnach protested. "And Maelgyn is injured. You cannot, in good conscience, demand that we kneel. The very idea runs counter to everything the Law of Swords was written to protect us from! We—"

He stopped when Maelgyn placed a heavy hand on his shoulder. While he wore a cape to hide the worst of his wounds, spider lines left over from his injuries were still quite visible on Maelgyn's wrist. "Let it go, cousin. We have more important things to discuss, today."

Arnach winced. They had anticipated 'Brode' would do things to deliberately provoke them – anything which might discourage future meetings between fake-Brode and the real Brode's relatives should be expected. Still, to demand that Maelgyn not just bow, but kneel, in his current condition was egregious.

But when Maelgyn was the first of the three of them onto one bended knee, it was hard to argue the point any further. Arnach found himself following suit – perhaps persuaded slightly be a push from Maelgyn's magic – and Sir Leno was not far behind.

'Brode' sighed impatiently. "Very well – make your petition."

When preparing for this meeting, it had been decided that Sir Leno would be the one to lay out their initial argument, and Arnach would take over after that. While El'Athras was their true spymaster, Sir Leno would be taking credit for his work before the Court. With their understanding of Porosian biases, having a Human as their spokesman would be expected. Portraying those of Royal Blood as having their hands clean of such tawdry concerns as espionage was necessary, however, so it could be neither of the Sword Princes. Arnach, however, would be better at articulating their arguments; Maelgyn's main job was to look as dignified as possible and not collapse from his injuries.

"Your majesty," Sir Leno began. "Recently, our agents discovered seven Sho'Curlan camps at which your subjects are being kept prisoner. These prisoners include large numbers of soldiers taken by surprise in Sycanth, nobles, and – we have learned – even the wife of one of your fellow Swords. Freeing these prisoners would greatly reinforce our army's numbers, increase morale, and strike a significant blow against our enemy. We request that you allow us to task our generals with this mission."

There was a long pause. 'Brode' seemed to be thinking it over at first, but then Arnach noticed that he was glancing over at someone else for a decision – the Royal Archivist, a middle-aged man named Lazark.

After taking the throne, 'Brode' made a number of appointments for vacant Court offices. Most, Arnach suspected, were like the Royal Physician: People raised or trained under Porosian traditions, and therefore unable to discern when Sviedan traditions were being overrun, but still generally loyal to Svieda. Lazark, however, was one of the two or three people they now suspected of being actual members of this Porosian Conspiracy that Maelgyn had uncovered.

And 'Brode' seemed to be taking cues from this man. A very subtle shake of the head – Arnach would have missed it if he hadn't been looking for it – and 'Brode' was quick to speak.

"Why do you come to this court with such trivialities? Svieda's armies still have not recovered from the last major attack the Sho'Curlans sent our way. The castle's defense is in shambles, and what offensive forces we have? Dwarves and Nekoji – useless creatures." There were murmurs of protest from the gallery... and not from El'Athras or Gyato, who must have been biting their tongue. Interesting. "To make any sort of offensive strike now would be folly."

"To sit here and do nothing while our enemies regain their strength is worse folly," Arnach said, though he feared his words were going to deaf ears. "The defenses here are secure – the Dragons will see to that. With only a small force of arms, we can rescue our fellow soldiers and bring the Royal Castle's Human defenses back to full strength."

'Brode' didn't even look for advice on this one. "Enough. Your petition is denied."

As El'Athras and Gyato had pointed out, they could not afford for a 'no' answer. He would have to draw things out some more, and hope they stumbled across some argument that 'Brode' – or more accurately, his Porosian leash-keeper – could not refute.

"Then I appeal your decision with the Sword's Right of Debate," Arnach declared.

The fake-Brode's eyes widened at that one. He sent a panicked look to Lazark, who seemed rather taken aback. The Sword's Right of Debate was a guarantee the Law of Swords granted any petitioner to appeal any decision made by a Sword to the Sword King. It wouldn't seem to make any sense to appeal the Sword King's own decision in this way, except the law demanded that the Sword King permit the petitioner to make their case for as long as they wished to speak. More than one petitioner over the centuries had won their appeal through the strength of filibustering the Sword King... but to appeal the Sword King's own decision using that right had never been done. At least, according to the official record it hadn't.

Lazark gave 'Brode' an indecisive gesture. Neither of them had been prepared for this kind of maneuver, clearly.

"I... don't know..." 'Brode' began.

Lazark must have felt that the impostor king was in over his head, because he was quick to intervene. "That right has always been granted to the Swords, it is true. However, I have never heard of the Sword King's own decision being appealed in this manner."

"I am not at all surprised you are unaware of it," Arnach said. "After all, you are a recent member of this court, and were not present during the reign of our father. But I am absolutely certain that Brode would never forget the time he made such an appeal of our father, Sword King Gilbereth II, on the decision of whether he would be permitted to defy tradition and marry a certain innkeeper's daughter."

The fake Brode looked stunned, but before he could say anything incriminating Lazark got angry. "There is no mention of this in the public record!"

"Because Brode dropped the petition when said innkeeper's daughter found the matter too embarrassing to bear, and requested that we quietly drop the matter and leave her name out of the records. The Royal Archivist of the time agreed to leave all mention of it out of the public record, but I am certain that there are any number of people from our father's Court still with us who remember it."

Lazark shifted uncomfortably, and this time he was the one who looked to 'Brode' for help.

"I am not sure that our father ever meant for that 'appeal' to be taken seriously. That was a personal matter; these are affairs of state," the impostor said, having managed to recover his composure.

"You may never have taken your personal affairs seriously," Arnach said. "But if you think that our father never once thought that the woman you brought into the family as a future Princess Consort was not an affair of state, you didn't know our father."

That was a slight jab that the real Brode would probably have laughed off. This fake, however, wouldn't know how many times they had said similar words in jest to one another – he would be immediately put on the defensive. But the only way he could save face would be to permit the appeal.

'Brode' gave a resigned sigh. "Very well... but if this debate is to take long, we should have refreshments brought to the court."

"Thank you, your Majesty," Arnach said, then glanced over at his companions. "And may I request chairs, so that I and my companions here – especially Maelgyn, who was grievously injured in defense of your throne, may rest?"

It was back to 'Brode' asking Lazark for direction, and a reluctant nod indicated their acceptance. "I suppose a concession to formality may be granted due to our cousin's wounds. But for all future petitions, remember that the petitioner should remain kneeling!"

Once again, that was in defiance of all Sviedan traditions, but this time Arnach was able to restrain himself from protesting. Hopefully they would find the real Brode before too long, and they would never again have to deal with this impostor's ridiculous demands.

Arnach had wondered how the fake-Brode would obtain the water he needed to maintain his illusory disguise should their appeal last long. Large jugs full of water being presented as their "refreshments" gave him that answer. They were lukewarm, and did little to quench Arnach's thirst, but that was an issue they didn't have to worry about.

For the next three hours, Arnach pushed forward with the desperate need to send rescue parties to these prison camps. He had Sir Leno provide an estimated break-down of who these prisoners of war consisted of, with what were hoped were accurate numbers of the number of able-bodied soldiers at each camp as well as names of the known prisoners. Arnach spoke long and hard about the nobles they believed were held captive, 'reminding' the fake-Brode of what many of them had meant to the brothers in their life. Sir Leno picked up the argument, after that, discussing what damage taking these camps out would do to the logistical structure of Sho'Curlas as it sought to re-organize its armies from this latest defeat. It was all very compelling.

What they did not do was mention Euleilla at all. Beyond that one brief suggestion that she might be mixed in with one of these prison camps, Arnach stayed well away from that topic. The Porosian Conspiracy did not seem to approve of mages in high positions, so that argument would likely be counter-productive.

Still, three hours in and there didn't seem to be any sense that 'Brode' (or rather, Lazark, who appeared to be the real decision maker) was letting any of the arguments get to him.

Arnach had paused for a moment to pour himself a cup of water. His throat was very dry after speaking for so long, and he figured it was safe to pause that long – Sir Leno could take over. Except it wasn't Sir Leno that continued the arguments for them.

Maelgyn stood up slowly. His hands were trembling, and he was obviously in pain, but when he made it to his feet he managed to steady himself... barely. His cloak fell away, revealing the injuries he had been hiding all this time. He had not been able to wear a shirt and was instead wrapped with bandages, under which poultices were strategically located. Arnach hadn't known about the poultices, but they and every other treatment – including scars where wounds had been stitched up – were now a visible reminder of what he had suffered recently.

The revelation of just how much Maelgyn had been forced to endure to save them in the siege caused a lot of murmurs to erupt in a gallery that had been growing disinterested with the debate. Some people had been wondering why Maelgyn hadn't shown himself since the battle, but now there was no question that it was due to his injuries.

"Brode... we've known each other since we were very small kids, right?" Maelgyn began.

'Brode' hesitated slightly, but again it would only be noticed if you were looking for it. "We have."

"My father pulled me from Mage training when I was nine, and you were the one who argued with him. You were the one who begged my mentor, Thoniel, to continue my training despite his demands... true?"

It was true, and 'Brode' must have decided there was no catch to this because he agreed. "True."

"When I was twelve and wanted training in swordplay, you were the one who trained me until a mentor could be found, yes?"

That was not true... or rather, it was a half-truth. Arnach had been the one who gave Maelgyn his first lessons, and Brode merely helped, but it was close enough to the truth that no-one would know the difference. Even the real Brode might have conceded the point.

"I suppose I did," 'Brode' agreed, a little more reluctantly than before.

"You have always been willing to help me. We both know this," Maelgyn continued. "And the reverse has also always been true. When my father caught you and your first lover, the innkeeper's daughter, it was Arnach and I who argued on behalf of your petition during that Sword's Debate. I defied my own father, who had forbidden you from talking to the Sword King about the matter."

Again, an outsider might think that was the truth, but the details were wrong. It was the Sword King himself, Gilbereth II, who refused to listen to his son. Brode was going to ignore his father's decree and marry the girl anyway, accepting whatever punishment he dished out – it would be impossible for the king to object if he could get the blessing of the priesthood on his nuptials, and barring treason or another high crime the punishments that even the Sword King could deal one of the other Swords was limited – but Arnach had talked him into trying the Sword's Debate first. Maelgyn had been a part of that, but had been cowed into near silence when Nattiel took the king's side in forbidding the marriage.

This fake Brode, however, hadn't even known about the incident, and so could not argue the point. He was smart enough to figure out something he could say in reply, however.

"Fat lot of good that did me, wasn't it? The girl left me."

"Yes... and then you went after some flower seller on the street," Maelgyn replied. "And I was the one who helped you hide that affair!"

Arnach didn't know the details on that one; he only learned of the flower girl after the relationship had ended. As far as he knew, though, Maelgyn was telling the whole truth this time. Once again, 'Brode' acknowledged it as true with only some hesitancy.

"I remember."

"Suffice it to say, you, Arnach and I have always been brothers, even if by birth we are only cousins. We know everything about one another. I was injured even before the most recent battle, yet I still fought for you. I was being held together by stitches and magic, but when I heard that you were under siege I did not hesitate to come to your aid. Do you deny this?"

"It would be foolish to do so," 'Brode' said, though he looked at Lazark uncertainly. "Your intervention, saving Our Royal castle, will go down as legend whether we prevail in this war or not."

"The survival of our kingdom is of equal importance to me," Maelgyn said. "I fully understand the reasons behind your refusal. Please, my cousin – my brother in all but the accident of our birth – please listen to the reasons why we ask this. I have a personal stake in this request, undoubtedly, but it goes beyond that. There are two generals and seven lesser officers that you have appointed to command your armies in this castle right now. Before this meeting I talked with them all... and unanimously, they insisted that our best chance to survive this war is to reclaim our soldiers from those camps, and they all agree that now is the best time to launch this strike."

Again, 'Brode' looked at Lazark, and more obviously this time. To most of the audience, it would appear that Maelgyn was making an emotional appeal. Those in the know, however – including both members of the Porosian Conspiracy and Arnach – would easily recognize his words as a threat to reveal the impersonation. Lazark seemed flummoxed, and 'Brode' had to act on his own.

"I know that you want us to save your wife from the prisons of

Sho'Curlas," 'Brode' said. "But those concerns must be set aside, for—"

He never got a chance to finish. Maelgyn just turned away and headed for the door. "With or without your consent, I will rescue my wife – I ask you now to remember our history, and recognize that I am not against you. What we all need, however, is for you to save my kingdom. My injuries must be attended to, so I leave the rest of the debate in Arnach's capable hands, but I have said... what needed to be said."

Gyato was stunned at Maelgyn's theatrical departure, as were most of the audience in the gallery. He had effectively threatened treason, demanding 'Brode' agree to approve of the assault or he would do it anyway. However, that little bit of blackmail proved to be the turning point of the debate – it turned from a debate of whether to do it into a debate on how to launch the assault. An hour later it was over and Brode had agreed to the rescue plan. Gyato filed out of the room with the rest of the gallery, intent on rushing to Maelgyn's sickbed to give him the good news.

He didn't find Maelgyn there, however. Nor did he find Wangdu, who had been hiding in that room for weeks, now. Wodtke was, however, and she didn't look happy.

"He's gone," were her first words.

"Gone?" El'Athras said, entering from behind Gyato. "What do you mean gone? Who's gone?"

"Maelgyn came in here and asked me to remove the poultices strapped to his body. Now, I hadn't strapped any poultices to his body, and I'm his doctor, so I did wonder where they had come from, but I figured I could get an answer about that out of him while I helped him. Turns out it was Wangdu's work... and once I had removed them, he showed up. A spray of some Elven magical dust of some sort in my face and I'm frozen stiff for several minutes while they left the room. From what they were saying, Maelgyn's heading out to rescue his wife, regardless of what Brode decides."

El'Athras stiffened. "Are you all right? That powder hasn't harmed you, has it?"

Wodtke snorted. "Yeah. They didn't do anything to hurt me – they just both knew I would try and stop them from leaving, so they stopped me from interfering instead. Maelgyn isn't fit to walk, much less assault a castle single-handedly. That's just what he left to go do, however."

"Hm." El'Athras turned to Gyato. "You're faster than just about anyone else in the castle, save perhaps one of your fellow Nekoji. Could you catch him?"

"They will be moving slow, and I am certainly faster than they are," Gyato replied. "Even with a full hour's head start, I could catch them... but only if I knew where they were. I have no idea where this castle is that they're going to assault. Even if you showed me on a map, I would need a guide to find the exact location. Any guide who might know what path they took or exactly where this fortress they're about to assault is would slow me down too much. So, for all practical purposes, no."

El'Athras sighed. Glancing back at his wife he seemed to think things through for a moment. "Well... so be it. All we can do is hope."

Gyato frowned, thinking about what he knew of Maelgyn. "He has constantly surpassed what was expected of him. He will succeed."

"He should," El'Athras agreed. A slight grin popped up on his face. "I wonder, though – do you think he'll remember that there are other prisoners in that fortress who might need rescuing?"

Chapter XV

Mussack didn't like his latest posting. True, he was permitted the sort of leadership role one of his birth deserved, but the facilities were far below what he felt was due a high-ranking member of Sho'Curlan royalty.

For example, the castle was overcrowded. This shouldn't have made one iota of difference to Mussack, but the local commander insisted that Mussack share a room with some of the other nobles, instead of allowing each of them a private suite. There were no proper bathing facilities befitting royalty – if you wanted a bath, there was a copper basin that you could fill with hot water and sit in, like some commoner at a traveler's inn. There were no good places for practicing your sword technique, save the post that common footsoldiers trained at, but if you wanted to learn the bow and arrow they did have one single archery range. Food was rationed, even though there was plenty for the prisoners – when Mussack noted that the prisoners were eating better than he was, one of the local jailers pointed out that their food had mild poisons in them to reduce any magical strength. Allowing the nobles, or even the footsoldiers, to eat that tainted food would not be a good idea.

The restrictions imposed because of the magical prisoners were ridiculous. Large portions of the castle were forbidden, even to him, because they "didn't want the unprepared near the mages." Upon his entry to the fortress, anything on him that was iron or steel – including his sword, which had originally been one of the Sviedan Royal Swords now replaced in Mussack's kit with a far inferior bronze blade – were confiscated and shipped elsewhere (Mussack was unaware of the fate of his Sviedan blade, but he'd been told it would be returned to him after he left). Even Mussack's favorite lodestone – something he had taken to wearing since learning that his boyhood rival, Maelgyn, really was a mage – had been confiscated and locked in a storage room because it "might be used as a weapon by some of the imprisoned mages." Really, lodestones were the soldiers best defense against mages, but mages could use them as weapons? Mussack feared for the prison warden's sanity.

The only place to exercise – unless you were practicing your skills with the bow and arrow – was along the outer walls of this fortress. In an effort to keep up his sword hand, he was sparring with some of the local spear masters – there were few swordsmen in this castle, as most of the infantry relied on some form of wood-and-stone polearm or poleaxe when dealing with the prisoners. Another result of these odd mage restrictions, but it resulted in people being highly skilled with weapons Mussack wasn't accustomed to facing. It was good training, he decided, though he seemed to lose more often than he felt he should. He was tempted to speak to the sergeant-at-arms about that.

He had just suffered such a loss – the spear master had pivoted his weapon off of a parry into a counter-attack that hit him in the back of the thigh with more force than was necessary – when one of the nearby guards on watch said, "Hello, what's this?"

Mussack raised his hand to call for a break in his training and limped over to the guard. "Something amiss?"

The guard glanced at him with something akin to disdain, but then recognized who he was speaking to. "Sorry, your Highness. I wouldn't quite call it amiss, but it is unusual." He pointed down the road that led from the castle gates to a juncture that intersected with the main roads criss-crossing Sho'Curlas. Mussack saw some movement, but his eyes were not the best and all he could make out were a couple blurs.

"What are we looking at?"

The guard's mouth opened and closed a couple times before he reconsidered what he was going to say. "Er, travelers, your Highness. Two men – one appears to be a cripple and the other his caretaker."

Mussack shrugged. "So what is the big deal, then? A cripple and his caretaker don't seem to be much cause for alarm."

"I didn't say there was cause for alarm," the guard said. "But it is still strange. This fortress was built as far away from civilian settlements as we could get it – it was a secret location to start the invasion of Svieda from, even if we're now merely using it as a prison – so there should be no foot traffic nearby."

"Is our location still supposed to be a secret?" Mussack asked.

"To a degree, yes. We keep some of the war's most important prisoners in our cells; we don't want that getting out."

Mussack nodded. "Then we should send some guards out to arrest these two and prevent them from spreading word of our whereabouts."

"Perhaps," the guard agreed, turning to Mussack's sparring partner. "Send word for the Captain of the Guard. While his Highness' suggestion is appropriate, I want to ensure we won't be accosting any important people I was unaware were coming."

"Right away, sir," the man said, running off.

Mussack squinted, trying to see if he could make anything of the two moving blurs. Both of them appeared to be in heavy cloaks, and they were holding heavy staffs or walking sticks of some sort. To his eyes, they didn't look threatening in the least.

"A bit of a fuss for a couple people who probably just wandered down the wrong road," he said.

"I'm not so sure about that," the guard said. "One of those people isn't Human."

"Really?" Mussack said, squinting even harder. They still just looked like two blobs to him. "You can see that from here? How can you tell?"

"The one on the right – we've been calling him the caretaker – has long, pointed ears. That tells me he's an Elf."

"An Elf?" Mussack replied, squinting even harder. "I've never seen an Elf, before."

"You haven't? Really?" the guard said incredulously. "But you're a member of the Royal family!"

"And what does that have to do with anything?" Mussack replied.

The guard didn't actually say anything. He did, however, cough, and the cough sounded suspiciously like "Hrabak."

Mussack rolled his eyes. "Oh, don't tell me you believe in that silly tale. Look, I have never met an Elf in my life. If my father ever has, it was on a diplomatic mission to some distant foreign country, not in our throne room. There is no crazy Elf secretly ruling our government from the shadows. I think I would have been warned about him by now, at the very least, if that were true."

The guard shrugged. "If you say so, your Highness."

They continued to watch the two travelers walk down the road. They were heading for the fortress – there was no question of that – and as they got closer Mussack started making out features on them.

"I can't see those pointed ears you were talking about, yet," he said. "But that other one – the cripple – reminds me of someone. I can't place it, but something about him...."

"What's going on?" the Captain of the Guard for the fortress said, jogging over from a nearby set of steps.

"Sir!" the guard said. "We have two people approaching on the road. One of them appears to be a cripple, but the other is an Elf."

"An Elf!?" the captain replied, heading to the wall. "Hm... I can barely see him, but I think you're right. Good eye."

"We should send a few men out to arrest them," Mussack said. "If this location is to be kept secret, they can't be allowed to see us and leave."

The captain turned to stare at him incredulously. "You want to engage an Elf in combat... on natural soil? That is not a stone road, your Highness. We go out there, he has all the advantages."

"It's one Elf!" Mussack said, unable to believe that someone so high in rank would display such cowardice. "What could he possibly do?"

"It would be far, far safer to allow him onto our grounds," the captain said. "This prison was designed to keep all kinds of unusual captives – Dwarves, high level Mages, Merfolk, and Elves. We can keep them in, if we are prepared. Keeping them out, on the other hand, might be a bit of a problem."

"But it's just one Elf and a cripple! I don't care how dangerous

Elves are rumored to be – if there's only one of them, it shouldn't take too much effort to capture him. If you're that scared, call up the archers and have them shoot him down before he gets too close, but sitting here in fear is ridiculous!"

The guard's lips pressed together tightly. "Sir... he's right. While I share your assessment of what an Elf can do to us, I'm not comfortable just letting him walk right up to our front door. We should do something, and archers sound like a good call."

The captain grimaced. "Very well, call the archers. But we don't shoot until we know he actually means to attack us, got it? I don't want to start a war with any Elves if I can avoid it."

The guard was equipped with three different horns, each one sounding a different kind of alarm. It took him a moment to find the right one and blow a long, loud note in it. Moments later, more guardsmen equipped with bows and arrows started running up the stairs, taking posts along the wall.

They were still settling into position when a call came booming out from the ground. It was the Elf speaking – the cripple was still approaching the gates. "Hail the castle, hail it!"

The captain and Mussack stared at one another in surprise. Mussack surrendered the authority to speak to the Elf with a nod – after all, this castle was under the captain's command, whatever his own position was ostensibly supposed to be.

"Hail and well met, stranger," the captain called back. "For what purpose have you and your companion come here on this day?"

Most of the archers, as well as the guard and the captain, were focused on the Elf. Mussack, however, had his attention on the cripple – the man was just so familiar, but he couldn't place it. It didn't help that he was covered head to toe in a thick cloak.

Also, for someone who was limping with what appeared to be such a slow and ponderous gait, the man was making surprisingly good time. Already, he was close enough that the archers on the wall would have a hard time finding a position they could target him accurately from – the stone mantle itself would obscure their shot.

"We are here to deliver an ultimatum, we are," the Elf called out. "Free the prisoners you currently hold, you do, or this fortress – and all of the Sho'Curlans currently in it – will be destroyed, it will."

Mussack laughed. "With what army, Elf? There are only two of you."

The Elf stared at him. "That is a 'no,' it is?"

"Correct – that's a no," Mussack said.

"There may be only two of us, there may, but we could destroy you all with just one of us, we could."

And then the cripple dropped his cloak. Mussack just had enough time to recognize him as Sword Prince Maelgyn, Duke of Svieda, when the staff he carried struck one of the large lodestone panels that made up one half of the fortress' gates. It rang like a gong, and then another as Maelgyn similarly struck the other panel. That was all the time he had to contemplate things before his whole world exploded.

Nattiel's attention was drawn back to the girl – Euleilla, he now remembered her name was – when she broke from her meditation and jumped to her feet without warning. She cocked her head as if trying to listen out of their cell's tiny window and allowed a wide, natural smile to appear on her face.

"What's going on?" he asked, slowly standing up from his own bunk.

"Opportunity," she laughed.

He had become familiar with her quirk of giving only one word answers over the weeks they had been incarcerated together, but this one he couldn't figure out.

"An opportunity? An opportunity for what?"

She held out her hand. A moment later, a tethered necklace Nattiel recognized as the sort of lodestone your average soldier might wear flew through the bars of their cell and into her hand. A moment later, that lodestone was rendered into iron dust... and then reconfigured itself into a key.

"Escape," she replied.

Nattiel gawked at her as she slipped her hand through the wooden bars of their cell door and fit the key into the lock. "If you could have done that all along, why have we been waiting all this time to escape?"

She sighed in resignation, even as the latch to their cell door opened. "To gather that much iron in secret takes some time. I could only safely collect a spoonful of iron dust in a week without revealing myself. We could have escaped earlier with the amount I had already gathered when we last spoke, but I wanted more so that

I could prepare some safety measures as well."

Evidently she decided matters were too important to keep up with the ambiguity of her little one-word game. He hoped that continued to be the case, as he still had questions.

"Well, then, what changed? If that sort of thing is too dangerous, then—"

He was interrupted when one of the loudest bells he could ever remember hearing rang throughout the prison. Then there was a second, followed by the sound of stone being ripped apart and collapsing.

"Opportunity, like I said," Euleilla explained. "No-one will notice in the chaos of the outer walls being ripped apart, as they are."

"Outer walls? I... but—"

Euleilla cut him off with an amused 'look,' removing the key from the lock and tossed it to him. She raised her hand and more iron sand – this coming from her fur pallet, evidently the filings she had been able to collect earlier – flew into it and formed a small saw, which she proceeded to take to work on their jail cell door.

"Go and unlock the other prisoners," she said. "Or at least the ones who are loyal to Svieda."

"And what are you going to be doing?" he asked.

She was cutting with inhuman speed – she must have been using magic to make her hands move that fast – and it was only moments before she freed one of the ironwood bars of their cell.

"Making a weapon," she said, as her saw transformed again into two iron end caps for an improvised staff. "I intend to retrieve my belongings even as my husband rescues me. He shouldn't have all the fun, after all."

Mussack had never understood why people were so afraid of Elves until that day. Vines, erupting from the ground, were ripping the walls of their castle apart stone by stone. Their archers tried to fire at their attacker, but a wall of wood and thorns shielded him from even the most precise shot. Anyone who got too close to one of the vines found themselves flung into the distance – that was how they lost both the sharp-eyed guard and the captain.

It was absolute chaos. Yet the Elf's vines were not erupting from the stone floors of the castle – it was only the soil outside that provided him those weapons. The captain had been right – it would have been a lot easier to deal with him if he'd already been inside the castle.

What was even more terrifying was what Maelgyn was doing. The words "You get the walls; I'll go in and find her" were said to the Elf as their lodestone gates were shattered into dust. That might have seemed overly brash, but Maelgyn was backing up his words – what was once their gate was now a whirlwind of iron filings, whizzing around him and responding to his commands. This iron dust was a mage's weapon of unprecedented power – it wasn't possible to carry that much iron with you wherever you went. It would take someone fairly remarkable to be able to wield so much iron dust, even if you did... but the iron was already here, even if it had been in the form of a lodestone gate, and Maelgyn had the power to wield it.

It wasn't fair! Magic wasn't supposed to work on lodestones, and these gates were built from the two largest lodestones in the world! Mussack couldn't comprehend how this happened, but what he'd thought was the greatest weapon for use against a mage was, instead, being used against them. In fact, they were making him stronger than he could possibly have been without them.

Anyone who got too close to the whirlwind found their armor ripped apart shortly before a big ball of iron flew in and killed them. Anyone who tried challenging him directly was shredded by the dust, like cheese over a grater. The Elf was ripping the castle apart as if it were paper, but this whirlwind of iron – even if not quite as destructive – was far, far more intimidating.

It only took two or three deaths that way before people stopped challenging him.

Mussack survived being thrown from the walls in the Elf's initial strike, but he was hurt. And dazed. He couldn't be seeing this correctly – even his father had never put on such a display of magic, and he was never one to shy away from giving significant displays of his power. This was... unbelievable.

And yet Maelgyn was limping for some reason. It was a fast limp – while he looked ponderously slow, he was actually moving through the hallways at a rapid pace – but a limp it was, nonetheless. There was no call for pretense, here...

Unless Maelgyn was genuinely injured. And if he was capable of this when he was hurt, what would he be capable of when fully healthy?

Scary as he currently was... this looked like the only opportunity they would have to take him down.

Perhaps Mussack wasn't thinking clearly. Perhaps he was thinking clearly, but was letting his love of his country overwhelm his common sense. Either way, he came to the conclusion that someone had to stop Maelgyn, here and now, before he recovered his full health. And with everyone else running away in fear, he needed to be that someone.

He drew his sword. The bronze one. Now he knew exactly why the people who ran this prison insisted on locking up his lodestone and denying him a steel sword, but he still felt a sword was a better weapon in this situation than a staff. Of course, he could also have used some better armor – if he couldn't have steel he wanted bronze, but they only had leather available. Perhaps it didn't matter – nothing short of dragonhide would be useful in this situation; both leather and bronze would offer but a few seconds of protection, if that.

He did grab a bronze shield on the way. It wouldn't hold those whirlwinds of iron off for very long, but like the armor it might add a few seconds. He should also gather a few of the other soldiers to fight alongside him – they might add a few seconds to the battle, themselves. Maybe, with enough of these "few seconds" put together, he might have enough time to attempt at least one attack.

He'd have just one shot at this, even if everything went according to plan, but that might be enough. Maelgyn wasn't wearing his own dragonhide armor – now that the cloak had been pulled back into a cape, he seemed to be bare-chested. His pants were unarmored, he had bandages wrapped around his ribs and shoulder, and there were spots on those wrappings where blood had seeped through. That meant Maelgyn was vulnerable – a single arrow, one swing of a sword, and he would be just as dead as those people he was grinding to a pulp. But he had to be sure that lone attack got through, and those whirlwinds of iron were as much of a shield for Maelgyn as they were a weapon.

He grabbed a couple of the castle guards, stopping their panicked flight, as he tried working out a plan they could act on before Maelgyn got to the inner keep of the castle. The guards looked as if they couldn't believe he was going to stand up to this monster of a mage, but they stayed with him. Before he was done figuring his plan, he saw the three Sho'Curlan mages assigned to help guard this fortress, looking lost.

Sho'Curlas was not known for producing many mages. Well, not at the same rate that Svieda could, anyway – Sviedan laws were written to encourage parents to send their just-weaned children to mage schools, whereas it was a burden for most parents in Sho'Curlas. In Svieda, the nobles and even some royals might be required to send their children to a mage school; even among the Swords, Maelgyn was not the only mage – the late Sword of Sycanth, King Gilbereth's sister, had been one, as was Sword Princess Idril. In Sho'Curlas, Mussack's father Hussack had been the first royal or noble who had been sent to a mage school in over seventy years.

Sho'Curlas might have three times the total population as Svieda, but fewer than half of the mages. Fewer mages meant fewer powerful mages, and the strongest mages were usually reserved for the defense of the capital, even in times of war. Three mages who were on the low end of average would stand no more chance against the whirling ball of death that was Maelgyn than Mussack would.

But three mages, even on the low end of average, could increase the strength, durability, and abilities that Mussack and his two reluctant meat-shields would have available to them.

The plan was starting to form in his head. He rushed over to the mages – they didn't have much time to stop Maelgyn, but with their help he might have just enough.

Maelgyn was really feeling his injuries, but they weren't getting any worse. Wodtke was an excellent doctor, and had put him on a treatment plan that, in all likelihood, would have him recover to full health without any long-term damage. It would have taken at least a year to be ready for combat, however, and he just didn't have that time.

But that month's worth of treatment she gave was enough to allow him some significant improvement. Enough that he could, unaided, limp around the castle for a bit, kneel before his supposed king, stand back up, and deliver a speech.

But it had quickly become clear that, even if fake-Brode was convinced to send out the army and free these prison camps, Euleilla would not be a priority. She likely wouldn't even be an afterthought;

instead, he feared, the Porosian agenda would leave her still imprisoned... or worse, dead.

Maelgyn almost wished they hadn't consummated their marriage when they did. One night. One wonderful night... and the next day off to war, again. Had they done so earlier – such as when they were in Mar'Tok (first an impossibility, as she was still ill and recovering, and then unwise, as he had yet to decide to keep her as his wife), Sopan (an impossibility, as he was still recovering from receiving his *schlipf*), on their travels over the water (not practical while they maintained the lie that she was not blind but seasick), or in the Borden Isles (an impossibility, thanks to the wounds he received in battle) – perhaps it would not have been on his mind so much. But having done so, it was almost all he could think of while in the doctor's care... and it was slowly driving him mad.

When Euleilla was with him, even before that wonderful moment, he felt complete. Making love to her magnified all of his feelings for her, however, and now that they were apart, he felt broken. It just made his injuries feel worse.

Perhaps to stave off the madness of his grief, Sekhar – reluctantly – gave him a way out. It accelerated the healing of his wrist and arm so fast that his *schlipf* arm was fully healthy before the swelling had even gone down in the rest of his body. The *schlipf* itself could not provide this healing to the rest of him... but an Elf could.

Wangdu didn't want to do it. The process of healing a person in this way was identical to the Elven process of "biomanipulation." Maelgyn wasn't familiar with the word, but it was described to him as the Elven magic that allowed them to form the centaurs and satyrs, change the Ancient Dragons into their three modern races, and enslave their original creations like the *schlipf* themselves.

Wangdu had sworn to never use this power on another intelligent creature, a vow he had kept for over three centuries. As an Elf, he claimed, the temptation to make "changes" in the subject would be too great, too intoxicating; like a sip of wine for an alcoholic, touching those powers would make him want to use them even more. Maelgyn spent a month talking him into breaking that oath, frequently using arguments he would not have known unless Sekhar hadn't coached him.

In the end, Wangdu agreed... but to keep his oath, he instead created "poultices" that were really a biomanipulated fungi that could do the work for him, instead of directly healing Maelgyn himself.

The process was painful, to say the least. Pains that would have instead been a long-lasting, but mild, ache were instead compressed into throbbing knots of agony... and while they were relatively short-lasting, these pains could still endure for over an hour without relief.

This was why Sekhar kept telling him that the more natural healing he could manage, the better. Maelgyn had waited as long as he possibly could allow, and finally – the morning before he was to make his petition to 'Brode' – he had Wangdu apply the "poultices."

All those hours he was standing, kneeling, or sitting in front of the "King" were spent subjecting himself to this process. It was only when he could no longer deal with it all that he stood up, got in his final word, and hurried as quickly as his injuries would allow to have the "poultices" removed.

He hadn't given them enough time to finish their work. He was, effectively, eight months into a year-long healing process, and he was feeling it. He could have worn his armor, but it would have been too great a burden to wear for the entire journey to this fortress. They had no beast of burden or storage space to spare for it, so he had left his dragonhide armor behind. He could hold a sword and use it, to a degree, but not to the level needed for combat. He didn't leave that behind – with Porosian agents in the castle, he was afraid of what might happen if they got their hands on it – but the Sword on his hip was more decorative than functional. The staff he was using was more of a walking stick than anything, and not a proper weapon at all. Even his schlipf wasn't working at full capacity – the "poultices" had an unexpected side-effect which rendered Sekhar unable to grow its usual vines or spikes, and diminished its ability to talk with him.

But his magic... he was in tune with his magic like never before. It helped that, with those ridiculously oversized iron doors (which were not as effective as he suspected the guards thought; a knock on them with his staff was enough to turn them from being lodestones into cold iron. He probably could have broken through them even if that had failed, however), he had access to more "magic powder" than any mage before him would have even attempted to wield. He had no weapons, but this cloud of iron at his command could become both defense and offense. Even when he was fully healthy, he knew, this would be a feat he could never manage again – he would never have this much exploitable iron to work with – but for now, it made him more powerful than ever.

The plan was for him to get into the inner keep, seal the door behind him to keep the guards (many of whom had been lured outside by the battle) from interfering, and fight through any stragglers still inside on his way to the dungeons. Then he would bust Euleilla out and break a hole through the back wall, getting her (and anyone else he could get along the way) out that way. He was walking slowly, though, both because of his injuries and because he didn't want to lose control of his magic; it was a surprisingly long path between the outer gate and the inner keep.

Much of the Sho'Curlan resistance had withdrawn after the first few guards met such gruesome ends. The more dutiful ones turned their attention to Wangdu, who claimed to be invulnerable and unbeatable while on fertile ground, at least from the weapons these people held. Others were running away, or at best were watching in stunned disbelief. There were a few, however, who hadn't surrendered to the inevitable, and were looking to mount one last, desperate defense. They were gathering in front of the entrance to the keep... and were led by a familiar face.

"Mussack," Maelgyn growled.

Mussack looked utterly terrified, but he was standing there with sword drawn and ready to fight. Honestly, it impressed Maelgyn – he never would have thought that the arrogant little pissant who he shared a tutor with for several years would have had the courage to stand up to the deadly forces being wielded.

"I c-can't afford to let you leave this fortress alive," Mussack said. "You're too much of a danger to my kingdom."

Maelgyn cocked his head. "If you think you can take my life... come at me."

As Maelgyn requested, Mussack started his attack. One of the guards charged ahead of him, and two others flanked his sides. He had evidently decided on a human shield approach, which actually was a sound, if rather cold-blooded, tactic. It wouldn't do him any good, in Maelgyn's estimation, but it was sound nonetheless.

The first two guardsmen, protecting Mussack's front and right flank, were brutally disposed of before they were close enough to be of any threat. The guardsman on his left flank managed to thrust his spear before being stripped of his gear and killed, but that was parried and knocked away by Maelgyn's staff without dealing any damage. Mussack was the only one who got close enough to attempt a direct strike.

Maelgyn saw the sword coming. Were he at full health, he could think of at least six ways to easily block the attack. As it was, he still had two. Both required some exertion of magic, but he could easily afford it.

He reached out with his magic, hoping to grab the blood in Mussack's arm and push it – and him – away. He sensed it, reached out, started to grab hold, and—

He was blocked! There were at least three different mages all working counter-magic to stop him from manipulating Mussack in any way. They weren't especially powerful mages, and under normal circumstances he could power his way through them as if they weren't even there, but his magic was spread too thin, and it was too late to pull any of it in.

Options flashed in Maelgyn's head as the bronze blade headed for it. He had no armor. His injuries left him too slow to draw his sword in time to counter the blow. His *schlipf* was still shaking off the effects of the "poultices" and couldn't do more than scream in his head about the danger. His staff had been pulled too far out of position by the flanking guardsman to be of any use. What did he have left?

He considered dodging, but any way he would dodge would have left him in lethal peril from his own cloud of iron dust. He could form that same iron dust into a shield, but he didn't have enough time to make it solid enough to stop anything. His only chance was to push through the counter-magic... and he already knew that would be too late to help.

Maelgyn's eyes widened, the blade heading for his throat. Visions of past mistakes flew in his head... and regrets for lost futures. Maelgyn closed his eyes, silently saying a last prayer that Wangdu would be able to follow on what he'd already done and complete Euleilla's rescue.

A crunching sound followed, and when Maelgyn realized he was alive several seconds later he re-opened his eyes.

"Hi, love," Euleilla said, standing in front of him with a wide grin on her face. She was wearing the same dragonhide armor she'd worn to the battle, an odd-sized staff in her hand. There was a little blood dripping from an iron end-cap on that staff, and Mussack was lying dead at his feet with a caved-in skull. "What took you so long? I was just about to rescue myself without you."

Maelgyn's mouth opened and closed a few times, unable to form words. When he started getting words out again, he didn't seem capable of connecting them into sentences. "I.. but... you..."

"By the way, I found someone you might want to talk to," she continued once he proved himself verbal again – if still inarticulate. "Allow me to present Sword Prince Nattiel, Duke of Rubick and your father. Nattiel, allow me to present my husband, your son, Sword Prince Maelgyn, Duke of Sopan."

Nattiel seemed just as stunned, looking back and forth between Euleilla and Maelgyn. "You married *her*? My *son* is your husband? This is— never mind, we'll talk about it later. Let's get out of here, first."

Euleilla nodded. Gesturing to one of the clouds of iron fragments Maelgyn still had flying around, she asked, "May I?"

The question and its obvious meaning galvanized Maelgyn into coherence. "Of course."

Euleilla assumed control of about one quarter of the iron that Maelgyn had flying around and sent it out into the stone debris that Wangdu's continuing attacks was producing. Stone brick after stone brick returned, gradually being piled into crude walls that lined the path between the keep and the outer gate. It took several minutes, but soon they were six feet tall. The iron itself started forming plates along the top, with Euleilla grabbing more and more of it as she worked. Soon, the path was fully covered.

"Whew," she gasped, the project complete. "I haven't pushed my magic like that in weeks. We'll need it, though."

"What do you mean?" Maelgyn asked.

"Well... Nattiel and I aren't alone." She whistled, and Sviedan prisoners started streaming out of the keep, slipping past them and heading for the gate. "We should probably go too, yes?"

Maelgyn shook his head. "Right. Come along, father, wife. We should probably get outside first and help Wangdu cover our escape."

Chapter XVI

'Brode' (for he had no name of his own. Well, no name that Human, Dwarven, or Elven ears could interpret) relaxed in his bath as the last of his attendants left. The crisis was over, so he could revert to his natural body. Water was absolutely critical to keeping his Human form, whatever its temperature, though he was still adjusting to the heat Humans preferred for their baths.

That had been a long session. He'd very nearly slipped back into his Merfolk form several times during the petition; subsisting only on the water you could find in a small jug was not sufficient to stay transformed for very long. He knew he had given in, partly, because he was so desperate to get more water in his system. He half-wondered if he'd imagined Lazark's consent.

The sound of a door starting to open had him quickly retake the 'Brode' form. Fortunately, even if he had been noticed, the person entering the room wouldn't have cared.

"Will this incident set us back too much?" 'Brode' asked. "Should we pull out now?"

"I've done what I can," Lazark said, shaking his head. The Porosian handler was not positioned to take much action, at the moment, but he could keep an eye on things. With the door secured behind him,

Lazark started pacing in front of the bathtub. "That lovestruck fool they call a Sword Prince left a lot of hints that he knew who you really were, but he was willing to let things go as long as we agreed to follow through on this petition of theirs. I was starting to think we should go along with a variation of his plan, anyway, so I figure we will not be too badly harmed if we let him think he managed to blackmail us into doing things his way. As we don't want Sho'Curlas to win this war any more than they do, it could even help us, and if he thinks we're open to blackmail we might be able to catch him overreaching."

"If this petition of theirs would help your cause, why fight it in the first place?" 'Brode' asked.

Lazark frowned. "Secrets are the bedrock of this operation, and it is a hard thing to keep a secret even between two people. Is there a reason you need to know?"

'Brode' pulled himself out of the bathtub, stepping over the lip to grab his robe... and a Sword. He was not wielding it offensively, but the threat was clear. "Every time I reject one of their plans, I run the risk of them exposing me and overthrowing our new government. We know it's going to happen, but we're trying to make them try it on our terms, when a chance for me to escape safely will be present. If you have motives that will require me to act in a way that makes it harder to impersonate this Sword King Brode, I think I have a need to know. Getting me killed was not part of our plans, and the other Merfolk will not be happy if I am."

Lazark winced. "It is true that I may sometimes require you to enact a law or make a decision that could prompt an early rebellion, but only if their is a big enough reward to justify the risk. We aren't in position, however, for a complete takeover, or even to set off a Sviedan Civil War. Deliberately provoking such a reaction would mean everything we've accomplished these past few months would be for naught. We must account for all the Swords, first. Gilbereth and his sister's death opened this possibility to us. We are fairly certain Ambrosius is dead, even if our associates never found his body. Our agents are delaying Idril and keeping all news from her. Our plan eliminates both Brode and Arnach as contenders for the throne. We're making progress, and we're close, but we have two issues still to address: Maelgyn and Wybert. We might be able to get away with assassinating one of them, but not both. If only that spy of yours had gotten Wybert during that sea battle... with Maelgyn lying vulnerable for a month, he would have been an easy target."

"We thought Wybert would die with his ship," 'Brode' replied, still brandishing his sword. "As did you. We later tried your plan with Maelgyn when he sailed to Largo, but our assassin couldn't even get close to him."

"True," Lazark admitted. "I was not blaming your people, my friend, just lamenting a lost opportunity. Unfortunately, those lost opportunities might cause us more problems."

"What do you mean?"

"He may effectively be crippled, but Maelgyn is no longer an easy target," Lazark said. "After his little speech, he left not just your court but also the entire castle. We also think that Elf in our jails went with him – at any rate, he's no longer in his cell."

"But... where would he go? For that matter, how would he leave? He was in no condition to ride out of here, not even in a cart."

"Apparently he just walked right out the front gate with the Elf. No-one stopped them – we had placed no orders with the guards to stop them."

'Brode' almost dropped his sword in disbelief. "But, as you said, he's a cripple! It didn't look like he would be able to walk out the castle gates any more than I could if my legs were still flippers. You can't fake that many injuries."

"No, but you can exaggerate them," Lazark said. "And with the help of an Elf, you can heal yourself pretty quickly. It's unlikely, even now, that he would consider himself fully healed – there are limits to what even an Elf can do, and some of those wounds we saw must heal naturally – but he's certainly in better health than the impression he made during the petition might make you think."

"So he is out of our reach," 'Brode' said, finally letting his Sword down. "But we still had no plan to deal with him, yet, anyway... so what has changed, really?"

"Ah, now here we get to the answer to your earlier question, 'why fight the petition in the first place.' I believe that Maelgyn is using that Elf to rescue his wife from that prison camp."

"So? Yes, she's a mage, and Porosian tradition doesn't easily accept mages of their caliber being put in positions of power, but we've long known there was only so much we could do on that front."

"If it were just that she was a mage, we would have agreed to the petition from the beginning," Lazark said. "As strong a mage as she is, I have no doubt she will find herself on the front lines of battle once again. She and Maelgyn, both. While they can greatly enhance the strength of any army they work with, however, even powerful mages are by no means invincible; we should have plenty of opportunity for assassinating her and blaming it on the fog of war, if it comes to that."

"Then what is the objection?"

"We have known the location of the prison Maelgyn's wife has been kept in for several weeks, now. The problem is that this is the same prison that also holds Nattiel – one of the Swords, whose prior defense of this castle has him popular enough that he could usurp your throne if we give him sufficient cause – such as you not being who you say you are. His freedom could undo everything we have been able to achieve, so far."

'Brode' nodded slowly, returning to his bath. "So if this Elf were to succeed in rescuing Maelgyn's wife..."

"We get one more Sword we have to deal with," Lazark finished for him. "And a more problematic one, at that. Strangely, he is probably more sympathetic to Porosian traditions than any of the other Swords alive today, but he is also fiercely patriotic and will object to any hint that Svieda should re-join Poros."

"If we can only afford to assassinate one of the Swords, he might be the one to target," 'Brode' suggested.

"Arnach will be done once we reveal your duplicity," Lazark mused. "Which means we'd be back to dealing with both Wybert and Maelgyn... but if we plan to remove Nattiel in that way, assassination would be completely off the table for them. It would appear too suspicious."

'Brode' sank down into the water, letting it infuse him. It was easier for him to think when he was surrounded by water. A moment of inspiration had him resurfacing just a second later.

"I am still uncertain about this Wybert, who I have yet to meet," he said. "But if Maelgyn really did free the Elf and go out on his own, we might have an opportunity, here...."

Wybert emerged from his tent in the morning and was surprised to see El'Athras had returned. The Dwarf was discussing something in low voices with one of his spies, so he held back from greeting him at first. At least, until they waved him over.

"Come on, come on – we've been waiting for you," El'Athras fussed.

"Count El'Athras," Wybert said, making use of the Dwarf's formal Sviedan title for the first time. "I had not expected to see you back here so soon."

"I hadn't planned to be back here so soon," El'Athras replied. "But Maelgyn's gone and done something rash – or not so rash, if he can really pull it off – and now we have to prepare for the aftermath."

Wybert frowned. "What's going on, then? What did my cousin do? Did he remove that charlatan of a usurper unheeded?"

"No, actually. He was the one who stopped the rest of us from trying that," El'Athras said. "We understood, after he explained why, however. I'm surprised you puzzled it out, though."

"Arnach did, really. He laid it all out for me, and I've been thinking about it ever since." Wybert sighed. "How are we supposed to handle this mess?"

"Well, first we need to handle the other mess that Maelgyn's getting us thrown into," El'Athras replied. "My aide, here, was just telling me that the Dwarves who were left behind in camp have been working steadily, and it now looks like things are in fairly decent shape. Is this true?"

"More or less," Wybert said. "The camp itself is now much sturdier, and some structures have been made permanent. We now have functional and low maintenance latrines, proper mess halls, bathing facilities, a hospital, and a large surplus of residences. The stored food supply could be better – not that salt-beef and similar camp rations are ever very good – and clothes are a little threadbare, but with the improvements that have been made we might be able to stretch the budget enough to take care of those issues in time. Why?"

"Suppose the remaining Dwarves and Nekoji pulled out, but were replaced by several thousand humans. Could those deficiencies still be improved and the camp sustain itself on its existing budget?"

Wybert whistled. "How many thousands?"

"We don't know, yet," El'Athras said. "We are in the process of making a quick strike against Sho'Curlas. Our hope is to free the survivors of the sacking of Sycanth and any other soldiers who they felt should be placed into their prison camps."

"None of those people will be in good condition," Wybert warned. "Our food supply is hardly adequate for their recovery right now, and we don't have enough proper doctors for the number of people we have."

"We're willing to leave behind all of our medical staff and any surplus food we might have," El'Athras said. "Those sorts of things will be available locally, where we're going."

Wybert hated this kind of question. It involved doing math, and he hated math; it didn't help he could only guess about so many of the numbers.

"If the number of our rescued soldiers is no more than ten thousand, we can probably handle it – at least for another year or so, with what stores we have on hand," he finally said. "You might be able to push it to twelve thousand, depending on just how many supplies you leave behind."

El'Athras blanched. "We're hoping for at least twenty. Damn! How do you guys feed your people normally, if you can't feed them now?"

It was a rhetorical question. Army encampments like this one, which couldn't be expected to live off the land, needed large quantities of long-lasting or preserved foods. Also, they were far more concentrated than normal, so supply lines needed to be able to get the food to that one specific location in larger quantities than the distribution system would normally expect.

Sadly, there was another answer to the question, and it wasn't one Wybert was happy about.

"While most of Svieda's provinces are considered self-sufficient, the bulk of our surplus food production has always come from the province of Rubick. Unfortunately, Rubick is in shambles and won't be able to supply anyone with any food any time soon. I'm hoping, with the waterways cleared and the Borden Isles back under our control, we might be able to import food from there and from Sopan to keep us going. Glorest and Happaso together might be able to keep the soldiers currently present supplied – barely – but if the large reserve force now in Largo comes here to fight with us we'll be forced into starvation rations."

El'Athras frowned. "Yes, that agrees with what I've heard. How long could this camp handle an additional twenty thousand people?"

Wybert quirked an eyebrow at him. "I already said that twelve thousand was pushing it. With twenty... not long. We'd be using food far faster than we could possibly replace it, at a minimum. Forget a full year – two, three months, maybe, but that's it. And that's pushing it. Even with the camp improvements, we'd struggle to find housing for that many people. And the illnesses and injuries I expect they'll have would be beyond what we could handle."

El'Athras nodded. "Right. So, more food, more doctors, and more housing. If those could be taken care of, what else would this camp need?"

Wybert wasn't sure where this was going, but played along. "Well, we don't even have enough proper clothing for the people already here. This is an army camp, so weapons, armor, and other gear will be important. Some more standard gear like mess kits, sewing kits, bathing supplies, oils for leatherwork and polish for steel and bronze armor and weapons, parchment and ink, musical instruments and games for keeping up morale, and... well, soldiers generally need to be paid, and we normally pay them twice a year. That's coming up, soon."

El'Athras turned to his Dwarven subordinate. "Did you get all that?"

It was only then that Wybert noticed that everything they were saying was being written down.

"I think so," the Dwarf said. "Food, doctors, proper clothing for all seasons, weapons, armor, mess kits, sewing kits, bathing supplies, oils, polish, parchment, ink, musical instruments, and sufficient money to work as a payroll. And some kit housing with engineers and tools to set it up."

"Food, clothing, and medicine should be a priority," El'Athras added. "Make sure that's the priority in the first shipment."

The Dwarf shrugged. "Makes sense, but it will have to be the second shipment. We've anticipated you, sir, and have already requested one shipment. It will contain food, but instead of clothing and medicine we are bringing in more construction gear, some engineers, and the funds to purchase additional supplies locally. We've been rather disgusted by the conditions we found here."

"Good, good," El'Athras said, looking a little happier. "We'll also need a new camp overseer. The current minders won't be here much longer."

Wybert's eyes widened. "What's going on?"

El'Athras grinned fiercely. "Like I said, Maelgyn did something rash. But that's okay – he's got Wangdu with him, he'll be fine. However, we can use Maelgyn's rash action to get our own rash plans off the ground...."

Maelgyn was having a hard time of things.

One would think that his father would be happy to be rescued. That he might be grateful to the young woman who broke him out of his cell, and to his son who gave her that chance.

One might even think that a father would be concerned for his son's health after that incident. Maelgyn had not re-injured himself in the slightest, and many of the effects of the "poultices" were continuing to accelerate his recovery even after they were removed, but he was still far from full health. Each time they stopped their march back to the Royal Castle, Euleilla was quick to get him off his feet and administer what treatment she could to help him heal... but not Nattiel. Nattiel had been in shock when they had first been reunited, but that hadn't lasted long.

Maelgyn had ridden partway to the prison on a pony, allowing him to rest his injuries longer. He'd had to match Wangdu's pace, and the Elf was a pretty fast walker when he wanted to be. They let the pony go about two hours away from the prison, however, as it would have been a target for their archers, and they weren't able to defend it while attacking. Traveling non-stop, it had only taken them only two days to find the prison. The trip back to Svieda would take them more than a week, as many of the rescued prisoners were ill or injured and needed frequent stops along the way.

It was at the first stop they made that Nattiel had his first real conversation with his son since that day he'd had to flee Svieda's Royal Castle. It was not exactly a pleasant reunion, however.

"I understand you got married," Nattiel said without preamble, approaching his son while the others set up a rudimentary camp. They had no food or other supplies, and Wangdu was leading a team of men out to forage while Euleilla helped set up campfires. Maelgyn had intended to do more, like assign some of their healthier rescued prisoners to keep an eye out for pursuers – the prison may have been destroyed, but they left several survivors who might be looking to recapture them – but Nattiel intercepted him before he could.

"I'm sure my wife discussed it with you," Maelgyn said, a little affronted. "You were sharing a cell in that prison, from what I understand."

Nattiel snorted with humor. "Actually, she never said much. I rarely got more than one word out of her, some days."

Maelgyn grinned fondly. "Yeah, that's her, all right. Still, I thought she would have introduced herself, at least."

"Sort of," Nattiel admitted grudgingly. "We were each too paranoid that the other was a spy to give much away about ourselves, at first."

"And later?"

"Well, after I had just spent weeks and weeks calling you an idiot for marrying some commoner mage girl, she wasn't about to admit to being that commoner mage girl, was she?" Nattiel said.

Maelgyn winced. "Father, I—"

"Don't think this... foolhardy rescue of yours changes anything, son," Nattiel said. "I still feel you married wrongly."

Maelgyn stiffened so quickly that he tweaked the still healing muscles in his back. Ignoring the pain, he shot a glare at his father. "And just why do you think that?"

"Come on, son, surely you know why," Nattiel said. "First of all, you married a commoner. That never ends happily."

"Agaev and Amberry," Maelgyn was quick to counter.

"A beloved couple in our history, but you can't say it ended happily. They were harassed by assassins all their lives, and then Queen Amberry was finally killed while attending her husband's funeral."

"I doubt they would have considered their marriage that unhappy."

"And do I need to remind you that the marriage of Ivari and Laimoth brought about a Sviedan civil war that lasted for decades?" Nattiel asked.

"And it was my marriage to a 'commoner' that gave us the chance to end that civil war, bringing the Borden Isles back into the kingdom when we need them the most," Maelgyn countered.

"Then there's the fact that she's a mage," Nattiel said, brushing Maelgyn's argument aside as if he hadn't said anything.

"And what's wrong with her being a mage?" Maelgyn asked. "I am a mage. *Mother* was a mage – you didn't seem to object to mages when you married her."

"Mages are fine people," Nattiel said. "But you never had the mind for politics that a good Sword needs. You avoided the subject as much as you could, according to your tutors, so you needed a wife who could teach you to handle the politics, not someone who will just encourage your commitment to magic and other things that will just be a distraction from politics. I didn't need that when I married your mother."

Maelgyn sighed. He was convinced his father was lying, but wasn't sure how to call him on it. It probably went back to the way his mother died, but he wasn't in the mood to drag a confession out of him. Arguing the real reason Nattiel objected to Euleilla would take more time than he wanted to risk for their rest period. Instead, he tried to refute the argument his father was currently claiming.

"Things would have gone a lot better in the Borden Isles if I had focused more on studying my magic and swordplay growing up," he said. "Our contact on that island, Uwelain, might not have died."

"You can't know that," Nattiel said. "For all you know, had you studied diplomacy and politics more you would have been able to talk your way through that mess."

Maelgyn snorted. "If you'd ever met Paljor, you'd know just how ridiculous of an idea that is."

"I'm sure that's what you think, but you don't know what a skilled diplomat is capable of."

"I had several skilled diplomats with me," Maelgyn said. "They never had a chance to get a word out before I was challenged to a duel with the fate of the Borden Isles at stake."

Nattiel rolled his eyes. "Uh huh. Well, regardless... son, I have to figure you married for love."

"Well... I married by accident, actually, but it turned into love," Maelgyn muttered, a little embarrassed.

Nattiel went on as if he didn't hear him. "But if that is the case, I should warn you that your love won't last."

"What!"

"Oh, I don't mean to say you two will fall out of love or anything like that," Nattiel said. "I suppose she'll be faithful to you. But she has made some sort of inhuman deal with the Elves or something, as she has a *schlipf* on her wrist. It is an impressive weapon... but it reduces the lifespan of any Human who uses it by decades."

Maelgyn was a little surprised to hear that his father knew about that. Had Euleilla's *schlipf* sprouted while she was in prison? He had been too busy to check since their reunion. "Usually true." He held up his wrist, revealing Sekhar to his father, shaking his head. "Not always, however. Sometimes it can extend your life... as it will for both Euleilla and myself."

Nattiel's eyes widened. "What have you done to yourself? This... this is a slow death sentence!"

"I think you aren't listening to anything I say," Maelgyn sighed. "As I grow older it's becoming more apparent that for someone who supposedly values academic study and diplomacy, you show remarkably little skill with either. First of all, I didn't have a choice – I acquired this thing while in a hand-to-hand battle with four Elves intent on assassinating me, and it was only because *it* chose to bond with *me* that I survived that fight. And, as I said, it can extend a Human's life just as easily as it can reduce it. It depends on whether the *schlipf* is a slave or a volunteer... and ours are volunteers."

"I have never heard of anything like that," Nattiel snapped. "You're lying."

"And of course everything you have never heard before is a lie. A line of reasoning worthy of a true scholar, I see..."

Vines quickly wrapped their way around Nattiel from behind, cutting off the discussion. Maelgyn almost drew his sword to respond until he recognized their source – Euleilla, who took the opportunity to step around between them.

"A parent is fully within their rights if they wish to object to their child's choice of spouse," she said. "But now you overstep. You are slandering the integrity of my husband – your own son! Maelgyn and I are married. No amount of argument will change that, now. Go much further and I might forget you are also his father."

Nattiel didn't bother struggling in the vines for long. They weren't tight enough to strangle him, but they didn't allow him to resist much. "You are mistaken, you know. There are ways to end your marriage, and it really would be better for the both of you. You would both get to find relationships more befitting your stations."

The vines tightened slightly. Maelgyn almost said something, but his father really was being impossible – as long as Euleilla didn't injure him, she could do what she liked. He was halfway to throttling the man, himself.

"We are legally married. We have consummated that marriage. We had that marriage recognized both by the leaders of Sopan and at least two other Swords." Another slight tightening of the vine. "I am not fully versed in the exact laws on royal weddings, but I am fairly certain that there is no way for someone to end our marriage without our consent, correct?"

"T-true," Nattiel replied, gasping slightly. The vines relaxed slightly, allowing him to breath. "Well, mostly true. There are certain conditions where one Sword may invalidate the marriage of another, even at this stage of your relationship."

"Which requires that both of those who previously recognized our marriage claim they only did so under false pretenses," Maelgyn said. "Not that Arnach or Wybert would, but what possible cause would you suggest they had for claiming false pretenses?"

"Well, I seriously doubt you told them that this girl's blind, did you?" Nattiel said.

Maelgyn closed his eyes and took in a deep breath. Of course he'd told Arnach and Wybert, but at this point he was convinced his father wouldn't believe him if he said so. Why was his father doing this to him? The more he thought about it, the more his temper rose, and he found efforts to calm himself were increasingly counter-productive.

A gentle hand touched his face. He opened his eyes to see Euleilla standing in front of him, caressing his cheek. "Enough, husband – it doesn't matter."

It took a moment for him to take in what he had been doing. Euleilla's vines had been withdrawn, but Nattiel was still on the verge of choking – in his temper, Maelgyn's magic had unconsciously begun restricting the movement of muscles that allowed him to breath properly.

Maelgyn was quick to rein in his magic. He took another deep breath, still trying to calm down. "Father," he said. "Using that against my wife is... unacceptable. I will not stand for it – do you understand?" Eyes bulging, Nattiel was quick to nod. The last of Maelgyn's magic slipped away, allowing the man to collapse. "Good. And don't be too quick to assume what we have or haven't told the other Swords. Not all of them are as closed-minded as you. We've 'rested' enough – let's get moving, again."

"But we just finished setting up camp!" Nattiel protested.

"Yes, well... thanks to you, I can't sit still right now," Maelgyn said.

It had taken some arguing, but Maelgyn let his tired refugees rest a little longer before moving again. He still didn't allow them much time, however – not then, nor on any of the other stops they made. The risk of pursuit was too great, so he couldn't let them bunk down for any night until they were in relatively 'safe' territory.

They were pretty deep into Sviedan territory before he relaxed that stance. The refugees were immensely grateful to him and Wangdu for the rescue, but by that point they would have gladly mutinied against him if they just weren't too tired to do anything other than rest.

They were making a final push to the Royal Castle that day, though. About a mile out, however, they were intercepted.

"Hail, Sword Prince Maelgyn," a familiar voice growled. Moments later, a Nekoji leapt down in front of the column, resolving itself into the form of Gyato. "Perhaps you should direct your companions, here, to stop for a moment."

Maelgyn was startled to see him, but did as he suggested. "Column, halt!"

Various voices echoed the command of "halt" along their marching order, and people were quick to break formation and start setting up camp.

"It'll take a while before I can get them moving again," Maelgyn said. "So I hope we're stopping here for more than a greeting in passing."

"Hardly," Gyato said. He nodded to Wangdu, who was already gathering a detail together to go foraging and hunting with. "You might want to remember that Wangdu will be arrested the moment he is seen by the castle."

Maelgyn winced. He had actually forgotten about that. "Of course. I'll send him to the camp in Happaso – 'Brode' doesn't seem to be paying much attention to what happens, there."

"Actually, I'm going to suggest that all of these men you've rescued head to the Happaso camp," Gyato said. "I'll guide them there. You still need to take your father and your wife to meet the 'Sword King.' Or rather, you need to take them to meet Arnach, and he'll tell you what the rest of the plan to deal with him is."

"You knew, then, that my father was in that prison, too?" Maelgyn asked.

"We did not have certain knowledge, but El'Athras received certain reports – which came after you left – that strongly hinted at it." Gyato nodded over at Nattiel. "I can smell the traces of a familial relationship between you from here, though, so I would have guessed anyway."

Maelgyn frowned. "So, why are you taking the refugees to Happaso, anyway? Has 'Brode' done something that would make it dangerous for them?"

"No," Gyato said. "But it's probably best they go somewhere where he won't think of them. Otherwise, he'll have them armed and defending the castle the moment they're within its walls, instead of giving them the time they need to recover their health."

Maelgyn thought about that for a moment and had to nod in agreement. Making sure they were not under that impostor's thumb was probably for the best. "Fine. Anything else I should know?"

Gyato shook his mane negatively. "Nothing I could tell you, no. But I'm aware there are others, ahead, with more information for you. El'Athras has a plan, but he made sure none of us knew everything."

"Why not?" Maelgyn asked.

"In case one of us were caught and interrogated. 'Compartmentalization,' he called it. Oh, and Onayari and I have been trading off the watch, here, since El'Athras made his plan. Let her know that I met you, so that she knows to join me."

"Is capture a real risk?" Euleilla asked, walking up to join them finally. "I thought we were safe, now that we were here."

Gyato bowed. "It is a fine thing to see you in good health, once again, milady. In my opinion, El'Athras is merely being paranoid... but there is a danger. Has Maelgyn told you about our suspicions concerning 'Sword King Brode?'"

"It's a lot stronger than just 'suspicion,'" Maelgyn muttered.

"Not in detail," Euleilla answered. "Merely that he thought 'Brode' was an impostor, but for the moment it was safer to leave him where he was."

Gyato nodded. "That sums up our concerns well enough. It is this impostor – or his associates, whoever they may be – that El'Athras fears may get word of this plan, not the Sho'Curlans. I believe that we are quite safe from them, for the moment – they have bigger things to deal with."

Maelgyn didn't really understand Nekoji body language, but there was enough that it prompted another question. "Did Arnach actually get fake-Brode to authorize the strikes?"

"All of them, yes," Gyato said. "But it was more your speech, in the end, which did it. After that, 'Brode' was no longer arguing about whether it should be done, but how." He paused. "Their offensive broken, the Sho'Curlans are in a period of disarray. This strike will extend that period, but it will not be long before the Sho'Curlans regroup and return, and in greater numbers than we can currently match. Were we to pursue their fleeing armies, we could regain a great deal of territory, but we could never hope to defend it. Your plan to rescue our imprisoned soldiers, Sword Prince Maelgyn, will help us prepare for our enemy's eventual return far better than that would."

"I might be tempted to suggest we also reclaim Sycanth," Maelgyn said. He reached up and scratched his beard – a beard he wasn't sure Euleilla knew about, yet. He hadn't shaved since her capture, and it was becoming a habit to stroke the new growth when he was thinking. "If the real Brode were in charge, anyway. We could use those gold mines."

"Suggest it to Arnach," Gyato said. "He might be able to convince 'Brode' to do so, anyway."

Maelgyn shrugged. "I'm not sure it makes much sense without someone reasonable in charge of the country, but I'll talk it over with him."

It was then that Nattiel finally noticed the person who had caused them to make camp. He had been avoiding his son each time they stopped, but his curiosity evidently demanded he find out what was going on.

"Hello, son. What... sorry, who is this you are talking to? A friend?"

Maelgyn closed his eyes and took a deep breath. "Father, allow me to present Gyato, former Emperor of Caseificio and now, since our treaty annexing his country, Count of the Province of Caseificio. Count Gyato, Nattiel, my father, Sword Prince and Duke of Rubick."

Nattiel's eyes widened as he came to realize just who he was speaking to. Maelgyn may have been a Sword Prince and Duke of Sopan, but he was still 'just' his son, in his head. This Nekoji, on the other hand, had no such familiar connection to him – being a former emperor and now a Count made him seem so much more important, even if Maelgyn and Nattiel himself both technically outranked him.

"Milord," Nattiel said, bowing. "Many thanks for joining us in our hour of need."

Gyato stared at the man for a few moments, unblinking. The gaze was very much that of a predator evaluating its prey. "It was not entirely altruistic. We merely pounced on an opportunity that might save my people from extinction; that it could help you save yourselves in your petty little squabbles is entirely coincidental."

Maelgyn was a bit shocked – he had never heard such sentiment from any of the Nekoji he had met. Then, when Nattiel had been sufficiently intimidated into looking away, Gyato gave him a wink.

Well, his father deserved it, though Maelgyn wasn't entirely sure how Gyato knew that.

"Now, you three, head off. Wangdu and I will look after things, here."

Taking his leave of the refugees, Maelgyn led Euleilla and his father away from the camp. They made it within sight of the castle before they were stopped again – and again, it was by something dropping from the sky.

The flapping of powerful wings presaged the landing of a golden-hided creature the size of a horse in front of them, now less than a quarter of a mile from the quite visible gates.

"Greetings, Sword Maelgyn. I have not seen you since before the battle," Khumbaya said, the draconic rumble in his voice a little haughtier than usual.

"I was recovering from my wounds," Maelgyn said. He didn't look to see how his father was reacting to his first encounter with a Golden Dragon. "And since I have been busy."

"Many of your wounds occurred because I and my people were

slow in arriving," Khumbaya said. "For that, you have my apologies."

"Apologies are not necessary," Maelgyn replied graciously. "We knew that it might be some time before your people could get here. I am thankful that you made it when you did – I would not have survived if you hadn't."

There was a puff of smoke expelled from the dragon's nostrils – perhaps an acknowledgment, though with dragons it was hard to tell – in answer. "You are welcome. My people, however, do have concerns."

Maelgyn winced. It was never wise to offend a dragon. "Yes?"

"Your nation, Svieda, is not as... stable as we were led to believe," Khumbaya said. "We joined in alliance with you because you had ended your civil war, and felt you were the best candidates to protect our nest when we cannot. Now we begin to wonder; we hear rumors that civil war is upon you once again."

"My nation is not as stable as I was led to believe, either," Maelgyn said. "But we have yet to reach the point of civil war. We still have high hopes that we can avoid one."

"See that you do," Khumbaya intoned. "Now, in the terms of our alliance, we agreed to fully defend six of your cities. The Royal Castle, here, is one, and your companion – El'Athras – directed us to another location. That leaves four cities remaining for my people to defend, and he said to leave those decisions to you. Where do you desire us to roost?"

Maelgyn's curiosity was peaked when he heard that El'Athras had already designated one city, but he held in his questions. "Well, barring an invasion from Oregal, my own province of Sopan is fairly secure; the mountain range of Mar'Tok and the Orful River provide it with strong natural defenses. We definitely need defenses in Happaso, Glorest, and Largo, however."

More steam erupted from Khumbaya's nose. "That leaves one remaining city for us to defend."

Maelgyn nodded, thinking. Rubick could not be defended, any more, even with the Dragons' help, so it would be pointless sending them there. The Dragons were already on the Borden Isles, and nearly a century of civil war had proven that it was almost impossible to invade there even without the Dragons' assistance. That left Stanget and Leyland, neither of which were all that likely to see heavy action unless something catastrophic happened.

But there were things to defend against other than heavy action.

"Are your people able to distinguish between Sviedans and people from other nations?" Maelgyn asked.

"By appearance, no. By smell, we can determine if one person spent much of their lives in one Human city or another – every city has a distinct odor."

"Perfect!" Maelgyn said. That was a far better way to identify a foreigner than mere appearance. "In the province of Stanget, about two hours march outside of the capital, there is the Great Library of Stanget. Perhaps the largest collection of scrolls and books in the world resides there – a repository of knowledge the likes of which does not exist elsewhere in the world. It is part of an academy, a small city in its own right dedicated to learning and thought. I want the library – and, I suppose, the academy around it – protected."

"It will be done," Khumbaya replied. "While my kind does not need such things as books in order to exchange knowledge, we respect your need for them."

"I'm not finished," Maelgyn said. "As you mentioned, Svieda is not as stable as either of us would like. Part of the reason why that is comes from a conspiracy of Elves and Humans from Poros attempting to undermine our heritage and replace it with one that will allow them to take our homes and our lands without us even being aware of it. I fear that they may try to infiltrate that library and replace that knowledge with their own propaganda. It may not be an invasion of soldiers you need to defend against, but individual spies."

"These people from Poros wish to rob you of your very heritage?" Khumbaya roared, steam pouring out his nose. "Unforgivable! Your Great Library will be protected, even should the rest of your nation be inflamed."

Maelgyn bowed to Khumbaya. "Thank you, my friend. And thank your people as well."

Khumbaya released one final blast of steam before taking off and flying away.

Maelgyn turned around to see his father, open mouthed in shock. "Well, now – how were my diplomacy and politics there?"

Chapter VII

Maelgyn had no more than stepped one foot through the gates of the Royal Castle of Svieda when he was accosted yet again – this time by a pair of familiar young Dwarves.

"Greetings, milord," Tur'Ka said – or was it Tur'Tei? Maelgyn didn't think they were related, but he couldn't tell the pair apart. "It is good to see you again. We've been trying to meet with you for over a month, now, but have not been allowed inside the keep."

Maelgyn barely knew these two Dwarves – and really only through their association with the late Tur'Ba – and had no idea what they might want to talk with him about. The fact he was stopped yet again on his way into the castle was wearing on him.

"I really would like a rest before beginning any kind of intense discussions."

Tur'Ka shrugged. "We can wait, but it would be better if we could talk with you now. If what I've heard is true, I doubt you will find much rest inside."

Maelgyn paused. "What do you mean by that?"

"El'Athras spoke to us before he left," Tur'Ka said. "We don't know what is going on, exactly, but we were told you would not be able to stay in the castle for very long."

"Just like Gyato," Maelgyn said. "Something is going on, but no-one knows what. Fine. So, if you aren't going to tell me what El'Athras' plans are, what were you hoping to meet with me about?"

Both Dwarves bowed formally, Tur'Ka in front of Maelgyn and Tur'Tei in front of Euleilla. Tur'Ka continued to speak for both of them. "Milord, Milady. When Tur'Ba left, he was not sure he would survive. He was convinced the two of you would, however, whatever the result of the battle. He told us of his last wishes, and asked that we enforce them should he fall."

"Tur'Ba fell?" Euleilla said, frowning.

"Who is Tur'Ba?" Nattiel asked.

Maelgyn winced. He had yet to fill his two companions in on what had happened during their absence. He had planned to tell them both the full story once they were well situated, but perhaps there were some things he should have mentioned before they got there.

There was too much to explain to his father, but Euleilla deserved a few words, at least. "Tur'Ba fell in battle with Hussack, but delayed him long enough that I was able to intercept him before he killed you. Hussack may have escaped, in the end, but it was thanks to Tur'Ba's sacrifice that your life was spared."

Her lips trembled slightly, but other than that Maelgyn couldn't see any reaction to the news on her face. When he thought about it, while he often saw her express happiness, playfulness, or other lighter emotions, that was the strongest bit of negative emotion he could recall her showing almost since they met. Even when she was wading through the remains of dead bodies after the battle at Elm Knoll, she seemed calm and at peace. Only twice before had she displayed any emotional vulnerability, and both of those times they were alone together. He would have to talk to her about this.

But later. First he had to find out what these Dwarves wanted with him.

"So, Tur'Ba made some requests of you," he said. "What were they?"

Tur'Ka again was the only one of them to speak. "First, he wanted us to continue what he started, and finish re-learning the lost skill of the Dwarven Axeman. Your ally, Wangdu, was his mentor."

Maelgyn nodded slowly. "Well, I am hardly Wangdu's keeper, but

I am fairly certain he will be willing to give you some pointers. But you need to ask him, not me, for that boon."

"We know," Tur'Ka said. "But there is another request he made of us. One that involves you and your lady."

"And that request was?"

"Tur'Ba had not found fulfillment in the roles you had granted him until you reached the Borden Isles. There he found himself acting as your lady's defender – her personal guardsman. You two are great warriors, but there are ways in which you are vulnerable – ways even you may not realize – and he knew a true Dwarven Axeman could cover those vulnerabilities. He was not brought up with any martial training or tradition, but he felt it was his calling nonetheless. He worried that his chances of surviving in that role for long was low, so he made arrangements. Tur'Ba has asked us to replace him, should he fall... and that is the boon we ask of you: Accept us as your personal armsmen, to defend your lives until we fall."

Maelgyn was flummoxed. He'd humored Tur'Ba by bringing him along on his travels. Doing so had gotten the young Dwarf killed... and now two others wanted to take his place?

"I... I don't—"

"My husband accepts," Euleilla said, putting a hand on his shoulder to stop him. Nattiel muttered something under his breath when she did, but Maelgyn couldn't make it out. "As do I."

"Very good, milady," Tur'Ka said. "Shall we accompany you into the keep? We are not permitted inside unless we are with one of the Swords, according to the guards here."

"Please do," Euleilla answered, starting for the gate.

Maelgyn shrugged and followed his wife. He still wasn't sure what he thought about these Dwarven 'armsmen,' but he wasn't about to argue about it with his wife.

Onayari stood amidst the ruins of the Sho'Curlan siege camp, keeping her eyes on the Royal Castle's gate. Like many of the Dwarves, she had not been allowed inside after Maelgyn left. Only Humans could enter without the direct invitation of one of the Swords, according to the orders of the fake-Human currently impersonating a king on the throne. It was just as well – when El'Athras explained her part in the coming plan, she knew she would be better off on the outside.

She was not the least bit surprised when the Golden Dragon landed beside her, but still she flinched a little. They were quite intimidating when dropping out of the sky like that, even when they were expected.

"Khumbaya," she said, nodding in greeting.

"Are they inside?" the Dragon replied without preamble.

"They just went in... and they took those two Dwarves with them."

"Good," Khumbaya replied, a deep rumble almost resembling a purr erupting from his chest. Onayari knew purrs, being a Nekoji, but hadn't been aware that Dragons were capable of them. "I trust that your people will be able to get him away from this place safely, but inside that building he has few allies."

"I think he has many allies in that building, actually," Onayari said. "But far too many of them are unaware of the viper in their midst. They will not be in a position to act when the inevitable happens... but they will be able to support our other friends who must, for now, remain inside."

"I cannot stay to see if Maelgyn makes it out unharmed," Khumbaya apologized. "I must return to the Borden Isles and inform my people where our forces are to be deployed."

"You have left plenty of your kin to help guard this city," Onayari replied. "And my people are more than capable of escorting him to the next."

"Let's just hope that the spies your Dwarven friend, El'Athras, has tasked for this job are as capable," Khumbaya said. "Until we meet again, farewell."

Onayari spared a moment to watch the Dragon take flight again, climbing higher and higher until he was amongst the clouds before turning south and flying off. She wondered, briefly, if all this subterfuge was necessary – it was entirely possible that, in his efforts to preserve his counterfeit identity, 'Brode' would do nothing. El'Athras didn't believe it, though.

And neither did Onayari. She pulled out a horn and considered it carefully. It was time to summon the others.

Maelgyn managed to lead his companions (now four instead of two) to his most recent suite without incident. He had been seen by many guards along the way, and undoubtedly it wouldn't be long before news of his return spread throughout the castle. He wondered who would be the first to congratulate him on his safe return.

As it turned out, Wodtke was the first person he knew who would speak with him, as she was waiting in his suite. She was tending several potted plants, which Maelgyn soon recognized as the remains of the 'poultices' that had been treating his wounds. Strange – he thought that Wangdu had destroyed those.

"So, you're back," she said, glancing at him a little hotly. "How are your wounds?"

"Better than you might think," Maelgyn said. "I didn't re-injure anything."

"No? What about your magic – did you overstress that?" she asked.

Maelgyn hesitated. He didn't remember feeling any stress with his magic, but he certainly was using it more than he ever had, before. "I... I don't think so."

"Uh huh – let me check you out," she said, waving her hands over him. He felt a mild medicinal touch wherever her hand passed.

"Keep it quick," Tur'Ka said. "We've been warned that, as word of his arrival has certainly spread by now, he should soon expect a Royal summons. It would be best if we could answer that quickly when it comes."

"I'm aware. Athy was the one to come up with this plan, wasn't he?" Wodtke said. Her hand finished with Maelgyn's limbs and started over his torso. "Interesting little things Wangdu conjured up. I just wish you had consulted with me when you started this treatment. Now we might have to—"

"A trio of armored guards is coming," Euleilla said. "They just turned down the hallway, and will be here any second."

"That would be my summons," Maelgyn sighed. He glanced down at Tur'Ka. "Looks like you were right – I'm not going to have any rest at all. Would the rest of you like to join me?"

"Take the Dwarves with you, if you must, but the rest of you should stay here," Wodtke said. "I'd like to look the two of you over, and make sure that you didn't catch any of the diseases common to prison camps."

"I was well treated and never exposed to the camps at large,"

Nattiel said. "Privileges of rank."

"Still, you were there long enough that you need a doctor to examine you, and I don't trust any of the quacks around here to do so," Wodtke insisted.

The door opened at that point and Vihanto entered the room, flanked by two other guards. "Sword Maelgyn, his Majesty Sword King Brode IX requests your presence immediately." He relaxed his stance. "And I'm glad to see you back unscathed, your Highness."

"Do I have a moment to make myself presentable?" Maelgyn asked. He had several days growth of beard to deal with, his clothes were stained and torn, and his hair was in bad need of a wash.

"You can have a few minutes, but I'm afraid not long. His Majesty is quite insistent that you attend him soon."

"Hmph... well, I'll see what I can do," Maelgyn said, slipping into the back of the room. The beard and hair would have to wait, but he could at least strip off his soiled cloak and replace it with something clean.

"Tur'Tei shall accompany his Highness as a personal armsman," Tur'Ka told Vihanto, gesturing to the other Dwarf. Tur'Tei merely grunted in acknowledgment before Tur'Ka continued. "I'll keep an eye on things here."

Vihanto gave a careless shrug, though there was a twinkle in his eye. "Well, his Majesty didn't say anything about forbidding Maelgyn from bringing his own armsman. You're welcome to accompany me. Sir Leno and Arnach will be attending, as well – they are probably already in the court, in fact."

Maelgyn hated having a beard, but there wasn't any time to do anything about it. He didn't want to deal with his armor right then, ceremonial or functional, but he had his Sword, at least, and similar accouterments of his office that were – while uncomfortable to wear in his current state – quite presentable. He was able to splash some water on his hair to try and get it back into some semblance of order, but that was the extent of grooming he could afford the time for.

"Very well," he said, stepping over to Vihanto. Tur'Tei immediately took position on his left flank. "Let's get this over with."

The job of courier was not highly regarded in Sho'Curlas.
It paid well, came with the right to exploit certain patches of land

that were near the various messenger service buildings, and allowed a man plenty of time to themselves (though not a woman – women were forbidden from being messengers for reasons few could remember). It was a lonely life, sometimes, as messengers tended to spend days or weeks at a time on their own, traveling from city to city, but some people liked that sort of thing.

The problem came with the job itself. Few people would employ a courier to deliver good news – maybe the odd freeman or peasant announcing a wedding or birth to distant family, but usually a town crier was sufficient for that. Much of the time, they were employed to deliver innocuous reports between landowners, nobles, temples, and the like. When those people wanted good news delivered, however, they generally employed their own court heralds to take care of it.

Bad news, on the other hand, seemed to be their specialty. Did someone die? Temples would hire couriers to inform all of the dead man's kin. Taxes fall short? The couriers were employed to relay that to whoever was next up in the chain of command. Someone lose a major battle? Again, it was the couriers who would have to let the rest of Sho'Curlas know.

No-one liked receiving these sorts of messages. Usually it would result in anger. Sometimes it would result in tears. Violence was not unheard of, and therein came the biggest drawback of the job. Especially when the person who might become violent was one of the highest-ranking Royals in all of Sho'Curlas, making it a crime for the courier to defend himself.

So it was with great trepidation that Thorell, son of Behal, knocked on the door leading to the chambers where he was told that Hussack, father of the recently deceased Mussack, was residing.

There was no reply for a long time. Thorell was starting to wonder if he had come to the right room – or if he really wanted to wait out here for so long just to deliver such undoubtedly upsetting news – when the door slowly squeaked open.

Thorell had never seen Hussack, before, but the man who answered the door clearly wasn't him. Hussack was known to have recently lost an arm, but he was also described as tall, powerful, and aristocratic. And Human – while attempting to disguise himself with a heavy cloak, this was clearly an Elf.

"Yes?" the Elf asked.

"Urgent dispatch for Prince Hussack," Thorell said.

"Hussack is still recuperating from his recent surgeries," the Elf said, grinning in a way that disturbed Thorell. The fact he was talking like a Human rather than a normal Elf somehow added to that feeling. "I've been helping him to recover, but he passed out a few minutes ago. Perhaps I can take your mail?"

Thorell hesitated. "I would like nothing better than to have someone else shoulder this burden for me, but I cannot. It is my duty to deliver these sorts of messages personally."

If anything, the Elf's grin grew more manic. "Oh, one of those kinds of letters. Well, come in, then, and we'll see if we can't get his Highness awake enough to receive it."

Thorell noticed blood staining the hand that was gesturing him inside and wondered if, perhaps, he should have been willing to shirk his duties just this once. He really hoped he wasn't about to be killed as the 'inconvenient' witness of an assassination.

The room was very dimly lit. Considering the widely-known Elven affinity for sunlight, Thorell was a little surprised at how comfortable this Elf seemed to be in the dark.

He was led past a blood-stained table, where unwashed medical equipment was still strewn. A few raised chairs were left in position for the seated to watch the table. An improvised operating theater, perhaps? But where was the patient?

They passed into a back room. There was nothing in the room except a lit fireplace and a rather large hole in the wall, which looked recently opened but structurally safe. The hole opened up into a large cavern – not an unusual feature in the Dwarven-built parts of the city, but rather strange for a bed chamber.

Thorell's trepidation grew as he was directed into the tunnel. Just where was this strange Elf leading him, anyway? In his career, Thorell had encountered a few Elves. Invariably, they were all crazed – a product of their longevity, he was told. None he met had been violently insane, but there was always a first time.

The tunnel wasn't especially long, but it was rough-hewn out of stone and difficult to pass through in some sections. At least it was dry – Thorell had been through a few ancient Dwarven caves that didn't have a dry patch in them.

Eventually the tunnel opened up into a larger chamber. This

chamber was very hot and stuffy. Smoke from numerous torches filled the air, making it hard to breathe. There were three other tunnels leading out of the chamber, aligned – Thorell suspected – on compass points; if the map in his head was right, he had been moving eastwards. Also, the floor changed from hewn rock to packed soil.

When the Elf entered the chamber behind him, vines grew up behind them and closed off the passageway they had come from. "When you leave," he said, pointing to the 'northern' tunnel. "You would be well advised to go that way."

Thorell hesitated, but couldn't keep himself from asking the obvious question. "Why that way?"

"Well, I don't want anyone else coming down here without me to escort them, so I've sealed off the way we came," the Elf said. "And if you go the other way, you will eventually find the reason I chose to make my home in Sho'Curlas: The ruins of the Tengu capital. The Tengu left traps that would slaughter anyone who was not a Tengu."

That left Thorell with so many questions he couldn't figure out how to ask them all. All he could come out with was one word.

"Why?"

The Elf laughed. "The Tengu killed themselves, you know – we Elves did not win, and while the Tengu could not defeat the Dragons there were never enough of those to matter. My people believe they killed themselves because they knew they would lose, and didn't want to give us the satisfaction of winning, but I don't share that belief. No... they must have had a plan. Either they didn't all die, like they claimed, or they have some way of coming back to life some day. Either way, there must be a secret to defeating them, so I continue searching their city for it. While I do, I hope to build Sho'Curlas into the greatest empire the world has ever seen, for when the Tengu return it will be the Humans who must fight them. My people are dying, the Dwarves are dying, the Nekoji are dying, the Dragons cannot grow very quickly... but a Human empire? Humans are a growing people, and they might actually stand a chance when the Tengu return, so I continue to search the Tengu city, in hopes of finding some weakness your people may one day be able to exploit."

Thorell had never even heard of the Tengu, before. He wasn't sure if these ramblings came from legitimate fears or if this Elf was completely delusional, though he doubted that whatever they were they would be 'coming back to life.' Assuming he got out of this delivery alive, he would have to ask another Elf if they really existed, however.

"Um... and Hussack?"

"Oh, right," the Elf said, frowning. "We were going to see him, weren't we? Well, come on, then."

He again led Thorell 'east.' This tunnel resembled one of those damper Dwarven caves Thorell had been thinking about, earlier, but again it was short. Eventually it rose to the surface, opening up to a small, outdoor meadow, bordered on all sides by some thorny bushes... all sitting on the edge of a cliff face.

Hussack was asleep, there, lying on a literal bed of flowers. The stump of his missing arm wasn't visible, as one of those flowers was now encasing it. Thorell wasn't even sure the man was breathing.

"Is he even alive?"

"In a sense," the Elf said. "He must be kept perfectly still while I work, so I have slowed his heartbeat until it nearly stopped. He is becoming my great experiment – a test of my greatest weapon against the Tengu." He went from laughing to sneering in a moment. "Not like any of my kin can be trusted to prepare for them. They cling to the belief the Tengu are all gone. Ha! If they were all gone, where did they go? They don't even have any grave-sites! How is that even possible, if they're all dead? Idiots! They just sit around and go madder and madder by the day. I am merely doing what our Ancient brethren knew must be done – anything and everything that can be done to stop the Tengu! I hate my living kin. Most of them won't even abandon their arrogance enough to drop their nonsensical bifurcated verbs, even when speaking in Human tongues! And they call me 'mad.' Ha! I and Lady Phalra are the only two Elves who have earned that designation, but my entire race is crazy. Phalra may buy into the belief that the Tengu are gone, but at least she has plans for this world that don't include diminishing the other races. No, she embraces them! And they call her *mad* for it! Those idiotic *lunatics!* They think her mad! They think me mad! They are the crazy ones! *They* are!"

His ramblings had gotten so intense that spittle was now flying and arms flailing. Thorell was afraid about what the Elf would do if he weren't interrupted – already, he noticed the thorny bushes acting as a safety rail around this outcropped meadow were growing taller, their thorns growing sharper.

"Um... can Hussack be awakened, then?" he asked, hoping not to set the Elf off further.

The Elf froze, arms in mid-air. "Well... briefly. That's right – you're here to deliver him an important message, aren't you?"

"A personal one, yes," Thorell replied.

The Elf walked over to Hussack's body. More vines slipped out from the bed and started encasing the unconscious Prince, holding his limbs tight. When that was done, a quick tap of his hand to Hussack's head was enough to awaken him.

"Wh-what?" Hussack said, eyes looking around wildly. "I can't move!"

"You cannot be allowed to," the Elf warned. "It would kill you. You should not be awake, but this man has an important message for you."

"What man?" Hussack demanded. "Where am I?"

Thorell stepped forward, getting close enough for the Prince to see him. It felt somewhat awkward, delivering a message to a member of the royalty that was currently encapsulated by vines, but he'd come this far. "Your Highness? I'm a courier. I bring news from the front."

"Well, it must be important. Otherwise, Hrabak would never have awakened me."

Hrabak! Well, that explained some things. It seemed the legendary Elf behind the Sho'Curlan throne was real. Thorell worried even more about surviving this encounter. He just hoped Hrabak would really let him leave after delivering his message.

"I never told Hrabak what your message was, but yes, your Highness, it is important," he said. "After your siege was broken at Svieda's Royal Castle, our forces were in disarray. Svieda took the opportunity to launch several quick strikes against us, freeing their prisoners of war."

Hussack frowned. "That is not good... but why awaken me? Were you hoping that I would be able to return to the front and set things in order?"

"Lord Knold is directing the front, for now, and he did not ask for you. I imagine your return to the battlefield would have been a great morale booster, however."

"According to Hrabak, that won't happen for a while," Hussack said.

"My message is on a more personal matter, your Highness," Thorell replied. "I regret to inform you that, n the process of trying to defend one of the prison camps, your son Mussack was killed."

Despite all of the vines holding him down, Hussack was able to turn his head and lock eyes with the courier. "Who?"

Thorell hesitated. "I... Mussack, your Highness, as I—"

"No!" Hussack snarled. "Who killed him?"

"Oh. We don't know for certain, your Highness – reports are unclear. There were three people it might have been: The Sword Prince Maelgyn, who evidently is now regarded as a High Mage. His wife, Euleilla, also a powerful mage, who was seen wielding an Elven weapon of some kind. And then there was an Elf."

Hrabak started at that news. "An Elf? Did you get a name?"

It was Hussack who answered. "If Maelgyn was involved, there's really only one Elf it might be. Wangdu, formerly of Squire's Knot. Our spies show he was instrumental in arranging Svieda's recent annexation of Mar'Tok and Caseificio, and is in the process became the Sword Prince's close friend."

Hrabak frowned. "Wangdu? Hm... interesting. He never dismissed my beliefs about the Tengu – if anything, he is one of the few Elves who think as I do, that they are still alive – but he has had moral qualms with the ways my Ancient kin went about fighting them. I have long held that that following his moral path at the expense of the destruction of the world was his form of insanity – all us Elves have one, you know. It just shows more on some than others. I doubt most Humans even know he is insane."

"Moral?" Hussack repeated, his voice eerily calm. It steadily rose as he continued. "How can an Elf claim siding with Svieda is the 'moral' path? Svieda is no nation of saints! True, we were the aggressors, but Svieda would have attacked us if they thought they had a chance. Don't tell me they wouldn't have! And now... now this 'moral' Elf kills my son! Unforgivable!"

"Calm yourself, Hussack," Hrabak warned. "You are in a very volatile stage of your healing. Paljor failed to calm himself, and he emerged with such a temper! No wonder his own people decided they were better off asking some outsiders to conquer them rather than stay under his rule."

"But—"

"As for your moral Elf... you would be surprised what someone might be able to justify as a 'moral' act. I make no bones about it – I am a monster. I care nothing for Wangdu's moral code. I'm only concerned about setting us up for the end game. I hate the Elves, but I would gladly use them if they would work with me for the greater good of us all. Wangdu... he used his 'morals' to justify treason, arranging for the death of all the Elves in Mar'Tok when he helped the Dwarves reclaim their homeland. Tell me – just how moral is treason?"

"He sounds more like a monster than you do," Hussack said, finally relaxing against the vines again. "Tell me, Hrabak – when you are done with this treatment, will I be strong enough to kill this Wangdu?"

Hrabak laughed. "I certainly hope so. My goal with you, friend Hussack, is to create a being strong enough to slaughter whole armies of Elves on their own!" He put his hand back on Hussack's forehead, sending the Prince to sleep. "Now rest... you have another year of this treatment before I can graft that arm onto you." He turned around, and was surprised to find himself alone. "Huh... I could have sworn I brought someone with me when I came here. Maybe it was another figment of my imagination, like last time...."

Thorell, having done his duty, fled when Hussack had started rambling about morals. He was now in the northern passage, hoping against hope that Hrabak had told him the truth about how to leave this place. He had no desire to stand near those two madmen.

He also had a particularly interesting report to give to his contact in the Dwarven spy service. He wasn't sure what El'Athras would make of this one.

For some reason, the glare that 'Brode' was sending Maelgyn made him nervous. He'd stood up to 'Brode' before, in this very court no less, and with more on the line. Perhaps it was that he had no idea why he had been called before his supposed king, but this felt like a far more dire situation.

"So. You've returned. Later than most of the other raiding parties we sent out, too, and they started after you did."

Maelgyn wasn't quite sure how to respond to that one. Was 'Brode' seriously going to try dressing him down for tardiness? "I was on foot, your Majesty. And I was and am still recovering from the injuries I suffered freeing *your* castle from the Sho'Curlan siege. That slowed me down, especially on our return trip."

'Brode' snorted. "Yes, your wounds were achieved honorably, but that means very little. One instance of heroism does not make up for another instance of treason."

Maelgyn ignored the gasps from the audience, though he couldn't help his eyes from widening at the accusation. What basis could 'Brode' possibly be using to come up with such an accusation?

"I am unaware that I have committed any treason... or were you merely speaking hypothetically?"

'Brode' stood from his throne. "You haven't? Were you not the one who was seen leaving the castle gates accompanied by the fugitive escaped prisoner, the Elf, Wangdu?"

Maelgyn cocked his head. "Wangdu has been a member of my court since I assumed my title in Sopan. What, pray tell, was the crime for which he was imprisoned?"

"He has done something to the Royal Archives. Documents may still be examined in the archival chambers, but cannot be removed for further study," Lazark called from where he stood, off to the side.

"Interesting," Maelgyn said. It was certainly that – they hadn't come up with any justification for imprisoning Wangdu when they'd pulled him out of the prison; evidently, they figured something to accuse him of after learning he'd escaped. He could exploit that. "You must not have done any questioning of him once you captured him. His 'crime' sounds like a very effective method of preventing theft. My own court archives were recently discovered to have been tampered with, and he likely was attempting to add security to prevent the same from happening here."

"Unimportant," 'Brode' said. "No-one had been granted permission to release him from prison, so he was a fugitive. You helped him to escape from the castle."

"We just walked out of the castle – we were seen by several guards, but no-one ever stopped us. And I did not release him from prison," Maelgyn replied. "If you'll recall, I was bedridden until the very day

I left, but I saw him walking the halls of the Castle for several weeks of my convalescence. I did know he was in the prison, but it seemed like a misunderstanding caused by the fog of war. I figured someone had released him from the dungeons once his status in my court was made known."

"If you were not the one to release him from prison, who was?" 'Brode' demanded.

From the audience, Arnach cleared his throat. "Forgive me, your Majesty, but I ordered him released weeks before Maelgyn left us. It was my understanding that he was only in prison because your guards did not know if he was friend or foe. As he was a member of Sword Maelgyn's court, and as I could identify him, there seemed no cause to continue holding him."

"And you did not bother to inform anyone you had done this?" 'Brode' asked incredulously.

"Why should I have?" Arnach asked. "Given the official reason for his arrest, I was perfectly within my rights."

Maelgyn knew that Arnach was lying – it was El'Athras and Gyato who had arranged for Wangdu's release, well before Arnach's arrival – but perhaps 'Brode' would respect Arnach's authority on this matter. Theoretically, those two should also have that authority, but with 'Brode' in charge it was difficult to say if it would be recognized. Best to get them off this topic before Arnach was faced with questions he couldn't answer.

"At worst, your Majesty, this sounds like a case of clerical mistakes; had the official charges included mention of Wangdu's tampering of the archives, Arnach would not have had the authority to release him and I would not have suspected his release was legitimate," he said. "I do not see any way this might reach the level of a treasonous crime, at any rate."

'Brode' turned to him slowly, a frown on his face. "For getting him out of the prison, perhaps. But as the guards were never informed of his release, he should have been captured before he left the castle. Yet he was, evidently, moving through the hallways of this, our home, unimpeded... for weeks! How is this even possible, unless he had some Royal assistance?"

It was a ridiculous question, and Maelgyn was on the verge of chucking the plan – a plan he still had not been clued in on – and proclaiming the fateful challenge of 'Brode's' authority that would get him arrested, even if it pulled Arnach and himself out of the ranks of the Swords. With Wybert safe in Happaso, Nattiel now free, and Wangdu's trick keeping the Royal Archives safe, perhaps Svieda was in no danger of being overthrown by the Porosian Conspiracy at this point.

But El'Athras did have a plan, so for the moment it was probably best to play along. However, that didn't mean he had to let 'Brode' run over him.

"How should I know?" he asked. "I was bedridden the whole time he was in the castle. We were unchallenged when we left, and I don't know why the guards would have missed us. And even if I had, somehow, convinced the guards to look the other way... what would it matter? Wangdu has not done anything against Svieda. There were no crimes attached to his name on the official record, and the thing you have accused him of in this session of court today was done for Svieda's benefit. Nothing I have done – even at the worst possible interpretation – constitutes treason."

A look flashed in 'Brode's' eyes, but it passed too quickly for Maelgyn to make it out. "So, you compound your crime with arrogance, daring to lecture me on what is and is not treason?"

Maelgyn started. Where did that come from? It took a moment, but Maelgyn eventually decided that 'Brode' had been looking for him to lose his temper. It wasn't much of a temper tantrum, but it apparently was enough for 'Brode,' who had been losing control of the debate from early on. Maelgyn had refuted any genuine arguments; all 'Brode' and Lazark had to work on him with, now, was pure bluster.

Fine, let him bluster.

"As one of the Swords, I have that right," Maelgyn said. "And given the circumstances, I think it's quite obvious that someone should."

"Enough!" 'Brode' snarled. "Your arguments may have some merit. If Arnach was truly the one to release this Elf, and if the Elf's crime really was an attempt to protect the archives, and if the guards really did do nothing to stop you from leaving, then perhaps your crime was not of treason but merely that of not following the proper order of things. However, none of this testimony has been sworn to, no investigation has been conducted, and failing to notify anyone of

Wangdu's release was still an impropriety of criminal proportions."

"Only if his incarceration wasn't also an impropriety of criminal proportions," Maelgyn replied. By this point, there was a lot of muttering in the audience – for one of the Swords to defy the Sword King so publicly, it was a little surprising those mutters were still so quiet – but they were making enough noise that he had to raise his voice to be heard over them. "Now tell me, 'Sword King Brode,' just who was it who ordered him imprisoned in the first place, and what were his *official* charges at the time?"

"Irrelevant!" 'Brode' snapped. "Sword Maelgyn, you are hereby under arrest for treason. Perhaps you will be exonerated at trial, but in the meantime you will not be able to assume your duties as Sword. Sopan's Sword will be considered vacant until such time as—"

"Excuse me, your Majesty, but you do not have the authority to do that," Arnach said, stepping out from the audience chambers.

"What do you mean, I don't have the authority?" 'Brode' said. "I am the Sword King. I have all the authority in my own realm."

"Except where constrained by the Law of Swords," Arnach answered calmly. By this point, Sir Leno had also pulled himself out of the crowd and was walking over to Maelgyn.

"Play along," Leno said, whispering in Maelgyn's ear once he reached his side.

"What are you talking about?" 'Brode' snapped, ignoring Sir Leno.

"The Law of Swords," Arnach repeated. "You know, cousin – the law that you, Maelgyn, and I had to study, over and over again, until we were almost driven crazy by our tutors. The law we were told we had to be familiar with above all others. You know... that law?"

"Yes, I know that law!" 'Brode' said. "What, in that law, says I don't have the authority to remove a treasonous Sword?"

"There is nothing that would prevent you from removing a traitor... if it was proven that said Sword was, in fact, a traitor," Arnach said. "But you cannot just declare someone a traitor, strip them of their power, and send them to prison to wait for whoever knows how long. There are procedures in place, and you have so far followed none of them."

'Brode' turned to Lazark, who seemed just as puzzled as he was. Returning his attention to Arnach, he said, "Enlighten me, then."

Arnach's smile turned predatory. "Of course, your Majesty...

though I'm surprised you don't recall, yourself. It all boils down to the fact that only a makeshift council, and not the permanent council for the Royal Province of Svieda, can be called upon."

"What does that have to do with anything? A permanent council only has a few things it can do that the makeshift council cannot."

"But those few things are critical to what you are attempting," Arnach stressed. "When our father was killed, Svieda was – by law – to operate under the Law of Swords' provisions for an interregnum. During a period of interregnum, the Swords are all to operate as autonomous, but allied, powers. Treaties enacted by any of the Swords hold weight across the country only after they are recognized by the other Swords, no two provincial armies are *required* to work together, etc., etc. Yes, these things are customarily affirmed, and any rejection of treaty or division of the armies would be unprecedented, but that is merely by tradition. The key part of the interregnum provisions most bearing in this matter is that, as long as a Sword is not directly responsible for the death of another – either by their own hands or by proxy – they may not be removed from their position as Sword by any of the other Swords. Even in the event of their death, they are still the legal Sword until the interregnum is over. Only the permanent council may appoint another Sword, and only after determining what the new line of succession is."

"Yes, I understand all that," 'Brode' said. "But I am now the Sword King, so the period of interregnum is over."

"You may now be recognized as the Sword King," Arnach replied. "But, according to the Law of Swords, that does not mark the end of a period of interregnum. Interregnum persists until there is a Sword King and the full complement of Swords is restored. As no new Swords can be appointed until the permanent council is appointed, and several of the other Swords have sadly lost their lives and must be replaced, the interregnum continues."

"But treason—"

"Is certainly punishable by the removal of your title as Sword," Arnach agreed. "So appoint a permanent council, redistribute the Swords according to the line of succession, and you can temporarily suspend Sword Maelgyn's titles while a trial is carried out. You have ninety days to begin that trial, at most, mind you, and it would take at least five Swords to agree with you to convict, but if you truly feel that what Sword Maelgyn has done merits such a conviction... well, you know what your option is."

'Brode' looked over at Lazark, who seemed rather flummoxed by the interpretation of the laws Arnach was describing. He clearly wasn't giving any answers, but 'Brode' didn't seem to know how to proceed without his advice.

Finally, 'Brode' risked a direct prompt. "And... how does our Royal Archivist see the law? Is this true, according to both law and precedent?"

Lazark coughed. "Actually, your Majesty, there is no precedent for this situation whatsoever. I... I believe that Arnach may be speaking truthfully about the law – until the interregnum ends, you may not remove Sword Maelgyn from his office, even temporarily." He paused. "But if we really still are operating under the provisions for interregnum, there is another option. Sword Maelgyn may be banished from any provincial territory you control – including both the Royal Province and your original province of Glorest – until he agrees to waive his right to a jury of Swords and to submit to a trial and sentencing by your own throne's magistrates."

Maelgyn was about to demand that such a trial happen immediately, as there was no way he would lose, but Sir Leno stopped him.

"Lazark controls which of our magistrates would oversee your trial," he whispered. "Accept banishment, but name a proxy to serve in your absence. That way, you will effectively lose nothing but your suite here in the castle. Arnach will remain here to act as our eyes and ears – we all figure he's the only one of the Swords they cannot afford to assassinate, because then there will be no consequence for accusing Brode of being an impostor."

Maelgyn wanted to ignore that advice. After all, he had done nothing wrong – why should he have to leave the castle? 'Brode' was an impostor – all he would have to do was bring that up before the Royal Court and even a makeshift council could depose him. But that would hurt Arnach... and the real Brode, if he was still alive somewhere. Which really was their only hope in all this mess – finding the real Brode.

"Very well," Maelgyn said. "If you will indulge me with enough of a grace period to pack up my belongings, I will leave. At least until such time as you regain your senses, you shall not see me again. But Sopan deserves representation before the court, and for that I shall name... um..."

Who to name as proxy, though? Sir Leno would be a good choice, truly representative of Sopan Province and knowledgeable in most affairs, but Maelgyn really didn't want to give the man up as a member of his inner circle. Nor did he want to appoint his wife, since it would probably be months – if not years – before he saw the proxy again in person. Most of Sopan's nobles and military officers were much too far away. That eliminated anyone who was actually from Sopan.

Wodtke was a doctor, not a politician – she was far, far more valuable in her chosen profession. He could do something radical and appoint someone like Gyato or El'Athras, but he had a funny feeling that they had their own plans that didn't involve sitting as a proxy – it needed to be someone who would be willing to do the job. He could go eccentric, point to Vihanto, and make the selection seem utterly random. That idea had some merit – Vihanto had proven himself to be a reliable ally, helping them keep secrets and finding them supplies and other support during their stay in the castle. By making it appear to be a completely random selection, 'Brode' and Lazark would think Vihanto harmless and likely underestimate him. Still, Maelgyn would feel guilty putting the young guard through that.

But then inspiration struck.

"I name Arnach as my proxy."

Arnach started. The decision suddenly gave him a lot more options – with the proxy powers of a second Sword, especially with so few living swords, he would almost be as powerful as the Sword King, himself. All of those powers in interregnum that required more than one Sword – for example, agreeing to a new treaty and having it confirmed – he could now do on his own. If a permanent council was formed, Arnach would have twice as much influence when advocating who should be on that council. If Maelgyn ever was tried before the court as a 'traitor,' those proxy powers would be retained – Arnach would have twice as much influence to reject any findings of treason.

It was a lot of power... and a lot of responsibility. But it could be used as a weapon against 'Brode's' excesses, and everyone in the room knew it.

"I accept," Arnach said.

'Brode' glared at both of the Swords. "If you insist. You have six hours to get your things together and leave – I won't tolerate your presence a moment longer."

Maelgyn nodded, delivering a mocking bow, before turning to leave the room. There were a lot of exits, thanks to its old design, and he picked the one that allowed him to cross paths with Lazark.

"We know who you are," Maelgyn whispered, leaning over to the Royal Archivist as they got close. "And you know that we've already foiled your plans. If you want to get out of all of this alive and without my exposing your Elven colleagues to the rest of the world, you would be wise to lead our armies sensibly in this war, and not force me and my allies to take action. If it starts to look like Sho'Curlas will win, you can bet who I will be blaming."

Maelgyn continued out the door. He never heard Lazark's reply – not that Lazark meant him to.

"Actually, young prince, I can assure you that preventing a Sho'Curlan victory has always been a part of our plan. You might not like how we plan to do that, however...."

Chapter XVIII

A gruff "in there" from Nattiel, complete with gesture towards the partition, was all the greeting Maelgyn got as he returned to his suite. He walked over to see his wife stripped down to a *fundoshi*-style loincloth and nothing else.

He may have seen the sight, before, but it was still a surprise, and it certainly wasn't one acceptable for his entourage.

"Ack! Sorry!" he said, retreating, shoving Tur'Tei back with him. The silent Dwarf seemed amused, but nodded and walked over to a corner of the room where Tur'Ka was sitting.

"It's okay, husband," Euleilla called, a hint of humor in her voice. "Wodtke just needed me to remove my armor so it wouldn't interfere with her examination. You might as well come and enjoy the view until she's done."

Flushing slightly, Maelgyn shuffled his way to her side. He wasn't able to 'enjoy the view,' however. They might be married, but somehow having another person in the room made his wife's nudity a lot more embarrassing.

"And I was just finishing up, so I'll leave you two alone," Wodtke said, turning away.

"You might want to start packing," Maelgyn suggested. He

went over to Euleilla, doing his own visual – and ostensibly clinical – inspection of her as the doctor started for the doorway. He thought of something just as Wodtke was about to leave. "We'll be heading out as soon as possible."

Wodtke froze. "Sounds like things went according to plan. So you were banished, then?"

"What!" Nattiel exclaimed. He attempted to charge past the partition, but was blocked by both Tur'Ka and Tur'Tei. "Get out of – oh, forget it. Maelgyn, come over here, son!"

Maelgyn sighed, pulled Euleilla to him, and gave her a quick kiss. "Get dressed. I know we just got here, but it seems we'll have to leave right away," he whispered to her.

"I know," Euleilla whispered back. "Wodtke warned me about that. Go deal with your father – I'll be ready in ten minutes. And if you have time, shave off that beard before I join you – it tickles when you kiss me."

Maelgyn flushed, but ignored the comment about his beard. "You don't need to rush that much – we have a few hours."

"Only if 'Brode' keeps his word, yes?" Euleilla said. "Better to keep him off guard. Ten minutes."

Euleilla grabbed her armored riding trousers and started slipping them on. Maelgyn briefly considered just ignoring his father and actually enjoying the view, as she'd suggested earlier, but another shout proved too distracting. He made his way through his two Dwarven armsmen and pulled his father out of the suite and into an empty neighboring room.

"Let's give my wife some privacy, okay?" he grumbled.

Nattiel only held his tongue long enough for the door to close behind them.

"What is all this about you being banished?"

Maelgyn rolled his eyes. He didn't have time to deal with this – especially if he was going to shave that beard off. "Father, there is a lot going on you don't know about. I might have discussed some of it with you, already, if you weren't in a snit over my wife—"

"I still say you should never have married her, and should allow me to dissolve your marriage. It really would be best for all concerned, and—"

"Stop talking *now*, father, if you want me to continue thinking about you *as* my father," Maelgyn warned.

Nattiel's mouth opened briefly, but he seemed to rethink what he was going to say. "If you refuse to discuss it now, we'll talk about it later, then. But what is this about you being banished?"

As annoyed as he was with his father, it wouldn't do to leave the man defenseless when just a brief word would protect him. "This is going to take some background, which I do not have time for, but here's the most important thing: Brode is a merfolk impostor, but we're all treating him with kid gloves and going along with it because the Law of Swords could tear Svieda apart if we don't handle it carefully."

Maelgyn, mindful of his ten minute deadline, summarized as briefly as possible everything he knew about the Porosian Conspiracy (which included a brief mention of how he acquired Sekhar), the situation in the castle, and Wangdu's trick that may have saved the Royal Archives.

Nattiel was suitably astonished at first, but after considering things for a moment, he gave a nod.

"Okay... I can see why you didn't immediately depose this impostor, but the situation has changed. Your Elf friend has protected the archives, I'm free and able to offer my Sword, and you are no longer lying defenseless and bedridden in that room over there. Why aren't you taking action now?"

Maelgyn stared at Nattiel in disbelief. "You, father, of all people? Advocating direct action over politics and diplomacy?" He held his father's gaze for a second longer to emphasize the point, before continuing. "El'Athras set up this plan in my absence, and he's my spymaster. I know better than to sweep his plan aside without finding out what else he knows and what his reasons are. I hope to get answers when I finally see him again, which should be soon. If I'm not satisfied by those answers, I may just turn right around and confront 'Brode' after all."

Nattiel frowned. "You trust this Dwarf more than is seemly."

"He has earned it!" Maelgyn exclaimed. "He ceded his kingdom to us and arranged for Emperor Gyato to do the same. If that weren't enough, he also was the one who helped me see the only realistic solution for bringing the Borden Isles back under Sviedan control – without him, we would have had no Dragons to counter the Sho'Curlan invasion, and Svieda might very well be in pieces by now. And he has given us resources that Svieda could only hope to have – our spy network has been entirely inadequate, considering we missed the gathering of a massive invading army on our borders. I trust him as much as I do because I do not believe we can win this war if I don't."

"It is true that we would have been in serious trouble without the Dragons, but now that they are once more defending us I'm not sure that we're in such dire straights as to need to rely on the Dwarves," Nattiel grumbled. "I don't like Dwarves – they can be bought far too easily to be trustworthy. The only Dwarf I ever met sold me out for just a few coins, and these will sell you out some day, too – mark my words!"

"Just like you don't like being attached to mages – they kill themselves far too easily?" Maelgyn shot back. "Mother may have accidentally killed herself, but her accident is not commonplace among mages. Some Dwarf may have betrayed you once for money, but that does not mean they commonly sell their friends out." He paused, realizing time was short.

"Bah," Nattiel said. "You are too trusting, son."

"And you are too stubborn, father," Maelgyn said. "Enough! I have told you what you need to know. I must get ready to leave this castle. Will you join me?"

Nattiel shrugged. "Someone must remain here to keep an eye on things. If this Porosian Conspiracy is this far along, already, they must be getting ready to make their move. I'll be here when they do."

Maelgyn nodded. "And I will be out looking for the real Brode – if we can find him and rescue him, chances are we can get out of this mess unscathed."

"A pretty big if, son," Nattiel warned. "You may think this advice misguided, but at least consider it: Do not trust these Elves and Dwarves you've befriended too far. They aren't Human – they don't think the same way you and I do."

Maelgyn drew in a breath of air to argue, but then just shook his head and let it out slowly. There was no point, and no time – he and his father would never see eye to eye on this issue. Worse, any sign of concession, of even agreeing to think about it, would lead Nattiel to believe he had won. When they met again – if they met again – it would only lead to further arguments. And the arguments reminded him of other promises he had made.

"Farewell, father," he said, turning away. "You may not trust my decisions, but I must ask you to consider them. My opinions are not those of a boy; they are based on real knowledge, and hard-won experience this past year. Please take care that your views do not lead you to inadvertently betray our country's cause to the Porosians. You value skill in diplomacy, logic, and reasoning. Use them! Keep yourself safe. And if you see my wife before I go, let her know I'm going to the archives – I have a promise to keep."

Maelgyn wasn't sure what to think when his father said nothing in return. The lack of response rattled him so much he forgot to shave.

Maelgyn hadn't arrived in the Royal City of Svieda with much, but it would take a wagon to haul all of his things out of it with him. Much of what was being loaded wasn't his, alone, but belonged to his whole party: In addition to the expected clothing and gear someone would take on a journey out of the province, Wodtke was taking the cuttings of Wangdu's 'poultice' plants that she had preserved; Tur'Ka and Tur'Tei had somehow found and brought with them Tur'Ba's effects; Sir Leno had several parcels of clothing that had been created for him by the local tailors and seamstresses, as he had arrived in town with nothing but the armor on his back to wear; and Maelgyn himself had two sets of armor, three swords, and a hastily repacked shaving kit after his wife made him pull it out to get rid of that beard he'd forgotten to shave.

There were also the basic stores required for their journey – far more than was necessary to get to Happaso, in his opinion, but Maelgyn hadn't been in charge of packing them.

Maelgyn also carried with him several artifacts that he had been in too much of a hurry to pack the last time he fled from the castle, including several books – historical texts he hoped could be used to help undo the damage that the Porosian Conspiracy had already done to Sopan's provincial archives. Maelgyn was a little surprised to find these volumes intact. Despite Wangdu's efforts to secure the Royal Archives, Lazark and his ilk were more than capable of removing or altering texts that weren't in the archives. He had checked, though, and the books in his old private suite were still present and unaltered.

Maelgyn was on hour five of his six hour window to leave, watching and waiting as porters loaded the wagon with all of their luggage. Wodtke, Sir Leno, and Euleilla were ostensibly supervising the work while they talked with each other. Tur'Ka stayed by Euleilla's side while Tur'Tei remained by his own.

He stood at the gates of the Royal Castle's inner keep, not really paying attention as Arnach and Vihanto were trying to lighten up the send-off. His father was no-where to be seen; perhaps he felt he had already said his goodbyes.

"You haven't heard a word I've said, have you?" Arnach said.

Maelgyn started, turning towards his cousin. "Sorry. I was—"

"Yeah, I can guess," Arnach replied. "Doesn't matter – I haven't told you anything you didn't already know, anyway. But I do need you to listen for this last bit."

"I'm listening, now."

"Good. I suspect you're planning to head back to the camp in Happaso and direct things there, correct?" Arnach asked.

"Initially, at least," Maelgyn replied. "That camp needs some help getting on its feet. I'm hoping that we'll have found where they're keeping Brode by the time I get that place sorted out."

Arnach shook his head. "Don't bother. A team of Dwarven engineers is there, now, helping settle things down. I wouldn't be surprised if, in a year's time, that camp has become a full-fledged city. Or part of a city – it may grow into Happaso City proper and merge with it."

"Happaso would then be the largest city in Svieda," Maelgyn said.

"It already gives Largo a run for its money," Arnach laughed. "At any rate, you aren't needed there. In fact, Wybert, Gyato, and El'Athras are already leading a general withdrawal of your combined armies. Once all the refugees settle in, there would be too many people for that camp to support. No, I'm going to recommend you head to a new military 'encampment' which has been in-progress for a few months, now. That's where your armies are going to be, and that's where you'll first hear any word of Brode."

Maelgyn frowned. "What about my people already here, in the Royal City? Where are they going to go?"

"They'll be joining you at the new camp," Arnach said. "The

moment you were sighted, Onayari started making the arrangements. It's not like any of them were ever actually allowed in the castle to begin with."

"Still," Maelgyn said. "With as many hits as the Royal Province has already taken in this war, I'd think we would be vital to its defense."

"Not with the Dragons here," Arnach said. "A direct assault on the city by the Sho'Curlans would be suicide, whatever their numbers, and they certainly know that by now. Our biggest problem will be maintaining supply lines for the castle. Despite 'Brode's' negligence in the matter, the generals are working fast to lay down as many supplies as possible before the Sho'Curlans think to attack them. If your people leave, that's less burden on the system, and a larger force outside to work on restoring those supply lines."

Maelgyn grimaced. "Okay, I suppose that makes sense. So where is El'Athras sending me?"

Arnach snorted. "He does seem to be sticking his finger in everything, doesn't he?"

"My father doesn't think he should be trusted. He believes every Dwarf is just waiting to sell you out," Maelgyn sighed. "I reunite with him for one week, and all he can do is pick fights with me over my friends, my wife, my mage studies...."

Arnach looked at him for a long moment. "Uncle Nattiel is a very... opinionated man. He does care about you, but—"

"No, I know. I don't question that," Maelgyn said. "And I'd really rather not discuss it. Sorry. Again, where does El'Athras think I should go?"

"To the new camp, of course," Arnach replied.

"Which is where?"

Arnach snickered. "Let's just say we think you'll be familiar with the place, but it's a surprise. Don't worry – Onayari will guide you... and lead your escort. Head to the old post station where we set out the last time we had to flee the castle – she'll be arranging things there."

Vihanto coughed. "Your highnesses, the carriage has finished loading. Sir Leno is calling you over."

Maelgyn clasped hands with his cousin. "Well, this is it – setting out on our separate ways yet again."

"Last time we were fleeing an imminent invasion that we thought we had no chance of defeating," Arnach said. "This time, we have a plan – a solid plan – to keep things in line. Don't worry – I'll keep an eye on our 'cousin' until you can return... and when you do, we'll take it to the Sho'Curlans *and* the Porosians."

"We shall," Maelgyn agreed with a nod that might have been just a shade too confident. He turned to Vihanto. "My cousin, here, is a Sword, and therefore able to select his own armsmen, but he's now also my proxy. That means I can do things to look out for him, like assigning him a personal guard to protect him in my stead. These are very dangerous times – look after Arnach until I return."

"I swear he will be hale and healthy when you return," Vihanto said, improvising a half-bow.

Maelgyn nodded, a little surprised at how seriously the guard was taking it. "Very well, then. I guess I'd better be going."

"Farewell," Arnach and Vihanto chimed together.

Maelgyn turned to go, his ever-silent Dwarven companion immediately lining up at his side. He broke from the keep's gate and made four steps towards the wagon when he heard a series of familiar soft twangs.

Danger! Sekhar screamed in his mind. The *schlipf's* call startled Maelgyn – he hadn't heard from it since Wangdu had begun his 'poultice' treatment – but it put him on the alert.

Arrow! was his immediate thought, recalling where he had heard that twang before. His magical senses immediately extended to try and deflect it, but he couldn't sense where it was coming from. That meant it was tipped with something that wasn't magically reactive, like bronze or stone. Were he in his armor, it would typically be a minor issue – he would have to protect his head, but anywhere else on his body would deflect such a weapon without a scratch. Were Sekhar in better health, it still would be easy to protect himself.

But thanks to the lingering effects of his injuries, he wasn't wearing his armor, and Sekhar was weakened by the Elven medicines that Wangdu had used on Maelgyn's joints. And magic couldn't stop bronze or stone arrows unless he had a lot of magic powder already prepared. And he had no idea who was shooting or what they were shooting at. He—

"Oof!" he coughed, as Tur'Tei tackled him to the ground.

"Look out!" half a dozen voices cried half a second too late, though he couldn't tell who all was saying it.

There was a brief "ping" as something bounced off Tur'Tei's armor, but then there were no more shots – Maelgyn was listening carefully to be sure.

"Anyone hit?" he called.

"Not seriously," Euleilla called back. "Tur'Ka and Tur'Tei acted quick enough to protect us all."

"And the shooters?"

"Gone," Tur'Ka said. Maelgyn felt Tur'Tei roll off of him as he continued. "There were two, but neither of them had many arrows – they ran after shooting their last ones. Five shots each, ten total. I didn't catch a good look at either of them, however."

Maelgyn was a little astonished – he knew there was more than one shooter, but he'd only heard a single shot before he was lying on the ground. Speaking of which, he really needed to get back to his feet.

"Were they ours?"

"They were not wearing any Sviedan livery I'm familiar with. They both had courier's cloaks on, however."

Maelgyn recalled a certain cloak he had borrowed, himself, several months before. They were certainly good for concealing one's identity. He almost wanted to investigate, but the reality of the situation struck him pretty hard. The attempt may have failed due to the quick actions of the Dwarves, but whoever they were had prepared for his and his wife's magical skills. They struck at the one time he was without his armor and would be vulnerable. They had enough people so that even if he saw one in time to stop him, the other arrows might still strike him. The planning behind the attack left him rattled; assassins of this caliber might have a plan B...

"In that case... I doubt Brode will actually investigate, so let's get out of here before they try to finish the job," he said, heading over to the wagon once again. He paused, turning back toward the gate where Arnach and his newly-assigned bodyguard were still watching. His cousin's mouth had dropped open, and he seemed unable to say anything, but a quick glance showed he was uninjured. "Vihanto – I have your oath. It seems someone is upping the game, however, so keep your eyes peeled. Don't let anything happen to him."

"On my life, your Highness," Vihanto called back.

With a nod, Maelgyn pulled himself up into the cart, where Euleilla and Leno were already waiting. Tur'Ka, after a moment's inspection, crawled in after him. Tur'Tei went ahead and took the reigns.

"It seems Tur'Ba was right – we are needed," Tur'Ka said as they got underway.

Maelgyn plucked a now headless arrow out from a joint in Tur'Ka's armor. "It seems he was, indeed."

This time around, Maelgyn was happy to be leaving the Royal Castle.

'Brode' frowned, watching the cousin of the man he was doppelganging ride away from the castle. He heard someone walk up the stairs behind him.

"I thought we weren't ready to move forward, yet," he said.

"We aren't," Lazark replied, joining him along the Royal Keep's tower parapet. "That wasn't us."

"Sho'Curlans, then?" 'Brode' asked in concern.

"I don't think so," Lazark said. "Assassination isn't exactly their style, though I wouldn't rule them out completely. There aren't too many other suspects."

"Either them... or a new player on the field," 'Brode' concluded.

Lazark nodded. "Exactly. And if there's one thing we don't want, it's someone else getting involved in this mess before we are able to act."

'Brode' walked over to a barrel full of rain water and pulled some out with a ladle. He was starting to feel parched, and if he didn't get more water soon he might have to revert to his Merfolk form. As it was, this much water wasn't sufficient to keep him from transforming for long – he had been kept away from his bath for too long, thanks to the legal requirement to "ensure the offending Sword had fully vacated the region when banished." It looked like he would have to remain there for a few minutes longer, however, since Maelgyn was taking a slow route away from the city. Stupid Human ceremonies.

"And our own plans?"

"Well, after that attempt on Maelgyn, the guards will be on high alert. We can't make our own assassination plans for a while. Just as well – with Nattiel back in Svieda and Maelgyn merely banished rather than deposed, it will take us some time to whittle down the Swords' numbers to a manageable size, again. We'd better start making new plans for Sword Idril, too, now – she should be back from her ambassadorial mission before the final stage, thanks to this delay."

"Or we should enact Plan Arrowhead," 'Brode' suggested. "Things are not going well, here. If we do keep going forward with the current plan, we'll need to bring in another Elf to undo the damage that Wangdu has done to our cause."

"You really don't want us using Plan Arrowhead," Lazark warned. "But you're right – things have not gone well, and we do need another Elf here. I shall send for one... but in the meantime, we must be patient."

"In Human – or even Merfolk – terms, we are being more than patient," he huffed. "We are not Elves and do not live forever. But I think even the Elves might wonder if we're taking too long. Maelgyn's faction will discover where the real Brode is before too long, and then everything will fall apart."

"Even if they find Brode, what will they be able to do about it?" Lazark said. "No-one will ever be able to break through what's guarding him."

"I would argue the point," 'Brode' said. "But Maelgyn is now out of sight and I'm struggling to hold my form. I need to retire for a while. We will talk more on this in the morning."

Lazark nodded, but thought over their arguments. 'Brode' might be right, and the only solution might be to enact Plan Arrowhead... but he'd better hope not. Not if the Merfolk wanted to survive his little role acting as the Sword King, that was.

Maelgyn wondered just how much advance warning Onayari had of his banishment. By the time he made it to the old post building, she had assembled the entire cavalry force he had brought to free the Royal Castle and organized them into a formation.

Lining both sides of the last mile or so along the path to the post building, members of that cavalry were standing at attention. The pattern went one Nekoji, one Human on his horse, and one Dwarf on his Wolf. As his wagon passed, each group of three pulled away from the road and went on ahead.

Maelgyn wasn't sure what to make of this unexpected ceremony. He still wasn't sure what El'Athras' plan was, but this looked like more than what he would have expected were they simply waiting for word on Brode. It almost looked more like a coronation than a ride off in the disgrace of banishment.

Finally they reached the end of the pathway, where those cavalry officers forming the line had joined the rest of the cavalry units in formations usually used for travel on long journeys. Onayari was waiting for him at the post station.

"Greetings, Sword Maelgyn, Duke of Sopan," she called. "Your escort awaits."

"This seems a bit much for an 'escort,'" Maelgyn said. "And I still don't know where we're going."

"We're headed to a new base we've established in Largo," Onayari said. "A staging area, of sorts. Truth be told, the Royal Province does not have the resources to support a larger force than what is already present. The reserve in Happaso was already too large for the resources they had on hand. We're working to supplement that, but the influx of Sycanthians freed from the prison camps might overwhelm Happaso if we were to go there. It is only a matter of time before Sho'Curlas tries outflanking our forces by striking us through the now undefended province of Rubick. So, we've established a third rallying point – a place where we can gather an army that will be powerful enough outflank the flankers."

Maelgyn nodded slowly. "Okay, I can certainly understand the need for that. But why am I going to be at this new location instead of Happaso?"

"Because, your Highness, it was voted on and decided. The Royal Province and Happaso camp, between them, have combined to become the Sycanth-Happaso-Glorest-Leyland-Rubick-Royal Army, holding the line here. With Idril nowhere to be found, we managed to convince the Regent of Stanget to send his army to our new facility and place it under your command. You will ultimately be the leader of the combined Sopan-Caseificio-Mar'Tok-Largo-Stanget Armies, charged with the defense of the interior."

Maelgyn took in a deep breath. "And Brode?"

"If you're referring to the impostor posing as the Sword King, he has no knowledge of this plan, but as he has delayed appointing a permanent council and therefore left us still acting under the rules of an Interregnum, he cannot object even if he hears of it. If you're referring to your real cousin, well... depending where we find him, you might need an army to rescue him, no?"

Chapter XIX

Arnach took a deep breath and stepped into the bathing chamber that now seemed to be the place 'Sword King Brode' was taking all of his informal meetings. It had been a few days since Maelgyn and his cavalry left the city – a rather demoralizing moment for the soldiers still in the castle, but one they would survive as long as the Golden Dragons remained.

For these first few days, Arnach had been concerned with creating his own inner circle in the castle, now that he no longer could rely on Maelgyn's. He would need people who could keep their eyes and ears open, monitoring 'Brode's' action, preparing in hope for the real Brode's return, and coming up with a viable alternative if the real Brode was never found.

Vihanto was his first ally. The young guard had proven reasonably capable of getting Arnach information about their army's leaders and plans. Since the raid freeing Sycanth's forces, Arnach and the military leaders of Svieda had largely been left alone by 'Brode,' Lazark, or anyone else connected with the Porosian Conspiracy, as far as he could tell. Instead, the war was being run by Castle Svieda's castellan, the regent of Rubick, the regent of Leyland, and a few military officers from Glorest and Happaso who had less aristocratic pedigrees.

When news of the war broke out, the regent of Rubick had brought most of Rubick's armies into the Royal Province to fight on the front and hadn't returned since, even as Rubick itself was sent into ruin – not a tactical decision that won Arnach's respect, nor gave him any desire to include the man in his inner circle, but possibly a sensible one under the circumstances. The regent of Leyland, likewise, had abandoned his home province to help fight on the front – though, in his case, he had been ordered to directly by the Sword, who had since gone missing and was presumed dead.

Surprisingly, his uncle, Nattiel, was the second man in his circle. While Nattiel seemed very set in his ways, and had huge disagreements with Maelgyn before both of their separations, he was very loyal to the country of Svieda. As a loyalist, he set his grievances aside... for the moment. Once this Porosian threat was no longer amongst them, he cautioned, he would have his say.

Other trustworthy allies in the court were harder to come by. Arnach wanted someone with regular access to the Royal Archives – an archivist not appointed by 'Brode' or Lazark – who could check any books for possible alterations and keep an eye on the safety measures Wangdu had left behind. Unfortunately, there wasn't anyone with those qualifications in the entire castle.

Arnach had briefly approached the Royal Physician – a man who had kept the secret of Wangdu's escape from the prison from 'Brode' even though the impostor had been the one to appoint him. However, he refused to have anything to do with any of the castle's politics – he was a doctor, first and foremost, and stuck by his principles to give everyone similar treatment and discretion, regardless of their political choices.

As inner circles went, Arnach didn't have many people on hand... but his search was still in its infancy. He had been about to approach someone new – a member of the kitchen staff, who just might be able to warn him if someone was ordering certain Porosian (or Merfolk, or Elven) specialties more often than was seemly – when a guard found him and told him that 'Brode' was demanding an audience.

Arnach wasn't sure what to make of the request. While he was certainly working against the impostor, even his attempts to recruit a staff of his own weren't threatening 'Brode's' plans at all. If 'Brode' was going to be drumming up some pretense for expelling Arnach from the castle, much as he did with Maelgyn, this meeting would have been before the Royal Court and not in such an informal setting as these bathing chambers. Instead, even though Arnach had brought Vihanto with him as a personal armsman, this meeting was being held in private – even the Royal Guards were leaving them alone.

Arnach really hoped they weren't going to be kidnapping him and replacing him with another Merfolk. Vihanto was on the lookout for that, and there would be bloodshed if anyone tried it, but such an attempt might force actions that would circumvent the plans that El'Athras had been making.

"Greetings, brother," 'Brode' called once the door was closed.

Arnach snorted. "Let's drop the pretense, alright? We both know you aren't my real brother, as does my guard, here. There isn't anyone else in this room for you to need to keep up this act."

'Brode' froze momentarily and then 'shifted' into a more relaxed pose. Arnach was a little surprised to witness him transform from Human into Merfolk.

"Thank you," the Merfolk said. "Even Lazark insists I keep up my transformation around him."

Arnach nodded cautiously. "You're welcome. Now... given that I know what you are, and you know that I know what you are, why have you summoned me? You must know I have no intention of allowing your plans for my country to proceed, or doing anything that would further them."

"True, but there are areas where my employer's goals are the same as your country's needs," 'Brode' replied. "We, too, want the threat of Sho'Curlas stopped, for example. As it is clear you know of our existence, we may as well work together when the situation calls for it. I'm calling on you for help in such a matter."

Well, that was unexpected. Arnach supposed he hadn't thought about it, much, but it was true that this Porosian Conspiracy wouldn't want the Sho'Curlans to win the war any more than Svieda did. A threat from Sho'Curlas could very well be a uniting factor between them.

Though with the real Brode still held hostage, it was a bit difficult to remain civil with these people.

"Very well," Arnach said, clenching his fist tightly. "What do you need my help with, then?"

The Merfolk stood up out of the bath and grabbed a robe, wrapping it around him as his fins turned into legs. "I suspect you think that my employers were the ones behind the assassination attempt on your cousin, Maelgyn. However, this assassination attempt was not our doing – in fact, it has worked against our plans."

"I find that hard to believe," Arnach said.

"We are trying to get rid of the Swords, as you undoubtedly already know," the Merfolk admitted. "So getting rid of one of you through assassination was and remains a possibility. But if someone starts assassinating the other Swords before the other parts of our plan are in place – parts which your Elven friend, Wangdu, has delayed – it will become harder and harder to resist the call to appoint a permanent council and reinstate the Swords."

Arnach wasn't convinced, but decided not to argue the point – at least not until he heard the Merfolk out. Still, he found it a bit ironic that they were asking him to find an assassin whose actions prevented their own attempted assassination of his kin.

"So you say you weren't responsible for this attack. That means you think that someone else did it – any idea who?"

"Not who it is, only who it is not. It is not us. It is not the Sho'Curlans' style. We believe someone new is entering the field." The Merfolk said. "But who that is, we have yet to discover."

"Another player?" Arnach said. He started trying to run down who it might possibly be.

Of course, this Merfolk could easily be lying or mistaken. This story seemed a bit too convenient... or would if Arnach didn't find himself believing it. The confession that the Porosians were planning their own run of assassinations made this seem all the stranger. Unfortunately, other possibilities for who to blame were far more disturbing.

There was Sho'Curlas. The obvious choice, considering they were at war, but the Merfolk was right – this wasn't their style. They might be willing to use assassination as a tactic, as they had with Arnach's father, but not like this. They would do it up close and personal, bragging about it in the face of the man they were killing – not shooting at them from a distance while hidden in shadows.

But there were other countries who might employ such tactics. The

Oregal Republic, for example – they often chose such assassination tactics against their enemies instead of all-out war. The target being Maelgyn, as the Sword ruling the province nearest their border, seemed to point to that possibility as well. There had always been peace between Oregal and Svieda, but there had been many occasions where tensions were high... but war was usually averted when some Sviedan official wound up dead under mysterious circumstances.

That didn't make any sense, though – Svieda was certainly not threatening Oregal at all. Perhaps if they were afraid that Sho'Curlas would win the war, Oregal might consider snapping up the province of Sopan in an effort to maintain the balance of power, but it wouldn't be in these opening stages of the war. After the Golden Dragons entered the fight, the likelihood of Sho'Curlas winning seemed far less likely. If Oregal was behind this attempt, something far more serious might be going on.

While the Porosian Conspiracy that this Merfolk and Lazark were a part of claimed not to be part of this attempt, each of the four countries that made up the perpetually warring major factions of Poros (nominally labeled "North Poros," "South Poros," "East Poros," and "West Poros" on most maps) would occasionally rise in power and stature to be considered a major power like Sho'Curlas, Oregal, or Svieda. In such a case, one of them might be thinking expansion, which would likely put them into conflict with Svieda. They might be acting in complete ignorance of the Elven conspiracy operating within their borders.

None of them were particularly ascendant right then, as far as Arnach knew, but he had to admit he hadn't been paying much attention to the situation in Poros until learning of the conspiracy Maelgyn uncovered. As that conspiracy was led by Elves, and those four countries were led by Humans, it seemed unlikely that they would co-ordinate their efforts. With Rubick a shattered ruin, there wasn't much to defend Svieda should they attack through that route – only Squire's Knot (which was still nominally an independent power, even after Sho'Curlas used it as a staging area for raids against Svieda) and the Bandi Republic (which shared most of it's southern border with Svieda's northern borders in Largo and the newly acquired province of Mar'Tok) would provide any other resistance should Poros start showing interest in expansion south.

But that would leave the question of "Why Maelgyn?" Was he just a target of opportunity? That seemed unlikely, given the level of planning done for the assassination attempt. Even the arrows used showed that they were targeting Maelgyn himself – they would have gone ahead and used steel-heads if it was someone who didn't have magic on their own, like Nattiel... or Arnach, himself. But why would the Porosians want Maelgyn out of the way?

There was one other possibility, however, that worried Arnach – the idea that this was an internal plot. That someone from Svieda itself wanted Maelgyn dead, and for reasons Arnach didn't know. He couldn't figure out the assassins' motives. Who would want Maelgyn dead?

Unless... they weren't after Maelgyn at all?

"I don't suppose your people know much about Maelgyn's new wife, Euleilla, do they?" he asked.

The Merfolk gave what was probably a grin, though it was hard to say on his inhuman face.

"What do you want to know?"

Wybert, leaning against a lamp pole, was astonished at the number of ships in Happaso's harbor. After the battle at Largo, he had been under the impression that Svieda's navy had been devastated; here was proof that more had survived than he thought. That, or the shipwrights had been working long hours rebuilding their Navy.

A lot of recognizable faces had already passed by. Gyato was one of the first aboard, even though the Nekoji ruler had never enjoyed boat travel. Maelgyn's new cook – Kiszaten – had bickered and complained about being stuck with "lousy salt-beef" again as he'd been herded on board by a group of Dwarves. Several of the Dwarves who had been making the camp livable traded places with another set of Dwarves who apparently were more skilled at that sort of thing – though how, Wybert wasn't sure.

It was fun people-watching. But it was also very strange, seeing as he was about to join them.

"Not long now before everyone is aboard who's going aboard," El'Athras said, coming up behind him. "You should probably queue up, too. With much of the cavalry going with Maelgyn, this will only take us one trip."

"These are all warships. Where did they all come from?" Wybert asked, astonished. "I was under the impression our Navy had been devastated. Even before then, though, I didn't think we had this many that could serve as troop transports."

"True, a lot of ships were lost in Largo Harbor," El'Athras agreed. "Between the battles and the fireships, there was effectively a naval stalemate – you'd wiped out their fleet, but you didn't even have enough ships left to protect your own ports. But that was months ago, and a lot has changed."

"They don't all look new," Wybert said. "In fact, most of them look older than the ships we lost in that battle."

"Not many of these are new ships," El'Athras agreed. "None of these are from that incident, however. Your surviving warships from that battle are still mostly being used in port defense, but every newly built ship since the fire ship attack is now here. But you've forgotten that you've earned new allies since then – Mar'Tok, for example, only has one port, and it is a small one, but we did have a few warships we could spare for the cause. Most of these are one more benefit of our success in the Borden Isles – they had been maintaining a navy that could challenge Svieda's, but they are now a part of Svieda. I'd say about half of the ships here, today, came from there. Maybe more. The rest are converted merchantmen, borrowed from traders and fishermen out of smaller ports, and will be returned to their owners once this operation has been completed."

"I didn't even think about Borden," Wybert said. "When I thought of the Borden Isles, I mostly thought of the need to bring back the Golden Dragons. I forgot about all the other assets bringing them back into the fold would grant us."

"The Dragons and this navy are but the first of many benefits. There are mages, and soldiers, and many other weapons of war that the Borden Islanders will eventually be able to send to the front, once the government has been stabilized," El'Athras said. "Their return will be a significant help."

"Shame we couldn't do the same thing with the former Sviedan province of Abindol," Wybert said. "Or re-capture Sycanth, instead of just freeing their captive soldiers."

El'Athras nodded. "Unfortunately, Sycanth is too far overrun to re-take without great effort, and the Grand Duchy of Abindol is held under a much tighter fist by the Sho'Curlans. The government is still loosely based on the laws set up by Svieda, but the people in power are mostly Hrabak's puppets. It would take a lot more to bring them back than what it took with the Borden Isles."

"Just a thought," Wybert said.

"And a good one," El'Athras replied. "I might suggest it to whoever the Sword King winds up being, once this mess with that impostor is cleared up. But it will require more complex planning. For now I must focus my attention on finding the real Brode – but I'll look into my network and see if I can't find an adequate advisor for the Sword King in this half of the country. If I start him on the problem, now, maybe by the time things are resolved he'll have a plan ready to go that the real Brode, or whoever is in charge, can work with."

Wybert looked over at El'Athras, quirking an eyebrow. "You make it sound as if you don't expect Maelgyn to return to the Royal City when his banishment has been ended."

"I don't," El'Athras huffed. "Not for some time, at least. Maelgyn... he's too powerful a mage to be sidelined by court duties. When the war comes to a head, he will need to be out there on the front line, fighting our enemies – not holed up in some castle, talking politics with his cousins. Even were he to become Sword King, I doubt he would stay locked away in some castle."

Wybert nodded. If he were honest with himself, he wanted to be out on the front lines, too – his pair of wooden legs and all – but he knew how unlikely that was, at this point. A young man like Maelgyn, with a decent sword arm and unheard of magical powers, would no doubt feel even stronger about it.

He continued to watch the ships loading, then glanced over to where a set of Dwarven engineers were already rebuilding the camp into a permanent settlement. "Your people are contributing a great deal, as well. Mar'Tok has been very generous to us. Your soldiers, your engineers, your spies – without you, we'd be in a right mess."

"We haven't been helpful enough, yet," El'Athras said, shaking his head. "Svieda is in for a rough time with Sho'Curlas, still... and it may be that this Porosian Conspiracy is a greater threat than the war. Nothing we have done, yet, has directly countered them – only Maelgyn's and Wangdu's actions have been of any help on that front, so far."

"We need more allies, then," Wybert concluded. "But who's left? Oregal? They're more likely to attack us than help us."

"I wouldn't be too sure about that," El'Athras said. "Oregal is very powerful. I doubt they'd send us any direct assistance, but they might be willing to try something sneaky to improve our chances of winning. They desperately want to avoid sharing a border with Sho'Curlas; war between the two of them would be inevitable, and while Oregal would likely win it would be a costly one. They much prefer war-by-proxy."

"What about Poros?" Wybert asked. "What would Oregal's reaction be to their ploy?"

El'Athras frowned. "I'm not sure. So much of what these Porosian Elves are doing is very secretive, and all of it is with the long game in mind. If they were to permit the Porosian factions to reunite, Poros would be the equal of Sho'Curlas or Oregal. That would be a great threat, but there are a lot of border kingdoms between Poros and Oregal that they would have to fight their way through. And Oregal has its own population of Elves who undoubtedly could counter those in Poros – it's the only place in the world where you'll still find fully Elven communities, I believe."

"Still, it seems unlikely they would intervene on our behalf, even if Poros were to take action," Wybert said. "So... who's left? Are any of the border kingdoms strong enough to truly aid us?"

El'Athras snorted. "No. All of them put together wouldn't equal the strength that you can still find in Sopan alone, even after moving so much of its army out of the province to fight in the war. Unless you include the Bandi Republic, that is – we've never considered Bandi one of those border kingdoms, but some maps do."

Wybert snorted. "Well, they are in that region, and their territory expands and contracts just as rapidly as most of the border kingdoms do – they have bumped up against Poros, Mar'Tok, Caseificio, Oregal, and some of the other border kingdoms over the years."

"But they are far, far more civilized," El'Athras said. "The central parts of Bandi are stable, and they have a relatively strong military. If they wanted, they really could expand out and take all of the border kingdoms without much effort. The only real efforts of expansion, however, come when one general or another finds disfavor with the Mad Lady Phalra. She tends to order those generals to take command of their worst company of soldiers and see how far they can go. Some generals have been more successful than others, causing significant expansion and retraction of their frontier. Trying not to be the company designated for such a suicide mission can be quite the motivator among her troops, though."

"Sounds like Bandi might make a good ally, then... if its leader wasn't so, ahem, eccentric."

El'Athras shrugged. "She's an Elf. All Elves eventually go insane – it's the price for their immortality. But despite that, she's been an effective ruler for over six centuries, possibly longer, and her people love her. I would bring her in as an ally if I could, but I couldn't get her to even talk with me when I was arranging the conference that led to Mar'Tok's own alliance with Svieda."

"Then what's our next step?" Wybert asked. "I mean in the war – obviously, locating Brode is our next goal. But even with all that we've done, we remain on the defensive. We have no options when it comes to adding more allies, and it's only a matter of time before Sho'Curlas launches another major assault. Where do we go from here?"

"Well, once Maelgyn's firmly installed in his new position, we start by rebuilding Rubick. Once that border is secure, we can strike back." El'Athras grinned. "The big problem at the outset of the war was that Sho'Curlas had a much larger army, they had trained a company of Black Dragons, and they've established enough of a support structure to grow both of those things faster than Svieda could.

"All of that has changed. The Black Dragons have been negated by the Golden Dragons. Sho'Curlas still has a larger army, but their defeat in the siege and the rescue of Sycanth's refugees has changed things; their campaign army is now the one that is outnumbered, albeit slightly, by the defensive armies here and in the Royal Province, and it will take them some time to assemble more forces from their outlying provinces. With the Borden Isles, Mar'Tok, and Caseificio all joining Svieda, they're no longer able to out-produce Svieda. Effectively, we've forced a stalemate."

"But not a win," Wybert noted.

"Not yet, no," El'Athras agreed. "But they have lost the tactical advantages they had at the start of the war, and we're now in a war of attrition. Suppose we do manage to recover Abindol without another war? Suppose one of their outlying provinces uses this as an opportunity to rebel? Suppose Oregal secretly does something I'm not even thinking about, right now, on our behalf? All of these are things that have a good chance of happening, with or without us helping them along. We just need to clear out this Porosian intrusion, first, so we can focus on *getting* these things to happen. My spy network is stretched too thin trying to combat the Porosians to try any sabotage of that nature."

Wybert frowned. "So just who is running the Porosian Conspiracy? I mean, I know it's Elves, but surely even among the Elves there's someone in charge. If we know who leads it, maybe we could target them directly. The old saying is cut off the head and the body will die, no?"

"I don't know – I haven't figured that out, yet," El'Athras said. "My spies can't seem to find much on these Porosians at all. That's partly why I've been having so much trouble finding where Brode has been taken."

"Are we sure that Brode is still alive?" Wybert asked.

"Reasonably. That's just about the only thing we've been able to figure out, so far. Well, that, and he's being moved around between Porosian bases. We won't just need to know where Brode is now, but where he's going to next, before we can act."

Wybert sighed, pushing himself off of his lamp pole and stumbling off towards the ships. "Well, let's hope you find out soon. If not... I hate to say it, but it might be best to forget about Brode and move on. He's a cousin of mine who I care about pretty deeply, but he's just one man. There has to be a way out of this mess without him, and if looking for him is going to prevent us from doing what is necessary to win this war...."

El'Athras shook his head. "I am not compromising the war effort to search for one man, however important that one man is. But the Porosian Conspiracy is a real threat – if it is left unchecked, things will be far, far worse. Finding Brode is only the tip of the iceberg; if we can get rid of the Porosian Conspiracy altogether, however, that's one less threat we have to deal with."

Wybert nodded, wobbling on his legs as he made his way down to the docks. "So why not make these Porosians react, instead of act? So far, we've been just trying to defend ourselves. We know what their goals are – or at least what they've told Maelgyn their goals are – so why don't we send people to Poros and get something going that they'll have to deal with on their home front? It can't be that hard, considering Poros has been in an unending state of civil war for centuries, now."

"Well, it's probably harder than you think. My spies have a hard time in their lands, and we don't even have a proper map of where all of their cities are any more. Sending people into Poros may wind up our only option, however...."

Chapter XX

Maelgyn was starting to get a bit antsy. He still didn't know where they were going, outside of somewhere in Largo, even after quite a bit of travel. This morning, as they were breaking camp, Onayari sent Sir Leno and Doctor Wodtke ahead to warn the camp that they were coming, and had told him that they would reach it that afternoon, but he was starting to wonder if she'd told him the truth. He and Euleilla – both without horses – were still riding in the cart that also carried most of their luggage. Onayari was sitting with them, which just made things even more cramped.

Maelgyn had given the Nekoji female some scrolls copied from the Royal Archives, on how to correct her improper mage training, and she was sitting in the cart, the readings spread out in front of her. It didn't help with the crowded seating, and with so little space, it had become a very uncomfortable trip.

Things had been looking vaguely familiar for some time, but, well, roads were roads – one patch looked largely like another. The foliage might be familiar, but he couldn't be sure he'd ever been down that road before.

Until he reached a certain stretch of the road that he didn't think he'd ever forget. It was the same section of road where, almost a year ago, he had encountered a young woman being accosted by a group of ruffians.

"Euleilla, I think we're back in Rocky Run!" he said.

Euleilla playfully bumped shoulders with him. "Yep."

"You might not recognize the place when you see it, though," Onayari said.

Maelgyn frowned. "What do you mean? Why... oh... my..."

They had reached a turn in the road, giving them a clear view of the town. To say it had changed was an understatement – it looked like someone had dropped a city on top of the sleepy little town that had been centered around a river ferry service.

Evidently, a temporary wooden wall had been erected around the town, but Dwarven workers were in the process of replacing it with a more permanent stone fortification. Also, the ferry was no longer necessary – now there was a very sturdy, and very permanent-looking – fortified bridge crossing the river. Many of the old wooden buildings in the town were also being replaced with stonework structures, and many more buildings were being added.

"How... how was there even enough time for all of this work to take place since I was last here! It should have taken years to get this far," Maelgyn said.

Onayari shrugged. "This fast, quality stonework is exactly what Dwarven engineers are known for. Though it's probably not as complete as you think – to the best of my understanding, almost all of the work they've done has been on this side of the river, and they still aren't quite finished. They have a lot more work to do, especially on the bridge, from what I've been told."

Euleilla's head cocked at that. "Bridge?"

"Yes," Onayari said. "Their intention is to add permanent stalls along each side of the bridge for the public to use as shops. But it looks like you can use it to cross the river, already."

Maelgyn frowned, wondering if the new town structure might confuse his wife. She was familiar with the old town, he was sure, but all of this work would change everything for her. "What's the point of all this? I was under the impression we were headed to a temporary camp, and we would be returning to the front before long."

"Well, the Dwarves are turning this small town into a fortified city, but they aren't done yet," Onayari said. "In the meantime, those temporary camps you're talking about are being set up outside of the fisherman's port on the other side of the river. It's a sight you might want to get used to. Without a decisive advantage for one side or another, this war could last for years. A great many more Sviedan townships and cities will need to be strengthened before it's over, even this far from the front."

Maelgyn held his tongue as the cart continued to roll its way into the newly built city. Euleilla was turning her head this way and that, as if looking at the new construction, though obviously that wasn't what she was doing.

"What do you think of all this?" he asked her.

She shrugged. "Few of the old wooden buildings in this village lasted more than a couple of decades before they had to be rebuilt, so there's not much history or sentimental value to what they're replacing. The cobblestone roads and alleys between houses appear to have been kept as they were, though, so the change is more superficial than you might think. The walls and the bridge are new... and, at least in the case of the bridge, long overdue. I never liked that ferry."

Maelgyn wondered how she knew where the roads and alleys were when his *schlipf* reminded him that she now had more than one way to sense where something was. That was something he'd been meaning to talk with her about for a while, now – ever since the prison rescue, in fact. He'd seen that her own *schlipf* had sprouted, and was wondering how well she was adjusting to the new abilities it granted her. However, that was a conversation to be had in private, and – much to his chagrin, even when bunking down for the night – they hadn't been alone together for more than a minute or two since then. They hadn't even kissed, making him wonder if he'd shaved for nothing.

"Well, I'm guessing the soldiers will be headed for the camps," Maelgyn said. "But I think my wife and I would like to stop at the Left Foot Inn for a while."

"That was the plan," Onayari agreed, as the cart continued down the road.

Nattiel sat at his writing desk, finally going through those belongings of his that had been salvaged when the castle was reclaimed. While some of his old possessions had been looted, many had been left behind when Brode and Arnach retook the castle. They had been crated up into storage while he was in captivity, but he hadn't learned that anything had survived until that morning.

Going through his stuff was vaguely disturbing. He knew a lot of things had been taken or destroyed by the Sho'Curlans, but what was left didn't paint a very pleasant picture of him as a husband or a father.

Some royal heirlooms – such as one of the three captured Swords and a couple sets of Dragonskin armor – had either been recovered or (in the later case) replaced with improved versions. Beyond those, however, none of his clothing, weapons, or armor had been left intact. What was left were pieces of furniture, candlesticks and lamps, his own personal set of cutlery, a particularly fine ink-pot complete with a set of copper quill nubs, and several similar items.

But none of it had any sentimental value at all. Nothing in his possessions, either those recovered or those that had been destroyed, even hinted that he had ever been a father. He never even kept his wife's effects after her death – not because it was too painful or anything like that, but because he never saw any use for it all.

And nothing he owned was manufactured by magic, save his recently-recovered Sword itself. Nothing was made of iron or steel by non-magical hands, either – not even any nails. He wanted nothing to do with magic after his wife's death – which was partly why he had dismissed Maelgyn's magic tutor before the training was complete. Nothing he could do would have stamped the magic out of Maelgyn, however.

And now Maelgyn was possibly the most powerful mage in the world, married to another powerful mage. Magic would always be a part of Nattiel's son's life... and to his shame he still couldn't stand the idea.

A knock on the door broke him from his thoughts. "Yes?" he called.

One of his door guards stepped in. "Sword Arnach to see you, your Highness. He says it's urgent."

"Send him in," Nattiel said, standing up. He was quick to close the crate that he'd been unpacking and stepped over to the door. He made it just as Arnach entered.

He and Arnach clasped hands in greeting. "Sword Arnach! Welcome. This is a pleasant surprise."

Arnach nodded in reply, not looking nearly as pleased to be there. "Uncle."

"So, what brings you here?" Nattiel asked.

Arnach glanced at the door, waiting until the guard had finished closing it behind him to answer. "I'm investigating the attempt on Maelgyn's life."

Nattiel frowned. "I heard about that, but I wasn't anywhere nearby when it happened. I don't know what you could possibly want from me."

"I just want to talk to someone who might remember a little local history from about thirty to fifty years ago," Arnach said. "And you're the only person old enough to remember that period that I trust."

"I lived in Sycanth until I reached my age of majority, though would occasionally summer here. I'm not sure what help I can be," Nattiel said, gesturing for Arnach to take a seat on one of his (recently unpacked) leather-upholstered benches.

"Do you remember anything about the infamous alchemist, Delbruck?"

That was a name tied to a popular movement in Nattiel's youth. Stories of Delbruck were quite popular, for a very long time, but shortly after Nattiel was invested they had stopped... and rather abruptly, he realized, although he had no idea what had stopped them. He didn't think there was any connection between his ascension and Delbruck, however.

"I know something, yes. I'm not sure how factual what I know is," Nattiel said. "I went to Rubick to have my provincial stewardship confirmed before the full extent of his treachery was revealed, and it was before my brother's ascent to the throne that he died. I might remember a rumor or two about his glory years, though."

"Tell me the ones you think are true," Arnach asked.

"Well, when I was born his fame as an alchemist was already widespread," Nattiel began. "He was in the process of founding the Delbruck Academy in Sycanth. He wanted great minds and talents from all over the world – not just Svieda – to join him, and many did. Not just alchemists, like Delbruck himself, but mages, herbalists, numismatics, architects, engineers, philosophers, and even poets –

scholars of all types joined him.

"But the academy was a scam to steal the advances by the people who joined it, and much of the work it supposedly did was a hoax. Delbruck made many discoveries that were shared with the world, it's true – studies on the importance of hygiene and proper medicinal dosing revolutionized medicine, for example. Delbruck was not nearly as altruistic as most believed, however, and most of those in the Academy didn't realize they were being hoodwinked until it was too late.

"Delbruck allowed 'his' scholars to release certain achievements to the world... but not all of them. He would allow those scholars to announce the discovery of two or three minor things, but if there was something major he really wanted for himself... well, a lot of those academics started having mysterious deaths right when they were about to make a breakthrough. Or, if he really wanted more advancement of these discoveries, he let them keep working on it, but refused to allow them to release anything – he would always say either the technology was not ready for the world, or the world was not ready for that technology. Until he tired of those deceptions and killed them, anyway.

"He hoarded knowledge. It was said he had the ability to harness lightning, store it, and use it in smaller doses to light lights, cook food, and more. I don't know if I believe any of that, but it was also said he knew how to turn naphtha oil into some sort of false tortoiseshell, and I know that one is true – a few artifacts made from that discovery survived the Academy's fall, though no-one has been able to replicate the process.

"But all of this knowledge was stolen, and those who discovered these things were killed by some kind of poison none of those great minds could find a way to detect. When people started wondering about these deaths, old Sword Prince Taygon of Sycanth, on his own deathbed, ordered his guards to investigate. Delbruck destroyed his Academy – and all of his stolen discoveries, as well as many of the scholars inside – and fled. Further investigation proved he had been selling weapons, mostly poisons, to the Borden Isles and other foreign powers. He was eventually captured, but took another poison that destroyed his mind even as it left him alive. He was imprisoned, and when it started to look like he might recover his intellect was tried and convicted of treason. My brother's first official act as Sword King was sanctioning his execution, in fact."

"How many survivors of the Delbruck Academy's destruction do we know about?" Arnach asked.

Nattiel closed his eyes, tipping his head back as he tried to remember. It had been a long time. "Not many, to be honest. It had thousands of members in its heyday, but fewer than a hundred survived when Delbruck used his alchemical skills to blow up the buildings. Why are you asking? I wouldn't think any of the survivors would have reason to try to kill my son."

"It isn't the possibility that a survivor from the Delbruck Academy would be after your son that has us worried," Arnach replied. "It's that we are wondering if your son was, in fact, the target... or if it was the daughter of two Delbruck Academy survivors."

Nattiel's eyes widened. "The daughter... that girl, Euleilla, you mean?"

Arnach nodded. "Believe it or not, that Merfolk impersonating Brode put me onto this possibility. He told me that—"

"And you trusted him?" Nattiel snorted.

"Not really," Arnach replied. "He tried to claim that an attempt to assassinate Maelgyn would work against Porosian interests because it would make it harder to resist calls to appoint a permanent council and re-establish new Swords, but I don't really believe that. I think it more likely that they don't know who the assassin is and they're worried that one of them could be the next target. At any rate, they seem genuinely rattled, and wanted me to help with their investigation. I think this might really be one of those 'we have a common enemy' situations."

Nattiel frowned. "I suppose that's possible, but I'd still take anything they said with a grain of salt. So, what did they tell you?"

"I specifically asked if their spies knew anything about Euleilla's background," Arnach said. "Well, it turns out her mother was a mage who was briefly a part of the Delbruck Academy... and her father was actually one of Delbruck's apprentices."

Nattiel sighed. "So I was right – Maelgyn shouldn't have married her."

There was a long pause, and it took Nattiel a moment to realize that Arnach was not in silent agreement with him – rather, he was staring at him in disbelief.

"Do you *seriously* think that anything I said should be considered an indictment of Maelgyn's marriage?" Arnach finally said.

"Well, if she's a child of traitors—"

"And just where did I say that?" Arnach snapped. "Very few people from the Delbruck Academy were partners in his treachery. Delbruck was certainly a traitor, yes, but most of his followers were no more traitors than you were for not slaughtering Hussack the moment he showed up here as the ambassador."

"Perhaps her mother wasn't, but her father—"

"Even his apprentices were largely ignorant of his treason," Arnach said. "And the Porosians have informed me of things about Delbruck's treason that I had otherwise never known."

"A suspect source, at best," Nattiel said, trying to regain some control after having been interrupted twice.

"Agreed, but it fits with information that they were unaware I already knew," Arnach replied.

"Which is?"

"Elven factions," Arnach said. "When the Elven nation dissolved, the surviving Elves spread across the world. Many of these Elves have settled down to live their own lives in isolation, but several of them grouped together to form factions. Each had a goal in mind, based on the lessons they learned from the actions of the Ancient Elves. One such faction is the Porosian Conspiracy, itself, but there are others. Some of those others are just as effective and secretive as they are. Thanks to Maelgyn – who learned it from Wangdu – I now know what many of these factions are."

"Why would he have told you of these?" Nattiel asked.

"It was part of his original description of the Porosian Conspiracy," Arnach said. "He listed a few of them. Among them was one that called themselves the 'Technologists,' a faction dedicated to preventing the rediscovery of what the Ancient Elves called 'forbidden technologies.' According to our Merfolk companion, this faction worked with Delbruck, allowing him to use certain technology as long as he guaranteed that it would never leave the Academy. It wasn't the first time they'd done this, and it probably won't be the last. And Delbruck justified it to himself by allowing any of the Academy's discoveries which were not on the 'forbidden' list to be released to the public –

discoveries which may never have been made without the Academy."

"All right, you've explained the reason Delbruck was the traitor he was," Nattiel said. "You have not explained why this apprentice of his was not a traitor, himself."

"Well, let's start with Euleilla's mother, first, instead," Arnach replied. "As I said earlier, she was a mage named Melka. Melka was a moderately powerful mage – not as strong as her daughter has become, but still at least a second rate. She joined Delbruck's Academy because she wanted to learn the mythical magical technique that allowed a mage to call forth lightning purely from their magic... but it turns out that said technique was on the list of forbidden techniques."

Nattiel stiffened. "Wait... the magical ability to call lightning has been 'forbidden' by some pretentious group of Elves... and they kill people to protect this secret?"

Arnach nodded. "I do not know this list of forbidden skills and technologies for certain, but the Merfolk claims this was one, yes."

"And... Euleilla's father?"

"Never participated in Delbruck's treachery," Arnach said. "But did learn of it. In fact, he was the one who sent word to Sword Taygon informing him of the treason. He did it because he had fallen in love with Melka, and she had figured out the technique to call lightning. Euleilla's father witnessed Delbruck attempt to poison Melka, diagnosed what he was trying to do, and saved her life, helping her flee from the Academy and into Taygon's protection."

"What was this man's name?"

"Well, Melka died shortly after giving birth to Euleilla – she was assassinated by an Elf in broad daylight. After that, Euleilla's father fled from place to place, changing his name whenever people started to figure out who he was. Surprisingly, we don't think it was this Elven faction that killed him; rather, we think it was another former pupil of Delbruck who stole his knowledge of poisons, using them to support a mining venture. Apparently they were afraid of the implications of an alchemical process for retrieving gold from certain crystals that Euleilla's father was working on. I believe that this Elven faction now has figured out who Euleilla is – if we could do it and the Porosians could do it, so could they – and that they believe Euleilla knows the secrets behind certain of these 'forbidden' techniques, thanks to her parents."

Nattiel took a deep breath. "I am quite willing to ally with the Porosian Conspiracy against this Elven faction, provided they are willing to accept a truce and put off their take-over plans until they have been routed."

"Well, we still aren't certain the Elves were the attempted assassins—" Arnach began.

"I don't care. This Elven faction must be put down, and I don't care what it takes to do it," Nattiel said.

Arnach looked at him a moment through narrowed eyes. "This is about more than the assassination attempt on your son and his bride, isn't it?"

"Much more," Nattiel said. "It is about the successful assassination of my wife – an assassination I've mistakenly been blaming on overuse of magic ever since."

Nattiel could see the puzzle pieces click together in Arnach's eyes. "Your wife was trying to discover the magic to call lightning, too, wasn't she?"

"And she succeeded... once," Nattiel said. "About a week before she died."

Arnach nodded. "Very well, then. We'll keep our eyes open when dealing with the Porosians, but for the moment... it looks like we're on the same side."

High King Fitz IV, ostensibly the ruler of Sho'Curlas, was once again regretting the accident of his birth that put him on the throne.

He had no desire to go to war with Svieda. That was Hrabak's order; he was just forced to follow it. He wasn't entirely sure why he was forced to follow it, but he had learned in the later years of his father's reign that saying no to their Elven shadow lord was impossible. Literally – their mouths wouldn't work if they tried.

Fitz believed that it was the throne, itself, that controlled the High Kings of Sho'Curlas. In fact, he was fairly certain of it – there was a pin-prick sized splinter that would mysteriously appear in the smooth-polished wood, about one a year. It would stab him and a brief moment of fire or cold would spread out through his veins, starting from the wound, while the area around it would go slightly numb. Then the splinter would break off and fall out of his arm. He would generally spend the next week or so feeling ill and in a daze, and was especially compliant to the Elf's wishes at that time.

It had been a while since the last time he'd encountered such a 'splinter.' He was probably due to receive another one the next time he sat on the throne, which went a long way towards making him want to pace around the throne room rather than take his seat.

He wanted to tell someone about it. Better yet, he wanted to destroy the throne and replace it – maybe with something that was pure stone or pure metal, so that no wooden splinters could possibly appear without explanation. However, even though he felt able to "tug at his leash" a little with as long as it had been since the last splinter, he couldn't do either of those things. It was all he could do to avoid sitting on the damned chair.

Had he not been born as the heir to the throne, Fitz suspected he would have gone all his life believing that Hrabak's existence was a myth. He'd never seen the Elf before his age of majority, and only saw him a few very brief times after that before he took the throne.

After taking the throne, however, Hrabak would show up at least once a week, telling Fitz how he should handle his rule. There were a few issues the Elf never bothered to instruct him on – usually minor decisions on ceremonial activities, appointing the likes of the Royal Dressmaker and the Royal Chef, the setting of standard weights and measures, and similar activities – but he didn't think he'd been allowed to make a major decision since he'd first sat on the throne.

And now it was costing him his family. He'd never had children of his own – his wife had proven to be barren, and one of the few decisions he'd been allowed to make was to not 'replace' her with a different wife who wasn't – but he did have a brother and nephew he was close to.

If he was honest with himself, he probably would not have been a friend of Hussack's were they not related. Hussack had been an arrogant whelp in their youth, and had merely coated that arrogance with the magical and physical strength to back it up and an aristocratic air as he got older. Fitz wondered how Hussack would react, should he ever discover the secret of their throne, himself.

Hussack had married a girl named Muen. She was not a native Sho'Curlan, but had been brought (or rather, bought, as the payment in exchange for a trade treaty) from the Grand Duchy of Abindol.

Muen was a quiet girl, living alone in her apartment at the castle; her husband hadn't bothered to see her since she'd given him a son. Fitz felt sorry for the woman, but it was not his place to keep her company – that would have resulted in a scandal. Still, he'd ensured that his wife befriended her so that she wasn't too lonely.

Then their was his nephew, who was every bit his father's son, but without the refined veneer that Hussack had even in his youth. Mussack (a portmanteau of his father's and mother's name, as was common among the Sho'Curlan nobility... though less so among the royalty) had all of the charm of a slug. He and Fitz rarely got along.

And yet he was still family. It still hurt when the news came in that Mussack had fallen in battle to the Sviedans – or rather, to a single Sviedan of such magical power that he could overwhelm an entire castle on his own (if the almost certainly exaggerated rumors were to be believed). But his death was an even bigger blow to the Royal bloodline – currently, Hussack was Fitz's only heir, but Hussack was only a year younger than Fitz. Even if Hussack outlived Fitz, he no longer had an heir himself.

The next closest relation in the line of succession was a distant cousin by a line descended from Fitz's great grand-uncle. Fitz had never met the man, and he wasn't likely to have been raised to be king. Not that it would matter, with Hrabak being the true power behind the throne, but still – the throne of Sho'Curlas was in danger.

Far more so with word of Hussack's own injuries. The doctors had amputated Hussack's arm, and it hadn't been so long since then that he was out of the woods from that. But then, after the amputation, Hussack had been – for lack of a better term – abducted... by Hrabak!

Fitz glanced at the throne with a sigh. Perhaps it was time to summon that cousin and prepare him for the facts of Royal life.

The doors to the throne room opened, and Fitz's majordomo scurried through. Fitz didn't like the man – he was far too much of a toady, in his opinion – but he did his job well.

"Your majesty," the majordomo whispered in his ear. "A delegation of Elves from Poros are waiting out in the hall. They wish to speak with you."

A delegation of *Elves*? Really? Fitz had enough problems with one Elf – what could a whole delegation of them do? Still, lacking Hrabak's specific instructions, it was his decision whether to admit them or not... and, knowing that Hrabak would probably insist he not admit them and wanting to rebel a bit, Fitz acquiesced.

"Send them in," he said.

Four Elves, dressed with concealing robes over elegant attire, entered the room. They looked very solemn – a far cry from Hrabak and his perpetual crazed grin. They also were very well armed, given the *schlipf* that three of them were bearing. Fitz had never seen a real *schlipf*, but he'd heard the description of them often enough. Curiously, the fourth Elf had a wound where a *schlipf* might normally be found, so perhaps they weren't quite as invulnerable as he'd heard.

The Elves waited until the majordomo had left. So, for some odd reason, had all of Fitz's guards. When the door closed behind them, he found himself alone facing four Elves.

"We greet you, we do, your Majesty," the lead Elf said. "We have a... proposition for you, we do."

"A proposition?" Fitz repeated, not entirely sure what to think of these Elves. They were like the Elves Hrabak constantly ranted about – speaking a strange dialect that featured their native language's bifurcated verbs – but he didn't know if that was a good thing or a bad one.

"We have set certain plans in motion, we have, that may allow you to greatly expand your kingdom, that might." the Elf said.

"I see," Fitz said, amused. Did these Elves really think he cared one iota about that? "And what would you ask in exchange for this... boon?"

"We wish merely to talk to your heir in private, we do," the Elf said.

Fitz nodded. A plan came to mind, but he had to keep these Elves talking. "I see. I suppose you know that I already... deal with, for lack of a better term, another Elf?"

The four Elves looked at one another. "We... suspected it, we did."

Fitz stepped over to the Elf that didn't have a *schlipf* and, using strength and reflexes which had been getting stale since he first took the throne, pivoted to throw him into the seat of the throne. The other Elves were startled, but that particular Elf was angry... for a very, very few seconds.

"Please," Fitz said. "Take the throne, just like Hrabak does. I have no say in anything worthwhile. I don't know where my brother is.

All I know is that Hrabak has absconded with Hussack, my nephew Mussack is dead, and as far as expanding the kingdom is concerned, I. Don't. Care. Talk to my 'master' if you want to get anywhere."

It looked as if the other Elves were prepared to attack him, but the Elf on the throne waved them off. Instead he stood, plucking a splinter from his shoulder and looking at it curiously.

"I see the truth in what you say, I do," he said. "And I forgive you for your temper, I do. But you had better not try that again, you hadn't – I can't hold back my friends for ever, I cannot." He handed the splinter to the first Elf who had spoken, who also took a close look at it. The Elves took turns examining it, but none of them said anything to the others.

The first Elf – the leader, it seemed, or at least the spokesman for the group – tossed the splinter into a brazier that was helping to heat the throne room. The splinter burned green for a brief moment before it charred through.

"You're playing a dangerous game, you are," he said, giving Fitz a rueful smile. "One where you'll need a great deal of help to survive, you will. But as much as we'd like to help you, we would, I do not have the authority, I don't." He paused, running his hand over the wooden surface of the throne. Another splinter came out, which again he tossed on the fire. Two more splinters removed later and he resumed speaking. "I have a suggestion, I do. For the next six weeks you should pretend that nothing has changed, you should. Even this throne will be safe for you during that time, it will, though perhaps it will not be for much longer than that, it won't. Then you should flee the castle, you should, to head into Poros. Once you are there, you are, you should find us, you should. Then we might be able to help you, we might."

"And Hussack?" Fitz asked, though he suspected he knew the answer already.

"If Hrabak has hidden Hussack away, he has, there is little we can do for him, there is," the Elf said, shaking his head sadly. "But we may be able to help what else remains of your family, we might."

Fitz gave the Elf a genuine smile. For the first time in decades he felt hope. "Thank you," he said.

"You must not say anything of our presence to Hrabak, you mustn't," the Elf warned. "But hopefully we'll meet again, we will."

Chapter XXI

"It's Euly! Euly's back! Euly's home!" Maelgyn couldn't distinguish the individual voices as he, Euleilla, and Onayari entered Rocky Run's Left Foot Inn, but he counted six of Euleilla's foster-siblings rushing the door to give her a hug. Tur'Tei stood to the side of the door and started taking up a silent guard. Tur'Ka was outside, attending to their cart.

Wait, wasn't it five last time? he wondered to himself. *Then again, there were at least nine people working here the first time I came to Rocky Run, and Ruznak said most of them were his foster kids.*

Maelgyn wasn't sure how many children Ruznak had fostered over the years, but there were a lot of them to keep Euleilla company as she was growing up. He had been introduced to a few of them, but he couldn't remember half of their names. If he was in Rocky Run for as long as he suspected he was going to be, though, he'd have to learn them all, soon.

Euleilla, unsurprisingly, knew all of their names already. "Kara! Nordh! Simek! Melen! Miceli! Novak! It's so good to see you all again!" she cooed.

Maelgyn boggled. While Svieda was a fairly cosmopolitan nation, there were at least four regionally specific names in that list – Nordh was usually Porosian, Miceli Oregalan, Melen Odenian, and Novak Sycantian. Looking the group over, he did notice a few ethnically distinct features from those regions on some of them. Evidently, Ruznak didn't discriminate when he found a child to raise.

Maelgyn felt a bit like an outsider, or rather an intruder. Here he was, the man who had stolen this wonderful young woman from their lives. It didn't feel fair to these young men and women who Euleilla was raised to see as her brothers and sisters.

"I was unaware your wife had such a large family," Onayari mused quietly to Maelgyn.

Euleilla heard her, however. She shot the Nekoji woman a smile over the shoulder of the young man she was currently hugging – Simek, Maelgyn identified. "Oh, this isn't all of them. When I lived here there were about a dozen who either lived in the inn or stopped by regularly, and another five or six who would still make the trip for special occasions. Gramps has been fostering children for decades, now, and we all view each other as brothers and sisters."

"It sounds much like a Nekoji orphanage – one dominant male raising as many parentless juveniles as he can," Onayari said, amused. "Of course, 'siblings' are rarely as friendly with each other in Nekoji circles. At least male siblings."

Nordh, Simek, and Novak all started laughing at that one, then turned to playfully threaten each other with various implements of their trade (a damp dishrag, an empty pewter pitcher, and a small log intended for the inn's fires, respectively).

"Enough of that," Euleilla said. "Where's gramps?"

The merriment went out of the foster siblings faces. "Well... he's in his room, asleep," Simek said. "He's been ill since he returned home. We're a little worried, and we've sent out for the others to come home. I...."

Euleilla sighed. "I'll wait for him to wake up. I didn't think I would see him again before he died, so the fact that he's alive at all warms my heart."

In an effort to regain the prior boisterous mood, one of the girls – Miceli, Maelgyn thought her name was – returned to hugging her long-lost foster siblings. "It's good to see you back... but are you sure you're the same Euly? You're actually saying real sentences! You sure you aren't an impostor?"

Maelgyn winced – the subject of impostors was a bit sore for him at the moment, all things considered – but Euleilla just laughed.

"Yes," she said with a smile.

Miceli turned to glance at Maelgyn, himself, her arms still holding Euleilla tightly. "I suppose we have you to thank for that, right? Now that she's speaking like a normal Human being, we may never get her to shut up!"

"Maybe," Euleilla agreed, setting the rest of the foster siblings laughing again.

Maelgyn relaxed slightly as Simek pulled him and Onayari aside and suggested a pitcher of their inn's 'famous' blackberry cider while the rest of the family got reacquainted. He also mentioned that El'Athras and a few other people Maelgyn would be interested in meeting with would be coming to the inn that evening, so he might as well enjoy himself while he waited.

Euleilla didn't seem to want to let him out of meeting the family, however, as she led the others to his table a moment later and sat down next to him. The conversation remained lighthearted and easy-going while they all waited for the new arrivals Simek had told him about.

Maelgyn gradually learned the foster siblings' names (he had a funny feeling that Euleilla was trying to help him with that, as she started calling them all by name every time she spoke to them, at one point), and heard stories of his wife's youth that he would not have expected. Like the time she was trying to figure out how to magically split a log but set it on fire instead, nearly burning their entire supply of firewood to ashes before realizing what she'd done. And how, when she got drunk for the first time in her life, she stole Ruznak's wooden leg and used it as a rolling pin for pie dough.

It was mid-way through the story about where Euleilla had gotten the idea for her armored riding pants (a story that somehow involved a donkey, three of her foster siblings, and ride through a roped-off garden path) that Maelgyn felt their allies arrive. Sir Leno, whose magical signature was great enough to act as a flare for those who could sense it, was approaching the inn; with him was Doctor Wodtke (with not nearly as bright a signature, but you could tell it was there if you were looking for it) and oddities in his magical senses that he had learned to associate with Dwarves and Elves.

"I hate to interrupt," Maelgyn said with genuine regret. "But the people I'm hoping to meet are just about to come through that door."

Simek laughed. "Did you manage to teach someone else that trick, Euly?"

"We've taught each other quite a few things," Euleilla said, a sly smile on her face. "That might be one of them."

Simek led the other foster siblings to their feet. "Well, we don't want to get in the way of your business, so we'll just get on with our chores."

As the siblings started moving away, Maelgyn turned to Euleilla. "Why don't you go with them to catch up some more? I'll let you know whatever gets discussed here."

Euleilla frowned. "Not necessary. We'll probably be here long enough for me to do plenty of catching up. I'd much rather be a part of the meeting that will help chart the course of my husband's future."

Maelgyn winced. "I don't think we'll be talking about anything that will be quite that significant, but okay. I just thought you'd enjoy spending time with your family."

Euleilla nodded. "I'm glad you're trying so hard to think of my needs, but this isn't necessary. You are my family, now – I will remain by your side as long as we still breathe. My being captured, once, should not change that!"

Maelgyn's eyes widened. "Euleilla... honestly, I wasn't trying to send you away. I'm not going to do that, no matter what happened in that battle. I already know you plan to stick by my side, meeting or no meeting, foster-siblings or no foster-siblings. Trust me, that wasn't why I was suggesting you visit your relatives."

"I... I'm sorry," Euleilla said, her voice cracking slightly. "Tur'Ba died, and I was taken from you, and you nearly got yourself killed – twice – trying to rescue me. And it was my fault for two reasons: One, I let myself get overconfident and pulled too far ahead of our guards. And two, I let the tacticians planning our strike talk me into not fighting at your side for that battle. It may have been the right decision, from a military standpoint, but personally it was a disaster all around."

Maelgyn nodded, putting his arm around her shoulders comfortingly. "We still haven't talked about it, have we? Things have just been too complicated. We haven't even had a night alone together since you were rescued."

Euleilla flushed. "Yes... that is something we must rectify, soon."

He would have followed up on that comment, but the doors opened up right then and Tur'Ka led in a long line of people. El'Athras, Sir Leno, Gyato, Dr. Wodtke, Wangdu, and even his new chef – Kiszaten – had all arrived from Happaso (though Kiszaten almost immediately went over to join Euleilla's siblings and talk about cooking). There were still others joining them, however – men and women who had come from Sopan, who had been setting up a temporary camp here when El'Athras' orders to make things a bit more permanent came down.

Maelgyn hadn't seen Rykeifer in a while, but the man still looked as competent as ever. Being able to keep your uniform tidy was sometimes a sign that you weren't in the thick of the action, but sometimes it was also a sign that you were well organized and good officer material. Maelgyn just hoped that the impression he got of him from his work in the Elm Knoll Militia held up as he took on more responsibilities.

Then there were the children of his regent, Duke Valfarn, who had joined the army for their march across Mar'Tok. Agaeb and Amberry – named after the former beloved Royal couple – were also quite well-attired. That, however, probably was due more to a lack of action rather than any statement on their organizational skills.

A cavalry officer Maelgyn recognized only from the heraldry on his armor was next through the door. This was the famed Baron Terekalo, the ostensible head of all the cavalry under Maelgyn's command. When Maelgyn was in Sopan, Terekalo had been too ill to attend, and had initially been left behind when the cavalry was sent out to the front. He still looked rather pale and sickly, but he evidently refused to be left out of the action for long.

Maelgyn was a little less enthused by the last three rounding out the meeting. Barons Mathrid and Yergwain had not exactly been the easiest to get along with of his officers from Sopan. Neither were particularly fond of him, his wife, or mages in general. Still, they were some of the highest ranking officers in his army, so he supposed their presence was necessary. Neither was he sure about the need for his chief steward, Reltney, and the stuffy ceremonial attitudes he wanted to insist on for everything, but it was a gathering of all his current brain-trust, so it seemed Reltney had been invited on his behalf.

"Khumbaya is outside, as well," Tur'Ka said, gesturing to the door. "But he would have had a hard time getting in the door, and I'm not sure a wooden inn is the best place for a fire-breathing dragon. He'll want to know the schedule for his kin's patrols before we retire for the evening, however."

"We'll take care of that before long," El'Athras said to him. "But you might want to keep waiting outside. We're expecting several more people to show up."

"Really?" Maelgyn replied as Tur'Ka went to do as instructed and the other guests started finding spots around the table. "Who?"

"Sword Wybert, who would have come with the rest of us but someone needed to stay behind and act as a guide," El'Athras said. "Duke Kunyk, his regent here in Largo. Your own regent, Duke Valfarn. Duke Rudel, who just arrived from the Borden Isles. Duchess Kassi, regent of Leyland. Duke Kousa, regent of Stanget. Baroness Mikko, general of the armies in Largo. And finally Baron Jank, general of the armies in Stanget."

Maelgyn frowned. "I understand why Wybert would be here, but why the others? Especially the regents! Surely their time is better spent dealing with the situation in their own provinces."

"They're going to be fine temporarily administering things from here," El'Athras said. "As far as why they're going to be here, they're all part of plan C."

"Plan C?" Maelgyn said, feeling like a toddler several steps behind his parents trying to catch up.

"Plan A is what we've already started," he said. "Keeping the remaining Swords all alive and their claim to the throne intact, circumventing 'Brode' and the Porosians for as long as we can without damaging the war effort. It was touch and go there, for a while, but by rescuing Sycanth's soldiers we've been able to give ourselves about a six month window where, we expect, there will be a pause in the war – three months where both sides are reorganizing their armies, and three more months where winter weather is expected to prevent major operations. Meanwhile, we attempt to find and rescue the real Brode and use him to overthrow the usurper."

"Six months? Really?" Maelgyn said. "That seems a bit optimistic to me."

"Which is why we came up with Plan B. The Law of Swords is written in such a way that, to remove 'Brode' from the throne, three of the Swords would lose their claim to provincial rule and the line of succession – Brode, as the man impersonated; Arnach, as the man who vouched for him; and the third Sword, the accuser – whoever that is." El'Athras grinned darkly. "I've been going over the full text of the law and found a loophole that'll mean we only lose two."

Maelgyn's eyes widened. He'd been trying to puzzle it out for months and hadn't come up with a solution to their current crisis, and he'd been intimately familiar with the Law of Swords for far longer than El'Athras. "How?"

"Simple enough," El'Athras said. "You were banished from the Royal Province, correct?"

"And from Glorest," Maelgyn replied, shifting uncomfortably.

"Which means you were able to appoint a proxy. Please tell me you did not appoint your father?"

"No, of course not – that would have been a disaster. I named Arnach."

El'Athras laughed. "Even better. Well, under the rules of interregnum, when a proxy is seated in the Royal City, they have most of the powers that any Sword would have in that city. However, if your reason for appointing a proxy stems from being physically or legally unable to attend court, you do not bear the consequences for the actions of that proxy; instead, those consequences are on the head of the proxy themselves. In other words—"

"—Arnach can be the accuser, and there can be no additional punishment," Maelgyn said. "Of course! But how were you so certain that 'Brode' would banish me?"

"We figured he'd try something – we just weren't sure when," El'Athras said. "We just had Arnach in place to ensure that banishment was the punishment he chose, rather than deposing you as a Sword or executing you."

Maelgyn shivered a little at the thought that he might have been executed if things had gone wrong. "Well... okay. I still prefer the outcome of Plan A, however."

"As do we... which is where Plan C comes in," El'Athras said. "Plan B is only to be executed if things spiral out of control in the capital.

Plan C is what happens if Plan A doesn't succeed in our six month window."

"Which somehow involves two Swords and four regents."

"And two additional provincial leaders," El'Athras said, gesturing to himself and Gyato. "Between yourself and Wybert, myself and Gyato, and the sitting regents of Leyland, Stanget, and the Borden Isles, we have the leaders of seven Sviedan provinces."

Maelgyn frowned. He knew the significance of that number, but there seemed to be one significant flaw to it. "Duke Kousa doesn't count. Idril would—"

"Idril is unavailable, just as Nattiel and Ambrosius are," El'Athras pointed out. "For the time being, her regent is ruling in her place. If she ever shows up again, we'll explain things to her such that she joins us."

"I'm not sure I like this idea," Maelgyn said.

"What idea?" Euleilla asked, reminding him of the others in the room.

"Sorry," he said, turning. He saw comprehension only on Sir Leno's face. Gyato looked as if he had some idea, but wasn't certain, while most of the others looked completely clueless. "It's a separate part of the Law of Swords – namely, the rules on how to suspend or amend the Law of Swords during a period of Interregnum."

"When the rulers of seven provinces are gathered together during interregnum, they can suspend or amend the Law of Swords for the purposes of ending that interregnum," El'Athras said. "It was intended to be used should peace be re-established before the Royal Province had been recaptured or a king had been appointed, but nothing in that section of the law forbids it from being used for other purposes."

"We might just be doing the Porosians job for them if we suspend the Law of Swords," Maelgyn warned.

"Not under Plan C," El'Athras said. "The Law of Swords won't be suspended long enough for the Porosians to even find out about it before we return it to being the law of the land. The declarations have already been prepared – we just need everyone here to sign them."

"What do the declarations say?" Maelgyn asked.

"First and foremost, that we find that the Makeshift Council was formed in a way that did not give them the necessary discretion to determine if Arnach was being coerced when he agreed to vouch for 'Brode' as the 'true and right Sword King of Svieda.' That's almost certainly true, by the way, but it would be hard to argue the point to a magistrate, likely one appointed by 'Brode,' while the Law of Swords is still in place. And it will protect both the real Brode and Arnach from being deposed as Swords."

"True," Maelgyn agreed.

"Second, that we depose 'the creature masquerading as the true Sword Brode' for having coerced his way onto the throne, such that it became impossible for other Swords to challenge him while the Law of Swords were in place."

"Also true."

"Third, we will be moving the capital of Svieda from the Royal City of Svieda to a new location – the rebuilt Rocky Run, in the province of Largo."

"Wait a minute—" Maelgyn began.

"And finally, we agree to recognize you, Sword Maelgyn, as having been the first Sword to 'reclaim' the new capital city of Rocky Run, making you Svieda's new Sword King."

It took both time and effort for Lazark to arrange a meeting with his superiors. They were very secretive, very important, and very cautious people. They were also Elves, and never quick to respond to a summons.

So it had taken him several weeks to get in contact with them, and even longer to arrange an actual meeting. Now, as he rode his horse past the burnt-out ruins of an old manor home belonging to a now-deceased Sviedan nobleman, he was wondering how long he would have to wait when he got to the meeting point for them to see him.

He was not expecting a vine to shoot out of nowhere and grab him, yanking him off of his horse and into a nearby cluster of bushes. He wasn't hurt, mind you – despite the jerking motion, neither the vine itself nor the fall did him any damage – but his breath was knocked out of him and he was left in the bushes, stunned.

The vine wrapped around his head, blindfolding him with leaves, and then he was pulled from the bush onto something wooden that started moving away from the road. Where to, he had no idea, but as he began to settle down he started silently cursing the paranoia of his Elven masters.

He wasn't sure how long the journey was – he drifted off a couple times, and he was pretty sure several hours had passed – but it was quite some time before the cart he was in came to a stop. Only then did the vine uncoil from around him and the leaf-blindfold uncover his eyes.

He took a few minutes to blink. He was in a meadow, of sorts, ringed in an unnaturally circular pattern of bushes and trees that blocked all view of the outside world. A few oversized tree roots were being used as seats by three Elves, and another was placed right in front of him.

Well, at least they gave me someplace to sit down, this time.

Lazark took off and folded his traveling cloak a few times to make a cushion before taking his seat. The three Elves – none of whose faces were visible, thanks to ebony masks they were wearing – stared at him intensely.

"So you summoned us, you did," the leader, identifiable by the red painted highlights on his otherwise black mask, said. The Elven contingent of the Porosian Conspiracy included four traveling teams, each of which were assigned to a different set of cities. He'd met some of the others, and each was very different. This was the only one that liked to wear masks, the only one that was a group of three instead of four, and the only one where only one of their number ever spoke. To be honest, Lazark wasn't sure why the other two were present. "And we have come, we have."

"Thank you," Lazark said. "I fear there may be some... competition, setting up in the Royal City of Svieda. I was hoping you might provide me with information on any local band of the Technologist-faction Elves."

Red Mask stared at him for a long moment. "No," he finally said.

That threw Lazark for a loop. "No? Why ever not? I would think tracking down these people is of great interest to our cause."

"It no longer matters, it doesn't," Red Mask replied. "We've decided on Plan Arrowhead, we have."

Lazark's jaw dropped. Plan Arrowhead was conceived of as a last, desperate chance, which would likely cost thousands of lives, and was only to be considered if something drastic had happened. "But...

I know we've had a few minor setbacks, but the current plan has a firm foothold. It may take a bit longer than originally planned, but Svieda will fall to us in a matter of years, as long as you can keep the real Brode on a leash that long. What have we done wrong?"

"It was not your doing, it wasn't," Red Mask said. "We learned something in Sho'Curlas, we did. The old plan will not work there, it won't. As Sword Maelgyn is now aware of our plans and working to counteract them, he is, we no longer believe anything can be salvaged of your operation, we don't. We know Plan Arrowhead is unlikely to succeed, it is, but we think we can use it to get a new plan to work, we do."

"Why not just kill Sword Maelgyn, and let me finish the plan as it is?" Lazark pleaded. He had thought banishing the man would be sufficient for his plans, but perhaps he should have stood his ground and forced a capital judgment of treason on him. Having his own people execute him would only weaken the Swords that much more.

"We have tried that twice, we have. When we struck him in Sopan, we did, he acquired one of our precious *schlipf*, he did, and his Elven ally arrived in time to chase us away, he did. Then we struck at him as he was leaving the Royal City, we did, but his Dwarven allies protected him there, they did. Had we killed him then, we had, things might be different, they might, but we now think Plan Arrowhead is our best option, we do."

Lazark grimaced. He had volunteered for this mission specifically because he didn't want Poros involved in Plan Arrowhead, but it looked like his hopes were dashed. "Should I return to East Poros, then, to help prepare for the reunification?"

"You still have one last task in Svieda, you do. It is time for our Merfolk 'ally' to die, it is."

Chapter XXII

Euleilla sat down at the side of the bed of her foster father, pretending to watch his chest rise and fall under the blankets. Ruznak was still alive, though his breathing was very feeble and congested. He had yet to wake since she'd arrived in town, and she wasn't sure how much longer he would be sleeping. Maelgyn had been here for a while, but he'd been poor company after the shocks he'd endured in El'Athras' impromptu meeting, so she'd sent him off to bed. She would join him, soon, but she wanted a little time here.

It felt odd sitting a vigil over Ruznak like this. Even when they were returning from the Borden Isles, her foster father seemed so strong and sure of himself, and not just for a man of his age. Honestly, that was the way she had always wanted to remember him. She had thought, when they parted, that it was the last time she'd ever see him, but had comforted herself that at least she wouldn't have to watch his health fail him.

As it was failing him, now. It had only been a few months – how had he fallen so far, so quickly?

"Hey, Euly," a voice called from behind her.

"Kara," Euleilla replied, not turning to look at her foster sister. Both of them knew it would just be play-acting if she had.

"He was really happy when he came back home," Kara said. Euleilla wasn't paying magical attention, so started a little when Kara's hand came down on her shoulder, however comforting the gesture was intended to be. "He told us all about your new life and your new husband. He talked about your adventures on the Borden Isles. He was really proud of you."

"'Was'?" Euleilla repeated, feigning surprise. "He's still breathing. Did something happen to make him no longer proud of me?"

"Sorry, I meant 'is,'" Kara said, taking a seat next to her. "He's still a strong man. I don't care what age he is, he'll get through this. He'll outlive us all... right?"

Euleilla probed her foster father one more time. Somehow, she doubted it – even if he survived this illness, he wasn't long for the world. She let the silence answer for her, however.

Kara lapsed into quiet contemplation as well. It wasn't long before Simek and Novak joined them. Their other siblings – Miceli, Nordh, and Melen – were needed to handle running the inn, but these three were likely to stay until the shift change. Euleilla sighed – it was far too quiet.

"So, you all have heard what my life has been like since I left – and had your fun telling my husband some slightly exaggerated tales of my youth – but we haven't talked about things around here. What have your lives been like since I left?"

Kara coughed. "Well, Miceli, Melen, and I have all been doing that late-start study on magic, like we were before you left. And we've started to really master the basics."

"Really?" Euleilla said, genuinely impressed. Late-start magic courses were rarely attempted, and even when successful led to mages who could never fulfill their full potential. It was time consuming, laborious, and dreadfully dull, and always left the trainee with disappointing results. It was a large waste of time for most people, but once she had learned the technique to do so Euleilla had been surprised to discover that her three closest foster-sisters were all sitting on high degrees of untapped magical potential. Ruznak immediately tracked down a tutor, and to Euleilla's surprise her sisters had stuck with it even after she had left.

A quick scan showed that Kara, at least, had managed to take modest control over some of it. She'd probably be able to act as a fourth-rate mage, in time, though had she been trained from birth she might have been a first rate like Euleilla herself. None of her male foster-siblings had enough potential to make the effort worth it, however.

Euleilla felt Kara magically reaching for a portion of the nickel powder that typically surrounded her feet to look for dips in the road and the like. It was a feeble bit of magic, but it impressed her nonetheless. She allowed her foster sibling to take a little of the powder for herself, though she kept a close eye on it. If Kara did anything weird with that particular powder, she wanted to recover it quickly – nickel powder was scarce in those parts. It might become scarce countrywide, with the mines of Sycanth cut off.

But no immediate need to reclaim the nickel powder became apparent, as Kara started flying it through the air in an intricate pattern. It took a moment to recognize the symbols, but soon Euleilla recognized it as writing in the air. It took another moment to read that writing. It was a simple message.

"Can you read this?"

Euleilla almost laughed. Retaking control of the nickel powder, she changed the letters around... to read one big "Yes."

Once the sound of Kara's giggles revealed she had gotten the message, Euleilla reclaimed the nickel and let it rejoin the rest of the powder around her feet. Then she took one of the several satchels around her waist and tossed to over to her sibling's lap.

"What's this?" Kara asked.

"Some magic powder of your own," Euleilla said. "As skilled as you're getting, you'll need it. That's iron powder, mind you – quality iron, processed to a fine grain, with anti-rust treatments and other protections included, but iron nonetheless. It won't be as 'pretty' as my nickel, but it'll probably work better for you."

"I've been meaning to get some," Kara said. "Our tutor lets us fiddle with his whenever he's in town, but he works with mages in a dozen small towns along the Largo River. We only see him – and get to work with the powder – once a month, now that we've gotten through the basics."

Euleilla shot her a grin. If that was all the training she was getting, then maybe she could realize still more of her magical potential, with proper instruction. She was already a borderline fourth rate mage –

perhaps Kara might make it to third rate, if she had enough help. "Well, if my husband and I stay here for a while, I suspect there will be several people able to help you train a little more often than once a month."

"I'd like that," Kara said.

"So will you be teaching her, or your husband?"

Euleilla thought about it for a second. "I was thinking of Sir Leno, actually, though of course both I and Maelgyn will... Gramps? You're awake?"

With a watery cough, Ruznak pulled himself into a sitting position. "I've been awake for a while, now. Surprised you didn't notice."

Nonplussed to be caught so inattentive, Euleilla nonetheless shot him a wide smile. "I've been waiting for you to wake up all day! Of course you choose the one moment I'm a little distracted to rouse yourself."

"Ever since you learned that magic trick where you could sense other people, I've been the only person who's ever been able to sneak up on you," Ruznak said, pausing only to cough again. "I don't plan on giving that up."

"What kind of illness renders you this sick this fast?" Euleilla said, concerned. "Just a month ago you were the picture of health! Now—"

"It's called old age, Euly," Ruznak said. "And maybe a touch of pneumonia. If this is the thing that kills me, there are far, far worse ways I might have gone."

Euleilla shook her head. "But you're still stronger than many young men I know! Why would you even have gotten pneumonia in the first place?"

"Probably because I've been spending more days on cold, wet ships than I should have," Ruznak said. "Child, you knew I didn't have long to live when we last parted. Why are you so upset?"

Euleilla took a deep breath, shaking her head. "I've already said my final goodbyes to you twice. I shouldn't be reunited with you just in time to have to say them a third time."

Ruznak sighed, turning towards Simek. With Ruznak ill, Simek would be running the inn. "So, just when did she and her husband get here, anyway?"

"About eight hours ago."

"And I bet she hasn't had one minute of rest since she got here?"

"Well, first we were all so happy about the reunion we had to talk, and then there was a meeting she attended where more than a dozen nobles and royals were all gathered, so I have to assume it was pretty important. And since then she's been waiting here."

"And her husband?"

Novak answered, here – he was in charge of finding rooms for everyone. "In bed. He tried to stay with her, but she decided he needed his sleep more than she needed his company."

Ruznak nodded. "Euly, you're too tired and you aren't thinking straight. Go join your husband in bed. I'm old and sick, but not that sick. I'll still be here in the morning."

"But—"

"Go. Or I'll have Novak drag Maelgyn out of bed so that he can talk you into it."

Euleilla pouted. "You don't play fair."

"Of course not. How do you think I've lived *this* long?" Ruznak laughed.

Kara stood up, offering Euleilla a hand. "Come on, Euly – I'll show you where we put that husband of yours."

She wasn't happy about it, but still felt the warmth of her family's teasing as she accepted the help out of her chair.

Home may have become wherever Maelgyn was, now that they were married, but there would always be a part of her that realized she had more than one home... and that all those homes were now in one place.

El'Athras gazed on as Ahttur'Gne, the head engineer on the Rocky Run project, guided him on an inspection of the latest work. His attention was wandering – Ahttur'Gne was rather long-winded, yet rarely seemed to actually say anything – but El'Athras was still impressed at how much work had been done in such a short span of time. And he wasn't the only one – accompanying him on the tour were Wybert, Gyato, Valfarn, Rudel, and the other dukes – basically, everyone (except the sleeping Maelgyn) who might rightfully be called a provincial leader. Oh, and Wangdu was following them from the shadows, but the Elf wasn't really part of the group.

Maelgyn hadn't said much once the actual meeting started. Just as well – the poor boy looked shocked at the situation El'Athras was putting him in. And yet he had dutifully signed the declaration suspending the Law of Swords along with everyone else. The declaration would be held at Rocky Run in secret until such time as it was needed. Assuming, of course, it was needed. Along with the other documents they all had signed, which would revise and then re-establish the Law of Swords in a matter of minutes should they ever be released. They would not go into effect until presented to the public, so until then these documents – all potentially evidence of treason – would be kept under lock and key, with a fast method of destroying them on-hand should the need arise (or should Plans A or B be completed successfully).

El'Athras knew that none of the signers wanted the declarations to be used, but he was starting to wonder whether it wouldn't be for the best if they were, regardless of Plan A's potential for success. The truth was that the Law of Swords – while an impressive document that had helped set up Svieda as the most stable government in Human history for the past several centuries – was showing quite a few shortcomings. Problems that needed desperately to be addressed by someone – if not by these declarations, than by the real Brode when he assumed the throne, or by, well, whoever became the new Sword King, should Plan B go into effect.

With two new provinces to account for now that Mar'Tok and Caseificio were merging in – neither of which could be properly represented by someone in the (very Human) line of succession to the throne, as the Law of Swords demanded – changes would need to be made, anyway. Probably more significant changes than the few already agreed to by the council of war El'Athras had set up the previous day. El'Athras could count on Maelgyn to give his people proper consideration, if he were leading Svieda when those changes were made. Should someone like, say, Nattiel take the throne... well, the Law of Swords might not get those changes at all.

That would be a disaster. It might be okay in the short run, but in the long term it would lead to the Nekoji and his people being regarded as second class citizens, not equals with the Humans. That sentiment would take some time to develop, so there was no rush, but El'Athras was concerned that someone who would ignore their concerns would end up on the throne at the end of this war.

"Milord?" Ahttur'Gne said.

El'Athras started, glancing up at the other Dwarf. "Sorry?"

"I asked if there was something wrong with the warehouse, milord? You look disturbed."

"Oh, no," El'Athras said, shaking his head. "I was thinking of something else. Please, continue."

Ahttur'Gne turned and started talking again about the type of lime used in the concrete – evidently, something about it had a significant impact on drying time or something like that – and El'Athras quickly phased him out.

"You are bothered by something, and I'm fairly certain it isn't the architecture," Duchess Kassi, Leyland's regent, said to him. "You fear that you haven't done enough to protect your people after embroiling them in this war."

Her words startled El'Athras, but she was being quiet enough and subtle enough to not draw attention to them. Kassi was an odd-looking middle-aged woman – horribly gaunt, but with kind eyes and a smile that instantly warmed you when she graced you with one.

And apparently, she was rather insightful.

"You have the advantage of me, milady," El'Athras said. "That is exactly why I may seem... distracted. I wonder if we shouldn't go ahead and suspend the Law of Swords, anyway – at least long enough to make the corrections needed to protect my people and the Nekoji."

"And yet, you didn't propose any such amendments among the set of changes we have already proposed," Kassi said, amused.

El'Athras sighed. "I trust some people to do the right thing for us... but there are scenarios where people who I do not trust take power. Maelgyn, I trust. His father, however..."

"Nattiel is hard to deal with and stubborn, but he can be reasoned with. Just not the way you think – he has a position, and will argue with you defending it. But if you make your point, while he won't accept your words at first, he'll come around to your way of thinking. A couple weeks later he will propose your ideas, and he'll be *convinced* that it was his plan all along." She leaned in with a conspiratorial wink. "Go ahead and let him think that. He'll be easier to deal with next time."

Euleilla undressed as quietly as she could manage – she didn't want to wake Maelgyn. Her armored riding pants were the most troublesome of her clothes, but she managed to keep them from making any more than a soft thump as she slipped them off.

She considered pulling on a nightgown, but she decided not to. She found herself more tired than she realized, and knew it would require more effort to put one on than she was comfortable with. She couldn't easily find her nightgowns, as they were the one set of garments she had that she couldn't realistically put iron markers in, and looking would make more noise than she needed to make.

She'd slept nude, before, but never with her husband – even the night when they had consummated their marriage, she had slipped on a nightgown before bed. Slipping into bed with him sans any kind of clothing felt amusingly illicit, and she was sure she would have ample opportunities for teasing him in the morning.

She was not expecting him to reach out and gently grope her the moment she finished slipping under the covers.

"I've been waiting for you," he whispered, pulling her to him and kissing the juncture where her neck met her shoulder. His breath on her skin caused goosebumps to rise. "Interesting choice of sleeping attire."

"I didn't think you were awake," she replied, burrowing into his side. She loved that place right under his chin, where her hair was just brushing his jawline. "I'll let you see my sleeping attire better in the morning."

"And why not right now?" Maelgyn shifted, pulling her more solidly on top of him. Both of them were very tired, but that just made their session of lovemaking a little slower and more leisurely than it would otherwise have been.

Afterward they snuggled together cozily, and Maelgyn sighed, not quite ready to let go of their private time together. "I'm exhausted, but still unable to go to sleep. Want to talk?"

"Hm?" Euleilla muttered. She was already drifting off, but she'd let him talk if he wanted.

"I noticed your *schlipf* matured while you were in captivity," Maelgyn said. "Did you ever come up with a name?"

She nodded, loving the feel of her hair rubbing against his chest. "Melka, after my mother."

"Your mother? You've never told me anything about your mother, before. I thought you didn't remember her."

"I have very few memories of her," Euleilla said. "I think she died before my father went into hiding, but I'm not certain about that. I know little about her other than her name. I think she was a mage, but I'm not even certain about that."

"Heh. My mother was also a mage. I probably have more memories of my mother than you do of yours, but she also died when I was young. Father thinks she died because she over-exhausted her magic, but that seems odd to me. It takes severe overuse to die of magical exhaustion, and nothing she had been doing in that time would have exhausted her like that."

Euleilla frowned. "Is that why your father so dislikes mages and magecraft?"

"I've wondered that, on occasion, but truthfully I don't know what makes my father act the way he does."

"I find it odd that both of us would have mages as mothers, and both of us would lose them at such a young age." She paused. "It feels oddly... coincidental."

"Well, if you're worried that we might secretly be long-lost siblings or something, I can assure you that our mothers were different people," Maelgyn joked. "My mother never left my father's side after marrying him, and they'd been married for many years before I was born. And she wasn't named Melka."

"What was her name, then?" Euleilla asked.

"Addiena. She was born in Leyland, and served as the Court Mage for her Sword before she married my father. She loved experimenting with magic, trying to discover some things that magical theory says we should be able to accomplish but which we mages have yet to discover – calling lightning, cooking food without heat, determining compass points, various medical uses, and so on." Maelgyn chuckled, pleasantly bouncing Euleilla against his chest. "What she saw in my father, I'll never know."

"My father told me that he met my mother at the Delbruck Academy," Euleilla said. "That probably means my mother was interested in experimental magic, too."

"It was a popular field back in our parents' generation," Maelgyn said. "Especially the question about calling lightning. The Delbruck Academy your parents met at was a large part of the reason why. It's fall from grace is why students in the field of experimental magic are so rare, nowadays."

"I've tinkered with experimental magic from time to time," Euleilla said. "As I'm pretty sure you know – after all, you've benefited from some of the things I've discovered. Now that I think about it, my father had a journal from my mother where she documented some of her experiments. I've never read it, but I wonder if it would have details of her experiments."

"Where is it?" Maelgyn asked.

"Hm... I'm not sure if it still exists. Father had it with him in Sycanth, and I think that was the last I saw of it. I don't believe Cawnpore took it with him when he collected me from my father."

"So it's still at your father's home in Sycanth?" Maelgyn said.

Euleilla hesitated before telling him. She never said anything, but she often wondered if the reason her father was murdered had nothing to do with the supposed 'mining consortiums' who were after his processing technique, but rather the secrets of her mother's journal. She was not naive – she knew there were factions in the world targeting the secrets that her parents had been researching. *Both* of her parents.

Maelgyn could be trusted, though – he was her husband, after all. "Underneath the floorboards in my father's bedroom. Though the building nearly collapsed after the attack which poisoned my father and blinded my first eye, so who knows if it still exists at all."

"Sycanth is currently held by the Sho'Curlans. Maybe when the war is over, though, we can go there and see if it still exists. Such a treasure should not be left neglected."

Euleilla nodded, though she didn't see any point in agreeing. The war was not likely to end for years, yet, and if he remembered this promise... well, she would have to wait and see.

Lazark had no idea where he was when the Elven transport dropped him off after the meeting. All he knew was that he needed to find civilization, and soon.

He thought they'd had years to get things done in. Now, he learned, he only had weeks. And he was to be the spearpoint for the move... literally. He rubbed his hand where a schlipf had been forcibly embedded in him. It was dormant, for the moment, but he had just two days to find shelter. He would need to stay in that shelter for a while before returning to the Royal Castle. When his *schlipf* became active, he would likely be ill for several weeks.

Once he had completed the forced bond, however, the *schlipf* would be his to command. A weapon said to give Humans a taste of the power that the Elves wielded... but just a taste. And one that would be shortening his lifespan considerably.

Taking on the *schlipf* had not been his idea. He had resisted most strenuously, in fact... but he could not hold off Red Mask and his two Elven compatriots. He was no warrior, and even if he had been there was no Human warrior on earth capable of fighting three Elves in their own chosen home and hope to survive. And the *schlipf* was now binding him to a course of action much as he would now be binding the actions of the *schlipf*.

But now he had a weapon. A weapon whose target he no longer was sure was the right group to target. If this was how his allies treated their supporters, perhaps they weren't his allies after all. No, perhaps he had misspoken earlier – he didn't have a weapon. He was the weapon. A weapon charged with destroying the entire government of Svieda... or at least as much of it as he could get in one attempt. Then he would drive Svieda into complete chaos, sending its armies into disarray and weakening Svieda's defenses severely – and he was not to worry about the Sho'Curlan invasion at all, counter to his instructions of just one week before. The Sho'Curlans could go ahead and take whatever territory they liked, and it wouldn't concern Lazark's masters in the slightest.

Poros was about to rise again... and it would do so by breaking the back of Svieda.

Chapter XXIII

It had been several weeks since Maelgyn, his wife, and his entourage reached Rocky Run. In that time, the small town continued the process of becoming a powerful fortress city, with new towers and walls being added ever day. The Dwarves were working at an inhuman pace (as one might expect, them being Dwarves and not Humans), and finally the first phase of reconstruction in the Eastern half of Rocky Run was complete.

The other side of the river was still much the same as it had always been, though, and the current debate among the townsfolk was whether or not to accept the changes that the Dwarves were planning. A hastily arranged meeting between the town's guild leaders and aldermen with the leaders behind the new construction – now dubbed the "Sviedan War Council" by the locals was taking place in the meeting hall. It was, perhaps, the largest building in the unfinished side of the burgeoning city, though the Left Foot Inn was giving it a run for its money.

Maelgyn found himself sitting on the side of the so-called war council, which consisted of all the visiting Dukes, Counts, and Barons, as well as his personal advisers like Wangdu, Rykeifer, and the increasingly infirm Ruznak.

Maelgyn sighed. Ruznak really was the only one of his advisers who knew the town at all, but his health issues left him with only about an hour each day where he was lucid enough to dispense any actual advice. This meeting was not taking place during that period of lucidity, however, and Maelgyn would have to brief him on everything, later. In the meantime, he had decided not to make any hasty decisions.

But he was somewhat unique, in that regard. It seemed as if everyone else in these meetings, on both sides of the debate, were pushing for quick, in his opinion unsatisfactory resolutions to complex problems – often in diametric opposition on most issues – and so the debate continued for far longer than Maelgyn thought made sense. Maelgyn wasn't sure what the locals were so concerned with, since any buildings demolished would be rebuilt as better, stronger stonework buildings. But Maelgyn suspected he knew why his own side was so adamant about keeping the debate going.

They were bored. Nothing was happening – no newsworthy events, anyway – and so these men and women who had been so great when the call for action had come now devolved into the creatures they became when they had nothing good to do: They became politicians.

Pompous, gregarious, self-important politicians.

Who had nothing better to do than to try and make their opinions heard, whether they made sense or not. Honestly, Maelgyn agreed with most of the positions they took, and when speaking with each of them individually liked them all a lot, but as a group they lost their minds.

What was the point of debating the *logistics* for a debate? Who cared about table size, who met who where, and so forth – this had gone beyond ridiculous long ago. Maelgyn couldn't think of a better word for the situation at all.

And my father wants me to become more *like these people?* he thought incredulously.

"...can't use local workmen for this job," Duke Kunyk was saying. "Believe me, I would like nothing better than to provide jobs for your people. But we can't afford the local workmen – the Dwarven workers are, quite frankly, faster and better equipped than any local we could possibly find, and they come at a remarkable price: They're free. Or rather, they're being paid for by the Mar'Tok war chest, and by law those funds may only be used to hire the Dwarves of Mar'Tok. We're also getting all of the materials for, well, not free, but far cheaper than any local granite mine or the like could afford to sell it to us for. These Dwarven stones are being mined and transported for a profit, it's true, but the cost for the Dwarves to mine and transport these stone is far, far less than what our locals could hope to mine it for. They're just better at it."

Tomas – a man who made his livelihood as a chandler but was now the town's senior alderman and the closest thing to a mayor Rocky Run had before Maelgyn's army swooped into town – led the response to that. "We don't care about which specific jobs are being talked about, but you've already ruined the ferry trade by building that bridge. What other business are you going to just ruin while we wait for these mythical advantages you are always talking about?"

It was at this point that Maelgyn's wandering attention was caught by a disruption in the back of the room. A young Dwarf wearing a traveling cloak and some kind of livery Maelgyn was unfamiliar with was standing next to El'Athras, whispering in his ear. There was no way to tell, from the expressions on the two Dwarves faces, what was being discussed, but it undoubtedly would be far more interesting than this dull meeting that would result in absolutely nothing decided.

Evidently, even El'Athras thought so. "Excuse me, everyone – we'll have to resolve this another time. We have news that must be attended to right away. The town council is dismissed. We will resume discussions on the state of the construction in the morning. The War Council should remain behind, however."

"This had better not just be a delaying tactic," Alderman Tomas muttered, but stood anyway and gestured for his fellows to join him.

The guild leaders grumbled a bit, and the junior aldermen a bit more, but they still filed out of the meeting hall dutifully. The last of them closed the doors behind them, and El'Athras stepped forward so he could be heard by the crowd.

"I've just received word," El'Athras said without preamble. "That the real Brode has been located."

All of those present had been told about the impostor on the throne. Most had learned before signing the documents that could be used to suspend the Law of Swords those several weeks before, and the rest – none of whom were involved in the signing – had it explained to them afterwords. Honestly, it was a bit surprising the rumors hadn't reached the civilian populace, yet, since many as were now in on the secret.

"Where?" Maelgyn demanded, standing from his seat. Finally, there was something to do that might save their country. Maybe these idiot politicians would once again become men (and women) of action.

"In a Porosian town named Sjouleber," El'Athras said.

Maelgyn frowned. "Never heard of it."

"Sjouleber is only on the most detailed of our maps," El'Athras said. "We know little about it. Our best guess is that is is about the size that Rocky Run was before we started fortifying it, maybe a bit smaller, but evidently the Porosian Conspiracy has been making it their headquarters recently."

Maelgyn nodded. "I see. If they're using a town of that size, they're probably relying on stealth as their principle defense. Depending on the terrain, it might be easy to take. Does the town have walls? Should we take a siege engine, or make a quick strike with our cavalry? What are our options?"

There was some muttering by the other lords, and El'Athras hesitated. "Your Highness... it would not be wise to attack the town. Sending an army there might be viewed as an act of war by powers who we would be wise to keep peace with."

Maelgyn frowned. "The Sho'Curlans pass through Squire's Knot as if it wasn't there without response. It seems to me as if they should allow our soldiers to pass, as well, if they want to make any pretense of neutrality."

"The people of Squire's Knot are not who I am referring to," El'Athras said, his voice strained. "Your Highness, I am actually referring to Poros itself. At this point, we have no proof that any part of Poros – not even West Poros, itself, where Sjouleber is located – is affiliated with the Poros Conspiracy. In fact, from what I understand it is more that the conspiracy is using the Porosians, not working with them. It would be... unwise, at the least, to start a war with Poros."

"If Poros were to unite, it were," Wangdu continued. "It would become a nation even more powerful than Sho'Curlas, it would. But if they are not provoked, they aren't, they will remain divided and out of our war, they will."

Maelgyn let out a deep breath, frustrated. "Well, at the moment, there's a member of a group we've been calling the 'Porosian Conspiracy' sitting on the throne in the Royal Castle, while the person who should be the Sword King is sitting captive in a Porosian town. These are both acts of war made by Poros, but we can't do anything because it might provoke a war with Poros. Surely you are not suggesting that my cousin must sit rotting in their prison and we must allow an impostor to stay on the throne?"

"Your temper is understandable," El'Athras said. "But we are fairly certain that the government of West Poros is unaware of the actions of the Porosian Conspiracy. Were it not likely to prompt his captors to kill him when provoked, we could ask that government to rescue Brode for us, and they would probably try to do so."

Maelgyn had a hard time believing that the Porosians were so ignorant of such a widespread movement acting in their name, but conceded the issue. El'Athras' spies were rarely wrong about such things. "So, we can't go into the town and rescue him because that might start a war, but we also can't ask Poros to rescue him for us because that might get Brode killed. What do you suggest, then? From what you've said, it sounds as if we can do nothing."

El'Athras stiffened a bit, putting his hands on his hips. "Come, come, your Highness – we've known each other for almost a year, now. I've been planning for this eventuality for months. Do you really think that I wouldn't have a plan ready for this?"

That struck a chord. Maelgyn took another deep breath and let it out slowly. "My apologies. No, you're right. I think it's the sitting around here, as we engage in pointless debate after pointless debate about our right to fortify this city while we sit on our hands when it comes to the war. It's starting to wear on me."

"Those Elves who sat through our government's political debates were always the first of us to go crazy, they were," Wangdu said, drawing a laugh from the other lords.

"Yes, well... hopefully I can escape them soon enough to preserve my own sanity," Maelgyn said.

El'Athras snorted, amused. "I'm afraid it has long since been too late to save your sanity, your Highness. Sane people don't go charging bandit attacks to rescue Dwarven Merchant Princes they don't know, or challenge several Black Dragons to single combat."

"Sanity is overrated, it is," Wangdu teased. "Most Elves are insane, we are, yet most of us survive and thrive in society, we do. It is only a relative few of us that you must watch out for, it is."

Maelgyn ignored the joke, focusing on El'Athras. "All right – tell me this plan, then."

"Well, rather than a full-scale invasion, the Porosian government may be willing to overlook the intrusion a small rescue party consisting of very powerful, very skilled warriors who understand the art of stealth or who can be taught it, considering the circumstances. As to how you'll get across that border, well, that'll have to wait – you might say that the plan involves the secret to my spies' success...."

Euleilla sat in a room, supervising a test of her three foster-sisters' magical abilities. She watched as the last of them, Melen, took her block of iron, magically flattened it out, and then folded as if it were paper with her magic. It was eight minutes into the exhibition – the target was ten.

The bit of iron started heating up, turning red. This was a crucial part of the technique, but it was also the most vital – the demonstration that one could manage two tasks at a time while concentrating on their magic.

The traveling magic instructor – the only mage in town licensed to issue official magical ratings – watched with her as the red-hot iron first formed a knife, but then – as if Melen had re-thought her plan, it changed into a shield.

The sand in the instructor's timer ran out. Ten minutes had passed.

"Congratulations," he said, smiling at them. "All three of you have passed your certifications as third rate mages. I'd like to take the credit, but I know you've had a much better teacher than I these past few weeks."

It was far better than most mages could manage who started late in life; even the few 'success' stories rarely became anything more than fifth-rate mages. They were lucky enough to know they had great potential, thanks to Euleilla – something most people who wanted to learn magic later in their lives couldn't say – but even so, to get even this far was remarkable. It was further proof, as Euleilla suspected, that all three of them might have been first rate mages had they been trained from a young age.

"I wouldn't say that," Euleilla said. "They were already fourth rates, certification or no, when I came into town. That was all your work – all I did was give them suggestions on how to build and maintain their magical strength."

"Well, it worked, whatever you did," the instructor said. "I'll fill out your certifications and get them to you before I leave town tomorrow. Good day, miladies."

All four foster-siblings curtsied (Euleilla rather awkwardly, as she was wearing pants) their farewell to the instructor, who bowed in return and left the room. His departure led to cheers – it was a happy occasion all around.

Euleilla had been the first of the girls tested, and passed her first rate certification quite easily. She didn't really need the certificate, now that she was married to Maelgyn, but since the others were being tested she figured she might as well join them. She only regretted Maelgyn was unavailable at the time the instructor said he would be doing the certifications – it would be amusing to see him try and come up with a practical High Mage test to use for the certification. And when Maelgyn passed that, it would be interesting to see just how the instructor filled out the certification form – there had never been a high mage, so no-one had ever designated what such a certificate should look like.

Still, it was nice to be able to show off to her sisters... and to cheer them on as they showed off their own burgeoning talents.

"Well," Euleilla said. "I'd say this calls for a celebration. Why don't I see if Maelgyn's meeting has ended, and we can return to the inn for your party?"

Miceli, Melen, and Kara started shifting around uncomfortably. Euleilla knew they were looking at one another, but not what facial expression they had on their faces – she had no idea if this silent communication boded ill or well.

"Actually... while we do plan to go to the party, we would like to talk with you about something else, first," Kara said.

Euleilla wasn't sure what would make them so nervous. They often talked about 'something,' and it often was very personal, as one might expect among sisters. Why would they be nervous about talking to her about... well, anything?

"Go on," she prompted.

Kara took a deep breath. "Well, we haven't just been boring ourselves silly by putting in hundreds of hours of time on studying magic – hours that many would say would be better spent managing the inn, or pursuing husbands, or even indulging in some other career or form of leisure – just because you claimed we had an undiscovered talent. We had a goal in mind when we started training... and now we think we're ready for it."

Euleilla was a bit surprised. Her foster-siblings were rarely this serious, and when they were it usually had to do with caring for one of their other foster-siblings or the operation of the Left Foot Inn. What would they need the use of magic for, when it came to those sorts of things?

"I'm happy you've managed to reach your goals," Euleilla said. "But why are you telling me all this?"

"Because you're a *part* of those goals," Kara said. "Euly... we want to enter service to the Province of Sopan. We would like to be your handmaidens – and protectors."

Euleilla took in a deep breath. The truth was when she married into the royal line, her foster siblings were to be left behind... at least as far as the rest of the world was concerned. It had, on occasion, passed through her mind that it would be politic if she did not publicly claim them as her family... but it had never come up, and she certainly wasn't about to reject them as family, either. She wanted to keep a connection with the family that raised her, politics or no politics.

And using a little quasi-nepotism to bring them into her service as handmaidens would be ideal... except she would, officially, be their 'princess.' She wanted them as sisters, not as servants. And the idea that they would be her guards, putting their lives on the line to keep her safe... that really disturbed her.

Especially considering how she had gotten the last person swearing to protect her killed.

"I already have a Dwarven Armsman. While I appreciate the offer, I don't think I need more protection than I already have," Euleilla said. "But as handmaidens... need we make it so formal? You are my sisters in all but blood – surely that is enough!"

Miceli snorted. "Tell me, Euly – who made your last dress?"

"I make my own clothes," Euleilla said. "You know that."

"No, you make your own armor. I asked who made your last dress – as in the formal-wear you wear in court?"

Euleilla hesitated. "They were provided by someone in Maelgyn's court. I don't know who – his court seamstress, I would imagine."

"And did this court seamstress know about the 'special needs' you require in all of your clothing?" Miceli asked.

Euleilla shook her head. "Of course not. I don't know that person – why would I tell them about that?"

"So... let me guess. While you might have been fully dressed, you felt naked on the floor of your husband's court, during a formal ceremony that likely was supposed to be one of his crowning achievements. Correct?"

"Yes," Euleilla admitted.

"Well... my skills may not be up to the standards of your court seamstress, but I have been training in tailoring clothes much of my life," Miceli pointed out. "Perhaps I couldn't design the gowns you need to wear in court, but as your handmaiden no-one would question it if I were to make a few minor adjustments to their fit... and perhaps those adjustments could include adding some small pieces of iron or nickel in subtle locations to help mark the edges of your skirts."

Euleilla pursed her lips. "That... would be nice, but—"

"Tell me, Euly," Melen said, not letting her finish. "Is everything in Sopan written using iron-gall ink? Or some other ink that's infused with iron?"

"Many official documents are," Euleilla said. "It's a fairly common ink."

"But what about books? Private correspondence? That sort of thing? Don't most of those use the newer, cheaper lamp black ink?"

"Not... not always."

"So, enough things that you could prove yourself literate... but you might sometimes have trouble reading some things for a reason no-one at court would understand. But would anyone question it if your eyes were 'tired,' and so you handed a letter you had just received to one of your handmaidens to read for you?"

"I—"

"You do know I can read in five different languages, now, right?" Melen asked. "And I also recently earned my license to practice as a scribe for official documents here in Largo – surely you or your husband could arrange for that license to transfer over to Sopan."

"You're a good one, too, from what I remember," Euleilla said. She could see the sense of what they were saying, and honestly wasn't sure if she wanted to keep arguing the point. "I'm certain that I could arrange something, yes."

"But now comes the big one," Kara said, taking her turn as the final of the three sisters. "Is your Dwarven Guard capable of learning that little trick of sensing magic, to know when you really are in danger of exhausting yourself and telling you to cut back?"

Euleilla sighed, shaking her head. "All right, all right! You've convinced me. I'll take you as my handmaidens, if you insist. But I don't understand – I'm more than happy with you three as my sisters, not as my servants. Why would you do this?"

"Because it means good jobs for the three of us," Kara said. "We wouldn't be commoners freeloading off of our foster-sister's good fortune; we would actually have jobs. Jobs that we could prove to any honest critic we are quite qualified for, regardless of our relationship with you."

Euleilla held her hands up in surrender. "Very well. I will talk with Maelgyn about the handmaiden jobs, but—"

She was interrupted by a frantic knock on the door. "Milady Euleilla, are you in there?"

Euleilla sighed. "As I was about to say, but if you wish to join my guards you will have to talk with my current armsman, Tur'Ka. That's him at the door."

Melen was quick on her feet and rushing to the door, but Miceli beat her to it. Tur'Ka didn't even notice the two girls, though as he ran to kneel at Euleilla's feet.

"Milady, you have been summoned to attend the War Council. It is urgent," he said.

"Urgent?" Euleilla repeated, standing from her seat and drawing herself to full attention. "Is it gra— uh, Ruznak?"

Ruznak's health was still very poor, but even so he was dutifully attending the War Council most days. Euleilla was afraid he was pushing himself too far – he was already exhausting himself past the point of lucidity some days, and his counsel seemed even more vital as he tired himself more. She was worried he was working himself to death.

"As far as I am aware, he has been excused from the War Council for the day, and should be home resting. No, milady, this has nothing to do with him."

That was a relief, but it didn't clear up anything at all. "Then what, pray tell, is so urgent? I made it clear I was taking neither side in the conflict between this town and my husband's war plans."

"And I believe everyone appreciates that, milady," Tur'Ka said. "This is something else related to recent news brought to us by El'Athras' spies."

"Intriguing," Euleilla mused. She turned to face her foster siblings. "Girls, it appears I am needed elsewhere."

"We understand," Kara said, then laughed. "You know, Euly, sometimes you really do sound like a princess. Makes me wonder where you learned such decorum, since you were raised a barmaid like the rest of us."

Euleilla snorted. "As if gramps would let any of us grow up to be mere barmaids. Now, as I was saying, it appears I'm needed elsewhere. I will accept you as handmaidens, but as I was saying, your other request must meet the approval of my head armsman. Tur'Ka? I'm off to meet with my husband, but my foster siblings want to discuss something with you...."

Every joint in Lazark's body was sore. His wrist hurt more than the rest of him – it was red and inflamed, and any touch sent lightning shooting up his arm. In all the pain he hadn't been able to sleep for weeks, now – well, not that he remembered. He probably drifted off once or twice, but even his dreams were of pain.

This was not how things were supposed to go. The Swords were supposed to slowly be eliminated, one by one, until only their mercenary from the Merfolk people was left. Then that last "Sword" could re-make Svieda the way the Porosians wanted. Their initial contingency plan would also result in taking Svieda without a single person being killed: Arrange things, using the intricacies of the Law of Swords, so that when the Merfolk impersonator was removed from office or killed, Svieda would be in such political disarray that they would revert to the old laws... laws which Lazark, as the court archivist, would have altered for the benefit of the Porosian plans.

Plan Arrowhead, though, was always intended as a last resort. Avoiding it was the main reason he had volunteered to go to Svieda at all. But now there was no question that they would begin Plan Arrowhead soon.

Lazark wondered just how desperate he was to prevent Plan Arrowhead from happening. He had left his family back home, journeyed thousands of miles, allowed the Elves to alter his face and voice with their particular form of magic, and learned in six weeks what a proper Sviedan Archivist would have spent years training themselves to know.

And now it was happening, anyway. And he was going to be the plan's opening gambit. And, worse, it looked like he would die in the effort of beginning it – his body was rejecting the *schlipf.*

He wasn't especially familiar with Elven lore, so he couldn't say for certain whether it was a common problem or not, but his body simply wasn't properly adjusting to having a *schlipf* embedded inside. The effect was horrible, weakening him and causing him to lose his sense of touch in his fingers and toes. He also was losing his senses of smell and taste, and even his eyesight was failing him.

He had no idea if these symptoms were typical of bonding with a *schlipf,* but he doubted it. The doctor in the village he was staying in had worried that he was suffering from an infection like gangrene, and wanted to amputate his arm, but Lazark was lucid enough to put a stop to that idea.

Some of those symptoms were starting to fade away, however. The fevers had gone down, and what had been sharp pains were now dull... except in his wrist. But that was not from his bonding being accepted by the *schlipf* – it was simply that his strength was returning. More or less.

He needed the *schlipf* removed to get rid of the pain. That was clear. But the only ones capable of removing the *schlipf* without doing Lazark any additional damage were the very Elves who implanted it on him. And they would only do so if he completed Plan Arrowhead's opening gambit successfully.

Lazark had wanted to prevent Plan Arrowhead with all his heart...

but he wasn't willing to die in slow agony to keep it from happening. Even though he suspected he wouldn't survive it all, anyway, he had no choice any more – there was only one way to get the pain to stop, now. If only he could sleep and think, maybe he could come up with a way out.

Pains or not, he would be heading back to the Royal Castle in a few days time. And then... well, then he would do what he must.

Chapter XIV

"Well, there's no real choice. I'm going with you," Euleilla said.

When he summoned his wife to their suite at the inn, Maelgyn hadn't expected any other answer from her. He'd needed to discuss the news about Brode, and El'Athras' plan to rescue him. The plan would work better the fewer people who were involved, so he figured he should at least ask if she wanted to remain behind, but he knew better than to argue about it.

As, arguably, the most powerful warrior in Svieda, there was no question that he would be part of the rescue mission. Wangdu would also be accompanying him (the only person in Svieda who might possibly be a greater warrior). And, quite frankly because he found it impossible to prevent them from coming, so were his two new Dwarven Armsmen.

As a practical matter, the team shouldn't be any larger than that – in fact, it should be smaller. It would be hard enough travelling unnoticed with just one Human mage, one Dwarven Axeman, and an Elf to contend with. His wife was now certain to join them, as was her own Dwarven Axeman, and unless he missed his guess the new trio of handmaidens she had just told him about. And so would Gyato and Onayari, at least part-way; they had to make a diplomatic trip to talk with Lady Phalra and the government of the Bandi Republic on behalf of their Nekoji people, so they figured they might as well tag along. And El'Athras would need to go at least part of the way to act as a guide, and Dr. Wodtke would undoubtedly join him. He would also be talking to Lady Phalra, representing the Dwarves of Mar'Tok. And if there were that many diplomats going, perhaps they should bring someone to represent Svieda's Human population – not Maelgyn, since he would be busy, but one of the other noblemen... who undoubtedly would have an entourage of their own. And one the party got this big they would need someone to act as a chef, people to manage their gear, etc., etc. The size of this 'clandestine' mission was getting frustratingly large.

And so Maelgyn had tried to ask Euleilla to stay behind. It wasn't that he didn't want her to join him, but if Euleilla didn't go, her trio of handmaidens wouldn't be coming. If they didn't come, they might be able to convince some of the others to stay behind, and the group might be small enough that they wouldn't need Wodtke or Kiszaten. That would make their chances of slipping into Poros undiscovered that much easier.

"Are you sure?" he asked. "It's not like when I was heading into the Borden Isles, or when we were going off to break the siege on the Royal Castle. I may be gone briefly, but if things go according to plan there will be little danger. Wangdu said he'll be doing any of the combat in this one – my role is basically to pick the lock of the door that Brode is being held behind with my magic. And I won't be gone that long – a week or two of travel in both directions, at most. You were held captive longer than that."

Euleilla put her hand on her hips. "And why do you think I might want to stay behind?"

"I thought you and your sisters would want to stay here with Ruznak. He needs care, and—"

"I've already said my final goodbyes to gramps... twice. I don't want to watch him fade away even more than he already has," Euleilla said stiffly.

Maelgyn could sense he was already in dangerous territory. He definitely did not want to annoy his wife with this. To be honest, despite his problem with the political side of the War Council, some of the best memories of his life had been made these past few weeks in Rocky Run... and Euleilla was a large part of the reason why.

They really were husband and wife, now. They had been in love, yes, and had the paperwork claiming they were married, yes, but now... now they were sharing a bed every night, and everything that went with it. Well, when they weren't too tired, anyway.

It was enough that, confronted with the idea of leaving Euleilla, he really didn't want to leave the city. This mission was too important to shove aside because of his own wants and desires, though, and he wanted it to go as smoothly as possible.

"I want to finish this mission as quickly as possible," he said. "I don't even want to go, myself, to be honest. I'd much rather spend the next couple of weeks in our bed. But it has to be done... and I'm worried that by taking you, the girls, the Dwarves, El'Athras, Gyato, Onayari, and so forth... well, I don't know how we can keep stealthy with that many people all together. If I could somehow convince everyone but Wangdu to stay behind, I feel as if we could be in and out quickly and quietly with minimal risk, and I'd be back in that bed we share in a week or less. If you all come with me, it'll be just like it was all those months we were on the road – we'd never be alone, we'd be in constant danger, things would take longer than were necessary, and—"

"—and I do understand why you're asking," Euleilla said. "But no matter what you do to try and convince me, you won't be able to stop El'Athras or Gyato from going with you as far as Bandi. You'll never convince those two Dwarven guards of ours to stay home. Or me – I could watch your back while you unlocked the door. Why are you not trying to convince, say, Gyato or Onayari to stay home?"

"Actually, I was going to, once I was done with you," Maelgyn said ruefully.

Euleilla sighed. "Well, you won't be able to make the diplomats stay behind, so I'm not staying home. I will talk to my sisters, though, and order them to stay here – I'll be able to come up with some excuse, and honestly I don't want to put them into harm's way, myself. Actually, I think they're the ones who need to stay at Gramps' bedside – not so much because they are ready for his passing, but because he's going to need their help. Maybe I'll ask Sir Leno to put them through their paces – they still have a lot to learn."

Maelgyn let out a long breath. Honestly, that was more of a

concession than he'd hoped. "Thank you. And you're right – I'm not going to be able to leave those others behind, so I might as well have you along." He paused. "I'm worried, though."

"Worried? What about?"

"It's just something that's sort of been hanging over me since I heard we weren't sending in a full army to rescue Brode," Maelgyn said. "Between you, me, and Wangdu, we'll have a fairly power-heavy team; we should be able to handle any normal guards we encounter. But... I have this feeling of dread hanging over me – something which makes me fear things are going to go wrong, and in a very bad way. If we could keep that element of stealth, that would make me feel a lot better, but without stealth, and without the backing of a full army..."

"I can see why you're so worried," Euleilla said. "But you have to work with what you've got. As you say, between the lot of us, we'll be able to handle most anyone we encounter. And we might be better off in the stealth department than you think – being part of a diplomatic mission should help keep our cover for at least part of the journey, and it might even work better when it comes time for you to scout out where the guards are."

"That's how we'll have to handle it," Maelgyn sighed. "But I still don't like this idea. We should either be going in with overwhelming strength or absolute stealth, and at this point it doesn't look like we'll have either. I don't see any option, though, so we'll deal with it as it comes."

"As we always do," Euleilla said.

Ruznak was dying and he knew it. Maybe he wouldn't be dying the next hour, the next day, or even in the next few weeks, but he didn't think he had much time left. He had been a fighter for ninety-eight years of life, but he didn't think he'd make it to ninety-nine. It was a good run, but even if he survived whatever illness he was dealing with now, he would be left weakened and vulnerable to the effects of old age.

True, he believed that he would be in a 'better place' when he died, and see the many loved ones who had gone on before him, but he wasn't entirely sure he was ready to go just yet. There were so many things he had yet to do before he died, even now. True, he had seen his most problematic foster child off (not that she ever acted up, exactly; just that finding a way to give her the life she deserved had always been a problem), but there was more work to be done.

To start off, he had at least six children (foster children, perhaps, but he thought of each and every one of them as his own) who still hadn't been weaned off the inn. Well, maybe just three – he knew of Kara, Miceli, and Melen's plan to enter service under Euleilla's husband, though he had yet to hear how that had turned out. He suspected it would wind up as a clash between three of his more headstrong daughters with his *most* headstrong child of either sex.

It didn't help that his illness required him to rest for so long each day. He had maybe an hour or two to get anything done, most of which time he spent trying desperately to mediate issues between the 'citizens' (read idiot guild leaders and puffed-up politicians) of Rocky Run and the new military government. It left him little time to think, and almost none with his children.

Even now, when the debates had been temporarily postponed, he found himself speaking not with one of his children, but with several of his son-in-law's advisors.

"Forgive my old ears," he said tiredly, not even lifting his head from the bed to look at them. "But I do not understand the question."

"It is simple enough," Wybert said. "The bulk of the decision-makers among the War Council are about to leave town with Maelgyn. I'm not sure I trust those remaining to negotiate a fair compromise with Rocky Run's mayor, and you're the closest thing we have to a neutral party. He's leaving in two days, so we need you to come up with something that satisfies everyone before then."

"You want a compromise... that satisfies *everyone?*" Ruznak said.

"Well, all of the people in Rocky Run, civilian and soldier alike," Wybert said.

Ruznak snorted, which induced a bit of a coughing fit. "There is no such a thing. Compromises never satisfy everyone, and they rarely satisfy anyone – the best they do is leave fewer people unhappy, and then usually because only one side surrendered on most of the sticking points just to get a few minor concessions that the other side never really cared about anyway. And then the winning side will point to those few concessions as if said compromise was a great hardship for them. Bah."

Wybert winced. "Yeah, I know what you mean. Perhaps

compromise isn't the best word, though – I mean, surely there is some way to satisfy the concerns of the village and still fortify it, like we need to?"

"Quite frankly, I would ignore the village's concerns, at this point," Ruznak said.

Wybert's eyes widened. "I... really?"

"There are few areas where the government really should have the right to ignore the consent of the governed," Ruznak said. "But in time of war, some concerns supersede it. Such as the construction of walls around the town – Tomas and his cohorts are being completely unreasonable. They are, quite frankly, complaining because you wish to improve the village. Perhaps not quite free of charge, for these people still must pay the taxes that pay for it, but they are getting their money's worth. Rarely does government action actually provide service equal to the amount of tax money taken from people, but this is one such case."

"So you're really saying to ignore the senior alderman and build the fortifications, anyway?" Wybert said. "I'm not sure your son-in-law will like that... nor am I sure I like the suggestion that I should ignore the concerns of my own people."

"Well, you asked for a compromise," Ruznak laughed, again slipping into a coughing fit. "As a ruler, you of course want to do whatever is best for your people. You've listened to the reasons they are against this, and done whatever was reasonable to address those issues – you've agreed to make arrangements for those who do not want to live in a big city or who do not want to be in a potential target of our enemies to have another place to live. You've created work for the people – skilled jobs for those whose existing skilled jobs are being eliminated by the upgrades, like the ferrymen, and positions and training for those who are likely to lose their jobs as unskilled labor. Buildings which are being demolished for the construction of the new fortifications, including both businesses and houses, are being rebuilt and replaced with newer, larger, more durable buildings. Quite frankly, at this point Tomas is only fussing because he'll lose a lot of political power if he concedes, and most of those with him are too much his lackeys to realize they'll be better off, too. It would cost ten times as much to use local villagers for the construction, it won't be half as well built if we insist on replacing wooden buildings with replacement wooden buildings, and so forth."

"Well, when you put it like that..."

"Of course, that'll make recruiting any new militia that much more difficult," Rykeifer warned.

"And without the co-operation of the local civilian government, we're going to have to handle our own needs for supplies, equipment repair, medical needs, etc.," Baroness Mikko warned.

"And the aldermen were already unhappy that we're hosting a patrol of Dragons. Nor do they like the Dwarves being nearby. How will we take care of these supposed allies of ours if things get even worse with the civilian populace?" Baron Mathrid warned.

Ruznak was wondering when the others would start making their presence felt. Tomas was only one of the hold-ups in reaching an agreement; the others were Wybert's and Maelgyn's advisers always pushing them to be more accommodating. These advisers may have made good arguments for mollifying Tomas' crowd, but frequently those arguments were contradictory. Nor did they always agree with reality.

"As I said, the real problem is not the civilian populace, it's the civilian politicians," Ruznak said. "I think you'll find that the bulk of our people are quite willing to defend their own homes, to take jobs that will support our military, and even to care for our Draconic and Dwarven defenders."

"But—"

"Out!" a voice snapped from the doorway. Ruznak winced – it was his son, Novak. The ward of a civilian innkeeper had just shouted at a general, three barons, two Dukes, and a Sword Prince. The fact that Ruznak wanted them all gone, himself, didn't help – it was never wise to anger such powerful people unnecessarily.

"Excuse me?" Baron Mathrid said, drawing himself up to full attention. "Who are you to tell us what to do?"

"I am the person who is currently responsible for seeing to it that my foster-father lives long enough to see his foster-daughter return from the mission she's leaving on in two days," Novak said. "I don't care who the hell you lot are. The unneeded pressure you're putting him under and the unwanted strain of dealing with your petty concerns are making my job that much harder. Now, leave!"

Wybert chuckled, glancing down at Ruznak with twinkling eyes.

"I suspect this isn't one of those times when the government should have the right to ignore the concerns of the governed, correct?" he said. "Very well then. Come, ladies and gentlemen – I fear we have already overstayed our welcome."

"But—" Baron Mathrid protested.

"No, Baron – we are a guest at this gentleman's house, and we're almost certainly asking more of him than we have any right to. It is perfectly acceptable for them to ask us to leave," Wybert said. He turned and sketched a polite bow to Ruznak. "And thank you, my friend – I believe I know exactly what you mean. I'll certainly take your advice to heart. Now, rest well – I will try to stay out of your hair for the rest of our stay, here."

The gathering all filed out the door, Novak glaring at each and every one of them. When the last of them was gone, Novak followed briefly. Ruznak heard the inn's front door close a moment later, and the heavy latch that locked the inn tight when it closed was quick to turn. Then Novak returned.

Stepping over to Ruznak's bed and fussing slightly with the sheets, Novak didn't quite meet his eyes. "Are you okay, father?"

"Better now that I know your head isn't going to be chopped off for annoying that particular group of people," Ruznak said wryly.

Novak rolled his eyes, heading over to the armoire in which the linens were stored. "No-one gets beheaded for kicking nuisances out of their inn, father. Not in Svieda."

"No?" Ruznak said, darkly amused. "Hm... maybe not under Wybert. I sometimes forget you were born after Sword Pennyweaver's reign. The jackass."

"It can't have been that bad," Novak said, pulling out some fresh sheets and a pillow. "There are laws which prevent the Swords and the nobles of Svieda from indulging in the excesses you see from the nobility in other countries. Those laws have been on the books for centuries."

"The laws as written, yes. But not the laws as they are now interpreted," Ruznak said. "You might want to read up on what the crime of 'Insolence to a Noble' was interpreted as meaning, prior to the magistrate's decision in the case of General Dier vs. Sword Pennyweaver, forty years ago. Before then, if Wybert – or even Mathrid – had taken enough offense at your remarks to draw their sword and strike you down, you'd be surprised at what the courts said your rights were."

"I'll take your word for it," Novak said, removing Ruznak's old pillow and replacing it with a fresh one. "That may have once been the case, but things are a lot better, now."

"Yes, they are," Ruznak said. "But angering a nobleman, or worse yet one of the Swords, can still get you in serious trouble."

Novak stripped Ruznak's bed and placed clean sheets over his foster father. "Perhaps. But if it keeps you around a little longer, I'm willing to suffer a few indignities."

"I can take care of myself – I'm not living that much longer no matter what happens," Ruznak snorted. "And I'm talking about more than mere indignities."

"Don't talk like that," Novak said. "We're all working hard to get you better, and then you'll be as strong as you were when you were our age."

That brought a congested laugh out of Ruznak. "I haven't felt that strong since I was in my twenties. Sorry, son – it's not going to happen. At best, I'll feel like I did in my fifties, like I felt when I was returning from the Borden Isles." He paused. "You're planning to take over the inn when I die, correct?"

"If Nordh and Simek don't, I will," Novak said. "One of us should, anyway. The others will keep working here, regardless. We have to keep your legacy going."

Ruznak grimaced. "And so which of you are joining the militia, and which the navy?"

"What?" Novak said. "What are you talking about?"

"If you truly wish to run the inn to keep my 'legacy' going, then – with so many children – I should have one pursue each of the careers I've had in my life. So, with three of you, one would join the navy – as I did in my youth – and one would join the militia, as I did after I retired, and one would run the inn."

Novak laughed. "Well, there is that. But it'll take all three of us to run the inn... and if I have anything to say about it, we'll have several years before we have to decide which of us will take on what part of your legacy."

Ruznak shook his head. Euleilla was the only one of his children who seemed to accept the reality that he was about to die. "I want you kids to do more than just run an inn, you know. You are all so much better than that."

"Why?" Novak said. "I'm a fair cook, Simek has a wonderful head for business, and Nordh... well, he may not like cleaning, but he does a pretty good job running the cleaning staff. Of course, now that the girls are entering Euly's service, we'll have to find a new cleaning staff...."

"Euly's hiring them, then?" Ruznak asked, amused. "Well, good for the girls! They, at least, are starting to find a place other than this rotting old inn to live their lives in. You boys should take their example."

"We like the inn," Novak said. "And it might be rotting now, but it'll soon be a nice stonework building."

"Oh? We're part of the fortifications, then?"

"Simek negotiated a deal with the Dwarves," Novak explained. "They'll be replacing the walls with stone in a way that allows us to stay in the building while they work, and they'll keep the noise down so you can rest. And they'll be adding upgrades, as well – a bathhouse with running water, better stables, and something they're calling 'baffles' that we can use to help keep the place warm in the winter and cool in the summer. Amazing workers, those Dwarves – if they can manage even half of what they're promising, we'll have the best inn in Largo by the time they're done."

If the Dwarves delivered all they were promising, perhaps his children shouldn't give up on the inn. Ruznak shook his head to clear it. He needed to think of something else.

"Will you be seeing Euly off, then?"

If Novak was surprised at the change in topic, he didn't say anything. He didn't look happy about something, though. "I think all of us will – even the girls. They were told that they needed more training before they could accompany Euleilla as her guards. They weren't exactly happy about it, either," Novak said, rubbing one of his ears wistfully. "Damn near popped one of my eardrums."

That, Ruznak knew, was Euleilla being protective of her sisters. She knew, as well as anyone, that he had personally trained each of his children how to fight, and fight well. He wouldn't spoil the excuse for her, though.

"It does take time to train a team like that to work together," he said, knowing that Novak would also have seen through the excuse for what it was.

Novak nodded. "I... I asked Euly if she would come see you one last time before she left. She refused – said she wanted to remember you as you were, not as she watched you die."

Ruznak snorted. "She always was the brightest of you lot. Look, Novak – don't be too upset with her. She said her goodbyes to me when she left to cross the Mar'Tok mountains. Then she said them again when we left from the Borden Isles. Then she gets here, and I'm ill and dying – and don't get started on me beating this illness, again, because we both know that there isn't really much hope of that!"

"There's plenty of hope. You're just being fatalistic," Novak insisted.

"There's not much difference between fatalism and realism when you're in my position, son," Ruznak laughed, again falling into a coughing fit. "I don't blame her for not wanting to see me. I wouldn't want to see me, either. I was happy to see her one last time, though – she seems so happy, considering she was in a Sho'Curlan prison not much more than a couple months ago. Healthy, too. Marriage agrees with her."

"True," Novak agreed, though he didn't seem to want to admit it.

"She'll be back in town. If I recover from this... whatever disease it is that's bothering me, well, it'll probably be before she returns. She'll see me then."

"And if you don't?" Novak asked.

"If I don't, she gets to remember me how I was, and not how I am," Ruznak said. "That's a fair trade, in my book. Don't begrudge her that."

"If you say so, father," Novak said, shaking his head. "If you say so."

Chapter XXV

Maelgyn stared at the hillside, not quite sure what to make of it. "So, you're saying that this is the secret to the success of your spy network?"

"Yes, yes it is. Magnificent, isn't it?" El'Athras said.

In the end, the group was about as large as Maelgyn feared. Euleilla managed to keep her sisters home, with instructions to train under Sir Leno's direction, but they were the only ones who either of them could prevent from coming on this trip.

El'Athras, Gyato, and – selected to represent Svieda's Human population – Duchess Kassi were going with him as far as Bandi. It was a purely diplomatic mission, but El'Athras insisted it could be used to explain their appearance in the foreign power before their detour to Poros and Sjouleber.

Each of them had at least one aide. Wodtke was coming for El'Athras, and Onayari for Gyato. Kassi, who had beaten out the other Dukes for the right to join him on the journey, brought several people with her – Sopan's Baron Yergwain (much to Maelgyn's disappointment – he'd been successfully avoiding the man since entering Rocky Run), Stanget's Baron Jank, and Baroness Mikko of Largo. The Duchess explained that she wanted to make it clear she was negotiating for all of Svieda, not just her own province of Leyland.

Then there were Maelgyn's bodyguards, Tur'Ka and Tur'Tei. No amount of arguing could get them to stay home – they claimed it was their duty to accompany him into any danger, and they wouldn't take no for an answer. Not even when Maelgyn threatened to jail them for insubordination – they just cited a little-known law in the Sopan Provincial Charter about the Sword's Guards having permission to countermand the Sword's own orders under certain circumstances... such as when he was trying to order them away from a danger they were duty bound to go into.

Of course, that wasn't all of them. There was Wangdu, of course – he was, perhaps, the one person in the group the mission would not succeed without. And, with so many people, they needed a cook – Maelgyn had selected Kiszaten, of course.

With so many people, Maelgyn felt like saying they might as well have brought the army. The little bit of diplomatic tact he'd inherited from his father helped him restrain that impulse, however.

And so it came to pass that El'Athras had guided over a dozen people to a point about a mile out of town, instead of Maelgyn leading a group of soldiers over the more conventional invasion route. Maelgyn was starting to wonder whether his Dwarven advisor was losing his mind, however, when he was so proudly pointing out a simple pile of rocks sitting on top of a hill.

"Uh..." he said, unable to quite find the right words.

Wodtke snorted. "Don't worry – none of the rest of us can see it, either. This is a secret entrance to the Dwarven cave system. It's 'magnificent' because it's so cleverly disguised."

"Actually, it isn't access to the full cave system, any more," El'Athras said. "But there used to be one that connected all of the great Dwarven cities. These tunnels run everywhere, from Sho'Curlas to Oregal. They're more like roads... but outside of my little group of spies, no-one would be using this one. In fact, any of these 'roads' leading into Mar'Tok have been deliberately closed off. We mostly use them for trade routes and intelligence gathering, though in a few of the more frequently used ones you'll find small, underground Dwarven communities, as well."

"This actually explains a lot," Maelgyn said. "I don't suppose one of these goes to the Borden Isles? And one goes to the Royal City of Svieda? And one goes to Sopan?"

El'Athras smirked. "Well, I suppose we might have occasionally used it to spy on your people... but we're part of Svieda, now. And we don't have exits in either Sopan or the Borden Isles – the former was never needed, and the later... well, it flooded a long time ago, and we haven't been able to repair it. Probably never will. This particular cave path, though, will take us as far as Bandi, and opens on the other end about five miles from the entrance to the 'road' that will take us closest to Sjouleber. We have no direct route to that small town, but there is a city about a day's ride away we can get to – I've already sent agents ahead to secure a safe house and some horses for you."

"And we don't just go overland... why?" Maelgyn asked. "At least as far as Bandi. I mean, if we're using the subterfuge of sending them a diplomatic mission, and they're one of our closest neighbors to the north, I don't see any real need for this kind of stealth."

"Ah... well, I think you'll find the answer to that inside," El'Athras said, pouring a flask of water into a cup-shaped rock that seemed to have a crack in the bottom.

Water slowly ran down the crack, and when it seemed to stop dropping he turned to a different rock, located in an indent a few feet below the first rock, and built a fire on it. Shortly thereafter, steam seemed to start blowing out of a third rock, and El'Athras gestured for them all to get back. The Dwarves and Wodtke seemed to know what was going on, and Wangdu seemed to figure it out, but the rest were all quite puzzled by El'Athras' behavior.

Or they were, until the last of the rocks in that pile – a roughly column-shaped stone the size of a man – started moving aside and revealed a lit passage and a set of stairs leading down.

"How... how did..."

"Steam power," El'Athras said. "And I'll thank you all not to mention this to anyone – there are certain Elves who are trying to prevent anyone from knowing about the existence of this sort of technology, and we'd rather word not get back to them."

Euleilla frowned. "Father – my birth father, that is – once mentioned that Delbruck had a similar mechanism that opened the door to his office."

"I'm not surprised," El'Athras snorted. "Delbruck had a lot of things he 'wasn't supposed to have.' I think the Elves worried about this technology know we have it, but they aren't overly concerned as long as it goes no further than it is. Now, enough gawking at the door – we need to hurry, because the door will close once the water used to make the steam has run out."

That ended further conversation as they all hurried down the staircase. Shortly after the last of them – Tur'Tei, bringing up the rear guard – was through, they heard grinding as the stone closed itself behind them.

"So... how would we get out?" Maelgyn asked. "Just in case we get separated, that is."

"We won't be getting separated down here," El'Athras laughed. "But if you did, there's another alcove up those steps that is well maintained with bricks of coal, some kindling, and several flagons of water. And a steam-lock that is far more obvious than the one outside. If, for some reason, you can't get a fire lit, there's a manual release for the door that will open it for five minutes. You don't want to use that, normally, because it seals things shut on both sides afterwords – we would then need to send a crew out to fix things, and that gets... tricky. Don't worry, though – they almost never fail, so we'll be fine. Come on – there's more."

It was a bit of a ways further down, then through an antechamber that had several stone benches, before they saw the next bit of Dwarven ingenuity. There, on two metal rails of some sort, lay a series of interconnected metal carts. There was something funny about the design of the cart in the front – it was much longer, and seemed to have a series of storage tanks and mechanical devices – but the others seemed to have been modified with jerry-rigged seats that looked much newer than the carts themselves.

"What... steam-powered carts, too?" Maelgyn asked.

"They'll run about as fast as the average horse gallops, but as long as you can keep feeding the engine coal and water they'll never need to stop or rest. Goes direct from here to Bandi and back," El'Athras replied.

"But this sort of technology... Mar'Tok was filled with all sorts of technological wonders, but this goes far beyond that! Why do you not have these things running throughout your cities?"

El'Athras flushed. "Well, it's a bit of a long story. There used to be some in Mar'Tok – and the other Dwarven cities, in ancient days – but... well, the Elves have sacked every Dwarven city at one point or another, and... um..."

"They do not understand the technology, they don't," Wangdu said, shaking his head.

"Well, we know enough to maintain things and keep them running," El'Athras said uncomfortably. "We can manufacture spare parts when needed. We probably could build them from scratch, but we... we don't think it would be a good idea to try."

"You've signed a deal with the Technologist faction, you have," Wangdu accused.

"We had no choice," El'Athras admitted gruffly. "If we didn't, they would have destroyed the surviving steam rails, and we'd lose touch with thousands of Dwarves around the world. Half of our supply lines would be gone. We... we can't fight the Elves again – not even as depleted as the Elves have become, and especially not the Technologists. It's bad enough we're going after this Porosian conspiracy while backed by the entire nation of Svieda – the Technologists are a much, much larger faction, from what we can tell."

"They are not as strong as you think, they aren't," Wangdu said. "But they're very good at appearing powerful, they are."

El'Athras shrugged. "Well, we're not willing to call their bluff, regardless. They've allowed us to keep these old rails running, at least. But only the ones that were running when we reclaimed them – there is no rail between Bandi and Poros; we'll have to walk that one. We'll be in Bandi by the end of the day, but it'll take us much longer to head into Poros, even though the trip is shorter."

Maelgyn was wondering about these rails. They gave him several ideas – this technology could be used for many things other than opening doors and propelling carts, surely, or else these Technologists wouldn't complain about it so – but now was not the time. "Then let's get going. I want to be done with this trip as quickly as possible."

Riding a cart from the border town he'd found himself in back to the Sviedan Royal City had done a number on Lazark. He would never bond with the *schlipf,* he knew – it was slowly killing him. His arm was fevered and sore, and every time the cart hit a bump it jostled the raw infection. He had vomited from the pain several times, and was feeling really weak by the time he arrived.

"Hello, sir," the guard at the gate said. "The Sword King has been distressed at your disappearance, and has anxiously been asking after you. Where have you been? You don't look very well, sir. Should I fetch the royal physician?"

"He can't help me at this point – it's just motion sickness," Lazark lied. He had picked the royal physician, himself – he knew just what the man was capable of, and treating an incompatible *schlipf* bond was not one of his talents. His only chance of getting that taken care of would be if he could complete his mission before the thing killed him. "I was called away as part of the investigation into the assassination attempt on Sword Maelgyn, and I have news for Sword King Brode. Could you let him know I'll meet him in his quarters tomorrow morning?"

"Of course, sir," the guard said. "I'm aware of just how bad those cart rides can be, especially in an old wreck like this one. Feel better."

"Thank you, soldier," Lazark said. He didn't think he was likely to feel better – he did feel guilty, however. While he was a supporter of Poros, he genuinely liked the people of Svieda. He mostly joined the cause because it seemed the only way to ever reunite the four countries of Poros – a reason many of the Human members of the movement had for joining. But he didn't see why reuniting Poros required destroying other Human-run countries. However, he'd sworn to bring down Svieda's government... and now, even if he was willing to break his vow, he had no choice.

Lazark didn't even remember walking to his suite, but he pulled himself out of his thoughts to see he was surrounded by the accouterments of his fake life as the Royal Archivist. Lots of scrolls and books – only a few of which he'd actually read or had any desire to read – lined one table. He had a warm fur rug under his feet, and had frequently kicked off his shoes to luxuriate in the feeling of walking on it. Instruments for writing, various wax seals, and other tools of his supposed trade covered the other table. Thinking about it, he really was far too disorganized to be an archivist of the level one typically associated with such an important position as he held.

And then there was the bed. A luxurious bed by his standards, though he understood that the down and cotton pallet he had was commonly used for bedding in this castle.

All of it would be going away in the morning. Even assuming he survived the current plan, he would have to leave the castle in a hurry and find the Elves again. That was the only way to get his *schlipf* taken care of, and he wouldn't be welcome here, anyway.

Well, he had one more night here, at least... and he was in desperate need of rest. Time to make use of that wonderful bed for the last time.

The trip across the rails had been fascinating at first, but after almost twelve hours where all of the sights were the same (cave walls, lit by 'eternal' gas lanterns on either side) it got a little monotonous. Simple rations were distributed every six hours, so they weren't hungry, but had they traveled by horse they might have had far better fare. Maelgyn was pretty sure he wasn't the only person happy to get out of the metal carts.

"Well, I understand why they haven't exactly caught on," he said as he started stretching his legs. "Not exactly the most comfortable form of transportation, is it?"

"It was not designed for people, it wasn't," Wangdu said. "When these were first built, they were, they were supposed to transport cargo, they were. A different sort of rail system was built for people, it was, but all of those are now gone, they are."

"We no longer have need to transport cargo between Bandi and what is now the province of Largo," El'Athras said. "So about thirty years ago, we changed most of these carts to be people transporters. There are still a few unmodified cargo carts, but they aren't on the tracks at the moment."

"Fascinating as this is," Duchess Kassi said. "I would like to get back to the surface soon. I must admit, I've been getting increasingly claustrophobic the longer I've been down here."

El'Athras nodded. "Right. Follow me!"

Once more they passed through an antechamber. There appeared to be more than one exit to this room – one (which they had just come from) was marked "Largo-Mar'Tok Border" and another was marked "Squire's Knot," though Maelgyn had trouble reading the faded Dwarvish characters on a third passage, which was left dark. Maelgyn knew that Mar'Tok's border used to be the river that Rocky

Run was founded upon, but that had changed nearly three hundred years ago. Evidently, the signage was fairly old, itself.

They went out the forth passage, marked "Exit," and for the first time Maelgyn saw the "steam lock" from the inside.

They all had to wait for El'Athras to start a fire and boil some water before their exit appeared. He struggled a bit, as the kindling had apparently gotten damp some time in the past and was now molding over; the extra water in the wood from the mold set them back quite a bit.

"Not exactly the fastest way to open a door," Kassi noted once the water started boiling.

"No, but unless you know exactly how to open it, it's impossible to gain entry to these tunnels," El'Athras said. "It took us one day – twelve hours – to cross nearly four hundred miles. Between stops for cooking, sleeping, caring for the horses, and the like, it would have taken at least three, maybe four days to travel the same distance by horse, and we were able to make the journey completely unseen. A few minutes extra to get the doors opened and closed are worth it."

Euleilla rubbed her rear end tenderly. "Perhaps, but I suggest improving the seating at some point. Those hard benches are torturous."

Maelgyn, briefly distracted by his wife's posterior, cleared his throat. "Well, we're here now, and we'll have ample time to stretch our legs during the next stretch of our journey. I think the door's opening, so let's get going."

The steps leading out this door were not as well maintained as the ones they had come from, suggesting that this was a less frequent destination (or at least less frequently maintained) than the Largo exit.

Maelgyn was momentarily blinded by the sunlight upon exiting the tunnel system. It was approaching dusk, but the sun was still in the air and the contrast in light proved rather significant. By the time his eyes adjusted, the rest of his people were also out of the cave.

Once the door closed itself and sealed the exit (now that he knew what to look for, Maelgyn could see and identify the outdoor components of the steam lock), it was Kiszaten – his cook, of all people – who instigated their next delay.

"We've been traveling all day," the cook explained. "And none of us has had a hot meal. Night it about to fall, so none of us are going much further, anyway – why don't we just camp here and I'll figure out a dinner – and maybe get a breakfast started for in the morning? That'll keep us all going for a while."

El'Athras frowned. "I'd like to move further away from the steam lock, first, but... well, no-one knows this thing is here other than my Dwarves, so I suppose it'll be okay."

They were in a wooded area, though Maelgyn was told they were in the ruins of an old city formerly belonging to the Plains Dwarves. The only hint he saw of Dwarven architecture were some heavily moss-covered stones which might have once been walls, but the city *had* been abandoned over a thousand years ago.

They hadn't brought that many provisions with them – enough for the day, and for those going into Poros, to be sure, but the plan had been for the 'diplomatic mission' (which Kiszaten was to accompany) to buy supplies for itself in the Bandi capital, while Maelgyn's team would rely on rations until they got to Poros and could buy additional supplies locally. This meal was unplanned, and resulted in some scrambling and foraging for ingredients.

Maelgyn reluctantly surrendered some of the grains that were originally to be his party's travel supplies. They were surplus supplies, but giving them up meant he would have no contingency if things went wrong on the next leg of his journey. Kiszaten was rather insistent, however, and Maelgyn gave in rather than futilely arguing with him.

Euleilla hunted a few rabbits as game. There were some deer, as well, but even with magic it was hard to take one of those down without a bow and arrow – they ran too quickly to be easily caught.

Wangdu went after root vegetables, wild fruits, and nuts. Being an Elf, he had a better idea than most what was safe to eat and what might be poisonous. He only spent about twenty minutes at it before returning with a sack full of them, but it was surprisingly more than enough to replace the supplies Maelgyn had contributed to the meal.

And Kiszaten, from his personal baggage, pulled out a variety of spices. Some of them Maelgyn had never heard of, before, and many that he could identify were only found in foreign countries. All of them were extremely expensive, and quite a treasure for anyone, much less someone with as little pay as a navy cook. Maelgyn wondered where they had come from, but decided not to bother asking questions. He'd be happy with whatever Kiszaten managed.

Maelgyn was expecting the rabbits to be spit-roasted over the campfire, but Kiszaten surprised him with a completely different method of cooking them. Just how the cook had managed to bring a large, cast-iron pot with a lid in his small allotment of baggage, Maelgyn would never know, but that was what Kiszaten used to cook the rabbits in. First, after the rabbits were dressed and cut into pieces, he browned the meat over a fire. Then some wild onions, carrots, cooking oil, spices, small beer, and a generous amount of water all went in with it, and the pot was set on a bed of hot coals El'Athras had been working up for them.

The smells of the roasting rabbit were wonderful, but each time Maelgyn reached for the food he found his hand stinging when a wooden spoon wielded by his cook slapped him away. "Not until the meat falls off the bone!" he'd been told.

It took longer to prepare than most campfire meals Maelgyn knew about – possibly because of the amount of rabbit that needed to be cooked, or possibly because of all the water in the pot. Eventually Kiszaten determined that it was done. Maelgyn almost found himself drooling as he waited for the food to be served. Bowls were distributed, and then the braised rabbit was dished out for everyone.

Maelgyn was just about to take his first bite when a call came out from behind him.

"Well, well. We'd been told that there was an increasing amount of Dwarven activity in this area – I didn't know Elves, Nekoji, and foreign Humans were also part of it all."

Maelgyn cursed under his breath. Of course they would be found right when he was about to eat. And how did whoever it was sneak up on them, anyway? Sekhar hadn't mentioned anything, and Euleilla hadn't provided any warning either. They both should have said something before whoever it was got close enough to call them out.

Several people, armed with bows and arrows, slipped out from behind the nearby trees and rocks. None of the weapons any of them had were a real threat to Maelgyn, but they all wore the colors of Bandi's forest rangers. They weren't here to start a war – far from it – so they would have to acquiesce.

"And this is why you don't bring a gourmet chef on a clandestine mission," El'Athras muttered. "We'd be on the move already if we'd just ate our travel rations, like we were supposed to."

"That gourmet chef isn't supposed to be involved in the 'clandestine' part of this mission at all," Maelgyn said, making sure that only El'Athras could hear him. He turned his attention to the approaching ranger and bowed. "Sir! Welcome. We're just having our evening meal."

"Using Bandi's rabbits," one of the foresters said, grinning slightly as he stepped closer in. Their hands were still on their weapons, but no-one had drawn their bows to shoot. "But poaching is a minor offense, here in Bandi – not like in some countries, where it's punishable by death. Now, what are you all doing here? Armed foreigners crossing Bandi's border illegally is a much, much greater issue."

"We're a diplomatic mission," Maelgyn replied, gesturing to those members who were intended to represent Svieda to Bandi. "I have representatives from almost half of Svieda's provinces with me, all just hoping for an audience with your government."

"Of course," the forester laughed. "Although I still wonder how you got here. Your embassy certainly wasn't by invitation of the Bandi government, and you didn't come here by crossing the Bandi border legally."

"And how do you know that?" El'Athras asked.

"Because there is a state of emergency across the land, and the Bandi border has been closed for several months, now. No-one may cross it going either direction."

Maelgyn frowned. "We were unaware; no word of your state of emergency has hit our lands. Because our travels have become somewhat risky with the war, we chose not to use the more conventional routes. I assure you that our intentions truly are diplomatic, and we are simply requesting an audience with your government."

The forester nodded. "I can believe that. With wars going on all over the place, now, I can certainly see how you may not have heard of our problems. So, then, where are you from?"

"Svieda. I am Sword Prince Maelgyn, Duke of Sopan, and this is my wife, Euleilla. We are accompanied by El'Athras of our new Dwarven province of Mar'Tok and his aide, Wodtke, Gyato of our new Nekoji province of Caseificio and his aide Onayari, and Duchess Kassi of Leyland, who is being escorted by Barons representing three of our remaining provinces. Oh, and our cook, whose deliciously prepared meal we would really appreciate being allowed to eat."

The forester shrugged. "No skin off my nose. This meal is technically the result of poaching, but the rabbits are already dead and I'm not the one who will judge the penalty for that. Eat. But why would Svieda be sending us a second diplomatic mission when the first hasn't left yet?"

Maelgyn glanced over at El'Athras, alarmed. He'd heard nothing about this, and it looked as if it were news to the Dwarf as well. "Forgive me, but we haven't heard of any prior diplomatic missions to Bandi. We are aware, however, of attempts to impersonate important people from Svieda using Merfolk shapeshifters. That is part of what our mission is here to discuss. Who is it that claims to represent my country?"

"Well, the Lady Phalra has confirmed the woman is who she says she is, and she is never wrong about such things," the forester said. "Please, finish your meal quickly. We will bring you to the Lady Phalra, and if she determines that you are who you claim to be, as well, perhaps you will learn who your other ambassador is."

Chapter XXVI

For a jail cell, Maelgyn decided, it was pretty decent. Clean, well-lit, with a separate privy, comfortable bedding (not enough of it for everyone present, which was further proof that Maelgyn was right about there being too many people on this mission, in his opinion, but they'd been told they were only being kept in the cell temporarily and bedding would be taken care of later), and fresh air through a grated window. It was still a jail cell, however.

Not one that could hold them without their co-operation, though. The bars were Human-controlled, Elf-made magical "trees" that – considering they had two *schlipf* and an Elf in their company, in addition to four or five high-level mages (though these sorts of bars really were, probably, the best way to contain a mage) – they probably could have broken through. With their own Elf present it would be quite easy to just command them to vanish, or their *schlipf* could convince them to open as well (these door-vines weren't exactly intelligent). Their captors knew it, too, but didn't seem all that concerned – they hadn't even bothered relieving Maelgyn and his company of their armor or weapons. Except for Maelgyn's Sword – while it was a crime in Svieda for anyone other than royalty to handle these weapons, they were not in Svieda, and he'd been required to surrender it (temporarily) to prove his identity, and as ransom against their escape.

Escape would be an act of war, anyway, and it wasn't a wise idea to start a war with a potential ally like Bandi. Of course, now they had to wait on the whims of a crazy Elf lady. Which was delaying their mission to rescue Brode. Maelgyn really hoped that this wouldn't take too long – the Porosians might move Brode if he wasn't rescued soon, and that could delay things for months.

Maelgyn turned to the others. "I don't suppose any of you have ever actually met the Lady Phalra, have you?"

"I've met her a time or two," El'Athras said. "State functions only, however, and we never really talked much. Most of the time, when I was dealing with their government, I had to talk with one or more members of their senate. She is a bit reclusive outside of this city, from what I can tell."

Gyato said something much along the same lines, but none of the others had much to say... until Wangdu stepped forward nervously.

"I'm familiar with her, I am," he said reluctantly. "I've known her for centuries, I have."

Maelgyn was greatly relieved. It was never a good thing to go into a negotiation without knowing who he was dealing with. "All right – tell me about her."

Wangdu took in a deep breath. "Lady Phalra is a complex person, she is. She has a brilliant mind, she has, but she rarely thinks like a normal person, she doesn't. She has been the Praetor of Bandi for its entire existence, she has, and—"

"Praetor?" Maelgyn repeated, unfamiliar with the title.

"Think cross between senator, military governor, and magistrate," Kassi said. "You'll find several of them in Oregal, where they command the regional armies and lead some lower courts. I've met a few during my time as ambassador there, but I was unaware there were any outside of that country."

"In Bandi, there is only one praetor, and that's Phalra," El'Athras interjected. "In her case, the title means she's something close to the general in charge of all the armies, head magistrate of the courts, and the only permanent consul, or senior senator, in the Bandi Senate. It doesn't quite equate her with a queen or a dictator, and she remains constrained by the dictates of Bandi's legislature, but she is the closest thing Bandi has."

"She's well known as the Bandi head-of-state, but I've never heard the term 'praetor' before," Maelgyn said.

"She translated the term from the Elvish, she did," Wangdu said. "When the Ancient Elves became the Modern Elves, they did, there were several Elven nations in confederation under one king, there were. The leaders of these nations were given an Elven title, they were, but Human historians now call them 'Praetors,' they do, as that is the term Oregal has chosen for similar positions, it is. Phalra founded Bandi, she did, to establish a Human preserve. As it was originally a part of this confederation, it was, she was given the title of Praetor, she was. And she has kept that title, she has."

"A... Human preserve?" Euleilla repeated.

"Poros and the Elven Confederation were at war, they were," Wangdu said. "The last war the Elves had fought led to the genocide of an entire race, it did. Phalra wanted to preserve humanity, she did, but it proved unnecessary, it did. The confederation fell apart, it did, and Poros became the first country to ever win a war against the Elves."

"The first, but not the last," El'Athras said. "Elves and Dwarves exchanged many victories across the centuries."

"So... the 'Mad' Lady Phalra likes Humans?" Maelgyn asked.

Wangdu nodded. "That may be an understatement, it might. It is partly why she got that appellation, it is. She has been experimenting, she has, to... to..."

"To?"

"She takes Humans as lovers," El'Athras snorted. "If she's been experimenting, I'm not sure I want to know what she's been doing."

"It's not like that, it isn't!" Wangdu insisted. "Well. That may be, it might, but that is not what I was referring to, it isn't. She is trying to make humans live longer, she is. She wants to find a way to make her Human lovers live as long as she can, she does."

"But she's an Elf. She's immortal."

"Which is exactly why she is thought to be crazy, it is," Wangdu said. "But while I do not think *that* is a sign of insanity, I don't, I believe her to be insane, I do."

Kassi spoke up. "I suspect many people here are more familiar with your Elven ways than I am," she said. "So perhaps they don't need you to spell it out for them, but why do you think her insane?"

"All Elves are insane, they are," Wangdu said, reiterating a point he had made many a time before. "But that is not what I am referring to, it isn't. I am not sure I could explain things well, I'm not, but I think you'll know why I made that claim soon after meeting her, you will."

"Just how well do you know this woman?" Kassi asked.

Wangdu flushed. "She is kin, she is."

"That doesn't tell me anything. All Elves claim to be 'kin,' from what I've seen. How, specifically, do you know her?" she demanded.

Wangdu shook his head. "You do not understand, you don't. She is kin, she is – she is my—"

"Brother! How delightful to see you again," a woman's voice called from outside of their cell.

"—sister, she is," Wangdu admitted, rolling his eyes. He turned to the door of the cage. "Phalra! It is wonderful to see you again, it is."

The Elf woman at the door took a moment to take in. Long, jet-black hair framed the front of her face, with wide, perpetually-surprised looking eyes (though she was narrowing them as she glared at Wangdu) looking out. She was adorned with Dwarven-style light armor made out of Golden Dragonhide and bronze metal accents, bound up using a burgundy belt or sash. And there was a live flower growing over her left ear, of all things.

"Still clinging to those archaic language forms?" Phalra said. "What a shame. I thought you might have dropped that when you started challenging the Elven orthodoxy."

"I do not agree with Elven philosophies, I don't," Wangdu said. "Nor with Elven insanities, I don't. But I do appreciate the search for knowledge, I do, and one of the few things I respect of our ancient brethren is their respect for knowledge, it is. I maintain the forms of their language in order to honor that study, I do. It is also why I can never make peace with the Technologists, it is."

"Well, I'm not Technologist, that's for sure," Phalra laughed. Maelgyn had to admit – the laugh did make her sound like a madwoman. "Now... about your companions. I understand one of them is alleging that certain members of Svieda's government are Merfolk impostors, and he fears the person currently sitting with *my* government is also one such impostor, yes?"

"We are suspicious, yes," Maelgyn said. "There is no record of our having sent you an ambassador recently, but it is possible that record was simply lost. When the Sword King was killed and the Law of Swords went into effect, I suppose one of the other Swords may have sent you an embassy. With the situation as it is, we had certain formalities that needed to be addressed to your government, so we formed a delegation to take care of them."

Phalra, who Maelgyn could only just see through the bars, glanced him up and down. She had a disturbingly flirtatious smile on her face as she surveyed him... until she saw Sekhar on his wrist.

"Foolishness. Why do you Humans cut so many years off your life to take on those trinkets my ancestors created?" she said, shaking her head. "Worthless trinkets!"

Worthless! Sekhar said, almost shouting in Maelgyn's mind in protest. *Just say the word and I'll show her just how 'worthless' I can be!*

Settle down, Maelgyn thought to him. *She's not entirely sane, according to Wangdu. We don't want to provoke her.*

Aloud, he said, "Actually, milady, this *schlipf* is a volunteer. I would rather not explain just how I acquired him, right now, but in these circumstances he will be extending my lifespan."

Not that it'll do you much good. Not as frequently as you've been banging your body about since you got me, Sekhar said.

You haven't spoken more than half a dozen words to me in months, and now you're being talkative? I need to convince this woman to release us, and you aren't exactly helping.

Well, the medicine and the healing left me a bit dormant, I have to admit. Plus it's a seasonal thing – I am a plant, you know. We like some seasons better than others. Speaking of which, what season is it, exactly? I've kind of lost track, and—

Hush!

Phalra's eyes gleamed when he mentioned extending his lifespan. "Is that so?" she... well, Maelgyn wouldn't even say he'd ever heard a Nekoji put as much of a purr in their voice. "The concept of the *schlipf* revolted me, so I never studied much about them. I didn't know they had that power. Interesting. Very interesting. I'm going to want to speak with you, afterwords, boy."

"Afterwords?" Maelgyn repeated. Somehow, that sounded...

ominous.

"You're alleging that Merfolk are impersonating members of your government, yes?" she replied.

"We really only know of one, so far," Maelgyn temporized, not liking where this was headed.

"One is one too many for comfort," Phalra said. "I'll hold onto your Sword until we prove it, either way. There are all kinds of tests I could make to determine if any of you are Merfolk. The easiest, though, is just to lock the lot of you up for a while without any water – eventually you'll have to reveal yourself. I know it won't be comfortable, but it'll be far less painful than anything else I can think of. And I believe that such discomfort would be adequate punishment for the poaching charge, as well."

Wangdu frowned. "If you are doing this to us for that troll-nut trick I played on you, I did, when we were still children—"

"Hm? Did you say something, brother?" Phalra said. "Oh, wait, I'm not sure you're really my brother, yet, am I? You might just be a clever and extremely well-researched Merfolk pretending to be him. I have to be careful about this, don't I?" She laughed, and again Maelgyn was struck by how insane she sounded.

Well, if she thinks I'm a 'worthless trinket,' she really is around the bend, Sekhar said.

Maelgyn sighed. *Months of little or no talking at all, and now I can't get you to shut up.*

Hey! I've been using all my strength trying to keep you alive, lately. You're such a handful I don't always have time to talk with you, any more.

"By the way," Phalra said. "Your suggestion of impersonators does trouble me, so I've decided to subject another 'suspicious' person to the same test."

A pair of guards dressed in Bandi livery came in, escorting a struggling person in fine clothes through into the jail. The cell door was opened, and the person was tossed in.

"Wait—" Maelgyn started to say, but the door was closed and locked, and Phalra and the guards both left his line of sight before he could finish his sentence.

Sighing, he turned his attention to their new guest. Her finery and disheveled hair made recognizing her difficult, at first, but once he took a good look at her face there was no denying who it was.

The woman stood up, dusted herself off, and straightened her hair. She then looked around before focusing on Maelgyn. "Oh, great. I should have known. What kind of a mess have you gotten me into *this* time, cousin Maelgyn?"

"Sword Indra?!" Maelgyn exclaimed.

Lazark knew this was a crazy idea. He was no assassin! And really, he was in far too much pain to think... or to plan either this move or his next. He tried, though – he really tried.

He'd started by trying to list his assets. He got as far as having some magical talent, third rate level, when he realized he didn't even have that, any more. With as much pain as the *schlipf* was leaving him in, he couldn't summon one iota of the magical strength he had spent so much of his youth learning how to wield.

Giving up on that idea, he'd tried figuring out what weapons he might have available to him... and only came up with the *schlipf.* Which he wasn't sure how to use. What was the point of all this, anyway?

He no longer had time to plan, and the best he'd been able to come up with was to get 'Brode' out of his bathtub. Merfolk were far, far too powerful of a creature to fight when in their natural element, and he knew his attack wouldn't last long once it began.

He hadn't been sure he'd be able to sleep that night, but he eventually just passed out. It was a troubled rest, to be sure, and he woke up feeling more tired and distressed than when he went to bed. Now he had to meet his 'partner' in usurping the Sviedan government and kill him. And any other ranking members of the government he could, including both Swords currently in the castle. Once the impersonator, all the Swords, and the leaders of the makeshift council were killed, he would then be allowed to leave and get his arm fixed.

It was a suicide mission, and one for a cause he didn't even believe in, any more. Well, he still supported the reunification of Poros, but not the people running this plan. He would have preferred to simply kill himself and be done with it, at this point, but the only weapon at his disposal (the *schlipf*) wouldn't allow itself to be used in that way.

As Lazark dressed for the day – his last day in Svieda, no matter how things turned out – he looked himself over in the mirror to groom his hair. When that task was taken care of, there would be no outward signs of his distress beyond the bags under his eyes. They formed dark shadows, making them almost look bruised, but that was it. His skin tone was fine; it wasn't pale, or flushed, or sweat-drenched, or any number of other ways it could show signs of stress. He'd somehow managed to dress himself immaculately. He wore gloves, preventing any sign of his infected wrist from showing.

He looked ready for a meeting with the Sword King... except he was sure anyone who saw him would know he was desperate for more sleep. Even with another day of 'rest,' however, he'd look no better, and he'd probably feel worse. No, best to just get things out of the way, and then maybe he'd have a chance to get the damnable *schlipf* out of him and move on.

That was a common refrain in his thoughts – get the 'damnable *schlipf*' out.

There was a knock on his door. "Master Lazark, his Majesty has agreed to your meeting this morning. He commands your presence as soon as possible. He will be waiting in his suite, as usual."

That was the guard he'd spoken to at the gate when he arrived a day ago. It felt like it had been a long time, yet not long enough. Lazark had no more time to delay, however; he had to begin his mission now.

"Thank you," he called out the door. "I'm just freshening up. I'll attend him momentarily."

"Very good, sir," the guard at the door said, before footsteps indicated he had left.

Lazark took a deep breath. "Well... this is it," he said to himself, turning away from the mirror. His hair was as good as it was going to get, not that it mattered any more.

He knew he was in bad shape with every step he took. His eyesight was being affected by extreme exhaustion; when he turned his head quickly there were afterimages where there shouldn't be.

When had it all gone wrong? Why was he even doing this? It was like he was operating on automatic, and no longer had control of his actions.

He made it to 'Brode's' suite without too much trouble, and wasn't surprised to find the Merfolk impersonator resting in his bathtub. There was a lone guard in the room who they would undoubtedly find some excuse to get rid of. Once they were alone, it would be the perfect time to strike... if 'Brode' was the only target, that was. But he wasn't.

"Lazark!" 'Brode' greeted him. "I've been worried about you. You disappeared without word, and you've been gone for weeks."

"I went to visit a contact," Lazark said. "I've got some vital information about the assassination attempt on Sword Maelgyn – perhaps we should contact the, uh, other Swords again and see if we can't pool our resources."

"Of course," 'Brode' said. "Guard, summon Swords Arnach and Nattiel. Request them to attend me presently."

"Of course, sire," the guard said, bowing before he went to attend to his task.

"So, what's the news?" 'Brode' asked when they were alone.

Lazark shook his head. Now would be a great time to attack, if he could just get 'Brode' out of the bathtub, but the other Swords were even more important targets in this assignment. Better to wait.

"I spoke with our Porosian superiors," he said. "I've received new orders... but I need the Swords here before I can explain anything. It's important."

"Really?" 'Brode' said incredulously. "There's nothing you can tell me in advance?"

"I'm very tired, still, and there is a lot to say. I really only want to explain things once," Lazark said, rubbing his eyes. "But the plans we've been operating under – the ones which put you on the throne? Those have been abandoned. Apparently, things with Sho'Curlas have changed."

"They're worried that Sho'Curlas might take advantage of our efforts and destroy Svieda?"

Lazark gave him a pained expression. That would make sense, if they weren't initiating Plan Arrowhead, but the truth was he had no idea what it was about Sho'Curlas that had them changing plans. "Could be, but I don't know. They haven't told me anything."

"Well, then—"

Any further discussion was curtailed when there was a knock on the door and the guard returned. "Swords Arnach and Nattiel are here, your Majesty."

"Send them in," 'Brode' said. "And then step outside. We will be discussing confidential matters."

The guard nodded reluctantly. That was hardly standard procedure for most of the Swords, but Lazark knew that 'Brode' had done it more than once. It was partly why the native Sviedans were starting to dislike the so-called 'Sword King.' That was something that, under the original plan, they would have needed to address, thanks to all the delays in eliminating the other Swords. Not that it mattered, any more.

The first complication, however, was that the guard's departure did not leave them all alone. Arnach's new armsman – Vihanto, Lazark thought the name was – remained with his Sword. There were no excuses that could get that guardsman to leave, as he had already been let into all of their confidences.

It was about as good as he was going to get... except 'Brode' was still in the tub. He had to find a way to get him out of the tub.

"I returned just last night from a meeting with my contacts regarding the Technologist faction, and their possible involvement in the assassination of Sword Maelgyn. The news is... disturbing, to say the least," he said, trying to stall for time. If he kept talking long enough, 'Brode' would eventually leave the tub so he could start pacing – a Human affectation he had developed in order to improve the believability of his performance.

"So they really were the ones who attacked Maelgyn?" Arnach asked.

Lazark shook his head. "That's just it – they weren't. But there is every reason to believe that they are keeping an eye on Maelgyn and his wife, anyway. My... contacts have let me know our plans have changed, and so it might have been best had we not chased Maelgyn away. Protecting him from the Technologists would have become a priority, if he were here – there is no love lost between those two Elven factions."

"We could always recall him," Nattiel said anxiously. "In fact, I will formally be making an appeal to end his banishment and bring him home – you can just listen to my appeal and 'agree' that you acted hastily. You could even claim this very attack we're investigating has prompted you to look at the evidence again and decide that things are not what you believed."

Lazark actually considered that. If Maelgyn were brought home, that would make his 'strike' that much more effective. But it would mean a longer delay, and he would not be able to survive that wait... and truth be told, he didn't think he could handle Maelgyn, *schlipf* or no *schlipf.*

"No, I don't think we can agree on that one. It would make 'Brode' look indecisive and easily misled – just the sort of thing our new plan cannot possibly permit. We need him to be liked by the Sviedan people... at least until the war with Sho'Curlas ends."

That was it – that suggestion drew 'Brode' from the bath. He stood up, reaching for a towel. Lazark had to be patient, though, until he was fully out of the water and too far away to dive back into it – if he struck too soon, all of this would be for nothing. He so wanted it all to be over, though.

"This is news even to me," 'Brode' said, wrapping the towel around his waist to preserve his 'Human' modesty. "It may sound odd, but I'm not really trained to be a likable leader."

"We can handle that for you," Arnach said enthusiastically. "You might need to change your philosophy on some minor things, but I think those are simply things you haven't grasped because of the different biases Humans of Svieda have versus what Merfolk expect. It—"

"Look out!" Vihanto cried, shoving his Sword to the ground.

Lazark glanced down, and was shocked to see his arm had raised itself and the *schlipf* was taking action without his knowledge. He hadn't been ready for the attack – yes, 'Brode' was out of the water, but he wanted him further away from the tub first. Had the *schlipf* really taken over, or was his tired mind so focused on getting through this that he was starting to act before he was ready?

His first target was not Arnach, however, who Vihanto had done a fine job of knocking out of the line of fire. Nor was it the other Sword Prince, Nattiel. No, it was his own ally, the Merfolk everyone knew as Brode.

It made tactical sense, though Lazark wasn't sure he would have picked him as his first target consciously. If the Merfolk got into the water before he was struck down, there were all kinds of powers he could use against Lazark. But he felt he could have struck down the other two without putting 'Brode' on his guard – they were ostensibly on the same side, after all, and there were no warning signs to the

Merfolk that Lazark was going to betray him, as far as he could think of. Another sign it was the *schlipf*, not he, who was in charge of his actions.

Perhaps because it was acting on its own, or perhaps because he was just so tired, Lazark's first attempt was too late. Vihanto's cry alerted everyone to his intentions, and 'Brode' had the chance to spin around and dive towards his bathtub for shelter, transforming into his Merfolk form as he went. He narrowly dodged a spiked vine heading his way.

With both Arnach and 'Brode' now under cover, there was only one target. Now taking charge of the attack, Lazark directed the *schlipf* against Nattiel. He consciously sent out the spear-like thorn, shooting it forward in much the same way as a ballista would fire a bolt, only with a tether at the end to retrieve it.

A *schlipf* was a powerful weapon. Nattiel might have been wearing armor made out of Red Dragonhide, as all the Swords wore, but that spike could pierce any shield or armor Humans could conceive of, given enough force. According to the stories, it was a similar strike that ultimately killed Sword King Paljor of the Borden Isles. There was nothing that could block that blow.

But it could be deflected. Vihanto had leapt across the room, sword drawn, and shattered his blade against the spike trying to parry it. While Vihanto was left weaponless, and he failed to damage the spike at all, he did shove Lazark's arm – and thus his aim – aside, so that the spike hit a wall.

It was only a brief reprieve. The spike seemed stuck, and he lacked the ability to pull it out of the wall with his natural strength, but the vine component of his *schlipf* could anchor him enough to retrieve it. He had to sacrifice the shielding ability of the *schlipf* to do so, however.

Nattiel seemed frozen where he was, and Vihanto was still down from his impressive leap, so there was a chance he could still get the Sword before he found cover as well. Lazark started the process, anchoring his body with the vine.

So there was nothing to protect him from the blade of ice that his former Merfolk ally spat out, severing his arm at the shoulder.

"Yaah!" Lazark cried in pain, falling away from his arm and to the ground.

The *schlipf* seemed to have a mind of its own, by this point, and continued recoiling from its initial spike. It turned itself to deliver one last blow to its attacker, somehow still able to move. 'Brode' was startled, and Lazark couldn't blame him – how could that thing keep going without a body or a brain to direct it?

It was Vihanto's turn once again. He had grabbed the Sword – that oh, so sacred heirloom of the Sviedan Royals – right out of Nattiel's belt and charged the *schlipf*. There wasn't much on the creature that was vulnerable, but somehow he found a spot – the base of the root system, underneath the skin on Lazark's former arm's wrist. While the blade was designed as a slicing weapon, it proved it could, indeed, pierce, as Vihanto spiked the root ball of the living weapon, just as it had been trying to spike 'Brode.'

The *schlipf* died with its spike falling less than an inch from a spot right between the Merfolk's eyes.

Silence reigned for a few seconds after that as everyone still living waited to see if any more attacks were coming. Finally, 'Brode' once more left his bath and walked over to Lazark, looking down at the man who had worked with him for so long.

"What is going on? Why did you attack me?" he demanded.

"It's over," Lazark muttered. He wasn't going to live, he knew it... and he felt like answering questions. "I've... been under the control of that thing... since my meeting with the Porosian Elves. It's been... slowly killing me for weeks."

"But—"

"Plan Arrowhead has begun," Lazark continued, desperate to get this out before he died. "I... the first strike was to break the Sviedan government. Sorry, 'Brode,' but you were to die, too. It... it wasn't my plan."

The Merfolk's eyes narrowed. "My death was part of the plan? Since when?"

"Since it was... conceived," he confessed. "That was... why I always warned you away... from calling it in." Lazark gasped, feeling lightheaded. He glanced at his side. The loss of an arm was sometimes survivable, but not the loss of so much blood. "The Porosians... were really the ones behind the attack on Maelgyn. Even I didn't know that. The Technologists... don't matter." He swallowed. "I... I thought this was such a grand effort. The reunification of Humanity's homeland.

But these Elves... they used me. Us. Us all. They care nothing for... ah! Oh, never mind. Just... it's happening. It's happening soon. The plan will..."

Lazark couldn't finish his sentence. Between exhaustion and a lethal loss of blood, he finally was able to drift off to a blissful sleep. He was so tired, and in so much pain, he didn't even care that he would never wake from it again.

Chapter XXVII

Maelgyn couldn't believe his eyes. Sword Princess Idril, his... well, cousin, of some sort (daughter of his great-uncle, whatever that made them) had been missing almost since the war started. Some thought her dead, though El'Athras' spies insisted that if she was, no-one on either side of the Sviedan-Sho'Curlan war knew about it. And here she was, fit as could be, dressing him down for getting her sent to a Bandi jail cell.

"What are you *doing* here?" he demanded, interrupting her rant.

"Me? I could ask you the same thing!" Idril replied. "You should still be in Sopan, not traipsing about in a foreign country accompanied by... well, I recognize a few of the Humans here, but not the Elf, Dwarves, or Nekoji in your company. How odd."

"How long have you been here?" Maelgyn asked incredulously.

Idril sighed, looking down. "Sword King Gilbereth must have had some warning of the impending invasion, but he didn't have time to act on it. I received a missive from him that had been sent before his demise, ordering me to come here, to Bandi, in secret, and negotiate a military alliance. I left as soon as it was possible, and I've been here ever since. I've made some progress with their senate, but Lady Phalra is still obstructing things. Her voice carries a lot of weight, here, and I fear I will be unable to conclude any alliance without her co-operation. I'm still angry that you've given her more ammunition to use against me."

"And in all this time, you've heard no news out of Svieda?" Maelgyn asked.

"Lady Phalra ordered the borders closed some time ago. We haven't heard any news, officially, and I have no assistants I can send to try and smoke out any rumors," Idril said. "Surely the war hasn't already ended, has it? Svieda hasn't fallen, has it?"

Maelgyn whistled. Bandi's border control must be good to hold back that much news. "We're actually in pretty good shape, for the moment, and you've missed... quite a bit. I honestly don't know where to begin...."

"How about with introductions?" Euleilla suggested.

Maelgyn winced. He'd forgotten that this was the one relative he hadn't introduced her to, yet... and it was the only one, other than his own father, that he feared her meeting. "Of course. Well, you already know Baron Jank, the general of your armies."

"I will ask why he is here and not leading those armies later," Idril warned, glaring at the Baron.

Jank shifted uncomfortably. "Of course, your Highness."

"Before berating him too much, Idril, keep in mind that you've been missing for almost a year without word of your whereabouts – some of us thought you were captured or dead, and we've been acting accordingly. Also present are Baron Yergwain, general of my armies, and Baroness Mikko, general of the armies of Largo. And you may also know Duchess Kassi, the ruling regent of Leyland."

"*Ruling* regent? Ambrosius finally got himself killed, then?" Idril asked.

Maelgyn grimaced. "Presumed dead, but not confirmed. He went missing during battle, but his body hasn't been found. You have also been regarded as missing, as I said, so Regent Duke Kousa is currently ruling Stanget in your absence."

"Indeed? I hope my province is still standing."

"It was when I left," Maelgyn said. He would have laughed, but he knew Idril wasn't joking; she genuinely felt she was the only competent leader in the entire Sword Kingdom of Svieda. "Let's see... here are Tur'Tei and Tur'Ka, my personal armsmen."

"Dwarves as armsmen?" Idril snorted a laugh. "When I return to Svieda, you must get in touch with me – I know some very excellent warriors who would do a much better job."

"Hey!" Tur'Ka said. "We're re-discovering the skills of the Dwarven Axemen of legend! You will find we are quite capable of fighting as warriors."Tur'Tei also looked offended, but as usual he said nothing.

If anything, Idril's smirk grew larger. "My apologies. You've researched hundreds of years of failed experiments to re-create their failures all on your own, I'm sure."

Trying to head off more of an argument, Maelgyn continued the introductions. "I should probably also introduce El'Athras. Or, as he now has the right to call himself, Count El'Athras of the Sviedan Province of Mar'Tok."

"Come again?" Idril said.

He drove ahead, deciding to bundle the explanation for two of them in one go. "I should also present Count Gyato of the Sviedan Province of Caseificio. We signed a treaty where both nations ceded themselves into Svieda. I'm surprised, even with everything else you missed, you haven't heard of it – there was a representative from Bandi to witness the signing."

"I... no, I hadn't."

"I would also like to introduce their assistants – Wodtke, our expedition's doctor and El'Athras' assistant, and Onayari, Count Gyato's aide-de-camp." Idril barely acknowledged the two with a nod. "Also our cook, Kiszaten." These she didn't even give that much of a reaction to the cook. He took a deep breath for the last introduction. Best to make this as formal as possible. "And finally, my wife. Princess Consort and Baronetess Euleilla." He paused when Idril froze, and decided to add one last detail. "She is to be invested as a full Princess, though honestly I've been too busy to see if the paperwork on that has been pushed through."

Idril stared at Euleilla incredulously. "You married a peasant? But you're one of the royals, a Sword even, and my cousin! How could you... you..."

If Euleilla was offended, she didn't show it. "Hiya!"

Maelgyn winced. He loved his wife, but this was not the time for her to play these sorts of games.

"And has this marriage been accepted by any of the other Swords?" Idril asked.

"Most of those still alive," Maelgyn said. "Of course, it helps when she's the foster-daughter of a major war hero, is a powerful mage, and that she was instrumental in helping me reclaim the Borden Isles while negotiating a new alliance with the Golden Dragons."

Idril's mouth opened and closed a few times. "Okay," she finally said. "I concede that I've missed out on a lot. How about you start from the beginning. Last I heard, *you* were the missing one – what did you do after our king was killed?"

"Ah, well, it started with my attempt to make it to Sopan without anyone figuring out who I was," Maelgyn replied. "As it turns out, I was pretty lousy at keeping myself hidden, since it seems I was discovered several times. One of those times was at a small village named Rocky Run, where I encountered a young woman being accosted by a group of ruffians...."

Nattiel, Arnach, and Vihanto had all joined 'Brode' as he stood over Lazark's dead body.

"So..." Arnach said hesitantly, looking at the Merfolk who currently was not wearing any disguise. "What now?"

'Brode' resumed his human appearance. "Well... things have certainly changed. As a mercenary, I have a rule: If my employer tries to kill me, I then turn around and work to kill them. However, I fear that my employers, in this case, are too powerful for me to defeat alone." He paused. "I have to think about my plans for the future. I realize that I have put you in a... difficult situation, now, by impersonating your brother. I will work to get you out of that situation."

Vihanto, breathing heavily, stepped on the severed arm of the *schlipf* and extracted Nattiel's Sword. He checked it for damage and, apparently satisfied, wiped it off on his pants before returning it to its owner.

"Your Highness, I apologize for borrowing this without permission, but the situation required immediate action," he said.

'Brode' turned his attention to the guard. The man had saved all their lives during this assassination – he pushed Arnach out of the way, deflected a blow meant for Nattiel, and finally killed the *schlipf* before it could hit him. He had never encountered a Human quite like him, before.

"I... you are pardoned for any crime that such an action might present," Nattiel said, still looking a little shocked in the aftermath. "Not that I think such a pardon is needed, under the circumstances."

"We can discuss such things later. There is much you need to know," 'Brode' said. "We must act quickly if we are to prevent a major disaster."

"Where is the real Brode?" Vihanto asked, turning to look at him. It seemed a non-sequitur, but the Merfolk suspected this was a sticking point for the man.

He didn't hesitate to answer. "I do not know. A captive of my former employers, as you might expect – kept alive, last I heard, but then I am starting to suspect they were lying to me about a number of things. I see no reason why they would have lied about this, however."

Vihanto nodded. He turned to Arnach and sketched a bow. "Your Highness, if you'll excuse me I would like to head to the quartermaster and get my sword replaced."

"I..." Arnach seemed more stunned by that request than he was by the attack. "I would rather you wait until the discussion here had ended."

"Of course, your Highness," Vihanto said, staring down at his hands. "But I will not be able to protect you from a similar attack until I am re-armed."

It was then that 'Brode' realized the man was in shock, himself. "Sit down," he ordered.

"But—"

"You have saved my life. You saved all our lives. Now sit down, and let the adrenaline work its way out of your system before you collapse – it would not do for us to let our saviors' heart give out because we wouldn't take care of him." When the guardsman just stared at him with distrust, 'Brode' gave a large sigh and reached to his belt. He always wore the real Brode's Sword – it was the symbol of the office, after all, and should be worn at all times – but he had other means of defending himself. Especially near water. He unstrapped the sheath and handed the whole sword belt to the guard. "If it will help you relax, you can hold onto this until you are satisfied of my intentions."

Vihanto stared at it for a moment before grabbing the belt and sitting on the corner of 'Brode's' bathtub. Moments later he started shaking all over.

"Was that your first time in combat?" Arnach asked him.

"I... yes, your Highness."

"You acquitted yourself far better than I did," Arnach laughed. The laughter help put the soldier at ease, but he was still trembling. It was the adrenaline, 'Brode' knew – there was no stopping the shakes as your system worked off the rush. "I wasn't even facing a real enemy – just a bear. We were hunting in the woods when I encountered the animal trying to steal our catch. I wanted to chase it off, but the beast swung at me, knocking me down and roaring in my face. If I hadn't been wearing Dragonhide armor and a decent helmet, it would have gutted me right then. Fortunately, my fellow hunters heard my screams and came to my rescue."

Nattiel, having come down off his own shock, was quick to join them. "Only person I know who performed nearly as well in his first action was my son, Maelgyn. A Red Dragon had flown in from the Eastern Wastelands, and was terrorizing some farms in Happaso. Maelgyn, fresh from mage's school and only in the beginning stages of his sword training, gathered several people together to try and hunt it down."

"I remember that!" Arnach said. "Idril found out about it and went to chase him down, taking a detachment of a hundred soldiers with her. Maelgyn only had a half-dozen people, but she didn't want him to be able to argue with her."

"Neither group ever made it to the Dragon before it flew back to its nest in the East, though Maelgyn says he got close enough to see it. And I suppose I believe him," Nattiel said grudgingly. "He ran into one of the old Abindol resistance cells – the kind that felt Abindol's border should have been based on the river, not on some old invisible lines drawn on the map of our old tax districts. Maelgyn, of course, charged in. Idril showed up with her hundred men and had to rescue him, but he had half a dozen of the rebels dead at his feet when she arrived, despite his lack of training."

Arnach glanced at Nattiel in surprise. "You know, that's the nicest you've ever spoken about Maelgyn in all the time I've known you."

Nattiel frowned. "Surely not. I—"

"Forgive me for the intrusion," 'Brode' said. "But there really are matters we need to discuss. Now that Lazark, here, is dead, we need to do something. Svieda should have a rightful king on its throne, and not a foreign-born impersonator like me."

"There are ways to do that, but we're giving Maelgyn a chance to find the real Brode first," Arnach said, glancing at the Merfolk. "If he can do so, it will remove several legal complications."

"Perhaps it would," the Merfolk said. "But I have a method that was previously unavailable to you, and it will remove all of them...."

"...and formed a War Council, now sitting at the new fortress I learned they were building in Rocky Run," Maelgyn said. "Which brings us to the, uh, diplomatic mission we began that brought us all here."

Idril was frowning. "And you say that there is an impersonator sitting on the throne of Svieda right now, while Brode is lying captive somewhere?"

Maelgyn nodded. "Exactly. Which is why we had some... concerns, to put it mildly, that some random diplomat we didn't know about was claiming to represent us to the Bandi Republic."

She arched an eyebrow at him. "Indeed. But it brings up the question of what we should do about it."

Maelgyn nodded. "Something we've been struggling with for months. But we have a plan, now – we've found the real Brode."

Idril almost smiled at that. "Of course you have – which explains why you're here, in Bandi, where he couldn't possibly be."

"Actually, he's due north of Bandi," Maelgyn said. "In a small Porosian town named Sjouleber. While this really is a diplomatic mission, a few of us were only escorting that mission this far before slipping north into West Poros."

"Really? How interesting!" a now-familiar cackle echoed from outside of their cell. A torch lit nearby, and Lady Phalra once more made her presence known, holding Maelgyn's Sword brazenly out in front of her. How Maelgyn hadn't seen or sensed her, he had no idea. "And, for the record, I am satisfied that none of you are Merfolk, now. But I'm not letting you all go free after admitting you plan to use our nation as a springboard in an act of war." She eyed Maelgyn again, glancing him up an down in a way that left him uncomfortable. "I am willing to be persuaded, however, that your actions are necessary, if you can convince me to be your ally. Guards, bring Sword Maelgyn to my private chambers!"

Maelgyn hesitated. "I am not the ambassador, Lady Phalra. The Duchess Kassi was to be my representative. I'm not really a diplomat."

Phalra smirked. "Well, I don't particularly care which of you came here to be your 'representative,' and if you are not a diplomat you shouldn't be on a diplomatic mission. But very well – I would be amused to see the reaction of your companions as we talk, ahem, terms. *You* will be doing the negotiating, but they may join us... at first. I will head to my chambers. Guards, I'll give them fifteen minutes to confer, then bring them all to me... except for the Elf. My brother isn't to be allowed out just yet."

"I knew this was about the troll nut incident, I did," Wangdu muttered as she left.

"Is she really gone?" Maelgyn asked once they heard another door close.

Euleilla frowned. "I... am not sure. I haven't been able to sense her, or any of the people in this room beyond our own."

Wangdu sighed. "Lady Phalra has a secret method for hiding the presence of her people, she does. No Elf or *schlipf* can sense her, they can't, but she can sense them, she can. Apparently it works against Human magical senses as well, it does. I do not know the secret, I don't, but I know she must prepare the area a year or more ahead of time for it to work, she must. After a millennia living here there is no part of Bandi that she hasn't protected, there isn't."

Gyato stood up straight. "There are other ways of finding someone that cannot be seen beyond Human or Elven magic. Onayari?"

The female Nekoji walked over to the bars and pushed her nose through them, audibly sniffing. "There are trace scents, as you might expect for someone who had passed through the room, but there are no female Elves currently nearby."

Maelgyn sighed. "Very well. I... wasn't expecting to have to do any negotiations, here, so what do I need to know?"

Euleilla, to his surprise, was the first to answer. "She is the most powerful person in Bandi. Your cousin, here, has been trying to conclude a military alliance with her for months, now, unsuccessfully. What sort of concessions has she been asking for?"

"She hasn't been asking for anything," Idril admitted. "She has simply been unwilling to negotiate. The other senators of Bandi have asked for trading or other economic concessions, and they wanted proof that we could actually contend with the Sho'Curlans before joining us, but she hasn't asked for anything herself."

"Well, she's negotiating, now," Euleilla pointed out. "And she's coming from the position of power. We want her to ally with us, but she could just as easily use our intrusion to declare war on us. Considering that, we will have to concede to almost anything that doesn't threaten Svieda's existence that she asks of us. Right?"

Idril snorted. "Well, it's clear you didn't marry a diplomat, cousin. Girl, as a rule, you never agree to whatever the first proposal is – you always negotiate and try to get them to agree to at least one more thing for your side. If you don't, they think they can walk all over you in future negotiations, even when things are otherwise in your favor."

Euleilla shook her head. "But these aren't proper treaty negotiations – this is a surrender! If we surrender because they've agreed to become our allies, that's hardly letting them walk all over us. And we need this to be over quickly. Any more serious negotiations will take longer, which means it will take longer to rescue Brode, which means it will take longer before we can return home. And I know we both want to return home as quickly as possible."

Maelgyn nodded slightly – she had that much right. Turning to Wangdu, he said, "You know the Lady Phalra best – what do you suggest?"

Wangdu gave him a long-suffering look. "With Phalra you can never know, you can't. She is the most unpredictable person I have ever met, I have, whether that person was Elf, Human, Dwarf, Merfolk, Nekoji, Dragon, or something else, they were. But she is good to her word, she is, so she will keep any agreement you make, she will."

Kassi coughed. "Since I was supposed to be your 'representative,' perhaps I may make a suggestion?"

Idril snorted dismissively, but Maelgyn turned to the woman with interest. "I would appreciate any advice you might have. You know more far more about this than I do."

"I'm not sure I truly know more," Kassi said. "But I think it would be wise if you went in there with at least some expectation of what she wants to ask from you. We have a few clues, though I don't know what they add up to, but perhaps we could make some guesses. To start with, she didn't know you were untrained as a diplomat and doesn't care. She does know that you are a Sword, however, and she wants you, specifically, to negotiate – that would seem to indicate that she must want to ask something that only a Sword can grant her. But she didn't care to discuss anything with Sword Idril, either... so perhaps she wants something that only you, specifically, can grant her. What can you grant her, as a Sword during Interregnum, that Idril cannot?"

"Perhaps something specific to Sopan," Yergwain suggested. "We hold a fairly powerful monopoly over all trade leaving through the Orful River."

Idril shook her head. "If it was just that, she could have at least talked to me about it, even though it would involve Sopan. Yes, I would have had to get Maelgyn to second the treaty, under the circumstances, but that's a minor thing."

"Perhaps something specific to him, that has nothing to do with being a Sword?" El'Athras suggested. "Maelgyn is a mage of exceptional talent. Perhaps there is something she needs his level of magecraft to accomplish."

"I'm a mage of 'exceptional talent,' myself – how many mages are stronger than a second rate?" Idril asked.

"Um..." Euleilla said, raising her hand. Smirking slightly at getting one up on his cousin, Maelgyn raised his hand as well... and even Onayari did, though she looked reluctant to get involved. "There's a reason that Maelgyn is a part of the team to rescue Brode. He is, quite frankly, the most powerful mage alive. And I say that as a first rate mage, myself."

"An exceptionally powerful first rate mage," Maelgyn said. "I may be number one – and I'm not bragging, there – but I think Euleilla may be in the top five for mages alive, today."

"But you were only half-trained!" Idril protested.

"After the battle with Paljor, Maelgyn was declared a High Mage," El'Athras explained. "But it wasn't until the Battle of Svieda's Royal Castle that he proved it in the traditional way, using his magic to kill three Black Dragons by himself."

Idril gawked at that.

"She's right, though," Kassi said. "If it was just magical talent that was called for, Lady Phalra should have at least considered Idril's talent. As far as I know, she is unaware that Maelgyn even has any magical talent, much less what it is."

"I still think it must be something specific to Sopan," Yergwain said. "If not an economic concession, perhaps a political one. Between Caseificio and us, we share a longer border with Oregal than anyone. We are best known for the economic stranglehold we have on the Orful River delta on our Eastern border, but our economy is also strong because of the trade we manage on the Sho'Mar river at our Western border, as well. While you haven't been in power long enough to know this, that river is almost as important as the Orful, because of its connection to Oregal. We control one bank of the river, they control th other. The Sword who controls Sopan must always maintain diplomatic relations with Oregal, sometimes even attending court in Oregal's capital itself. Perhaps she wants you to get her an invite."

"She has a standing invite in Oregal, she does," Wangdu said. "They really like her there, they do. Much of their government was based on Bandi's example, it was, and they know she was the one to set up that government, they do."

"You wouldn't know it from the way Oregal treats its people," El'Athras snorted. "They may provide a home for Elves, Dwarves, and Nekoji to live alongside Humans in peace, but any non-Humans are still treated as second-class citizens by them."

"She will not allow any other Elves to settle in Bandi, herself, she won't," Wangdu noted. "They are just following her example, they are."

"How did this become a discussion of Oregal?" Idril huffed. "We're working on a treaty with Bandi, remember?"

"Well, then, if it isn't political concessions from Sopan, my magic skills, trade concessions from the Orful River, or my negotiating power as a Sword during Interregnum, what does she want from me?" Maelgyn asked.

"She wants your presence," a guard at the gate said, interrupting them. Maelgyn glanced over at Onayari, who looked a bit sheepish at having not thought to keep a nose out for new intruders, but didn't say anything. "Your time is up – the Lady Phalra commands your presence."

"Already?" Maelgyn said, surprised. "Very well, then... let's go see what the Lady *really* wants."

Chapter XXVIII

The 'chambers' that Lady Phalra chose to meet them in were actually her bedchambers, it turned out, and the 'bed' in that word described the dominant feature of the room. It was elegant, made of a dark, well-polished wood, gold leaf trim, and topped with a soft-looking mattress and satin sheets made of a rich purple silk. It screamed both opulence and comfort. And it was huge, taking up almost half the room by itself.

And it wasn't a small room. There were at least ten bear fur rugs on the floor, surrounding the bed. There were no windows, but there were enough candles to provide plenty of light. The walls were lined with benches, and a four foot by four foot planter box stood in each corner. There were somewhat realistic oil paintings on just about every available surface, each one portraying a different male Human, nude and in intimate detail. It all made Maelgyn feel that much more uncomfortable with the situation he was in. Just what kind of a person was this Phalra?

Well, whatever kind of a person she was, she wasn't immediately visible. There were a couple doorways leading to additional rooms (perhaps a store room in place of an armoire, or perhaps a private privy? Maelgyn had heard of such things in some castles, though

Svieda's royals had never gone for such ostentatious frivolities), so maybe she would be entering through one of them. The door that had given them entry into this room was now closed and locked.

Euleilla gripped his shoulder and gave him a reassuring squeeze. "Remember," she whispered in his ear. "We need this treaty, so you need to agree to anything she asks for. First offer, no negotiation."

Maelgyn was about to say something in reply, but she drew away just as Lady Phalra entered the room from one of the side doors. A Lady Phalra who, while recognizable, looked nothing like the woman who had been standing outside of their cell door. She stepped inside the room, and almost slithered into the bed, spreading herself out seductively.

She had the same face and same hairstyle, of course – she was clearly the same person. But the armor was gone, and her skin was now glossy with scented oils. She was wearing clothes, but they were designed to emphasize areas normally covered up in polite society. She had a slight smile on her face, and she had a dangerous twinkle in her eye, as she held Maelgyn's Sword in a provocative way, offering it to him. *Seriously, what kind of person is this woman?* Maelgyn wondered again as he took it.

An Elven female attempting to flirt with a Human male, Sekhar thought to him. *You had better be careful – Elves don't understand the more subtle methods of Human seduction, so they can be somewhat... blatant.*

Seduction? Maelgyn repeated. *But I'm married!*

She doesn't know that, I don't think... and I doubt she even cares.

But—

"So," Phalra purred. "You want an alliance with my nation, yes?"

"It would certainly be helpful," Maelgyn replied cautiously.

"And you wish to know what I ask in return for that alliance, yes?"

"Remember, first offer," Euleilla again whispered in his ear.

"As you seem to be the person best able to help us get that alliance, yes, I do," Maelgyn replied.

"Good," Phalra said, her lips curling into an even wider smile. "Now, you say this *schlipf* of yours will extend your life and not contract it, yes?"

"Um... correct."

So whatever she wants has to do with you, and not me, Maelgyn thought to Sekhar. *What can you do that an Elf like her might want?*

I don't know – the Elves created and control my kind. There is nothing I can do for her that she can't do herself, as far as I know, Sekhar replied.

"How long will it do so?"

Maelgyn paused. "Come again?"

"How long can your *schlipf* extend a human's life? It is a simple question."

Well, do you know? Maelgyn asked Sekhar.

Not exactly, Sekhar said. *But I know I can keep you from aging or dying a natural death for as long as I live. You'll still be vulnerable to swords, arrows, spears, falling off dragons...*

I get the idea, Maelgyn said, mentally rolling his eyes. The few times they had talked since the siege of the Royal Castle, Sekhar never failed to bring that one up.

"I... my *schlipf* believes it will be able to stop me from aging for as long as it remains alive, itself. I can still be killed by other means during that time, of course."

"Interesting... very interesting," Phalra said. "You know, some trees live for thousands of years. Unless I miss my guess, when the Ancient Elves created those things, they made sure that they would live at least as long."

"I'm not sure what I think of that," Maelgyn said, wondering at the non-sequitur. "After all, your own people start to go mad once they reach a thousand."

Lady Phalra laughed. "Yes, yes. And I am mad, too, you know? I accept that truth. But we Elves have learned to channel insanity so that it can be used productively. Now, usually we're insane by the time we decide where to channel that insanity, so you'll get megalomaniacs like Hrabak or the truly bent like Prusek and his Technologists, but it's an easy enough trick. I'll happily teach you how to do so."

"Um... thank you?" Maelgyn said, not sure what to make of that offer.

"Now, for my request," Phalra said. "I will ally my nation with yours in the current and all future wars. Trade between our two nations will be untariffed and unchecked. The Republic of Bandi will become a self-governing autonomous province of Svieda. And I, personally, will join you on your quest to free your cousin from these Porosians you were talking about."

A nudge from Euleilla was all that stopped him from gaping at that. She seemed to be the only person in Maelgyn's company that wasn't thrown for a loop at that offer. Idril was speechless, and even the unflappable El'Athras looked shocked. It was everything they were asking for and more. Bandi, while not on the level of Oregal, Sho'Curlas, or Svieda itself, was a powerful nation – one of the strongest. Their potential contribution could help more than Mar'Tok and Caseificio's assistance, combined. And having another Elf, even an insane one, would greatly increase their chances in Poros. Especially if she could manage those tricks that made her own people so hard to detect.

"And in return?" he asked, knowing that it had to be something more than he was willing to offer in exchange. Possibly more than he could offer on his own, which would explain why she refused to negotiate with Idril; certain things required more than one Sword to promise in a treaty, even during Interregnum.

Phalra gestured around the room. "See all these portraits? Human men, all of them. Beautiful, weren't they? Oh, of course, you wouldn't see them as such, but surely even you can tell they were all quite attractive examples of their gender. All of them were my lovers for a time... and all were great men. Each one of these wonderful men, however, could only live so long. Most would only last for twenty or thirty years before they could no longer keep up with me. They would usually die after forty or fifty. After over a thousand years of this... it gets more and more painful each time. But I continue to take Human lovers."

"Why?" Idril asked. "Surely you would be happier with your own kind."

Phalra laughed. "You really think so? Have you met any male Elves?" She shook her head. "No. I am not saying there are no good Elves out there, but as lovers they are... unenthusiastic. When the Ancient Elves became the Modern Elves – and yes, it was a decision; we 'changed' ourselves as part of the process – there were some unexpected side-effects. Among them was a complete lack of interest in sex and procreation. You'll find very few young Elves – my youngest brother, Wangdu, is also among the youngest of our kind. My own children may very well be the youngest, and it's been centuries since I last spoke to them.

"My parents, while also disinterested in procreation, were afraid that the Elves were on a path to extinction. And we are. But in the process of trying to 'correct the problem,' they engineered me to be born with the libido that none of my fellow Elves had. Not even my other brothers and sisters, like Wangdu, showed any signs of sexual interest, and my parents soldiered on to produce eleven children over the course of their lives, trying to repeat the experiment that resulted in me each time.

"I tried an Elven lover, once, but it was... horribly unsatisfying. For both of us. While I had a pair of children with him, we eventually decided that neither of us were happy with the relationship... and then I started to take Human lovers. I haven't stopped, since."

"No Dwarven lovers, then?" El'Athras muttered. Wodtke elbowed him.

"Dwarves don't like me," she laughed. "First of all, I'm an Elf. Second... well, let's just say few Dwarves find someone like me attractive."

Euleilla shook her head, frowning. She seemed disturbed about something, and now was grabbing onto Maelgyn by the back of his armor. "All of this is very interesting, but it doesn't answer the question: What do you want in exchange for this alliance."

"Oh, you haven't figured it out, yet?" Phalra laughed. "Sword Maelgyn, your *schlipf* may not quite grant you immortality, but it gives you something fairly close. You are, from what I can tell, a good man, and you certainly look nice enough. So, in exchange for this alliance you crave, you must also take me as your lover and consort for all of your remaining days."

Euleilla sputtered. "You know, Maelgyn, just ignore everything I told you. Idril was the one with the actual diplomatic training, and she did say never to accept the first offer...."

If the discussion wasn't so serious, Maelgyn would have laughed... but Phalra was a mad Elf, and chances were she meant that demand seriously. Laughing in her face – even with Euleilla's words echoing in his head – would not be a good idea. Neither would accepting, however – not unless he wanted Euleilla to kill him.

"Forgive me, Lady Phalra, but that will not be possible," he said.

"No—" Idril protested.

"I am already married, and to a woman I love."

Phalra frowned. "Married, you say? A... Human marriage, yes?"

"Of course," Maelgyn said.

She shrugged. "A minor issue. Humans, in addition to the concept of marriage, also have something known as 'divorce.' You can simply 'divorce' this Human woman and stay with me."

"I—" he started.

"Oh, but you did say you love her, didn't you?" Phalra said, laughing. "Still, you humans have affairs all the time. I am willing to accept a lesser position as your mistress, at least while this Human woman of yours still lives. After all, while I have a libido, I do have other interests. We cannot spend *all* our time making love – she may have you when I am busy with other matters. Or we could share, I suppose, if you feel yourself capable of it – I have had other women in my bed, before, though always with one of my more virile man."

Maelgyn *almost* looked over at Euleilla to see her reaction to that suggestion, but thought better of it. He knew what it would be: She would hit him for even considering it.

"Lady Phalra, that is hardly an ethical thing to ask in exchange for this kind of alliance."

"Really? Why?" she asked. "You Humans frequently conclude political alliances by arranging the marriage of respective royal families. I am not even asking that much of you."

"Royals may not marry other royals in Svieda. It is against the law," Maelgyn was quick to point out.

"And I am merely the praetor of a republic, not the queen of a kingdom, so I am not royalty. So what is the issue?"

Maelgyn knew he was losing the argument, and wasn't sure where to go from there. An outright refusal would undoubtedly be bad – perhaps even start a war between Svieda and Bandi – but he was running out of excuses for putting her off short of a flat refusal. He glanced around the room, looking for some inspiration that might give him an argument against this... this... proposition. His eyes fell on Euleilla. Even though he knew she couldn't see it, he sent her a desperate plea for help with his eyes.

"What's this?" Phalra said, rolling over on the bed. "Is this woman your wife? Why, of course she is – just look at how familiar she is with you. You didn't say your wife was here with you! What, you can't accept my offer out of loyalty to this small-chested, mousy little thing?"

Maelgyn instantly felt a wave of magic he could barely withstand burst out near him, though he was able to withstand it. Several of his other companions were not so lucky, including all three normally-magic-resistant Dwarves, Duchess Kassi, and the Barons, who all were knocked off their feet. Gyato seemed to struggle, as well, but Onayari appeared to be shielding him.

"Small-chested?" Euleilla repeated. Despite the magical reaction, her voice was soft and quiet... which somehow made it feel all the more dangerous. "Mousy?"

Phalra laughed. "She has fangs, too! You found quite the powerful little mage girl... but you would be better off with me." She gestured to her body. "I am more toned, skinnier, smarter, and better looking. And she is far, far too young and inexperienced to even comprehend the sorts of things I could do for you. She really can't compete."

"Wrong," Euleilla snapped, her temper slipping. Maelgyn was going to agree with her – Euleilla was at least as striking, and not at all flat-chested. He'd seen both women well enough to know that better than anyone. It probably would not be a smart thing for him to say, though – that would imply he'd paid enough attention to compare.

"That's all you can say? Wrong?" Phalra snorted. "Not much of an argument, is it? Come now, girl – know who your betters are and step aside. Or if you must challenge me, know that you'll find no better time. I'm unarmed, in a room with a stone floor and stone walls. I'm not even wearing armor. As you – and your husband – can plainly see, I'm not wearing much of anything! In this situation, I'm not much more dangerous than your average human warrior... I just have an Elf's strength and reflexes... and more than a thousand years more experience than you could possibly have. So... do you want to challenge me just to keep me from your husband?"

"Yes!" Euleilla cried.

Maelgyn felt the magic warp and fold around the room, but he somehow missed it when Euleilla formed a solid chunk of iron in the shape of a fist out of her magic powder and sent it flying at the Elven woman. To just about everyone's surprise, it connected with Phalra's jaw, sending the Elf-girl tumbling out of bed.

Phalra was not badly hurt by the blow, however, rolling to her feet and taking a defensive stance. "Whew. I wasn't wrong when I said you were a powerful little mage, was I? That wasn't bad... not bad at all! Still, it was a fairly weak blow, even if it was made of iron. You should have used a knife or a spear – this fight would be over if you had."

Euleilla cocked her head towards the Elf, grinning madly. "That would kill you," she said. "I can't do that – it would be unforgivable, and probably would start a war, but I'm fairly certain I can get away with knocking you senseless. Even your own hand-picked senate has to know your reputation. If I make the charge of 'manstealer,' they would know it was justified. They will pardon me when I point out that you were the one to provoke my wrath. But only as long as I leave you alive at the end of it."

Phalra laughed. She seemed to be enjoying herself too much for Maelgyn's comfort – an Elf wouldn't be happy in this situation unless they were in complete control, and if she was in control that meant Euleilla was probably in danger. "Too true," she said. "Very well. A fight – winner gets Maelgyn!"

"No deal," Euleilla said. "Maelgyn is my husband regardless of this fight. The only thing on the line in this challenge is pride."

Phalra frowned. "Your kingdom needs this alliance more than you might suspect, and if you do not surrender Maelgyn to me, or accept that he is the spoils of our little duel, that alliance will be off the table. Come, girl – you know you need to accept my deal."

"Well, now I know you were holding something back when you let me hit you," Euleilla said. "This trick won't work. I said it before, and I will say it again – Maelgyn is mine."

"I already offered you the boon of sharing him," Phalra said. "And I would have made that offer again when I beat you. But no – you want to prove yourself too badly for that. I will not share any man of mine with you... and you will lose Maelgyn, anyway. You will regret your pride."

Euleilla laughed. "Nope."

"You really think you can win, then?"

Euleilla shook her head. "Nope."

"Then you're surrendering?"

"Nope."

"Then how do you plan to stop me from just taking your husband?"

Euleilla smirked. "Magic."

Maelgyn wasn't liking this. Euleilla was playing the one-word game, Phalra was trying to provoke a larger fight, and looking around everyone else was as stunned as he was.

Sekhar, you know Elves better than I do. Is there anything I can do to stop Phalra without starting a war or getting my wife killed?

Well, you could always agree to take her as your mistress, but your life-mate may not like that.

No, I don't think she would. Any other options?

Well... if you can get these women to calm down, you could suggest an alternative to yourself – but it would have to be another Human male who would be able to stay alive for a thousand years or more that she could take as a lover. Not many of those around, are there?

Maelgyn was about to ask Sekhar another question, but Euleilla grabbed his attention when she started removing her dragonhide armor.

"What are you doing?" Phalra said.

"Guess!" Euleilla said, dropping the cuirass and releasing the greaves. She still had her armored riding pants on, and she didn't remove the tunic she wore under her armor, but she was now just as unprotected as Phalra.

"If you think you need to remove your armor to give me a fair fight, then—"

"Nope," Euleilla said, grinning. She finally removed her sword belt and dropped it to the floor.

"Well, then... you seem to have gone as mad as I'm purported to be," Phalra said. "Because I don't know why else you would be surrendering your advantages."

Euleilla reached out, feeling her way a little uncertainly. It was only then that Maelgyn remembered that her magic and *schlipf* senses were unable to detect Phalra's presence. She must have gotten this far by using the sound of Phalra's voice... but that still didn't explain what she was doing now. Phalra was so confused by Euleilla's actions she just watched placidly as the Human girl reached out and grabbed her by the netted shirt she was wearing.

"Gotcha," Euleilla said, almost playfully.

Phalra, her eyes widening in panic, reached out to grab Euleilla's hand. Before she could, however, Euleilla stepped in, twisted her hips, dropped to one knee, and threw the Elf woman onto the ground. Euleilla dropped down onto the other woman, straddling her waist, and leaned forward to place her elbow at Phalra's throat.

Phalra struggled underneath her, but then stopped resisting. She looked at her combatant and laughed. "So do you think you've won?"

Euleilla shook her head. "Draw."

That threw Phalra for a loop. "A draw? You have me at your mercy, or so it seems. Why do you think it's just a draw?"

Euleilla sighed, her smile dimming. "You will attack me with the Elven weapons you have hidden in your planters around the room."

"How—"

"Because it's the only thing that makes sense. I cannot beat them. Nor can I do more than pin you down from this position, even using magic to enhance my muscles as I have. But while I have you pinned, I can rely on my *schlipf* to counter any vines that could be sustained in that small amount of soil."

Phalra gaped. "You have a *schlipf*, too?"

"Of course," Euleilla said. "I would never want my husband to endure what you have – the death of lover after lover, until he has to be wondering if it is still worth it any more. I resolved to endure the same bonding he has. And surrendering him to you would now also condemn me to the same torment you have endured all these centuries. So you can see why I simply cannot accept you taking him from me, yes?"

Maelgyn could see understanding dawn in Phalra's eyes. If anything, she shrank in on herself, and immediately stopped any kind of resistance. "No! I... I would... no. You... I accept your reasons, and withdraw my request. I would never sentence someone else to endure that, no matter how much I hated them. It is... it is a horror that you cannot imagine."

"Oh... I can imagine it," Euleilla said, rolling off of the Elven girl. She offered her a hand up. "Which is exactly why I will not allow it to happen. To either my husband or myself."

"No. No, I can see that," Phalra agreed, taking the hand. Once she was on her feet, she dusted herself off. "But that leaves you with another dilemma."

"Yes," Euleilla agreed. "We now have nothing to offer in exchange for your alliance. I am sorry, but this is one thing that is not negotiable."

"Agreed," Phalra said, looking rather shaken. "I had hoped,

though... finally..."

Maelgyn coughed. "Um, if I might offer a counter-proposal that we maybe can agree to without getting into any more fights?"

"Certainly," Phalra said.

"Perhaps," said Euleilla, a bit more hesitantly.

"The ability to extend a life is a talent that any true volunteer *schlipf*, not just ours, can manage," Maelgyn said. "According to my own *schlipf*, most Elves are unfamiliar with this fact – Elves don't need this power, and *schlipf* rarely agree to bond with a Human uncoerced, so it rarely occurs to them."

"So all I have to do is find a *schlipf* that will voluntarily bond with a Human?" Phalra asked. "They may be rare, but surely—"

"Milady, you don't need to find one – you have one. Or rather, I can provide you with one. Euleilla's *schlipf* is too young to produce any seeds, but my own will agree to provide an offspring that would would know its role as a true volunteer. There is a catch, though," Maelgyn said.

"Yes?" Phalra said, almost desperately.

Maelgyn rubbed the back of his head, embarrassed slightly. "Well... it's not my condition, but one required of my *schlipf* – Sekhar. He's... it may have been hundreds or even thousands of years since you endured this, yourself, but parents do have a strong emotional attachment to their children. Sekhar knows that this child is to be hosted in your lover. He... demands the right to approve of your host, to ensure that the bond will truly be voluntary. And he trusts my judgment, at least to a degree, so I have to approve of him too."

Phalra gaped at him, and then started laughing. "Well, well, then! I will agree to the previously discussed alliance – including, now as a requirement, the provision that I will accompany you on this rescue mission – if you, Sword Maelgyn, agree to be my matchmaker."

Maelgyn shot a smirk over at his cousin, Idril. "I'm no diplomat, but I've been told I should never accept the first offer during these kinds of negotiations. It's a sign of weakness, you know."

Phalra caught on to his playfulness and responded in kind. "Fine. I throw in a bag of troll nuts for Wangdu, provided you can convince that wife of yours not to toss heavy iron fists at me again."

"Euleilla?"

"Can I still use a nickel fist if she annoys me?" Euleilla asked, walking over to her breastplate and picking it up, trying to figure out which side was the front.

"As long as you keep those nickel fists non-lethal," Phalra agreed, laughing. "By the way, why did you remove your armor, anyway? What you did, with those magically enhanced reflexes, I'm sure you could have done them even without taking off that breastplate."

Euleilla shrugged. "I had to be able to look at you and watch my back at the same time, but even my *schlipf* cannot detect your plants by itself. I could, however, detect disturbances in a cloud of magic powder. I wouldn't have been able to sense that powder very easily through dragonhide, however."

Phalra whistled. "Again... Sword Maelgyn, my friend, you found yourself a real powerhouse as a bride. I'm not sure I really *could* have won against her."

"Well," Euleilla said, smiling. "I'll let you think you stood a chance."

In the end, the only people that High King Fitz was able to take with him into exile from the Sho'Curlas throne were his wife and his son's wife, Muen. Any guards, former friends, or even pets belonging to them had to stay behind.

But he was able to slip out of the castle without being seen, he thought. Muen had proven quite talented at being 'invisible,' and she seemed to know secrets about the city that its life-long residents were unaware of. Fitz had a feeling she had been planning an escape like this for some time, but just had never figured out where to go.

Once out of the city, it was a fast journey to the west. While their destination was some distance away, the roads were well-maintained and they had a stolen cart to hide themselves in. That cart made the going easier, but they couldn't use it for the entire trip. The most hazardous part of the journey was the mile, on foot, they made to cross the border... but once on the other side, an Elf appeared as if he knew to expect them. They were shepherded into yet another cart and were quickly taken further into the country.

It was here he met the same Elf he first encountered in his throne room several weeks before.

"You're early, you are," the Elf said, sounding a touch surprised. "But that's a good thing, it is."

"Oh? Why is that?" Fitz asked, holding the hands of his wife and his daughter-in-law with relief. They were finally safe. He would never have to sit in that damned chair again.

"We have a plan, we do," the Elf said. "A plan which we had to change, we did, when I offered you refuge, I did. But now that you're here, you are, Plan Arrowhead can begin, it can."

"Plan Arrowhead?" Fitz repeated uncertainly, starting to wonder if he had pulled himself out of a gilded cage and landed into the middle of a pack of wolves.

"I suspect it will matter little to you, I do, but I can give you the gist of it, I can. It starts with the reunification of Poros, it does...."

Chapter XXIX

"Are you sure allowing him to do this is a good idea?" Nattiel whispered, leaning over so that no-one could hear him speaking to Arnach amidst the many courtiers who were filing into the ornate Royal Council chambers. Seating was in a chevron pattern, with a long carpeted path splitting the room in the middle in which most of the council members were standing and chatting; they were in the wings, trying not to be seen until it was time. "That attack may have been staged to convince us to offer him this opportunity."

"I seriously doubt that," Arnach said softly, glancing impatiently to make sure there was no-one within earshot. Happy to see that they couldn't be overheard, he added, "And if he did, it's poor planning on his part. He only has any ability to change things as long as we support him – if we object to anything he says, he immediately loses all his power."

"It won't go well for us if we do have to object," Nattiel warned.

"True... but then the kingdom will probably fall to your son's rule. We could be in worse hands."

"Well... better than the present rule, at any rate," Nattiel agreed. "It helps to have someone at least loyal to the crown in charge."

Some of the Sviedan Provincial barons started approaching

them, taking too great an interest in their conversation, so Arnach gestured for Nattiel to be quiet. More people were filing in – this would perhaps be the largest assembly of the court since the invasion started, with the entire makeshift council and several additional nobles present.

Vihanto, filling the part of Sargent-at-Arms for the day, stepped into the room, and paused formally. "All rise for his Majesty, the Sword King, Brode IX!" He stepped aside, still at attention, and Arnach and Nattiel joined the rest of the courtiers in standing at the call, all conversation ceasing and all heads turning to face the throne.

Finally, the Merfolk impostor stepped out from the Sword King's private antechamber, and took his seat in front of the chevron. There was some brief confusion as the councilmembers rushed to find their seats.

"Please, be seated," 'Brode' said. "Call the council to order."

That call to order was unusually timed. Normally the council meeting should have been the final order of business in Court, after various ceremonies such as knightings were completed and all petitioners had been heard. It was rarely the first. By calling the council to order now, he was refusing to hear any petitions or conduct any of the king's other courtly duties.

But Vihanto was prepared for it and made the call. "The Second Makeshift Council of Svieda will come to order. The Court of Sword King Brode IX attending."

While the permanent Council would operate somewhat independently, a makeshift council ran under the direct control of the Sword King. He set the agenda, proposed laws, called for votes, and ultimately could veto most legislation the Council passed. In contrast, while a Sword King had some of those powers (setting the agenda and vetoing legislation), he rarely exercised any on his own volition during sessions of the permanent council.

Arnach looked around, sensing a shift in the mood. He shook his head, catching a few whispers that were perhaps louder than decorum should have called for. The peculiarities of the day had made some of the councilmen hopeful that he was about to declare the Council permanent, thus elevating their status. The Council would have to vote to ratify that decision, but only the Sword King could call for the vote.

Arnach knew they were about to bend quite a few laws in the next few minutes, but hopefully the temptation of being named as permanent council would convince the more political animals in the crowd to accept those twists.

"Men and women of the Council," 'Brode' began in formal address. "I must begin this meeting with some news: The Royal Archivist, Lazark, is dead, slain while attempting to assassinate myself and several other Swords in this very castle. It was only thanks to the fast actions of one of the Royal guardsmen that we were all saved. I would be asking for the Council to approve special honors to be added to his name, but other business takes priority. He acts, today, as our Sargent-at-Arms, and we expect he will receive further rewards in the future." Vihanto flushed at that proclamation, as several of the council members turned to look at him, but otherwise remained stoic.

"What business is more urgent than an attempt to assassinate our Swords?" Councilor Lemir, likely to become the head of the Council of Commons once the makeshift council was formalized, asked.

"A very good question," 'Brode' said. "One with a very complex answer. Lazark had not been acting alone until recently – he had co-conspirators. Sword Maelgyn discovered this conspiracy several months ago, in his own province of Sopan, but was unaware that elements of it were present here, as well, until recently. This conspiracy has done considerable damage to the government of Svieda, but Lazark's death has given us an opportunity to repair that damage."

"I... don't follow." Arnach gave the councilman an appraising look, considering his words. Arnach and the real Brode had selected Lemir and several of the other Council members from among the survivors of the previous council before reclaiming the castle from Sho'Curlas, but Arnach had had little time to observe him directly. Perhaps appointing Lemir had been a mistake.

"And it is just as hard to explain," 'Brode' said. "Lazark and his conspirators were attempting to pervert the Law of Swords against its own purpose. From what we have learned, the only remedy against the problems they were causing requires us to suspend the Law of Swords, itself."

"That makes no sense." That voice belonged to Baron Enebak, the presumptive head of the Council of Lords upon the re-establishment of the Permanent Council's two houses. Arnach had never liked the man, who hated the fact he was actually ranked under Lemir in most of the Makeshift Council's meetings, but was his ally in trying to get the council made permanent. Arnach didn't anticipate many problems from him in the long run, but he would be difficult to handle once they could no longer bribe him with the restoration and leadership of the two-house, permanent council. "The only way to prevent our enemies from breaking our Law of Swords is to break the Law of Swords ourselves? Is that what you're saying?"

Arnach decided he didn't blame the councilman for his confusion on this point – it seemed a little farfetched to him, too, described that way. He was tempted to interject and clarify – he felt he could have done a better job of things than 'Brode' had been doing. Before they began, however, they had decided that 'Brode' should be the only speaker at this stage. Interrupting him at this point might confuse things.

"I am about to tell you something critically important," 'Brode' continued. "If I do so with the Law of Swords in effect, one of the Swords might feel themselves obligated to challenge my Royal standing. They will lose their status as a Sword. Sword Arnach – who vouched for me – will lose his standing as a Sword. And I could, potentially, lose my standing as the Sword King. With no permanent council, there will be no replacement Swords. With so many other Swords dead, missing, or banished, a single assassination could throw the government into complete chaos... and we already know there are assassins at large. Lazark was not the first, nor only, assassin in these walls – the men who attacked Sword Maelgyn escaped undetected."

"There would be no Sword King, no eligible Swords, and no permanent Council!" Lemir exclaimed. "There are no modern laws for what to do in that circumstance that I am aware of. We would have to go to the archives to find what laws were in use before the Law of Swords..."

'Brode' nodded. "And Lazark was the Royal Archivist, who had been trying to alter our historical records before an Elf in service to Sword Maelgyn started protecting them. There may have been damage done before this protection started, however – it will take years for our scholars to compare the historic record in the Royal Archives against comparable untainted documents housed in the Library of Stanget, looking for any differences. Until then, we cannot trust those records."

Muttering broke out among the councilmen. The damage done by the Poros Conspiracy had finally been brought out into the open.

Arnach knew that the situation wasn't quite as bad as 'Brode' was painting it, but that was – in fact – the worst case scenario. It didn't have to be that bad, even without suspending the Law of Swords. He could be the one to challenge the Sword King, using his proxy status as Maelgyn's representative, and that would leave both Nattiel and Wybert (and Maelgyn, although his banishment would make things difficult for him) eligible for the throne.

Still, it was close enough to the truth to convince the council of the danger, and the panic it instilled could be used to make them act as their plan required.

"So why don't you name the permanent council?" Enebak asked. "We could bring the Swords back to their full complement, and this issue goes away." Arnach frowned. The suggestion on its face might have been reasonable, but he couldn't shake the feeling that Enebak offered it to elevate his own status.

"For reasons which shall become clear soon, my naming a permanent council would not be considered legitimate," 'Brode' said. "So, here is what must be done to get out of this situation: I spoke with Swords Arnach and Nattiel before this meeting, and they have agreed to support a resolution to suspend the Law of Swords for forty-eight hours. I request that you lend your support to them, since only unanimous agreement by the council will allow that resolution to stand. During that time, I will transfer my crown to Sword Arnach, and he shall – in turn – direct a few minor changes to the Law of Swords which he will call upon the council to pass. The moment that the Law of Swords is re-instituted, he will appoint a Permanent Council, who can then appoint the necessary Swords. In this way, we feel, the damage done by these conspirators can be repaired."

"That answers most everything, except... why are you leaving the throne?" Lemir asked. The question was reinforced by several murmurs around the table; that question cut through quickly to the heart of the matter.

"Again, a very good question," 'Brode' said. "But if I answer you before the Law of Swords is suspended, it would cause the very issue we're trying to prevent. It does relate to my relationship with Lazark, however, and why he attempted to assassinate our Swords."

"But... a Makeshift Council cannot suspend the Law of Swords with only three Swords' approval," came a third Councilman's voice. That was Baron Arundel, a smart young man Arnach had knighted, himself, from his sick-bed following the battle that reclaimed the castle. He'd fought hard to get the man on the Council, and he'd become quite the vocal leader since then. "How will we do that, unless you make us a permanent council now?"

"We actually have the votes of five Swords and proxies, as Arnach and Nattiel are also the named proxies for Swords Wybert and Maelgyn. With so many of the Swords dead or missing, that is all that that is required for suspending the Law of Swords. It will take unanimous approval by the Makeshift Council to allow for the changes we need to go through, though."

"What changes do you have in mind? The Law of Swords is a very complex law. In the past, the council was always given years of time to study the ramifications before making any changes." That was Enebak again. Strange that he was asking for a delay, as eager as he was to have the permanent council restored, but that call was in keeping with how he treated other laws brought before him.

"With the war, this conspiracy, and other threats on the horizon, we don't have years," 'Brode' said. "But if it helps your decision – it is my understanding that Swords Maelgyn and Wybert departed with plans to form a war council consisting of all the ruling regents of the other provinces. If we do not do something, soon, Sword Maelgyn will be forced to act in our stead. If he is forced to act... well, I would not be at all surprised if the seat of the Kingdom's government was forced to move, as well. This makeshift council would then become irrelevant, save for the governance of this lone province."

That was a threat, and painted Maelgyn as something of a rogue. Arnach wasn't happy about that, but it was something they had discussed for a possible last-ditch effort to convince the council to act quickly. Arnach had plans that would help restore Maelgyn's reputation... he hoped.

It appeared the debate was over, however, and in the following silence Nattiel stood up. "With my Sword and the proxy of Sword Wybert, I hereby call for a suspension of the Law of Swords."

Arnach was quick to stand as well. "And with my Sword and the proxy of Sword Maelgyn, I second that call."

'Brode' rose to his feet. "As the current Sword King, I accept the call, and put it to the Council for a vote." While he was about to lose his authority, and never should have had it in the first place, Arnach knew that history would (perhaps grudgingly) admit that he had the authority to make this call. He really was the Sword King – if he had been revealed as an impostor and murdered before the Swords and the Council had the opportunity to displace him, his murderer would have been prosecuted for regicide. The laws he enacted as Sword King would remain in place even after his revelation and removal, even were they not suspending the Law of Swords. He would be regarded as a usurper, yes, but even if he acquired the throne illegally, he would still remain in the records as the Sword King, however brief his rule.

The councilmen, however, might be a bit miffed when they learned the truth. Hopefully, they would not be so upset that they refused to help save the country, and would still be willing to accept the changes Arnach wanted to put through.

The vote was called. Unlike a permanent council, which had two houses that had to agree with each other to pass any laws, a makeshift council was usually formed of a group of 'yes-men' who would approve any laws put forth by the Sword King. That hadn't quite been Arnach's and the real Brode"s criteria for selecting them, so there had been fewer unanimous votes among them than most people would expect of a makeshift council, but they needed one in this case. With Arnach and 'Brode' working together again, thankfully, the council saw reason. After a few tense moments they consented to the plan unanimously.

"Enter this vote into the record, scribe," 'Brode' ordered.

That was important. Everyone would have to sign the record – it was verification that the vote was true and authentic. Until the signatures were added, someone might still be able to change their mind, so more tense moments were had.

When it was time for Baron Arundel – the junior-most and therefore last of the signers – to put his name on the paper, he hesitated. "Your Majesty... why *are* you resigning?"

'Brode' stood firm. "Sign it and I'll tell you."

The councilman took a deep breath and put pen to paper. Once the scribe had collected the document, Arnach let out a deep breath of relief. The hard part may have only just begun, but the biggest hurdle had been overcome and the outcome was now clear – 'Brode' would be leaving the throne, and one of the real Swords would be back on it.

And the current plan was for that Sword to be him. Maybe this wasn't such a good idea, after all.

"Very good," 'Brode said, leaning back in his seat. "Now, men and women of the council, Lords and Ladies of the Court... I tender my resignation as Sword King. You all accepted me as your king with faithful and honest intent, and I have been ruling you with the legal backing of your Law of Swords, but I never deserved the throne nor should I have been given it. For you see..." he changed into his merfolk form. That stunned the council, the courtiers, and even the guards into breaking the solemn silence that was expected of them when their king spoke. "I was never one of the Swords. I never should have been eligible to be your king. At the time of my coronation, I was in the employ of the conspiracy that Sword Maelgyn unearthed, and Lazark a part of. And yet I too was betrayed, and though I was under no obligation to inform the Swords of my role, my switching of allegiances, or any other part of my deception, I have done so.

"All I want, now, is to return to my people and the waters of my home. I could have left and you all would be none the wiser, thinking your king had abandoned you. But I felt that it would be wrong for me to leave without at least attempting to repair the damage I caused your people. So, as I leave the throne, know this: The real Sword Prince Brode is still alive, but he never sat on this throne. By all rights, it should have been Arnach, and not myself, who was named Sword King."

The councilmen weren't sure how to react to any of this. There were a couple sputtering in rage, some just staring blankly with disbelief, and one or two with a thoughtful look. Arnach hoped that they could get on to business before the forty-eight hour suspension of the Law of Swords ran out, because he had a lot of things they wanted to cover.

Before they calmed down enough to even approve of 'Brode's' resignation, however, the doors burst open.

"My Lords, your Highnesses, Sire," a man said, bowing. It was not someone Arnach recognized, but his tattered livery showed him to be in the service of the Duchy of Rubick – not a soldier's armor, but the sort of uniform the head of a local town militia might wear. Considering how devastated Rubick was at the moment, it was a little surprising to see someone wearing it. "I bring news from the border."

No-one else seemed to know how to react to that, but Nattiel was already heading to the man. "Well, speak up, then, man, speak up!"

"Squire's Knot is overrun, and soldiers are entering Rubick as we speak," the militiaman said. "But our enemy is not who we were expecting. These soldiers... they're Porosian! The four warring factions of Poros have rejoined, and for their first act as a unified people they've attacked us!"

Arnach nearly fell into his chair. They were too late. They hadn't had time to remove the stain of Poros from their land before the Porosian Conspiracy acted.

Well, they'd been expecting someone to take advantage of that weakness for some time. The war was hardly lost already... though Rubick might be. But they were prepared, and Arnach had a backup plan. Once again, though, he would need the Council's approval....

Maelgyn and his companions were once again standing around the hidden entrance to a network of Dwarven tunnels. It was a much smaller group than he'd started the journey to Poros with, thankfully, though he had more people with him for this stage than he'd planned, and Wangdu wasn't even there, yet.

In addition to Euleilla, Tur'Ka, and Tur'Tei, El'Athras had also come with them as a guide. He insisted that he wouldn't go much further than the tunnel, but since he was no longer needed as a diplomat he would be staying in the tunnel until they were ready to return. Apparently, there was a small enclave of Dwarves living in that tunnel permanently, and he was going to inspect it while Maelgyn attempted the rescue.

Of course, with El'Athras coming, Wodtke was also joining them. Maelgyn was actually happier about her being nearby – she was a doctor, after all, and it was entirely possible they'd need one once they found Brode.

And Lady Phalra was keeping to her word and joining them on their mission to rescue Brode. Since he was bringing so many others, he supposed he was happy to have her along – another Elf would be an immense help should things come to a fight. But it was still another person to keep disguised or hidden during their 'clandestine' mission.

And when Wangdu finally showed up, there would be eight people (counting Maelgyn, himself) entering these Dwarven tunnels heading to Poros. Perhaps he had made a mistake sending Kiszaten home with the diplomats – they might still need a cook after all.

At least he'd been able to convince Idril to go home. When she heard about the mission to rescue Brode, she insisted that as a second rate mage she would be a true asset in his rescue, but Maelgyn desperately didn't want her around. He pointed out that someone needed to 'escort' the return trip for Kassi, the Barons, their Nekoji companions, and Kiszaten, since their part of the mission had been completed. The truth was that Maelgyn recalled Idril as a rather incompetent warrior outside of her magic, and even that was best used in non-martial ways. If the diplomats were attacked on their way back to Rocky Run, he strongly suspected that it would be Gyato and Onayari who protected them all.

Phalra was glaring at the apparently random configuration of rocks marking the tunnel entrance while they waited for the last member of their party to show up. Wangdu's absence was her fault (she didn't explain just what she had done to keep him away, but she claimed he would show up before they had to enter the tunnel), and she was using the delay she had caused to discuss the other things she was learning about her new companions.

"So these are the tunnels that you Dwarves have been using to travel under my country, undetected, for centuries?" she asked.

"They were built by the Cave Dwarves, milady," El'Athras explained from his seat, resting against the rock spire that marked the entrance. "So it's actually been here for millennia. But we did only re-discover them a few hundred years ago, looking for relics of our ancient forefathers."

"I don't know what to think of the fact that foreign Dwarves have been living underneath my country for hundreds of years without my knowing about it," Phalra said.

Maelgyn snorted. "Neither do I, but we both have to remember we have annexed Mar'Tok, and so all of its properties – including these tunnels – are now part of our country, anyway."

"Your country," Phalra reminded him. "Bandi is still independent until you find me my mate. Unless, of course, your consort has reconsidered and agrees to share you with me, after all."

Maelgyn winced. While the verbal agreement had been simple, when Kassi (who really was the best person to handle such things on Svieda's behalf) and Phalra sat down and converted it to a written treaty, it – by necessity – became more complex. Most of the details that it added were insignificant. For example, the specific weight of the nickel fist Euleilla was allowed to hit Phalra with, including a provision which said such a blow must be non-lethal, actually wound up in the treaty at Phalra's insistence, with her claiming that "a bargain was a bargain." Phalra, if hit by such a bobble, was not permitted to retaliate physically or politically, but may "shout expletives, as warranted, upon being struck."

Among the details in the treaty were specific conditions that would activate some of its provisions. Bandi was bound, now, as an ally for the current conflict, but Bandi becoming a permanent ally and autonomous province of Svieda would only happen when Maelgyn completed his matchmaking duties. There were several ways that might be concluded, and again Phalra had insisted on including the option that Euleilla agree to 'share' him as one of those methods. Maelgyn wasn't happy about that provision, and Euleilla used her new right to throw nickel fists around to express her own displeasure. But it was written into the treaty, nonetheless.

"My job is merely to approve of your lover, not to find him for you," Maelgyn said. "And you can rest assured that I am not available."

Phalra pouted. "What a shame. You don't know what you're missing."

Euleilla looked like she wanted to smack the woman with another nickel fist, but instead she just sighed and shook her head in disgust. "How much longer do we have to wait here, anyway?"

"We have to wait for Wangdu to show up," Maelgyn said. "I don't suppose you know why he's so late, would you, Lady Phalra?"

"I ordered him to retrieve something from my gardens before joining us," Phalra said. "He should be here shortly... though he might be a little worse for wear."

"He's on the way," Euleilla said. "About five minutes out, as fast as he's moving. I only just sensed him"

Maelgyn gave her a slight grin. "So you can find him from this distance? I'm having trouble using magic to sense even the people one or two feet in front of me."

"You still haven't figured out how I hide my people from your special senses, have you?" Phalra said. "You'd probably be able to sense him by now if you had."

"Afraid not," Maelgyn said. "It's remarkable, though, I have to say – since learning this little trick of Euleilla's, no-one has been able to hide from me for long."

Phalra nodded. "The Ancient Elves were very interested by the science of sound, or acoustics. In their writings I learned of a little trick they employed called 'white noise.' It has several meanings, but in this case I mean a sound that your ear discerns as background noise and filters out. It can be played at a loud enough volume to hide other noises, making you unable to hear them even as you are unable to hear the white noise itself. I figured the trick should work on mystical senses, such as magic and the sixth sense that a *schlipf* grants some of their users, if I could just find the right frequency. Your *schlipf* probably senses a lot of danger around him, actually, but dismisses it all as background threats. With that, people can move about unobtrusively, and you'll never sense any but the most powerful of mages or the greatest of threats."

"It can get quite annoying," Euleilla mused.

"Could we take something like that elsewhere?" Maelgyn asked.

"Not easily, no," Phalra said. "The 'white noise' is being generated by the vegetation I have planted around Bandi. My soldiers and I also wear jewelry that can emphasize this, making it even harder to detect us, but nothing I know of can replace the work of that vegetation. It takes about a year for a plant to become sufficiently cultivated to work. With the root system it needs, it cannot just be put into a pot and carried somewhere – it has to spread to be effective – so I'm afraid it won't be useful for this mission."

"Just as well," Maelgyn said. "As skilled as Euleilla is with magical detection, it will hurt us worse than them."

"Especially since she's bl—" Phalra started to say.

Maelgyn's eyes widened. Euleilla stiffened, and El'Athras looked utterly horrified. The only people present who were unaware of the secret Phalra was about to blurt out were Tur'Tei and Tur'Ka, who undoubtedly could be trusted, but it was still a shock to hear the Elf woman speak so blatantly about it.

Before she could finish her sentence, however, Wangdu called from the edge of camp. "I'm finally here, I am!" he said. "I was not sure I would be able to make it before you left, I wasn't."

Glad of the change of subject, Maelgyn quickly seized upon the opening. "What kept you, then?"

Wangdu came jogging up, sending a glare over at Phalra. "Someone sent me to harvest some supplies, she did, and without telling her brother that some of those supplies would be troll nuts, she did."

"Troll nuts?" Maelgyn asked. He had been slightly curious about the incident the two Elven siblings kept referencing, but hadn't asked any questions. Asking those questions now would be ideal for helping distract the others from the secret Phalra had almost blurted out.

"Troll nuts were a creation of the Ancient Elves. Harvesting them can be dangerous to people who are not Elves, but is merely unpleasant for us," Phalra explained. "It is a common Elvish prank to send another Elf to get them. The last time my brother and I met, he pulled that prank on me."

"And now she's returned the favor, she has," Wangdu said. "I suspected she might do this, she might, but I knew they'd prove useful in the future, they could."

El'Athras stood up from his perch and dusted himself off. "As fascinating as these white noise plants and troll nuts might be, I'd like to get us down into the tunnels before nightfall. So lend a hand, and help me find myself some kindling...."

Chapter XXX

"I have to say, this may not be in the same category as those steam locks or the rail thing we've also been introduced to in these tunnels, but it's no less impressive," Maelgyn said, admiring the view.

Upon opening the steam lock and making their way down into the tunnels, Maelgyn had been looking carefully at everything, wondering if he might see other secret Dwarven technologies that the Elves had been forcing them to hide. The antechamber they had entered included several more tunnel openings than the rail tunnel they had encountered last time. (one was sealed off, listed as being the route to Sho'Curlas itself. Another sealed tunnel was labeled as the route to Mar'Tok. The open paths were labeled as heading for Squire's Knot, Caseificio, Rubick, and a few other names Maelgyn didn't recognize but – he'd been told – were towns or regions in Poros and Oregal).

El'Athras explained that the rails were still working to Squire's Knot and Rubick, but that others in the system were damaged, either partially or completely. Often, these rails had been cannibalized to provide repair parts for the surviving rails, but if the tunnel itself was intact they kept it open. If it wasn't, they sealed it. Sometimes they might not have a rail system for a tunnel's entire length, but could provide transport to an underground Dwarven city that was part-way to their destination.

Such was the case with the tunnel they were taking. A quick rail trip (fascinating Phalra, who could not recall ever encountering such a device, even when the engineering feats of the Ancient Elves were still prevalent in the land) took them to one such Dwarven town, and it was that town Maelgyn found himself gawking at.

The air was thick and warm, unlike any natural cave he'd been in, and while not quite what he would describe as 'fresh' it wasn't stuffy, either. There were some pools of water, though Maelgyn couldn't see what was feeding them. There were some gardens, though what they were able to grow underground by the light of the gas flames they were using throughout the settlement Maelgyn couldn't tell. And, in addition to the gardens, various animals were also being farmed – sheep, goats, chickens, and donkeys, just in the sampling that Maelgyn could see – in farms and ranches that stretched out for quite a ways. The donkeys appeared to be these Dwarves beasts of burden, but Maelgyn's group had passed an abattoir where all the other variety of livestock were being dispatched for food and skins. It appeared this underground Dwarven colony was self-sufficient, at least in terms of food.

Some buildings were hewn out of stone, as they had been in Mar'Tok, but others were built of brick, still others built of bronze or copper... and the central buildings were, by far, the most astonishing. They appeared to be built of crystal, mostly amethyst and quartz, and looked to have been grown out of the floor. They were somewhat see-through, though what you could see was too distorted to distinguish any details. It was a type of architecture Maelgyn had never seen before, much less never imagined.

The Elves in his party, however, weren't nearly as astonished. Instead, they looked horrified.

"Where... where did you get these buildings from?" Phalra demanded, grabbing El'Athras by the collar of his armor.

El'Athras pulled out of her grip, looking somewhat ruffled but unsurprised. "When we reclaimed Mar'Tok from your kind, we found several structures like that in our city caves. We couldn't use them as residences, and the traditional government houses had survived the occupation intact. We weren't sure what to do with them until someone suggested moving them to become the government houses of our other underground communities, such as this one."

"They should never have been in Mar'Tok, they shouldn't," Wangdu said, shaking his head. "It should not be possible, it shouldn't."

"What's wrong with them?" Maelgyn asked. "They look... amazing."

"They're indeed amazing, they are," Wangdu agreed. "But no-one alive should be able to make them, they shouldn't. Such constructs were common in ancient times, they were, and many an Elven city were built in ways much like that building, they were. But when the Ancient Elves became the Modern Elves, they did, they lost the ability to make them, they did. It was something we sacrificed in the transition, we did. But the occupation of Mar'Tok occurred after that transition, it did, so there should not be anyone alive who could create them, there shouldn't."

Maelgyn frowned. "Well, you Elves are immortal. Wouldn't it be possible for an Ancient Elf or two to have avoided the transition and still have been around?"

"It's unlikely. All Elves were required to go through it, so any who didn't would have had to hide themselves. If he had been caught making these things, he would have been forced to undergo the transition," Phalra said. "The fact that these were not just made, but placed in a public area like Mar'Tok, and neither Wangdu nor I have even *heard* about them is troubling."

"A mystery for another time, perhaps," Maelgyn said. "After we have rescued Brode, I'll gladly take you both to the Library of Stanget. It has the most complete historical record in the Human world – if we have anything on the subject of these crystal structures or evidence of still-living Ancient Elves, it will be in there."

"We just hope that is all it is, we do," Wangdu said, staring at the crystal building again. "Anything else we know of that could build these, we do, would—"

"Would not be something we should talk about in public like this," Phalra said.

Wangdu seemed a bit startled, but then narrowed his eyes and nodded. "Yes, we should not discuss it here, we shouldn't."

El'Athras snorted. "A good thing, too – we've got other matters to attend to. Come – I'll take us to the local merchant's shop. We need to replenish our supplies before we continue for the next stretch of this journey."

If the local Dwarves were surprised to find Elves, Humans, and Nekoji in their secret tunnels, they didn't show it. El'Athras introduced Maelgyn to a pair of Dwarves who would have been their guides, had he still been stuck in Bandi – he'd sent word ahead to get preparations made for Maelgyn's arrival. Some food (though they had already replenished a portion of their expended supplies in Bandi), firewood, some camp gear, a few building materials, and some riding gear. It was only then that Maelgyn realized they would be riding donkeys, underground, from this nameless Dwarven settlement all the way into Poros.

Maelgyn had nothing against donkeys. They were strong working animals – pound for pound, they were far better pack animals – with other talents as well, but he absolutely hated riding them. It was very different riding a donkey and riding a horse; they responded differently to the riding cues he was used to, they were far more stubborn, and they couldn't exactly gallop. Then again, for a long ride, you don't want to be galloping a horse, either, but the other two things were true.

Then again, there were reasons to prefer them when not riding into battle. They were stronger, ran farther, needed fewer meals and less rest, and weren't nearly as skittish as even the best trained warhorses could be sometimes. And, considering they were underground, it was probably a good thing they were shorter, too, on average (a few were as large as some ponies, but that was about as big as they got). But all of that didn't make the idea of riding one pleasant.

Two days of riding later, when even his own wife was laughing at his discomfiture with the creatures, he found a renewed dislike for the animals, and was starting to wonder about those foreign dishes he'd heard of that required donkey meat to make. He'd have to ask Kiszaten if he knew how to prepare any of them when they got back to Svieda.

But they weren't in Poros, yet. It was the end of the second day's ride that El'Athras told them about the next leg of the journey.

"Well, we're as far down the original tunnel as we're going to go. We could go on, but it doesn't stop until you're almost at Lake Poros.

Sjouleber is closer to the western border of Poros, so we're going to need to take a detour."

Phalra frowned. "Western border? Hm. One reason I closed Bandi's borders was that there were a lot of Elves trying to cross through Bandi to get to a small town on the western border of Poros."

Maelgyn raised one curious eyebrow. "A lot of Elves, you say? That's... troubling. Just how large is the Porosian Conspiracy, anyway?"

"If they have more than a couple dozen Elves in their employ, they do, I would be shocked, I would," Wangdu said. "But they are traveling all over the land, they are, so it may appear as if there are more of them than truly exist, it may." Phalra didn't look so certain of his assessment, but she didn't seem willing to argue the point.

It was Euleilla who had the next question. "So, if we aren't going to take this tunnel all the way to Lake Poros, what are we supposed to do? Do you expect us to dig our way out of this tunnel?"

El'Athras snorted. "No need. There's already a route out... but you'll have to go the rest of the way on foot."

Maelgyn glanced over at his donkey. *Finally!* he cheered.

"It's also as far as we're going," Wodtke warned. "El'Athras and I will be here, taking care of the animals, while you go on ahead."

"But first, I'm going to be helping you guys build a staircase," El'Athras said, unloading the construction materials they had acquired back in the Dwarven settlement and setting them on the ground. "See, with a tunnel system like this, between the steamworks and the gas lanterns and all the people, the builders of this place had to include a lot of ventilation so that people could still breathe down here. It is through one such ventilation shaft that you will have to travel, for about one mile, in order to get to the surface. My people are able to climb up to it using a set of rope climbing gear, but we don't have enough sets of that for you guys."

That didn't seem like much of a chore, as far as Maelgyn was concerned. And it wasn't – with three Dwarves, two Elves, and four humans on the project, it didn't take long before a very rudimentary staircase had been put together.

It was then that Maelgyn discovered that travel by Donkey wasn't going to be the worst part of this trip. While the Dwarves, and even Lady Phalra (the shorter of their Elves), were able to walk through the passage standing up, none of the others could. He, Euleilla, and even Wangdu had to hunch over. Maelgyn, the tallest of the lot, had to hunch over more than any of the others. And walking more than a mile hunched over like that wasn't exactly pleasant.

And then there was the little matter that, at the end of their little detour, there didn't seem to be any way out of the vent. El'Athras had failed to provide them with instructions, and so they made camp and sent Tur'Ka back to find out just how they were supposed to open the darned thing.

Maelgyn just hoped that this was the last thing that would go wrong in their effort to rescue Brode.

There was only so much looking after you could do for a guy wrapped up in a cocoon. Hrabak had decided that it was safe enough to leave Hussack for the moment, now that his hibernation was stable, and return to civilization where he could hear the news, and give orders as appropriate. What he found was utter chaos.

Guards were posted on every doorway. More guards were running through the hallways, searching every room... and searching them again, later, just to be sure. Courtiers were weeping – outright weeping! – as they walked through the hallways. Something was very wrong, but Hrabak was finding it hard to figure out what.

His usual source of information came from sitting behind the king (he literally was the power behind the throne – he often hid in a small alcove no-one knew about but him, that allowed him to connect with that 'special' Elven wood that the throne was built with) as news was delivered to him, but there was no king to hear that news. Other than the silent guards stationed inside, with occasional search parties checking in to confirm that "he" hadn't returned, there was nothing.

Hrabak tried Fitz's suite, but there was no-one there... again, with the exception of a pair of guards on high alert. The Elf was starting to get a pretty good idea of what was going on, but he needed to talk with someone to confirm the details. And that could prove problematic – the guards seemed more likely to attack him than to answer any questions, as frightened as they seemed to be. His habit of rarely showing himself to anyone but the king himself was coming back to bite him.

Though there were a few people who did know Hrabak on sight.

With that in mind, he made his way down to the Royal Surgeon's office – that was the last Human he had seen (well, outside of that courier, but Hrabak knew that he would not be returning to the castle any time soon) and therefore the man most likely to answer his questions.

When Hrabak didn't want to be seen, he was as good as invisible. He slipped from shadow to shadow, then waited until the surgeon was alone. After a moment to reassure himself that the door was closed and locked, Hrabak stepped out of the shadows.

"So what's been going on while I was away?" he asked without preamble.

The surgeon jumped, nearly toppling over a nearby chair. It would have been a disaster, as his scalpel and several other sharp implements were on the table he fell against, but Hrabak caught him before he impaled himself.

"You! You startled me...."

"Of course I did," Hrabak laughed. "Now, tell me what has been going on. I haven't heard anything since we chopped off poor Hussack's arm. Well, except for the tiny bit of news that courier brought, but that wouldn't explain what's going on in the castle now."

"How is Prince Hussack?" the surgeon asked. "I've been worried about him since we finished that amputation."

"I did ask first," Hrabak said. "But okay, I'll tell you. He's currently in a cocoon. Now, are you going to answer my question, or am I going to have to show you why Elves are feared?"

The surgeon worked his mouth a bit, clearly biting back more questions. Hrabak laughed internally – he loved doing this kind of thing. It was always more satisfying when he was able to throw someone for a loop like this.

"Uh... right, well... I suppose I don't really know what's been going on in the war, so I can't help you, there," the surgeon said, shifting slightly on his feet. "But I can tell you some other news."

"I'm not interested in the war – the generals at the front can take care of that," Hrabak said. "But I'm very interested in this other news. Please – explain to me what's got this castle in such an uproar."

"Well, that's an easy question to answer," the surgeon said. "High King Fitz has disappeared, together with his wife and daughter-in-law. And with Hussack missing and Mussack dead, no-one is sure who should be giving orders right now."

"No-one? The Castellan should be in charge," Hrabak said, frowning. Where would his puppet have gone?

"The Castellan is trying to take charge, but many other of the higher-ranked noble courtiers aren't willing to let a low-ranked noble give them orders, and insist we seat a regent. With Hussack missing as well, there's some debate as to who should take that role – while Lord Knold has served as regent when Fitz was ill or otherwise temporarily unable to fulfill his duties in the past, he's now on the front lines of the war with Svieda. Whoever is next in line for the throne after Hussack is in dispute. The Captain of the Guard is only concerned with finding Fitz, and he's not having much success... though one of the guards told me that he may have been seen leaving in the direction of Poros, which just announced its reunification. That's also pretty big news, mind you, but with the king missing it's not something many of our people are thinking about."

"Hm," Hrabak said, amused. "Well... looks like those idiots have made their move. I guess it's time to make mine, and come out of the shadows."

El'Athras was grumbling about people "not knowing how to open a simple door" as he was brought back from his camp – Tur'Ka had caught him engaged in certain intimacies with Wodtke, much to his annoyance – but he quickly shut his mouth when he saw the vent exit. He then profusely apologized, saying that there usually were more intuitive ways to open these vents, and demonstrated a hidden catch that allowed the improvised exit to open. As an apology, he spent the next hour guiding them to the closest Porosian town, and found the contact Maelgyn had been supposed to look for to take them to their safe house.

That contact, an elderly man with a bronze prosthetic arm named Ganz, quickly ushered all of them – including El'Athras, who was insisting he needed to return – to a nondescript warehouse, where he locked the door behind them.

"Milord El'Athras," he said once they were all in private. "It is good that you are here. I have very important news."

El'Athras sighed. "Oh, very well. But I must return, soon – I am already further into Poros than I had any intention of coming. And

Wodtke will be wondering where I've gone."

Ganz nodded. "I know that you weren't intending to wait here, milord, but we must discuss this immediately. Earlier today, we learned that High King Fitz IV of Sho'Curlas slipped into East Poros last week. His arrival prompted a meeting of the leaders of all four Porosian factions, and the gathering was attended by some masked Elves we suspect are part of this conspiracy you're worried about. Immediately after that, the civil war which has split Poros for millennia ended... and Porosian armies began gathering along our southern border."

Maelgyn's eyes widened. "We don't have much time, then," he said. "Svieda needs its true king back. We have no time to rest – we need to head to Sjouleber tonight."

"That is another matter... um, whoever you are," Ganz said, looking a little confused.

"Maelgyn."

Ganz frowned, shaking his head. "We shouldn't use true names, here, but I think that was on the list of possible contacts I was given. There are more of you than I was told. I was expecting only one or two mages and an Elf."

"That was the original plan, but it got expanded," Maelgyn said, shrugging. He had been arguing for a smaller team from the beginning. "We now have two Elves, two mages, and two Dwarves. Well, three Dwarves with El'Athras, but he'll be returning home before we go to Sjouleber."

Ganz sighed. "It'll be hard to get you all into Sjouleber. Even harder if we leave right away. We've learned things about that town that suggest you might need those extra people, however. Especially if it comes to a fight."

"What's going on?" El'Athras said. "It's supposed to be a small town."

"That's just it," Ganz said. "It should be. That's what all the maps say, and what residents of nearby cities say, and what we've all believed. When we first learned that this Brode you're looking for was being held captive in that town, and that the Elves were using it for their headquarters, we thought it was just this small farming town, and that they were hiding out there because it was so obscure.

"But we were wrong. It isn't a small town any more – it is a fortress, made of materials we have never seen used in construction before. Moving through that town undiscovered will be incredibly difficult, and worse – it isn't just a small village militia and a few guards you have to worry about. We now think that the Elves who were part of the conspiracy have taken up permanent residence and put the town on a war footing. We've seen a lot of them coming and going, including those Elves we recently saw meeting with the Porosian leaders."

Maelgyn grimaced. "How many Elves?"

"We can't get close enough to tell," Ganz said. "We are fairly certain this Brode person is there, but we have no real knowledge of what is inside that town, how it's defended, or where within the town he might be. We've identified at least five teams of three or four Elves, each, who periodically enter and leave Sjouleber, and we've identified at least four other Elves who will stand guard on Sjouleber's walls, but that's the best we've been able to see."

"Wait, Sjouleber has walls?" Maelgyn said. "The plan was to slip into the town from the surrounding woods – if they've got walls, that doesn't seem possible."

Ganz nodded. "No, it isn't. The only entrance is the front gate. And that's only half the problem – they don't allow any strangers inside. No supply carts, peddlers, or travelers of any kind. So... it won't be easy getting inside, but we think we've got an idea how to get there. Of course, once inside, it'll be hard to hide the fact that you're all strangers, and that you've got a couple Dwarves with you." He paused. "It might be better if you try some other way of recovering this man. This rescue attempt may not be possible."

El'Athras frowned, then glanced over at Maelgyn. "This doesn't sound good. I know that no plan is perfect, but we haven't even gotten to the start of the plan and it's already fallen apart. I recognize that rescuing Brode is important, but perhaps you should retreat for now and wait until we have a better read on this 'small town' that is suddenly so much more than we realized."

Maelgyn knew he should have done this with an army. He glanced at the others, gauging whether this news was concerning them much. Tur'Tei and Tur'Ka looked resigned, Euleilla reasonably confident, and... he really couldn't read what his Elven companions were thinking. There wasn't really enough information to make his decision, however. "Brode is my cousin, and I'm not about to leave him in captivity if I can avoid it. If the Porosian Conspiracy is making its move now, as it seems, I'm not sure we'll get another chance. I'm not saying we should necessarily go ahead and make the rescue attempt, but I would like to get close enough to Sjouleber to make my own assessment of the situation."

El'Athras grudgingly agreed. "I suppose that makes some sense. But you mustn't take any unnecessary risks, Maelgyn. I felt you should be part of this mission because of your unique skills, but that was when we thought there would be little opposition to rescuing Brode. If there are more than a dozen Elves in Sjouleber, as Ganz suggests, I am not sure it's wise for you to put yourself at risk. If you were captured...."

"I know," Maelgyn said. "But I'm a High Mage, Euleilla is a First Rate Mage, and we've got two Elves of our own." He paused, glancing at his armsmen, who looked a little perturbed at not being mentioned. "Plus, I've got two personal guards who will die before they allow anything to happen to us. We are in good hands, so we should be safe. The question is more whether we can get Brode out, I think, than whether or not we are in much danger."

El'Athras frowned. "Your Highness... it is unwise to become overconfident. You may be a High Mage, which – yes – would make you the most powerful mage in the Human race. But there are more powerful beings out there than Humans, as you are well aware – if there are dozens of Elves in this town, you would be in *great* danger."

Maelgyn winced. "I... well, of course. Together, the seven of us could probably only handle four Elves at a time, ourselves. We—"

"The lot of you might be able to handle a dozen Elves, if they're the right Elves. Conversely, you may not be able to handle even one Elf, if it's the wrong Elf. Please, your Highness – while I agree you need to check out the situation, and that there really might not be another change to rescue your cousin, he would not appreciate it if you killed yourselves trying to rescue him. Once the Porosian Conspiracy reveals itself, and it sounds like they will be doing so soon, there will be other ways of recovering Sword Brode. Negotiations, prisoner exchanges...."

"Assuming they don't kill him, or pretend they don't have him to hide the fact they've got a spy on our own throne," Maelgyn said.

"Look, I'm not going to go in if I don't think we can handle it."

El'Athras looked to the others for support. Maelgyn checked, as well – of his people, none of them looked unwilling to try. Only Ganz seemed sympathetic to El'Athras – even the other Dwarves seemed more on his side than El'Athras' side. Still, this wasn't about a popularity contest.

"Just... be careful. It's more important that you live than that you rescue Brode now. We can always return here after we've had more time to assess the situation – the Dwarven tunnels aren't going anywhere."

"Of course," Maelgyn said.

El'Athras sighed. "Well... this is where I take my leave of you, then. I think I will send Wodtke to this safehouse, so you'll have a doctor on hand, and go back to Svieda myself. Our people all need to be warned."

Maelgyn nodded. "Yes – it's looking that way. Poros is probably siding with Sho'Curlas, and will be striking at us through Rubick, soon. Our forces need to prepare."

"I can probably get word to Rocky Run, but the invasion will happen before we can send news to the Royal City," El'Athras said. "So keep that in mind when you return; go back home the way you came, and don't try taking Brode straight to the throne. We'll be better off sending him there by ship."

Maelgyn's eyes widened. "I'm not sure we'll be rescuing him, now – if Sjouleber proves too dangerou—"

"Your Highness, I know you too well," El'Athras said. "I've done my best to warn you about the danger of going in, but I know you will, anyway. And I know you'll succeed. Just... try not to lose anyone when you do."

Chapter XXXI

Ganz directed them to a "rear approach." Evidently, the town was built backing into a short cliff; a natural wall that he thought Maelgyn and his people would be able to climb down in secret, with as small of a group as they had. Ganz hoped they would be in an ideal position to survey the town from the top of that cliff, though he warned them that he didn't know what threats they might find going down that path.

It was a steep cliff, but it wasn't especially tall; it was a hill-side cliff, and not a mountain, that Sjouleber was backing into. Maelgyn spotted some wooden watch-towers covering their route, but not enough to fully cover the approach – even a party Maelgyn's size could slip passed the watch, once twilight descended.

But when they reached the cliff, there was no question about going in. The Elves wouldn't let them leave.

"We must go in and see what is going on, we must," Wangdu insisted.

"I think we need to do more than just 'see what's going on,'" Phalra said. "We need to act."

Maelgyn was surprised it was the Elves who were being so hotheaded, and not himself – Brode was his cousin, after all, and one would think that a mission to rescue Brode might be his concern more than any of the others.

That was until he saw the walls that Sjouleber had built around itself. As with the administrative building in the Dwarven tunnel town, Sjouleber's walls were made of giant crystals – mostly amethyst, and grown out of the ground.

Honestly, he wasn't sure he was comfortable with the idea of entering the town. It wasn't quite city-sized, but it was much larger than he'd been told, and there were people everywhere. Armed people – it looked like several brigades, if not an entire army division. And there was no way of knowing exactly where Brode was being kept, from what he could tell – the only way they would be able to find him would be to search from building to building.

But now it seemed as if Wangdu and Phalra were desperate to go in. Something about those crystalline walls really angered them.

"Okay, you two really need to explain just why this alarms you so much," Maelgyn said. "It can't just be that this is a lost technology, or you wouldn't be panicking like this. What about these crystalline walls has you so upset?"

Wangdu and Phalra looked at each other in silent discussion. Maelgyn couldn't quite read all of the body language, but it ended with a brief nod from brother to sister.

"It has to do with the process through which crystals of this size are created," Phalra said, hesitating. "Small crystals are easy to produce – you can grow these crystals inside an emptied eggshell, if you have the right materials – but these aren't small crystals. These are massive things, and that process won't work for them. For crystals of this size, you need a lot of heat and a lot of pressure. To create the necessary pressure, you needed a very thick-walled stone or ceramic chamber. The best of our technology can create forges or kilns that will easily reach those temperatures, but not in the thick-walled vessels of that size. No, to make crystals that large, you need a very large Dragon-fired crystal kiln. Enslaved dragons. We were supposed to give up enslaving dragons upon transitioning to our modern selves, and that forced us to give up this style of traditional Elven architecture."

Maelgyn winced. "Well... there are trained Black Dragons, so perhaps—"

"No, the Black Dragons have relatively cool fire. So do Red Dragons. Golden Dragons might manage it, as their fires are the equal of their Ancient kin... but only if you have several of them concentrating on one kiln. However...."

"However, no Golden Dragon would ever consent to work with an Elf – not after the centuries of captivity your people held all dragons in," Maelgyn said, frowning. "Perhaps the people here figured out some other way of producing these crystals? If the problem is the temperature of the fire, maybe they've found some new fuel that burns hotter than the charcoal-fired kilns and forges we use in other industries."

"Possible," Phalra admitted.

"But that is very unlikely, it is," Wangdu said. "At least finding one that gets it *that* much hotter, it is. We need to investigate, we do."

"If they are enslaving dragons, they must be stopped," Phalra said. "The only reason the Elves are still alive is that we negotiated a peace with the Golden Dragons, assuring them we would never enslave a dragon of any breed again – we are even forbidden from riding Black Dragons, which your people are not. While our people no longer have a true government that represents all of them, that is one law established when we transited from the Ancient to the Modern Elves that we must keep. It was biomancied into our very bodies as a part of the transition. It should not even be possible for an Elf to enslave a dragon!"

"Unless that Elf was never a part of the transition, he wasn't," Wangdu said slowly. "And does not respect the treaty, he doesn't. I did not believe any survived, I didn't, but perhaps you are right, you are, and there is some other way they've discovered to make these crystals, they have. We must investigate either way, we must. It is in our nature, it is. And if a dragon were to see these walls, it was...."

"I understand the situation, but I hope you have a plan to get us inside that fortress without being spotted. And you know what you're looking for. Look, I want to go in – I really do – but El'Athras was right; it is far too dangerous for us to enter that city, as things are." Maelgyn said. "Maybe if we made a concerted effort to get more spies here and get an idea of the layout of this place, we could do something, but as it is...."

"You did not think it too dangerous to storm a fortified stronghold by yourself, you didn't," Wangdu said, not taking his eyes off of the city below.

"Did he, now?" Phalra said, amused. "I'm going to have to do some catching up to learn just what my new ally and matchmaker is capable of."

"That was a somewhat different type of fort," Maelgyn pointed out. "And I wasn't by myself – you were there. And there were no Elves on the opposite side. And I had a pretty good idea what I was getting myself into. And we had a plan. And I still almost died, and would have if Euleilla hadn't already pretty much escaped on her own in time to save me."

"I think I can grow a vine ladder down to that spot over there, behind the houses, where none of the lights are shining," Phalra said, pointing. "Care to assist?"

"You had better make it stronger than your usual ladders, you had," Wangdu cautioned. "I'll reinforce them where I can, I will, but these Dwarves are too heavy despite their size, they are. They weigh nearly four times what Maelgyn does, they do, and you know Humans weigh almost twice what a similar-sized Elf does, they do."

"Right – I'll make it strong enough to hold an army of trolls," Phalra said.

"So you're seriously—" Maelgyn started to say.

"Be a dear and magic up about fifty iron steps for me, would you?" Phalra asked him. "About so long and so wide, one inch thick at least, with two holes an inch in diameter on either side."

Maelgyn frowned. "I'd need some spare raw materials for that. There's barely enough iron in these parts for one step like that, much less fifty."

"He's right, he is," Wangdu said, walking over to a nearby tree. He examined it briefly. "We'll make do with wood."

That said, the tree started, well, Maelgyn might call it 'shedding' lengths of board in the correct size and shape for what Phalra had asked. It only was able to provide about a dozen of them before it started looking a little thin, but Wangdu went to another tree and it started providing the same wooden steps to him.

Maelgyn huffed, looking over at Euleilla and the Dwarves. "Well?"

Euleilla shrugged. "If the Elves have lost their minds over this, we're in trouble no matter what we do. We might as well follow them and see if we can't find Sword Brode while we're there, though I'm not keen on searching house-to-house for him."

"I'll follow your lead, but it seems to me we should go in, since we're here, and try and get some grasp of the kind of war machine they're building here," Tur'Ka mused. "Bandi is our new ally, and any soldiers posted here are well positioned to target them. Is the force here purely defensive, or do they have enough of an army to launch an attack? We do need to know that."

Euleilla frowned. "It's a shame I've never been around the real Brode, before – it would have helped me to find his magical signature. But... tell me, did that Merfolk truly look like him?"

"If it weren't for his behavior, I would have been fooled," Maelgyn said. "Well... there were some differences in body language. But appearance-wise? He was a perfect duplicate."

"Then perhaps I can do some searching, anyway. If I can get within about a hundred yards of him, even if he is behind closed doors, I will be able to find him."

"So not house to house, but more like block to block," Maelgyn sighed. "Well, it's something. If we're really careful, we might be able to avoid detection... as long as our Elven siblings over there don't give us away with their fanatical search for whatever is creating those giant crystals."

Tur'Ka coughed into his hand. "I know it's not my place to advise, your Highness, but..."

"Go ahead," Maelgyn said, acknowledging the Dwarf with a wave. "And please, both of you, feel free to speak your minds. You undoubtedly know more about the kind of high-risk clandestine work we're getting involved in, here, than any of us."

Tur'Ka shared a look with Tur'Tei and nodded. He pulled out his dagger and walked over to a patch of dirt under one of the trees, where he started carving something in the dirt. It took a moment before Maelgyn realized he was drawing a map. "Well, your Highness, if we apply a little logic, we might be able to give your lady's search a greater chance of success, and minimize the risk to ourselves. Now, we're approaching from the rear of their defenses, here. They have buildings backing up into this cliff.

"From a soldier's perspective, this location is a tactical nightmare. I get the funny feeling they know that, but they're counting on their obscurity to give them time to build up defenses more sound than those watch towers – this crystal wall production technique those Elves of yours describe sounds slow-going, so they erected their first defense against accidental intrusion by shutting off the frontal approach... but they have those watch towers, so they know they're in danger from up here.

"The defenses they've already established are likely designed to go after archers and siege weapons – they don't expect infantry to come over the cliff in the first wave of attack. Any infantry descending from here will get in, sure, but they lose the advantage of the high ground. So their defenses will mostly be anti-archer archery batteries. But since they have seen no army – the thing that those watch-towers are guarding against – they probably aren't concerned about a few people like us approaching from the cliff side, like your Elves are preparing for us to do. They will likely have some kind of force that can respond to attacks from our direction, but it, too, isn't likely to be on the alert just yet.

"So if you exercise a little bit of caution against the unexpected or the lucky eye, you don't need to worry about their defenses. Not really – if you get spotted, things will start happening too fast and too hard for any sort of plan to be effective, so let's just plan on *not* being seen getting into town. Instead, you need to think more about where they might keep a high profile prisoner, and how to get there without raising any alarms."

Maelgyn nodded slowly. "Okay... that makes sense. Assuming we actually go with those crazy Elves at all, that's what we should do."

"Well, that means we want to check out these banks of buildings, if at all possible. From our vantage point, we've been able to see street patrols covering this area here, this alleyway, these streets...."

Maelgyn listened with a little surprise as Tur'Ka continued to lay out a strategy they might use to search for Brode, aided by the occasional grunt or gesture from his fellow Dwarf, Tur'Tei. It wasn't so much surprising that he could come up with such a plan – though it was further evidence confirming Maelgyn's suspicion that Tur'Ka's career before becoming his bodyguard involved a little more work in espionage than he had admitted to, so far – but rather that he was making the attempt seem plausible.

Sure, the whole premise (getting into town and being able to move through those crowded streets undetected) seemed unlikely, but it looked like the usually level-headed Elves were going to go in no matter what they said. Better to go with an implausible plan than no plan at all.

Speaking of the impossible, Maelgyn couldn't help but glance over at Phalra, who seemed to be growing vines of unnatural length and girth out of ground that didn't look fertile at all. He'd not seen either Elf with any seeds, either (outside of those 'troll nuts,' whatever they were), so these vines must have come out of something growing locally.

Elf magic. Maelgyn wasn't sure he would ever understand it, even with Sekhar's internal guidance.

A couple hours later, they had their plan, they had their ladder, and the night had grown darker. Maelgyn didn't even get that one last chance to try and talk the Elves out of it like he'd hoped for – they were already heading down the ladder before he noticed. They didn't even really need those steps they'd put on it, themselves – those were entirely for the benefit of the Humans and Dwarves, it seemed.

Well, they had a plan, and they couldn't let their Elves go in alone, could they?

With a sigh and a few hand gestures – no longer willing to risk vocal cues, even though they were probably out of earshot of any Porosians – he led the others down the ladder, using his magic to keep watch for any arrow shots that any observant watchmen might send their way. It seemed they managed to avoid prying eyes, however, and they were now on the small strip of grass that was between the cliff face and the village.

"All right," Phalra whispered. "You take your people and go look for your missing man. Wangdu and I need to investigate things."

"Are you sure that's a good idea?" Maelgyn whispered back. "How will we find each other again once we separate?"

"We'll meet back here, we will," Wangdu answered for her. "We need two hours, we do, so you can use that time for your search, you can. We can take care of ourselves, we can, but you had better stay safe, you had."

Maelgyn just sighed at the audacity, looking away and counting to ten in his head to rein in his temper. By the time he looked back up, the Elves had slipped into the shadows and vanished from sight.

Shaking his head, he again started using hand signals to direct Euleilla and the two Dwarves as they started their search. It was slow going – Euleilla could pick out the 'appearance' of a person inside the range she said, but it took her a while for it to get clear enough to identify everyone. Maelgyn was trying to help using his own version of the technique, but he feared that all he was doing was redundantly checking areas she was able to check faster and more thoroughly than he.

It was after about an hour of searching that she first indicated anything, but Maelgyn had noticed some strange things in his own search that he figured she would want to discuss. However, when she stopped them it was with a wide smile on her face.

"I found him," she whispered, pointing two buildings down. It was a nondescript wooden building – the kind of building they might have overlooked if they hadn't had magical assistance to speed themselves up. "Two guards, both inside. Humans, and I think one of them is asleep."

Maelgyn nodded. He was trying to keep in his elation, but it was hard – he had given up on his cousin after seeing Sjouleber from that cliff side, but this gave him new hope. Maybe they would be able to save Brode, after all.

He slipped around the alley to check out the street in front of that building's door. There were a few people in the distance down the road, but as dark as it was they were just silhouettes. They would have to be careful, but it should be possible to get into the building without being seen.

"Euleilla," he whispered. "Get the lock. I'll keep a lookout."

Euleilla and the Dwarves followed him out of the alleyway, trying to keep from looking too conspicuous. Maelgyn shook his head – the Dwarves were doing okay, but Euleilla was telegraphing "we're doing suspicious things" with every bit of her body language. If anyone saw them, they would know right away that they weren't supposed to be there. He kept an eye on the distant silhouettes.

Every noise was getting to Maelgyn. A dog barking in the distance, a night bird's call, even an insect's mating call was making him jumpy. He had a funny feeling he was telegraphing just as much as his wife.

"The lock is open," Euleilla whispered.

Maelgyn concentrated on the people inside. Yes, there were just three – one person asleep, one behind prison bars, and a third who was sitting at the door. Of course, opening the door would waken the sleeping person, so they had to account for both of them... and before any alarm could be made or Brode could be killed.

"Tur'Tei, open the door, and go in fast with Euleilla. Tur'Ka, you follow behind me and close the door, then I'll re-lock it – we'll have most of an hour to wait in here before we can return to the rendezvous point."

"Got it," Tur'Ka said. He was the only one of them that spoke.

Maelgyn raised his fingers, counting down from five. When he got to zero, he shook his fist and tapped Euleilla to indicate it was time to act. The door slammed open and they rushed in, Tur'Tei and Euleilla in front... a little faster than he'd planned, actually. By the time he was through the door, Euleilla had already grabbed the 'awake' guard and pinned him against the wall with her ironwood staff, and she was delivering a punch to his jaw that knocked him out.

Maelgyn didn't have time to admire her handiwork, having to deal with the other guard who was pulling himself out of bed. A handful of magic powder was used to help pin him into his sheets while he made his way across the room. Maelgyn didn't want to run the risk of the noise drawing his Sword, but an armor-gloved hand and a magic-enhanced fist could do wonders. Moments later, the second guard was unconscious or dead from the blow, and Maelgyn didn't really care which – if he was unconscious, it would be some time before he awoke and caused problems; if he was dead, he would never be a problem again.

Tur'Ka finally slipped into the building, almost slamming the door behind them. A quick moment to fix the lock and they were secure. Maelgyn gestured to Tur'Tei, who along with Tur'Ka started tying up the two guards.

And then Maelgyn finally risked a glance at the cell door, just to be sure they had rescued the right person.

"Who... Maelgyn? Maelgyn, is that you?" the prisoner said.

He was in what looked like a battered nightgown, with no other clothes or possessions in his cell. He looked a bit thinner than Maelgyn recalled him, and had started going prematurely bald though what hair remained was growing fairly long. He also didn't appear to have shaved in months, given the size and shape of the beard... but underneath the beard, the hair, and the bad clothing, it was clear that this was unmistakably the real Sword Prince Brode, Duke of Glorest.

Maelgyn grinned. "Hello, cousin. Long time no see."

Wangdu was starting to feel a bit guilty. He and his sister had already almost been caught four times, and they were far better at hiding in the shadows than Maelgyn would ever be. He had charged himself with keeping Maelgyn and the rest of the royal Sviedan bloodline safe (or at least to keep their kingdom out of the clutches of the likes of Hrabak), yet here he was almost forcing Maelgyn to take part in one of the riskiest operations he'd ever attempted.

"Have you seen how many Elves there are wandering these roads?" Phalra whispered to him.

Wangdu nodded. "It's certainly a lot more than the two dozen we were estimating, it is. I have to wonder if all of these Elves are a part of the Porosian Conspiracy, I do. I have heard nothing about any conclave of Elves, I haven't. Have you heard anything about this, have you?"

Phalra shook her head. "Like I said, we've noticed a lot more Elven traffic around Bandi, lately, but I knew nothing of this. There must be hundreds of Elves, here."

"And all of the Elves I see seem to be of a more martial persuasion, they are. This does not bode well, it doesn't."

Phalra nodded, pointing over at a building with a decidedly Elven theme. It wasn't crystalline, but it did resemble the architecture a lot of Elves used for new construction in the more modern Elven kingdoms. And it looked old. "They've been here for a while, too. The town walls are plainly new, though, and they clearly haven't finished with them. Whatever or whoever is making them must have arrived here recently."

"I have not seen anything that could make those wall-crystals, I haven't," Wangdu sighed. "And we are running out of time, we are. We should head back now, we should, so that we can help Maelgyn with his escape, we can."

"I think... uh oh."

Wangdu frowned, glancing over at his sister, waiting for her to continue on. When she didn't say anything for several more minutes he started to get worried. "Is there something wrong, is there?"

Phalra sighed and pointed. Wangdu looked over and saw she was pointing at an Elf in a very peculiar set of armor. He thought he vaguely recognized it, but he couldn't tell for sure what was so special about it. It was clearly Elven, and perhaps living – maybe it was an artifact of the Ancient Elves, even – but he saw nothing beyond that which was a cause for alarm. He waited for her to give him more information.

"I was very young when I last saw him," she whispered. "But I would recognize him anywhere. That is Lord Ajiro."

Wangdu's eyes widened. "That cannot be, it can't! He died before I was born, he did!"

"But not before I was born," Phalra said. "And it appears he isn't quite as dead as was believed. Remember, he refused to participate in the ritual that changed the Elves from Ancient to Modern. Three Elven kings captured him swearing to make him undertake the ritual, and three times he was released and became the general of the next king's armies instead."

"Hrabak was the last person to see him alive, he was," Wangdu said, his mind working fiercely. "That was supposed to be before he went insane, it was. But suppose Hrabak was insane even in that time, he was... would he have any reason to lie, would he?"

Phalra didn't answer for a long moment. "I don't know what's going on with these crystals – I know Ajiro swore an oath, binding on his Elven magic, never to enslave a Golden Dragon, which was the only way even he was able to escape the ritual so often. But—"

"But suppose Ajiro enslaved a Dragon that wasn't a Golden Dragon, he did," Wangdu said. "Suppose he found and enslaved a different type of Dragon, he did... or suppose he created and enslaved an entirely new type of Dragon, he did. He would not be violating his oath, wouldn't."

Phalra shuddered. "If Ajiro is here... this just became an entirely different kind of war."

Chapter XXXII

While they waited nervously, Maelgyn tried to relieve the tension by regaling Brode with the tale of his impostor's actions in Svieda. Brode was getting more and more anxious to leave, as if getting out of the prison now would get him his seat on the throne any faster. They couldn't risk leaving the building yet, however, and Euleilla was reporting to them more worrisome news every few minutes – the guards were out in force, for some reason, and it was looking increasingly unsafe to leave.

As it was, they would be late arriving at their scheduled rendezvous. That worried Maelgyn more than anything. Brode, though, wasn't worried about schedules – he simply wanted to escape after so many months in that cramped cell.

"Well, I'm not pleased to hear that there's been a Merfolk fooling everyone into thinking he was me during these months I've been in captivity," Brode said. "But I'm free, finally! I hope you have some kind of weapon for me, though – I would rather go out fighting than be stuck in that damned cell, again."

"It doesn't look like they've been treating you that badly," Maelgyn said, looking his cousin up and down. "Though you could stand a shave."

Brode chuckled half-heartedly, scratching a spot under his beard. Maelgyn recognized that nervous habit from when he had his own beard. "Yes, well, that's partly my fault. They gave me a razor to shave with when I first got here, but I tried using it to hold my guard hostage and force my release. They didn't even bargain – they just killed the guard for being captured and took away my razor. I haven't had a knife for any of my meals, either, which has made eating a bit difficult, sometimes."

"What's with all the Elves?" Tur'Ka said. "Your guards, here, were human, but we've had to avoid scads of Elves sneaking through the town to get here, and there are more outside."

"I don't really know," Brode said. "I do know they have a leader named 'Lord Ajiro' who appears to be something of a legend even among other Elves. And there are more Elves here than any gathering of Elves I've heard of since the fall of the last Elven kingdom, that much I'm fairly certain of. But beyond that? I have no idea."

Maelgyn considered this, recalling Wangdu and Phalra's rationale for coming into the city. "What about Dragons. Have you heard of any Dragons flying about?"

Brode flinched. "What makes you ask that?"

"We came here with two of our own Elves," Maelgyn explained. "They were looking for an Elf who may have been illegally enslaving some Dragons. They were very worried of the repercussions if one of their kind were to be caught doing so."

"Well, I haven't heard anything flying overhead," Brode said. "But there was—"

"Clear!" Euleilla called.

Maelgyn caught himself mid-response; it would have to wait. "Tell me later. We need to go, now, if we want to have any hope of leaving this place."

"Don't have to tell me, twice," Brode said, walking over to one of the trussed-up guards. There was no time to don any armor, not that what the guards had on would fit him, but he did grab a sword and shield. "Let's get going, then."

They slipped out of the door and Maelgyn immediately knew something unusual was happening. It was the middle of the night, and there were multiple armed patrols running around the street. Mostly Humans, but he was noticing at least one Elf with each group of soldiers. None of them were close enough to identify him, he hoped, but it would be hard to hide from them for very long.

"Hurry up," he ordered, gesturing for his people to slip through the same alleyway they had come from.

He feared they had been seen, and so redirected them down a different set of alleys, even crossing through a garden instead of letting them be seen on the street, and moving in a sort of zig-zag pattern until they were several turns away from where anyone would have seen them leaving the prison. There was a problem with this approach, however.

"Okay, now that I've gotten us completely and thoroughly lost, can anyone figure out how we get back to the rendezvous point?" he asked quietly. They were already late, and now Maelgyn was realizing his maneuvers to keep from being seen were going to cause worse problems. This was not good.

Tur'Tei grunted, gesturing to follow him. Maelgyn had never been happier about having accepted the two Dwarves as armsmen as he was at that moment – but getting them all killed or captured because he got his people lost was not an epitaph he wanted on his tombstone.

The silent Dwarf was doing an exceptionally good job of guiding them down various side streets, keeping everyone out of sight. Once again, Maelgyn was reminded that these two Dwarves did have experience as spies... and he was starting to see how the Dwarves could be so effective in that role, even in communities where the presence of a single Dwarf would have been seen as remarkable.

They finally made it to the stretch of grass behind the village, and Maelgyn couldn't see any people on the grounds. Waving everyone past, he sent everyone at a run towards the rendezvous point. He just hoped that Wangdu and Phalra would be there when they arrived, because he didn't have time to wait for them if they weren't.

He caught up with the others at the base of the cliff, where their ladder to freedom was supposed to be... only it wasn't there.

"Are we in the wrong spot?" he asked, looking around.

Euleilla shook her head. "No... there are iron deposits nearby. I noticed them when we came down the cliff. They're still here."

"Then... where's the ladder?"

"And where are Wangdu and Phalra?" Euleilla asked, herself.

"Not here, obviously," Tur'Ka said, slowly loosening his axe. "But if the ladder is missing, they're the only way we have of getting out of here."

Brode frowned. "All right, then – who are Wangdu and Phalra?"

"Two Elves. Spearmaster Wangdu, who I met in Mar'Tok, and Lady Phalra, Praetor of Bandi," Maelgyn said.

"Lady Phalra? Are we sure we should be relying on a crazy woman like that?" Brode asked.

"There's a lot we still have to fill you in on, cousin," Maelgyn said. He glanced around, extending all of his senses including his magical and *schlipf* senses. "You know, I don't see anyone here watching us, but the missing ladder has me spooked. We can't just sit here, waiting for some kind of trap to be sprung."

"Well, where do you suggest we go, then?" Brode asked dryly. "Should we just stroll through the town and leave out the front exit, or maybe see if we can't find a nice inn to spend the night in?"

"Well, if we can't find Wangdu or Phalra or some other sympathetic Elf, I fear that's the only thing we can do." He paused. "You've been here a while. I don't suppose you know your way around the streets?"

"I was never allowed out of my cell – not even to bathe," Brode said. "I'm surprised you haven't complained about the smell."

"We'll have to make for the wall," Tur'Ka suggested. "And follow it all the way to the exit. And we can't afford to be subtle at that point – we'll have to fight our way out."

"That must be why there are so many patrols on the road," Brode said. "They found your ladder and removed it. They know we can't get out that way, so they're going to post extra guards on the exit and they want to catch us in the town."

"Well, then, let's *not* go to the exit," Euleilla said.

"You mean you think we should just stay here?" Brode asked.

"No. I think we should find Wangdu and Phalra. And rescue them, if necessary," Euleilla said.

Brode stared at her incredulously for a moment. "You married a real firebrand, didn't you, cousin? There's an army of Elves out there. How will we even find them?"

"The same way we found you," Maelgyn said. "Logic. Tur'Ka – we know roughly where Wangdu and Lady Phalra were going to look for this possible enslaved dragon, and you probably remember the map of Sjouleber you were making better than I do. Suppose they are on their way back here, but the extra patrols are making them take a detour. Where would that detour take them?"

Tur'Ka looked at him, frowning. "You aren't asking much, are you? I... well, maybe I can begin to guess, but the number of options is pretty large. There are dozens of places they may be holding up."

"Well, there's only a few more hours until dawn – we'd better get started," Brode laughed. "Lead the way, friend Dwarf."

"We need to hurry up, we do," Wangdu said. "Maelgyn is undoubtedly waiting for us by now, he is."

"We left them the ladder," Phalra said. "They should be able to make their escape without us. We need to see who else is here. I've already identified Soudek, Doshkin, Jennike, and Volek. With Ajiro, that's five of the twelve generals of the last Elven kingdom. What is going on here?"

"It certainly doesn't fit the story that the 'Porosian Conspiracy' Elves told Maelgyn, it doesn't," Wangdu said. "But we must escape, we must, and we should warn the others, we should."

"I... that's Salmi! That makes six of the old generals!"

"If I were to make a guess, I were, I would say this looks like the beginnings of a resurrected Elven kingdom, it does," Wangdu said, frowning.

Phalra frowned. "Why, though? The Elven race is dying, however immortal our people are. We may have a birth once a century, probably fewer, and as powerful and immortal as we are, dozens of us die each year. When the Elven King died, we foresaw our entire race dying out, however many thousands of years it will take. We thought it best to use our time to guide the other races – or lesser races, as some of us thought of them – to replace us. Why—"

"Ajiro is still one of the Ancients, he is," Wangdu said. "As long as he survives, he does, the transition to Modern Elves can be reversed, it can." He paused. "The Ancient Elves bred more frequently, they did – perhaps they were not as fertile as Humans, they weren't, but fast enough. Elven numbers would increase again, they would."

Phalra shook her head. "Not like this. We made the change for a reason, and I would never go back... whatever my 'libido issues' may be. In the last moments of our sanity as a race, we knew we should never be entrusted with that power again; I will not question it now that I know we are all insane."

"I see another of the Elven generals, I do," Wangdu said. "I think it's Terao, I do."

"Terao!" Phalra exclaimed. "The five remaining are Sawada, Kuji, Kondo, Yakura, and Farynuk. Kondo fell when the King died. Sawada and Kuji led the rebellion to preserve the kingdom, and were executed after they were captured. When *Ajiro* captured them. That leaves Yakura and Farynuk."

"Farynuk was the one who proposed dissolving the Elven kingdoms, he was," Wangdu said. "He would not be a part of this, he wouldn't."

"And Yakura led the opposition... which consisted of all the other generals. Sawada and Kuji may have been the only ones to raise arms against the idea, but the others—"

"Went into a secret council, they did," Wangdu said. "And then they all withdrew themselves from the world in protest, they did. But suppose they didn't really withdraw, they didn't. Suppose they just started working in secret, they did..."

"This many of our greatest generals... Wangdu, can the Human world stand against all of them?"

Wangdu sighed, scanning all the Elves he saw. "Trained Elven warriors are a force to be feared, they are. I am not a trained Elven warrior—"

"You reached the rank of Spearmaster, brother. The only reason you aren't a 'trained Elven warrior' is that you had to teach yourself. There are a lot of 'trained Elven warriors' I know who you are more powerful and more skilled than. I am a trained Elven warrior, and you're more powerful than me."

"—I'm not, but I know it takes more than a year or two of training to earn the title of Elven Warrior title, I do." Wangdu gestured to where the Elven generals were in discussion with various small gatherings of other Elves. "Not every Elf is a trained warrior, they aren't. Not many true Elven warriors survived our civil war, they didn't. They may have a few dozen, they might, which may be why that's all the Elves we saw acting for the conspiracy, it might. Few of these Elves would count as warriors, they would. Most of them are no better fighter than an average Human mage, they are." He shook his head. "Even when the Elves had trained warriors, they did, they lost wars to Humans and Dwarves on many occasions, they did. Svieda has more mages than any other Human nation, they do. And the Golden Dragons will help them, they will."

"Svieda can probably handle the footsoldiers, yes," Phalra agreed. "It takes good fortifications and a lot of preparation, but an Elven Army can be defeated. But the Twelve Elven Generals themselves? The last surviving front-line soldiers from the Tengu wars? Only another Elven general has ever beaten one of them in battle. And with Ajiro, the last of the Ancient Elves?" She shook her head. "You and I may be 'Elven warriors,' but he is on another level."

"Then we will need to find another one as well, we will," Wangdu said. "Farynuk is still out there, he is. But Svieda will need to stand until we can find him, it will. And Sho'Curlas is not going to stop their war just because of this, it won't."

Phalra sighed. "You are right, brother... we need to get back to the rendezvous. He must be warned, Bandi must be warned, Svieda must be warned, Oregal must be warned... perhaps even Sho'Curlas must be warned."

"It might be wise if someone did, it might," a third voice said. Phalra and Wangdu spun around, seeing a third Elf wearing a red mask. "But you will not be the ones to deliver that warning, you won't."

Phalra's face twisted, though whether that was in fear or anger it was hard to tell. "I see you still hide your face, Yakura, and yet reject your armor. The only one of the Lords who refuses your traditional armor. You still are more afraid of being seen than being killed."

"And that makes all of them, it does," Wangdu said reaching for his staff. "I suppose we shall see just how much of an Elven warrior I am, we shall."

"I can sense something," Euleilla said, pointing. "A group of Elves are fighting each other over there. I'm finding some very confusing things, but I think one of the people fighting is Wangdu."

Brode snorted. "Great. Our saviors are in even more danger than we are." He glanced down at his sword and shield. "Should we go rescue them, then?"

"We might as well," Maelgyn said flippantly. "It's just about the only way we've got of getting out of this alive."

"Oh, good – the odds are in our favor, then," Brode laughed.

Euleilla patted Maelgyn affectionately. "You get weird when you're with your cousin," she said. "I like it."

Euleilla started leading them towards the action, but they only got within distant eyesight of the fight when a half-dozen Elves just appeared out of the shadows. All were wearing a mask of some kind, and all seemed very well armed.

Sekhar? Maelgyn asked, wondering how they snuck up on them.

It isn't like the situation in Bandi, Sekhar replied. *I can sense them. But they somehow hid from my danger sense until now.*

Great, Maelgyn sighed, mentally shaking his head. *It figures the Elves wouldn't be so quick to allow a weapon like you go unless they had some safeguard against you.*

The battle began with vines shooting out of the ground, aiming for Maelgyn's wrists and ankles. He quickly drew his Sword, slicing through all four aimed at him without issue. He threw his wrist out, and Sekhar dispatched one startled Elf before they realized he had a *schlipf* on him.

That was the first time I ever killed one of those Elven bastards! Maelgyn thought.

I killed that one, actually, Sekhar replied. *And don't you forget it.*

Another Elf, sword drawn, was advancing on Euleilla's flank. Maelgyn was quick to intercept him, running in with magically enhanced speed. A swing of his Sword pinned the Elf's arm. A magically enhanced punch bruised the Elf's jaw, though on a Human it would have broken it. Another swing, and the Elf was dead.

That one is definitely mine.

We shouldn't be beating them this easily, Sekhar said. *These Elves cannot be trained warriors. But the ones fighting Wangdu and Phalra are.*

Maelgyn frowned, looking around. The Elves that had surrounded them were either being dealt with or already dead. Yet Wangdu – the man who had helped him rip apart the walls of a fortress – was struggling in a fight, even with Phalra's assistance. He wasn't sure what was going on, but he knew who it was who needed his help the most.

It was a sprint to get to Wangdu and Phalra's side. They were dueling with that Elf in the red mask. Maelgyn had never seen

Wangdu wield his spear with such speed or precision, yet the Red Mask was more than keeping up with him. Vines were erupting from all over the ground, then withering away before they could do anything. Maelgyn couldn't quite tell what was going on, but he knew which Elf was his enemy.

Sekhar—

I know you aren't going to like me saying this, but things are too blurred. I'm not sure which Elf is which... they're all dangerous.

I'm on my own, then?

Well, I can still work as your shield. Just don't expect me to provide any offense. I can't target anyone accurately enough.

Good enough, Maelgyn thought, stepping into the fight.

"Wait!" Phalra cried, but it was too late. Maelgyn was in the battle, and once in it wasn't possible for him to get back out safely. He focused all of his magic internally, enhancing his strength and reflexes to their utmost. And he found he could keep up – perhaps he couldn't will vines away like the Elves, but he could move fast enough to slice them off at the root. And he was moving faster than Phalra, Wangdu, and even the Red Mask. Swords were not really designed to 'clash,' even when parrying, though at the speeds they were dueling it was inevitable. There were several times Maelgyn's Sword and the Elf's blade sparked at their contact.

Your senses are dulled, but mine aren't. Use my eyes – I need an edge, Maelgyn thought.

I'll be slower than usual, and you'll lose my defense.

I can parry his sword myself, and Wangdu and Phalra are doing a good job with his vines, but I need some edge to beat him. So get it for me!

The argument between Maelgyn and his *schlipf* was interrupted, however, when a fresh sword appeared... coming out of Red Mask's chest from the other side. The masked Elf collapsed, falling into a pool of his own blood.

"One down!" Brode called out, fire in his voice.

Or I suppose Brode could get it for me, instead, Maelgyn thought.

"You... you killed Yakura?" Phalra said in shock.

"What, you wanted him alive?" Brode asked.

"A Human was able to kill Yakura?" Phalra replied, though it seemed she was speaking more to herself in wonder than to the rescued Sword.

"We don't have time for this, we don't. We have to move, we do!" Wangdu said. "Why did you not already leave by the ladder, did you not?"

"One of the Elven Generals... defeated?"

"The ladder was gone," Maelgyn said. "Our only ways out are for you to craft another, or to fight our way out the front gate."

"At this point, leaving out the front gate would be just as easy as the missing ladder," Euleilla said, walking up to join them.

"A Human? Killing one of the Twelve?" Phalra muttered.

Wangdu frowned. "If they knew we were here, they did—"

"We're being surrounded," Euleilla said, leading the others over to them. "My *schlipf* is having trouble sensing them, but my magic isn't. The bulk of them are Humans, but there are hundreds of Elves mixed in with the ranks."

That shook Phalra out of her stupor. She glanced at Wangdu. "Time for the troll nuts?"

"Troll nuts?" Brode said.

"We're lucky they're in season in Bandi. They don't grow in this region," Phalra said.

"Is this really the time to pull some kind of Elven prank?" Maelgyn asked.

Phalra shook her head, dismissing his ignorance. "The prank is in collecting the nuts. But when you use them..."

"You get an army, you do," Wangdu finished, pulling a handful of troll nuts out of the bag on his belt. "Which direction is the town exit, is it?"

Euleilla pointed. "That way."

Wangdu tossed the handful of nuts in the direction she indicated... and nothing happened.

"What—"

"Come on," Phalra said. "We're getting out of this town."

She started running. Maelgyn wasn't sure where she thought she was going, as the mob of Elves and Human soldiers was growing plainly visible even without Euleilla's senses, but he followed, and he prompted the others to follow her as well.

Maelgyn wasn't sure what to think when giant trees erupted from the ground in front of them. Those trees grew arms and legs and even faces of a sort, and started charging the Porosian ranks alongside them.

"Treants?" Maelgyn said. "I thought you said those things were *troll* nuts!"

"That's because we use them to keep trolls out of our gardens!" Phalra shouted back. "These are much better than trolls. The Elf who plants them can even control them, to a point."

Whether they were treants or trolls, Maelgyn was glad to have them on his side. They plowed into the Porosian forces, and started sending them flying. It didn't matter what was facing them – Humans, Elves, or even small buildings – they were going forward.

"We must avoid the Generals, we must," Wangdu called. "The treants can't stand against them, they can't."

"Generals?" Maelgyn asked.

"The last living warriors of the Ancient Elven era," Phalra explained. "The Elf in the red mask we fought earlier was one of them. They are exceptionally powerful even for us Elves, and as you might imagine given their age and experience, are better trained than your typical Elven warrior."

"And they have the power to wrest control of the treants from me, they do," Wangdu warned. "Which is why I said to avoid the Generals, I did."

"How will we tell these Generals apart from all the other Elves we're fighting?" Brode asked.

"You'll know them," Phalra said. "They wear the *thkunch*, a cousin the the *schlipf*. Instead of a shield and a weapon, the *thkunch* is living armor that binds itself to the wearer, and is easily identified. Once bound it can never be removed, and they were driven extinct before the transition to Modern Elves. Only the *thkunch* bound to the Generals still exist."

"*Schlipf*-like armor. Got it," Euleilla called in almost hysterical alarm. "Which means we should avoid that Elf right in front of us, right?"

Phalra looked where Euleilla was pointing and shrieked, almost physically pushing Euleilla to the side. "Lord Ajiro! Of all of them, he's the one we need to avoid the most. We have to move!"

She turned them away from the exit, only to see another of the Generals. Then another.

"They're surrounding us," Brode said. "We'll have to go through one of them."

"Then we should take the most direct route," Maelgyn said. "I'll hold off that Ajiro guy and catch up with you."

Maelgyn didn't give the others a chance to protest, breaking free from them as he charged past the treants and through the Porosian lines. He avoided combat where he could to preserve his strength. From what he'd been told, Ajiro would a powerful opponent, but Maelgyn was now a true high mage. He didn't have to win this battle – just delay the Elf long enough for the others to pass through, and he was confident he could manage that much.

The Elf lord didn't even seem to notice his approach. He was standing on his own, with no other Porosian within ten feet of him. Maelgyn broke into the ring, Sword ready, and swung.

Ajiro reached up and casually caught the blade between his thumb and forefinger.

"And so a challenger appears, he does. But he does not know what he is up against, he does not." Ajiro flicked a brief glance at Maelgyn. "You are a nobody, you are, and you stand in territory that is ideal for me, you do. You should surrender now, you should, if you do not want to be utterly destroyed, you don't."

Maelgyn didn't usually care much for accolades, but being called a nobody? Really? That demanded some response. He had titles and powers he had earned, however rarely he used them, that even an Elf should respect. Besides, the longer he kept the Elf talking, the better – it would give the treants more time to work.

"I am Sword Prince Maelgyn, Duke of Sopan. High Mage, liberator of the Borden Isles, and Dragon's bane!" He pulsed his magic, sending a ring of people around them falling to their knees... though Ajiro stood unaffected. "Do not underestimate me."

"You are merely Human, you are," Ajiro scoffed. "Magic is but a trifling skill we granted you Humans eons ago, we did. Why we Elves ever thought your kind worth bothering with, we did, I no longer remember, I don't, but we tried to leave the world to you, we did. But we did not have to leave it to you, we didn't. I went into seclusion for a thousand years, I did, while the works of Elves were still regarded as great wonders, they were. But Humankind has slowly let our memory vanish, it has. The world has forgotten that we were its steward, it has. You seem to think your magic matters to me, you do, so you evidently have also forgotten what we are, you have. You must be reminded of it, you must."

Maelgyn snorted. "Arrogant bastard, aren't you? You are a dying people and you know it. You were *poor* stewards of this world, and you know it. We haven't forgotten you – we remember you just fine – but not because you were 'great.' And we've gotten stronger. Magic may have been something you 'granted' us – though I'm not convinced that's true, as you Elves are famous for your propaganda – but we have learned how to use it better than you could have imagined."

Ajiro cocked an eyebrow. "And you call *us* arrogant, you do? I guess I will give you a lesson on Elven greatness after all, I will."

Phalra's eyes widened in panic when she heard Maelgyn say, "I'll hold off that Ajiro guy and catch up with you."

"Wait!" she cried, reaching out to stop him, but she was too late. Maelgyn was gone, slipping past the line created by their treants and into the mass of Porosian soldiers.

Euleilla tensed. "What's wrong?"

"He's going after Lord Ajiro," Phalra said. "He is a legend among Elven legends. The last of the Ancient Elves, and the greatest of the Generals. Maelgyn was barely able to keep up with Yakura, one of the weakest of the Generals, with both Wangdu and I helping him."

"And Ajiro is already turning our treants against us, he is," Wangdu said, pointing. The two treants in the middle of their line had frozen, briefly, but now were turning to fight against them.

"Maelgyn is hoping to hold off Lord Ajiro, but he won't be able to," Phalra said. "Any of the other Generals and he might have at least been able to distract them, but—"

"Then we need to go rescue him," Brode declared, his voice full with the authority of a Sword Prince. "Dwarves! We need a path cleared."

"But—" Phalra started to say. Considering the opposition in front of them now consisted of two of Wangdu's treants, now co-opted by Ajiro, it was a bit surprising how quick Tur'Ka and Tur'Tei were to follow Brode's orders and charge ahead.

It also shocked Phalra to see how quickly those two Dwarves took the corrupted treants down.

"I haven't seen anything like that since the *real* Dwarven Axemen were fighting us," Phalra said in astonishment.

"They *are* real Dwarven Axemen," Euleilla snorted in disgust. "They were trained by the Dwarf who rediscovered the skill, and there was no-one better than him."

With that, she ran off after them, followed by Brode.

Wangdu put a comforting hand on his sister's shoulder. "You have much to catch up on, you do. I have been teaching them to be real Dwarven Axemen, I have."

"That's forbidden! The Covenants of Dissolution—"

"I am hardly the only Elf to ignore those covenants, I am," Wangdu said, gesturing to the Elves around them. "But we do not have time to discuss this, we don't. They will reach Ajiro before we do, they will, if we do not hurry, we don't."

Phalra nodded, drawing her own sword. She never thought she would have to face one of the Generals, especially after the Elven kingdom dissolved, but it looked like she would be doing it for the second time in less than an hour... alongside her brother, a pair of Dwarves, and a trio of Humans.

Maelgyn couldn't figure how to keep Ajiro talking much longer, and figured his best bet at survival was to make the first move. Again, he focused his magic entirely on increasing his strength, speed, and reflexes. There really wasn't much that magic could react against in the area, anyway.

With superhuman speed, he darted in, Sword at the ready. Ajiro almost casually blocked his first several swings, but after three or four attacks Maelgyn was able to direct the Elf's arm slightly out of position. It was enough of an opening for him to ram his armored shoulder into Ajiro's chest, with the idea of either knocking the Elf down or staggering him, either of which would leave Ajiro vulnerable to a follow-up attack.

Only Ajiro did not fall down, nor did he stagger. In fact, Maelgyn found himself bouncing off of his target, and he was the one who stumbled back from the blow. He stared at Ajiro in shock – he could have knocked a hole in a foot-thick stone wall with that hit, and even Paljor at his strongest would have been knocked to the ground, yet Ajiro didn't even seem to notice.

"Ancient Elves such as myself can draw strength from the very earth we stand on, we can, by rooting ourselves into the ground, we do," Ajiro lectured. "Your strikes are as pointless as hammering dirt, they are."

Sekhar, I think it's your turn, Maelgyn thought to his *schlipf.*

Sorry, but I can't get through that armor. Even if I did... he has some control over at that distance – not much, but enough to soften my thorns and slow my vines. It would be like trying to pierce him with the frayed end of a rope.

Really? Maelgyn thought back in wonder. *But—*

We were bred to fight for the Elves, not against them. Do you really think they would allow Humans to control a weapon such as us if we could be used against them? It's a power most of them lost when they changed themselves from Ancient to Modern Elves, but Ajiro never underwent that change.

Can you still work as a shield? Maelgyn asked.

You will have to direct me, as before, but yes, Sekhar said. *He can cloud my senses even at this distance, though.*

Maelgyn gritted his teeth. Sekhar was his most powerful weapon, but he was neutralized. His magically enhanced strength didn't seem to matter against this Elf. That left him with just his Sword – a fine example of Human craftsmanship, to be sure, but Ajiro's own swordsmanship was better than his own. And if Ajiro could take the blunt force of that shoulder attack Maelgyn tried, would he even be vulnerable to a blade?

Well, only one way to find out...

Maelgyn altered the balance of his magic, increasing his sword-arm speed even faster by sacrificing some magical enhancement of other parts of his body. And when he swung that blade, he was moving with such speed even he couldn't see his own arms moving.

Ajiro seemed able to, however, and blocked his swing. Not once, not twice, but three times in a row. And then, in a moment that must have been a calculated insult, he yawned.

Maelgyn didn't care if he was yawning just to taunt him or if he was doing so because he was genuinely bored and tired of the fight, he was going to take advantage of the Elf's inattention. Targeting Ajiro's legs, which appeared unprotected by any armor, Maelgyn swung his Sword with as much speed and power as he could muster.

Except the living armor breastplate that Ajiro wore grew a sheet of bark to cover that spot, working faster than even Sekhar could to protect its wearer. Maelgyn's Sword struck... and bounced off, leaving Ajiro unscathed.

But not the Sword. A chip of the dragon-blood tempered steel went flying as Maelgyn stumbled back, knocked back by his own attack. He paused, looking at his blade in disbelief.

The Swords were centuries old, and despite heavy use had never been damaged once. Yes, Maelgyn had been cautious with the Sword of Sopan in the past, not willing to risk it against another of the Swords in his duel with Paljor, but he never seriously thought it might be damaged even then. Perhaps it was the quality of the manufacturing, or the dragon-blood tempering, but they always appeared unbreakable. And until he chipped one on Ajiro's Elven armor, he knew of no proof that was wrong.

"That Sword is one of the finest weapons Humans can make, it is," Ajiro said, glaring down at him. "It is a pity you damaged it, it is. But it is also more proof that the best that Humans can manage is no match for what we Elves are capable of, it is."

This time, Maelgyn had no answer for the Elf. A quick sweep of his magic and Maelgyn was able to retrieve the small shard broken off his Sword. It might be possible to repair it later, though it was unnecessary for the moment – most of the blade was still intact and sharp, and it was still a viable weapon – but Maelgyn wasn't concerned about that, now.

Even against Paljor, Maelgyn had always felt there was at least a chance of winning the fight. When he found himself facing down five Black Dragons, Maelgyn at least had a plan. But Ajiro... how could he fight Ajiro?

Legends of Elven defeats crossed through Maelgyn's thoughts, but they were ultimately useless. Successful wars against Elves by Humans or Dwarves always came down to choosing the right type of battlefield and coming fully prepared; this battlefield was the Elves' choice, and Maelgyn hadn't been able to 'fully prepare' for a battle against Elves without an Army to back him up. That sort of preparation required specialized weapons requiring wagon trains carrying them to be effective. He knew they might be facing a few Elves, but he'd hoped to avoid a confrontation with them. And he questioned whether even those methods would work against Ajiro.

His real plan for fighting Elves on this mission had involved using his magic to magnify Wangdu's own fighting abilities, as in the fight against that Red Mask guy. He had thought he might even be able to take on an Elven warrior by himself, if necessary, and the fight with Red Mask only encouraged that belief... but Ajiro was as far above your average Elven warrior as Maelgyn was the average Human footsoldier, it seemed.

Maelgyn came to the realization that his only chance was to run, but his inattention while reaching that conclusion only took that chance away. Just as he turned to run, vines leapt out of the ground encircling his legs and arms, knocking the Sword out of his hands and preventing Sekhar from taking any action. He was fully restrained in seconds, unable to do much more than squirm. He was caught, and probably would soon replace Brode in that cell.

All he could now do was hope that he had been successful in giving Euleilla and the others a chance to escape. If they could just get away and warn Svieda of the severity of this threat, perhaps that army he'd wanted to use to sack Sjouleber could be brought in, complete with anti-Elf war machines, and he could be released then.

"I'm sorry, but my cousin came to your lovely town to bring me home. It would be rude of me to leave without him," came a call.

Maelgyn's eyes shot open, seeing Brode in the lead of the party, apparently having pushed through the enemy army to reach him. Euleilla was at his side, and the pair of Dwarven Armsmen were ready with their axes.

It was a sight that, any other time he was in a battle and the situation was this dire, he would have been glad to see... but right now it terrified him.

"No!" he cried. His voice broke with his panic, and he off-handedly wondered if anyone would think him a coward for trying to run from this fight, but he knew now it was the right call. "Get out of here!"

"Not going to happen, cousin," Brode called, leading the charge in.

Ajiro just shook his head. "Pitiful," he said.

The Dwarves were clearing the vines from the path, but the ones holding Maelgyn down were far sturdier than the others. In fact, they hardened even more as he watched Brode literally leaping into the attack, bringing his sword down with the added assist of gravity. Euleilla's magic was even assisting him, trying to add speed and strength to Brode's strike.

It was a good attack, but with Maelgyn's own experience fighting Ajiro the result was all too predictable. He could only watch in horror as Brode's sword shattered on the reinforced vines.

"Wha—" Brode started, rolling into his fall to roll up on one knee.

"This is growing tedious," Ajiro said, waving his hand. A fresh set of flowering plants grew – plants that Sekhar was quick to identify for Maelgyn.

"Shields!" he cried.

Euleilla didn't question him for a second – her own *schlipf* quickly weaved a shield to protect her. The Dwarves' weren't equipped with shields of their own, but they ducked behind her, using the heads of their axes to supplement their defense. Brode was on the ground, and hid as best he could behind his shield.

Making only a soft whistle of sound, sharp wooden needles shot out of the newly grown flowers, aimed at his wife and friends. The initial volley was deflected by the shields, although he saw at least one needle sticking in the armor that Tur'Tei was wearing – deep enough it might have broken the skin. As these needles would inject a paralyzing poison, Maelgyn hoped not, for his Dwarven armsman's sake.

"Get out of here – he's too much for you all to take on unprepared," Maelgyn called.

"I am not leaving my husband behind," Euleilla said, stepping forward as her *schlipf* retracted. She casually waved her hand, using some of the magic powder surrounding her to shred the archer flowers that had attacked them. "You should know that."

Ajiro snorted. "Another Human that believes being strong in their pitiful form of magic makes them strong, they do. You are even weaker than this one, you are – you stand no chance, you do not."

"Against you? My husband is a lot more powerful than I am. I believe I am more skilled in some areas, but not so skilled that I'm likely to best you where he failed," Euleilla said. "But he did come to rescue me against overwhelming odds not too long ago, and he succeeded – I think I have at least enough skill to return the favor."

With that statement, she opened one of the bags of magic powder on her waist. Then another, then another, until all six of them were opened. Iron and nickel powder mixed together as it flew out of the bags, blending together and slamming into the vines holding Maelgyn secure. To his surprise, Maelgyn felt the powder slide down his skin, in between the vines and his wrists and ankles, before expanding outward.

Maelgyn was, to his astonishment, free.

Slipping out of the vines before they could once again constrict over his limbs, he ducked and grabbed his Sword. "All right," he said. "I'm free. Now, let's get the heck out of here."

"And what would make you think that any of you are permitted to leave, would it?" Ajiro said. He reached into his pocket and pulled out a handful of what Maelgyn recognized were troll nuts. He lobbed them over Maelgyn's head to land behind their party, and soon four new treants were rising out of the ground, boxing them in. They even seemed a bit sturdier than the treants Wangdu had grown. "It was amusing to see you using an Elven weapon I helped design against our army, it was. Perhaps it was futile, it was, but you made good use of them, you did. You might be interested to know that these are a more advanced version, they are."

In a choice between battling Ajiro again or facing off against the four enhanced treants, Maelgyn chose the treants. But just as he was about to attack them, all four withered away and died unexpectedly.

"You may have invented the treants, you might, but you are not the only Elf who knows of them, you aren't," Wangdu called. Maelgyn couldn't see where his Elven companion was until he fell from the sky to land between Ajiro and the others. Just where he had come from, Maelgyn couldn't tell. "I have studied counters to all of your ancient inventions, I have."

Ajiro drew himself up and, to Maelgyn's surprise, gave Wangdu a courteous bow. "It is surprising to meet the Elf known as Wangdu, it is, on a battlefield such as this. I bid you greetings, I do."

Wangdu slowly returned the bow, his eyes not leaving the other Elf's. "I demand safe passage for my Human and Dwarven companions, I do."

Ajiro's eyes narrowed. "You surrendered the right to make those demands a millennia ago, you did."

Maelgyn didn't understand that comment, though Wangdu glanced back at him nervously. He wasn't about to ask any questions, however – they didn't have time, and Wangdu needed all of his concentration focused on this Ancient Elf.

"Svieda is under my protection, it is," Wangdu stated. "You broke the oath when you captured Sword Brode, you did. It is not I who is the honorless one, it isn't."

"Matters are too great for nostalgia to dictate where I set my eye, they are," Ajiro said. "Had you let my plans take their course, you had, there would have been no bloodshed, there wouldn't."

Maelgyn was expecting more debate, now no longer sure where he should go or what he should do. He couldn't fight Ajiro, but he didn't want to leave Wangdu behind... and Wangdu seemed to be negotiating their release. He didn't want to do anything that might provoke Ajiro into outright rejecting the request.

But then Wangdu and Ajiro switched to speaking Elvish – a language Maelgyn couldn't understand. And as the two Elves argued, a third – Lady Phalra – appeared behind him from out of the shadows.

"Run!" she snapped.

Maelgyn had absolutely no desire to be captured again. "You heard the lady – let's get out of here!" Maelgyn cried.

They started running again – at this point, it didn't matter in what direction, as long as it was away from Ajiro, since the Porosians were relatively inconsequential compared to the Elven General – but they had waited too long to take advantage of the opening Wangdu had given them. Ajiro's dormant vines once more rose from the ground. They didn't seem to be quite as strong as before – Wangdu or Phalra must have been trying to weaken them – but they were still quite numerous, and seemed to be targeting Maelgyn above the others. In no time at all, he found his ankle once more caught by the entangler vines.

When the others paused and looked back at him, he shook his head. "Go! I'll get myself free and catch up!"

Brode shook his head. "That didn't work the first time, cousin, it won't work now." He turned back and charged for Maelgyn, wielding his shield as a weapon. While not sharp, it was made of fine steel and had a beveled edge. Plunging it down onto the vine around Maelgyn's ankle, it acted like an axe. Maelgyn was free, but the shield was then stuck in the ground.

It was just the wrong moment to be without a shield, however – more archer flowers were sprouting, sending their needle-like spikes flying. Maelgyn's schlipf and dragonhide armor were enough to protect him, but they seemed to hit even harder than the first volley.

When it was over, Brode looked him in the face and shot him a pained smile. "Sorry, cousin... I think you'll have to handle that impostor on your own."

Maelgyn's eyes widened. Sekhar had protected him, but hadn't been able to sense the attack well enough to protect Brode – and Brode's own shield had been used to free him from the vines. As his cousin fell to his knees, Maelgyn saw a half-dozen spikes from the archer flowers stuck in his unarmored back.

"No!" Maelgyn cried, reaching to keep Brode steady. Euleilla was suddenly at his side, helping to hold Brode up. "I... you're still breathing, right? We can fix this! It... we just need to get you to a doctor. I—"

Brode snorted incredulously, then coughed up some blood. "I'm already dead, and we both know it. Don't worry about me – just get out of here!" He coughed again. "Honestly, better dead than back in that horrid prison again...."

And those were his last words. He went rigid, his eyes bulging, and then his breathing stopped.

"No." Maelgyn shot a hateful glare out at Ajiro, who didn't even see him – he was too busy dueling with Wangdu. "No!" he cried again, sending out a powerful wave of focused magic, aiming at the slight bit of Elven blood that could be effected by it.

And this time, the Elf felt it. Perhaps not enough to harm him, but it distracted him from the fight with Wangdu. A second blast of magic went not against Ajiro, whose protections were too great to be seriously harmed by it, but at Wangdu, adding every ounce of power and speed he could to Wangdu's own strike. Maelgyn watched as Wangdu's staff whipped through the air from above, cracking Ajiro on the back of the head with a loud crunch and sending him crashing to the ground, stunned.

Wangdu looked momentarily startled at making contact before noticing Maelgyn and Euleilla standing there, watching him. He sprinted in their direction. "That will not stop him, it won't! We must escape while we can, we must!"

Maelgyn felt like going another round with Ajiro, but had to concede he didn't have a chance to win. He turned and ran, taking

Euleilla with him, as Wangdu acted as their rear guard. Between Phalra, the Dwarves, and some more treants, it wasn't difficult to make it to the city gates. Said gates, Elven tree-like bars in nature, responded to Wangdu and Phalra's controls and opened. Maelgyn and his party were free, leaving Sjouleber without further casualty.

But Maelgyn had never felt so defeated in his life.

Chapter XXXIII

The trip back to Rocky Run was a somber affair. Maelgyn barely noticed his surroundings the entire time. He had not just failed; he had gotten his cousin, who had been relatively safe even if he was being kept in a cell, killed. That hurt him, personally, but it also placed all of Svieda in danger – with the real Brode dead (and with the complete inability to reclaim his body), how would they ever deal with the impostor on the throne?

Worse, it seemed his understanding of the enemy had been incomplete and mistaken. The Porosian Conspiracy had seemed to Maelgyn to be quite dangerous and powerful, but he had imagined it was a small group of influential manipulators. And perhaps they did have groups of influential manipulators, but now it seemed as if they also controlled an army that rivaled Sho'Curlas or Oregal in size – and directed by fell Elven warriors the likes of which he had never seen. How could Svieda hope to win the inevitable war with Poros while still trying to fight back against Sho'Curlas?

They would need new allies, but there were none with enough strength to matter. Not who they had a reasonable chance to call upon – Oregal could help, but they were more likely to open a third front against Svieda than they were to help. Bandi was now their ally, but they were not strong enough to counter what Poros could bring – especially with that massive army of Elves, untrained in the art of war or not. It would only be a matter of time before those untrained Elves learned the things that made Elven armies so feared. Who was left? The worthless border kingdoms? Even if they could reach some sort of alliance with the chaotic despots and anarchical factions in those lands, they weren't likely to be able to provide enough resources to make much of a difference.

Euleilla had tried comforting Maelgyn. She refused to let him go, sitting near him and holding his hand for the whole journey, and spoke to him in soothing tones... though he hadn't taken in a word she said, and barely noticed when she tried to hold him.

El'Athras and Wodtke had met them at the entrance to the Dwarven tunnel system, and it was only then that Tur'Tei collapsed from the paralyzing poison that had been in his system since the first volley from the archer flowers. Maelgyn briefly feared that his inattention had cost him another Dwarven friend, but Wodtke was able to treat the silent Dwarf successfully. El'Athras later explained that during Tur'Tei's "previous job," he had been inoculated against the worst effects of several Elven poisons. There were some poisons that one could never build up a resistance against, but the poison of the archer flower wasn't one of them. Still, it was never a good thing to let that sort of wound go untreated.

From the conclusion of that crisis and the completion of their second rail trip, none of Maelgyn's companions had been able to get a word out of him. Euleilla was getting increasingly worried about him, but he remained oblivious to her concerns until Wangdu and Lady Phalra decided it was time to intervene on her behalf.

"I am sorry for the loss of your cousin, I am," Wangdu began, taking the opportunity to approach him while El'Athras was dealing with the steam lock. "I am afraid it was my fault, it was."

"And it wasn't mine for being too weak to stop Ajiro, myself?" Maelgyn said. "Is that what you're going to tell me? I know that already. It's not my fault. It's not your fault, either, and you know that. But that doesn't mean I'm any happier about my cousin dying, or any less worried about what Ajiro might do next."

Wangdu flinched. "As I said, I did, I am sorry for your cousin, I am. But you should not be asking what Ajiro will do next, you shouldn't."

"No?" Maelgyn asked. "He's reunited Poros almost overnight after a civil war which has gone on for over a millennium, which should give him access to an army of Humans that might rival Sho'Curlas for the world's largest. He's adding to that by raising an army of Elves for the express purpose of invading my country. Why shouldn't I ask what his plan is?"

"We already know those plans, we do. We have known of those plans since your encounter in Sopan's library, we have. Perhaps we do not know the specifics, we don't, but that is for your spies to determine, it is," Wangdu began. "The question you should be asking, you should, is what *you* are going to do next, it is."

Maelgyn frowned. "Me? Well, if the armies of Poros are going to invade alongside a battalion of Elves... I'm not sure there are many options. The only Human tactic which ever worked in Human-Elf Wars was to retreat behind our walls and employ fire, magic, poisons, and arrows to reduce their numbers by attrition."

"It might come to that," Phalra said, joining the conversation. "But there is a brief period of time where most of the Elves in this upcoming war won't be much better fighters than their Human counterparts. You have perhaps a year or so before they start to outstrip the average trained Human soldier. It is during this period you must act."

"And do what?" Maelgyn asked. "What hope do we have when we are about to face off against the two largest countries in the world, there's an impostor in service to one of those enemies on our throne, and their leaders are that much stronger than I am?"

"You might be surprised," Phalra said. "Svieda has stood against the might of Sho'Curlas for a year now – they have gotten weaker while Svieda has gotten stronger. And Svieda hasn't brought its full force to bear, yet."

"Neither has Sho'Curlas," Maelgyn pointed out. "And that's most likely the weaker of the threats against us."

"A year ago you wouldn't have believed Sho'Curlas was so weak," Phalra pointed out.

Wangdu nodded. "But we should address these other threats, we should. If you are still afraid of the impostor on the throne, you are, you have forgotten that we have already taken steps to negate him, we have."

"True, but—"

"And when it comes to fighting Poros, it does," Wangdu said. "You should have noticed that we have been preparing for them, you should. Why do you think the Dwarves have been fortifying Rocky Run, do you?"

Maelgyn frowned. "I was under the impression that was to help protect us from the inevitable strike against Rubick's undefended border."

"And who do you think would be best positioned to attack Rubick, do you? It would not be Sho'Curlas, it wouldn't – we've been preparing for an attack from Poros, we have!" Wangdu pointed out.

"Perhaps, but even if we were prepared for an attack from Poros, I doubt we've been ready for a whole brigade of Elves to be a part of that attack!"

"That is true, it is," Wangdu conceded. "But a brigade of Elves who have never fought a battle before is not a true brigade of Elven warriors, it isn't, any more than a brigade of Dwarves armed with axes they've never used before are a brigade of Dwarven Axemen, it isn't. When we deployed our treants in Sjouleber, we did, we took down quite a number of them, we have. It is very possible to win this war, it is – to cut the number of Elves down to the small number you originally envisioned the Porosian Conspiracy having, you did, before they become a more serious threat, they do."

"I'm not too sure of that," Maelgyn considered. "Even if it takes them a year or two to get those untrained Elves up to fighting form, that is a very short timespan to give us to win a war of this size. And even if we can reduce the Elven numbers before they become a more serious threat... well, I'm not sure if Ajiro isn't strong enough to win this war all on his own." Maelgyn contemplated his hands. "It seems *I'm* not strong enough to beat him, anyway."

Phalra laughed. "I know Ajiro well enough to know he made you think you were nowhere near his level, but that isn't true. No, you couldn't get through his armor... any more than his spikes could get through your own schlipf. Yes, his vines were strong enough to entangle you, but if he hadn't had months – if not years – to prepare the battlefield, they would never have been able to contain your magically enhanced strength. He is powerful and quick, no question about that, but he was even faster and stronger than normal because he was able to focus only on you and not so much on growing those vines and archer plants that you had to also deal with. Ajiro was at the peak of his strength, and was fighting you in his home using defenses he'd had ages to establish. Fight him anywhere but Sjouleber, he's not much better than Wangdu would be if he had that fancy armor, too."

"I am not that strong, I'm not," Wangdu demurred.

"Oh, yes you are, brother," Phalra said, smirking at him cheekily before turning bat to Maelgyn. "And another thing – Prince Maelgyn, what makes you think that you've reached the limits of your own abilities? You may have been named a High Mage, you may have fought Dragons and conquered castles almost by yourself, but you're still not much more than half-trained in both magic and swordsmanship. You have a lot of untapped potential that with just a little more training we can get you to tap."

"And there are still other allies we might call upon, we might," Wangdu said.

"Like Farynuk – the one member of the Twelve Elven Generals who wouldn't ever be a part of Ajiro's conspiracy," Phalra suggested. "...and who happens to be our uncle."

Wangdu winced when that subject was brought up, but was quick to change the subject. "We might call upon our family, we might, but we can look for other allies as well, we can. And there are other things we can work with you on, we can... but they must be kept secret, they must."

"Why is that?" Maelgyn asked.

"We intend to teach you things no Human has learned since the days of the Ancient Elves, we do," Wangdu said.

"For example, we can work with you to rediscover how to throw lightning at your opponents," Phalra explained. "Something like that would definitely even the scales between you and Ajiro... but it might bring the Technologist faction of Elves into the fight. The last thing you need are more enemies."

Euleilla coughed. Maelgyn and the two Elves looked over at her, none of the three of them realizing she had been listening to the conversation. "If you need to know the way to cast lightning, I may know how you can find out."

"Do you know how?" Maelgyn asked, astonished.

Euleilla shook her head. "No... but mother did. She wrote down the procedure in her notes... which, if my memories from when I was a very young girl are correct, are still hidden in the ruins of the Delbruck Academy."

Maelgyn nodded. He still didn't like their odds, but throwing lightning around? That might help even them. "All right, then – we'll have to find the Delbruck Academy."

General Doshkin, one of the so-called Twelve Elven Generals (though that appellation was increasingly incorrect), was not particularly happy as he returned to his "home" town. This was where he had stashed High King Fitz, after uncovering how Hrabak's mechanism had controlled the Sho'Curlan kings for all these centuries, and he was starting to wonder if he'd done the poor man more harm than good by offering him refuge.

Ajiro was pushing the Porosian Elves into war. Doshkin had originally agreed with the ideals Ajiro had founded his group on – reunite the Elves, reunite the Humans, preserve just one nation, each, for the Five Major races, and then end conflict between them through what he had called a council of nations. The ultimate goal was peace, and to allow races other than Humans a chance to thrive again.

Doshkin hated the Humans of Poros, and from their example felt confident that Ajiro's philosophy isolated them from the other races was just. The Porosians Doshkin knew looked down on Elves, Dwarves, Nekoji, and even other Humans with a talent for magecraft. Poros, alone, had nearly driven the Nekoji to extinction. The Humans of the border kingdoms, the only other Humans Doshkin knew prior to joining Ajiro's cause, were even worse – completely uncivilized, no appreciation for any culture including their own, all fighting with each other hoping to make something of themselves by stepping on the backs of others.

But Doshkin's views started to change when the missions Ajiro was sending him on exposed him to Humans in other countries. His first experience was in Sopan, meeting that Sviedan Sword Prince. Doshkin didn't think much of the boy, but he'd done well for himself during that little skirmish... and then one of the *schlipf* decided that this Sviedan Sword Prince was actually worthy of wielding it.

Doshkin couldn't imagine such a thing. A *schlipf* would never voluntarily bind itself to someone like these Porosians he so despised. The proof, however, he had seen just a short while ago, while Doshkin was in Sjouleber. There, to his astonishment, was Sword Prince Maelgyn, wielding that same *schlipf* and fighting alongside a pair of Dwarves and a pair of Elves. Had the *schlipf* not willingly bonded with Maelgyn, he wouldn't have been able to fight like he had. While Maelgyn undoubtedly thought he had done poorly in that fight, Doshkin knew how impressive it was to even survive a fight against Ajiro. That Human had real potential.

Doshkin had also been to Oregal, where Elves, Dwarves, and Nekoji all lived in harmony alongside Humans. True, the non-Human races in Oregal were considered somewhat second-class, but only in terms of their rights to governmental offices and positions in the army – their Human neighbors, when not involved in the government, generally treated them as equals.

And then there was Sho'Curlas. This was a land dominated by an Elf – a mad Elf, true, but Hrabak wasn't really that much crazier than any other Elf of a certain age. Well... maybe a *little* crazier. Still, it gave Doshkin a hint of what an Elf-ruled Poros would be like, should they succeed in making it the "only home for the Human race."

King Fitz's situation was so bad that Doshkin felt even Ajiro would have had mercy on the Humans of Sho'Curlas. But instead of using Fitz to end the Human wars and bloodlessly create a different "single Human civilization" that might be more sympathetic to its fellow races, as Doshkin had expected, Ajiro instead used Fitz's escape to prompt a war of conquest, plain and simple. The plan to take over the Human world with a series of largely bloodless coups now lay abandoned.

Now Ajiro would conquer as much as he could of the Human world, starting with Svieda, and then "surrender" to King Fitz... and would replace Hrabak as the Elven puppeteer behind the throne. With so much of Human society under one throne, there was little chance of any other Human nations – even Oregal – withstanding his plans to re-establish powerful Elven, Dwarven, and Nekoji kingdoms. Except... it probably wouldn't work that way, and Ajiro would probably just supplant Hrabak as the shadow dictator of an even larger, more oppressive Human regime.

Perhaps Doshkin should help Fitz escape one more time, and instead take him to Oregal, or that Sword Prince Maelgyn, and see if he couldn't help teach Fitz the right way to integrate the other Major races into Human society.

He would have to come up with a new plan. One he could execute with the resources he had on hand. And he would have to do it quietly – Ajiro wouldn't tolerate such dissent, and not even another Elf wanted to go up against Ajiro when he was angry.

Hussack was drifting in and out of consciousness as Hrabak watched. His arm – the one that wasn't there – hurt tremendously, but then it always hurt tremendously. Hrabak had warned him (a bit too late for Hussack to do anything about it) that it wouldn't stop hurting until his 'new' arm was successfully grafted on, a process which would take three years. Well, a little less than that, now.

The pain was constant, though, and because of that he was starting to get used to it. At least until the next twinge – the moments when, as Hussack explained to him, a nerve in the Human part of his arm fully connected with a nerve in the "Tengu" arm.

It was a slow process. Right now, he could move one thumb on the Tengu arm, though he had no control of his other fingers, the muscles in his hand, his wrist, or his elbow. Not even with magic.

That was an interesting find – the Tengu arm wouldn't respond to any magical influences, similar to a Mage trying to work magic through Dragonhide. Tengu arms weren't like Dragon arms in other ways, however – they could still be burnt. Hrabak had saved him when he sat his Tengu arm into a cooking flame three times, now, but Hussack couldn't feel the blisters from those burns.

Hrabak was leading him to a new chamber of the tunnels he had claimed for himself – this one showing off floor-to-ceiling sized gemstones so dark and shiny they reflected like an obsidian mirror.

Hussack was surprised when, without preamble, Hrabak grabbed him and tied his good wrist to one of the obsidian-like gemstones. Hussack knew better, by this point, than to ask any questions while Hrabak worked. Soon both of his legs were also tied to different gemstones, spreading them wide and lifting Hussack into the air. Perhaps the Tengu arm was tied up as well, but he couldn't feel enough from that arm to be sure.

"Comfy?" Hrabak asked, his insane laughter bubbling out as he spoke.

Hussack shook his head. There was no point in either lying or telling the truth... but there was in saying something. Hrabak punished him when he avoided a question like that.

"No," he answered, though honestly being tied up this way was more comfortable than the bed on which he had rested while the Tengu arm was first being grafted onto him.

"Good!" Hrabak laughed. "We're about ready to begin boosting your magical talents. By the time you've got that sword arm of yours up and working again, you will be quite the powerful mage. Maybe even as powerful as the person who cut that arm off of you will be."

Hussack's eyes narrowed, remembering the news of his son. "Only 'maybe'? I thought the point of all of this was to make me stronger than Maelgyn, once and for all."

"You'll definitely be stronger than he is now," Hrabak said. "But Maelgyn will be growing in strength, too. Don't worry – once your new arm is working, I'll help you learn how to use this new magical boost more effectively. There are techniques you Humans have forgotten that your magic makes possible – you should be able to boil water remotely, throw lightning, and more. Once you learn these things, it will be interesting to see which of you really is the strongest."

"Yes, we shall see," Hussack replied, fantasizing about the final battle he was hoping for. He would always think of the young man as that scrawny kid, remembering their years together in the Royal City. "And I hope you'll be able to see that it is me, as I wring his scrawny little neck with this new arm you've given me, too."

Three years of enduring all the tortures Hrabak could imagine would be worth it if only he could manage that.

After spending a few days in Bandi, recovering from their wounds, word arrived that Poros was on the move. Wangdu and Phalra accompanied Maelgyn and his companions back into Svieda. Maelgyn had been expecting a sober homecoming, considering the circumstances. After all, as they learned from a traveler on the road back into Rocky Run, they had been preceded by the news that Poros had invaded. Rubick had, as expected, fallen with little resistance.

Only a few pockets of resistance remained in Stanget and Leyland, as the bulk of their armies were either fighting against Sho'Curlas or gathered with the armies in Rocky Run and the rest of Largo. Most of that resistance would likely be overwhelmed, soon, though – in the one piece of good news Maelgyn heard – the Dragons had come through for them and were holding the Library of Stanget securely. That facility would only fall if the Dragons abandoned them.

On top of all that depressing news, it should have been clear to everyone that Maelgyn had failed, since Brode wasn't with them. The fact he was bringing back word that Brode wasn't just still a prisoner, but was now dead, shouldn't have encouraged any sort of enthusiasm for his return.

So the cheers greeting him as he entered town were something of a shock.

"What's going on?" he asked, looking around. He wasn't sure who he was asking, but he was hoping someone had an answer.

"I don't know, but I think I know some people who might," Euleilla said, pointing to where a cluster of people – including Euleilla's foster-sisters and Maelgyn's cousin Idril – were heading to meet them from the direction of the bridge.

Nodding in agreement, Maelgyn went to meet the welcoming party. He was astonished when the entire group – including Idril – gave him a bow.

"What—"

"A courier arrived a few hours ago," Idril explained stiffly. She didn't seem happy about it, but she pulled a parchment from out of her belt and presented it to him anyway. "He gave us this."

Maelgyn frowned, first at his cousin and then at the parchment. It was now broken, but the evidence of a royal seal was quite apparent. It was not, however, from the fake Brode, but rather Arnach.

"*A Royal Proclamation:*

"*BE IT KNOWN!*

"*The Apparent Sword King Brode IX has confessed to being an impostor. This confession, however, was made only after the Law of Swords had been temporarily suspended. The impostor, due to his co-operation in resolving the current crisis, is to be pardoned. Unfortunately, he has explained to us that the real Brode – while possibly still alive at the* time of this proclamation – will likely be executed now that his confession has been made public. We are all saddened at his loss.

"The Law of Swords has been amended to reflect the current situation. The reality is that we are no longer one kingdom. Invaders from Poros have split the kingdom of Svieda in two. While we hope to reunite with our western half, we know that maintaining leadership in the meantime is essential.

"IT IS RESOLVED!

"Sword Arnach will be appointed two positions: Sword King of Eastern Svieda, and High King of All Svieda. Eastern Svieda shall compromise the provinces of Sycanth, Happaso, Glorest, and the Royal Province of Svieda. Should Svieda be reunited, Arnach will retain his title as Sword King.

"Sword Maelgyn will retain his title of Sword Prince over all Svieda, but also will be appointed Sword King of Western Svieda, ruling from the new capital of Rocky Run. Western Svieda will include the provinces of Largo, Sopan, Stanget, Mar'Tok, and Caseificio.

"The provinces of Rubick and Leyland are recognized to be fully in foreign hands. They, and the province of the Borden Isles, are to be considered the joint responsibility of both East and West Svieda.

"Other changes to the Law of Swords include the following...."

Maelgyn skimmed the rest of the missive, noting that there were dozens of changes to the Law of Swords – including interim methods for dealing with the laws of succession while Svieda was split in two and new methods for how to handle situations where an impostor might be on the throne – but nothing of great importance in light of the other news.

"But—"

"We know that Brode died," Idril said, her mouth puckering in what she must have thought was a sympathetic smile. "And the circumstances of his death. But you are our new Sword King, and you do bring tidings of the new treaty with Bandi – a treaty the council approved for Western Svieda just this morning. All hail the new Sword King!"

Maelgyn could only watch as the chant Idril led was taken up by the other people in the town. Humans, Dwarves, the Elves, even his own wife and Sekhar were all hailing him as the new Sword King – a title he had never felt he deserved less. But the royal seal on the letter was true. He really was Sword King...

....so now what was he supposed to do?

Also From Fennec Fox Press

The Law of Swords Series

Genre: Heroic Fantasy, New Adult

The Law of Swords: A set of laws written to prevent infighting among Svieda's Royal Heirs if the King dies unexpectedly. One of these laws has never been needed... until now.

I. In Treachery Forged

When Svieda is betrayed and invaded by a former ally, Sword Prince Maelgyn must travel to the province of Sopan to take command of his armies and help repel the invaders. Along the way he rescues a Dwarven Caravan, forges a badly needed alliance, and accidentally gets married. And then he learns about the dragons...

NOW AVAILABLE!

Ebook: $5.99 retail

Print: $18.99 retail

http://www.fennecfoxpress.com/

II. In Forgery Divided

With the defeat of Paljor, Maelgyn proved himself the strongest Mage in the Human world, but there are more powerful things than Mages for him to worry about. He returns home to find that his old enemies can still hurt him, while new enemies threaten to tear his kingdom apart from the inside. The Law of Swords is supposed to protect them from this sort of thing, but it is actually helping his enemies. And then there are the Elves to deal with....

Hey, this is the book you just read! Hope you enjoyed it.

III. In Division Imperiled

Still coming to grasp with his new status, Maelgyn finds himself fighting a war on two fronts.

Coming Soon

The Inari's Children Series

Genre: Heroic Fantasy

Once magic was plentiful and the world was dominated by a singular empire whose name has long been lost to history. In its time, the great wizard Inari developed his greatest creation: The kitsune. His enemies were quick to copy him, and soon the world was populated with many different types of this remarkable creation. Two thousand years later these different breeds of kitsune are fighting amongst themselves, and the rest of the human world is about to join them.

I. The Kitsune Stratagem

To avoid being used as a political pawn against her father, a young kitsune vixen named Kieras must leave her homeland. She soon gets caught up in the fortunes of Mathis, a vagabond hunter from Ekholm, a once sleepy little town on the verge of becoming a small city. To find a way to return home, Kieras must first help Mathis save Ekholm from threats both inside and out.

Ebook: $5.99 retail

Print: $18.99 retail

http://www.fennecfoxpress.com/

II. By Claw and Arrow

Mathis and Kieras return to Ekholm. They don't get to stay for long, however, before the Myobu Priesthood approach them with a mission that sends them to the ancient ruins of Eskesa. Yulaev takes Kobach to Erixonite lands, while Kazdri and Heshka resolve the issue of just who the reigning King of Kassia is, anyway.

Coming Soon

Nine Tales of the Kitsune

A collection of nine stories focusing on the history of Norre, Inari, and the creation and evolution of this world's Kitsune.

Coming Soon

The Shieldclads Series

Genre: Space Opera

During an Academy exercise, an Earth Navy student invents a new system for energy shielding warships. This revolutionary technology is immediately put to the test when Earth is hit by a surprise attack. The new enemy reveals that they have energy shields of their own... but where did they come from, and how will Earth respond to this threat?

I. THE MERRIMACK EVENT

When a real war breaks out during a Naval Academy wargame, it falls upon a squadron of cadet-crewed warships commanded by a former Army officer to strike back, resulting in the first ever battle between shieldclads.

Coming Soon

Other Works

This Book Cannot Possibly Make Any Money

Genre: Multi-genre Collection, Humor

An anthology of experimental fiction, inside jokes, story fragments from the cutting room floor, and high school poetry, all of which conventional wisdom says cannot possibly make any money. Production to be featured on the Fennec Fox Press blog.

Coming Soon

TO THE RINK OF WAR

When Alexander Zednik accepts a warehousing client named Anita Condon, he finds himself fighting off a rogue mercenary intent on destroying her cargo. A short story.

Ebook: $0.99 retail

www.ingramcontent.com/pod-product-compliance
Lightning Source LLC
Chambersburg PA
CBHW021841010726
47493CB00005B/1493